PENGUIN BOOKS

# The Damage Done

James Oswald is the author of the bestselling Inspector McLean crime novels. His books have been shortlisted for a National Book Award, the Crime Writers' Association Debut Dagger and the prestigious Dagger in the Library Award, recognizing an author's entire body of work. His debut, *Natural Causes*, was the winner of the Richard and Judy Summer Book Club in 2013. He has also written an epic fantasy series, *The Ballad of Sir Benfro*, as well as comic scripts and short stories.

In his spare time he runs a 350-acre livestock farm in North East Fife, where he raises pedigree Highland cattle and New Zealand Romney sheep.

# The Damage Done

## JAMES OSWALD

PENGUIN BOOKS

PENGUIN BOOKS

UK | USA | Canada | Ireland | Australia
India | New Zealand | South Africa

Penguin Books is a part of the Penguin Random House group of companies
whose addresses can be found at global.penguinrandomhouse.com.

First published by Michael Joseph 2016
Published by Penguin Books 2016
001

Set in Garamond MT Std
Typeset by Palimpsest Book Production Limited, Falkirk, Stirlingshire
Printed in Great Britain by Clays Ltd, St Ives plc

A CIP catalogue record for this book is available from the British Library

ISBN: 978-1-405-91713-1

www.greenpenguin.co.uk

MIX
Paper from
responsible sources
FSC® C018179

Penguin Random House is committed to a
sustainable future for our business, our readers
and our planet. This book is made from Forest
Stewardship Council® certified paper.

For Stuart MacBride, who many years ago suggested
I stop writing fantasy and turn my hand to crime.

# I

Silence fills the old house like a pool of stagnant water. Sunlight filtering in through the thick ivy clogging the fly-spotted windows picks out motes as they dance and spin in the heat. There is a stillness to the air, as if nothing has disturbed this place in decades. Only ghosts walk these abandoned rooms. Only spirits haunt the long, cobwebbed corridors. Even the rats avoid it and the only bird anywhere near lies dead in the hallway, trapped and starved and rotted to feather and bone.

She treads lightly on the wooden stairs, footsteps leaving imprints in the dust. Light fingers caress the bannisters as she descends from high above. If she notices the dereliction around her, she doesn't show it, stepping across the litter-strewn hallway without a care. She walks through a library filled with rotting bookshelves, their books collapsed into piles of decaying paper and leather on the floor; broken furniture worn down by time more than use. The fireplace in the drawing room is filled with ash and twigs, a small sapling growing where its parent was long ago put to the fire. The dining room is laid out for a meal, the food on the plates half-eaten and now turned to dirt. A fern unfurls in the corner where water has leaked in through a broken window. Its primeval fronds are delicate and pale, a home for insects and spiders. She stops for a moment, taking one leaf lightly between finger and thumb like a seamstress eyeing up a piece of fine cloth.

'I heard a noise. Did something disturb you?'

She turns slowly, recognising the voice of her brother.

'I woke up. I was asleep for so long.' She stretches like a cat, long arms reaching for the cracked, damp-spotted ceiling. The bones in her back and neck click and pop as if she has not moved in a very long time. She yawns wide, revealing pure white teeth in a mouth as black as the night.

'We are needed in the city.' He emerges from the shadows, her double. She leaves the fern, steps through piles of dried leaves and the skeletons of long-dead animals until she is standing directly in front of him. Together it is clear they are twins, but the embrace she drapes around him is far more intimate than any sibling greeting. He wears her like a coat for long moments before drawing away, pushing her back. He is dressed for the road and lifts a heavy leather bag as if its meaning is obvious. 'We are needed in the city.'

'I know. I felt it too.' She wipes at her lips with a slender finger, slips it into her mouth as if to taste whatever is there. The slightest of pauses as she looks around the derelict room, then with a shrug of her shoulders she turns for the door.

# 2

'All units check in.'

Detective Inspector Tony McLean sat in the driver's seat of the unmarked police car, staring across the dark street at a row of Georgian terrace houses. A few lights shone out through chinks in the curtains, but most of these buildings were offices, their workers long since gone home. Further up the street, scaffolding clung to a facade like ivy, skips filling up with seventies Artex-covered partitioning and mile upon mile of outdated wiring. Whether it was being turned into flats or just one rich person's home, he couldn't tell, but slowly this part of the New Town was being reclaimed as residential.

'Everyone in place. Might as well get this show on the road.' Beside him, Detective Chief Inspector Jo Dexter stared at her chunky airwave set. In the confined space of the car, all McLean could smell was stale cigarette and mint. Not overwhelming, but enough that he'd rather be outside. In truth, he'd far rather be directing the operation from the front, but that was sergeant work.

'All units proceed as planned.' Jo Dexter placed the airwave set on the dashboard in front of her, tuned to the channel designated for the operation, then settled back in her seat.

'Christ, I could do with a fag right now.'

'Thought you'd quit,' McLean said, even though he knew better.

'Aye. Thought I had too. Thought you'd gone back to CID as well.' Dexter peered out of the windscreen at the activity across the street. A dozen uniforms poured out of an unmarked Transit van, their hi-vis jackets reflecting the street lights as they clattered up the stone steps and in through the front door their colleagues had just rammed open. A few muffled screams of alarm wafted out on the night-time air.

'Seems like none of us get what we want these days. Except maybe DCI Spence. Never thought I'd look back on Dagwood's reign with fondness.'

Dexter opened her mouth to say something, but her airwave set squawked an interruption.

'Scene secure, ma'am. You might want to come over now.'

McLean climbed out of the car, feeling the autumn chill in the air. At least it was fresh. Across the road, the house that had been the centre of attention was ablaze with light now, shutters thrown open and curtains drawn to reveal whatever sordid secrets lay within. He looked up and down the street, only slightly surprised to see another car parked with two people sitting in it, the silhouette of a long lens. This raid was meant to have been kept quiet, but someone always told the press.

'Paps?' Dexter asked, seeing the direction of his gaze.

'Almost certainly. Nothing like getting a snap of someone important being hauled out of a knocking shop by the rozzers, is there?'

'Aye, well. We can send a couple of constables over to

4

distract them. Let's go see who's been caught with their troosers down first.'

The inside of the house was warm and bright. McLean stepped through the front door into a large reception hall filled with bustling police. Comfortable sofas lined the walls, low tables in front of them scattered with magazines and a few half-empty glasses. It might have been a posh boutique hotel rather than somewhere people paid for sex. Chances were that would be a line the lawyers would try, if it got that far.

Detective Sergeant Kirsty Ritchie spotted them and pushed her way through the melee. She wore a stab vest over her dark blue suit, but it was hanging open. If there had been any threat it was now long past.

'Exactly what we were expecting, sir, ma'am.' Ritchie had an airwave set in one hand and shoved it into her pocket as she spoke. 'There's a couple more reception rooms on this floor, a dozen bedrooms upstairs. We're still working on the basement.'

'I thought you said the scene was secure,' Dexter said.

'Oh it is, ma'am. Very.' Ritchie smiled, something McLean hadn't seen much of lately. 'It's going to take a while to get some of the people out of their . . . restraints.'

'Anyone important?' McLean asked. 'Only the press are here already. We'll need to be careful getting people out. You know what the lawyers are like. Any suggestion we've set someone up and the whole operation's bust.'

Ritchie's smile faded into a frown. 'Press? How the fuck did they find out?' She shook her head. 'No matter. We can get a van in the back, take everyone out that way. I'll sort it.'

'Good. We'll need to talk to them all first. Keep them separated until we've taken statements.'

'Shouldn't be a problem. All the johns are in individual rooms. Well, most of them. I've got a uniform on each door. No one in, no one out.'

'Good work, Sergeant.' Dexter gave Ritchie a friendly pat on the shoulder, then turned to McLean. 'Guess the sooner we get started, eh?'

McLean looked around the hallway. A few of the girls had been brought through and sat on the sofas. Some were in tears, some defiant, most just head down and shoulders slumped in resignation. What struck him most was how ordinary they looked. They weren't especially young or particularly old, not noticeably thin or fat. Some looked like they had dressed for a particular kind of party, but mostly they were just a bunch of women, shocked and frightened by a visit from the local constabulary in the middle of the night.

'Top down or bottom up?' he asked, getting a look of puzzled horror from Dexter and Ritchie both.

'Shall we begin with the basement and work our way to the attic, or do you want to do it the other way round?'

'Oh, right.' Dexter let out a short bark of a laugh, startling a couple of nearby uniforms. 'Let's split up. I'll take Ritchie and start at the top. You can have the basement. I'm guessing DC Gregg's still down there?'

'She was last time I saw her.' Ritchie gave McLean a naughty wink as she and Dexter headed for the stairs. 'Have fun, sir.'

He watched them go, then asked one of the constables for directions to the basement. Through the back of the house, the decor was much the same, a couple of large

6

reception rooms either side of a narrow back hallway, window looking out on to what might once have been a garden but was now a concreted parking yard. Steps worn smooth by age led him down into a stone-walled corridor, neatly arched ceiling surprisingly high overhead. The flagstone floor had been covered with a narrow strip of dark red carpet, and what looked like heavy iron sconces hung at regular intervals like an unconvincing film set. The torches in them flickered in a way flame never would, and closer inspection showed them to be made of plastic with electric bulbs concealed in their tops.

McLean was looking for the wires when a shriek of alarm distracted him. He rushed to the nearest open door, and as he took in the scene beyond it, he understood Ritchie's wink.

It was a large room, with a vaulted ceiling held up by squat stone pillars and lit by more of the fake torches. Two uniformed officers, one male, one female, stood with their backs to the door, staring at a metal cage suspended from an iron ring set into the ceiling. Perhaps a little over six foot long and cylindrical in shape, it was only just large enough to contain the fat man locked within it. His feet were a few inches off the ground and apart from a black leather face mask he was completely naked.

'Ah, sir. I was hoping someone senior might get here soon.'

McLean dragged his attention from the dangling man, seeing the familiar form of Detective Constable Sandy Gregg emerge from the shadows on the far side of the room. As his eyes adjusted, he saw yet more strange apparatus and what appeared to be another man.

'What's going on in here, Constable? Why's this man still locked up?'

'Key's snapped off in the padlock, sir. Don't know if it was done on purpose or not.' Gregg walked up to the cage and rattled the offending article, close to the man's flaccid member. Perhaps feeling the movement, he threw his head from side to side, mumbling something.

'Think he's gagged under that hood.' Gregg let go of the padlock, reached up and patted the man's arm through the bars of his cage. 'Try to stay calm, sir. We'll have you out of there in a jiffy.'

'If he's gagged, who made that noise?'

'Oh, that's Mr Jefferies.' DC Gregg pointed over into the dark corner, where McLean could now clearly see a man leaning uncomfortably over something that looked a bit like a coffee table made of Meccano.

'What's wrong with him?'

'I think he's taken too many little blue pills, sir. Either that or he's just really turned on by a uniform. We've been having difficulty, um, extracting him. Attached by a rather sensitive part. Doctor's on the way.'

McLean looked from one man to the other. No doubt the women who had been ministering to them were in the group upstairs. Well, these two weren't going anywhere in a hurry. He could come back to them later. He turned to the uniformed officers.

'You two stay and wait for the doctor. Gregg, you're with me. Let's go and see what other delights this place has in store for us.'

# 3

'You've got no right. This is a private house. We've not done anything wrong.'

If McLean had a pound for every irate man who uttered those words as he worked his way slowly up the building, he'd have had enough for a half-decent bottle of wine. He'd have needed something considerably stronger to erase the sight of puffy white flesh, the smell of things best left unidentified. People were endlessly creative in their sexual adventures, it would seem, but ultimately it all boiled down to the same thing. This man was like all the others he had interviewed so far, nondescript, swore he had no previous record. Even his name was average, so much so that they'd had to check his driving licence when he'd told them. John Smith. Utterly ordinary, except perhaps for his sexual proclivities and his estuary Essex accent. Two women had been in here with him, although from what McLean had heard they'd been more interested in each other.

'You deny that you were paying this woman—' McLean consulted his notes. 'Sorry, these women, for sex?'

Mr Smith sat in his boxer shorts and shirt on the edge of a large, comfortable-looking bed. The room they were in was large, too, with a floor-to-ceiling bay window that looked out on to the darkened street. Or would have done had not the shutters been closed and a heavy set of curtains drawn. Given the situation he had been found in, it was perhaps for the best. As yet he hadn't shown any sense of shame at his behaviour, something McLean had noticed of the other clients he'd interviewed.

'There's no law against it, you know?' Mr Smith's voice rose at the end in the tiniest hint of a question. It was the first sign of doubt McLean had heard all night, other than the endless loop of it going around in his own head. There was something very wrong about this whole set-up, and he had a nasty feeling the raid might well backfire on the police if they didn't play things very carefully.

'Against paying for sex? No.' McLean studied Mr Smith's face for signs of embarrassment, found none. 'But brothels are illegal and your use of this one will have to be noted. Your name and details will go on record with the sex industry department.'

Now Mr Smith looked worried. 'What does that even mean? Can you do that? I mean, I've not committed any crime here. This isn't a brothel.'

'So everyone keeps telling me, and you know what? I don't believe them. As to whether or not you've committed a crime here? Well, Mr Smith. We'll see about that. Once we've got the results back from the PNC check.'

'Look, you've got it all wrong. These girls. I wasn't paying them.'

'Lucky you. It makes no difference.'

'No, see. They're not prostitutes. I've not done anything wrong.'

Almost word for word it was the same claim he had heard in all the other rooms. McLean didn't want to think of the implications should it turn out to be true. He turned away, spoke to the uniform PC on the door. 'Let him get dressed, then bring him downstairs. Everyone's going out the back to avoid the press. We'll carry on this conversation back at the station.'

'The station? Press?' Mr Smith's voice rose an octave. Well, everyone had something to hide. 'But you can't . . . my rights . . .'

'Your rights, Mr Smith?' McLean paused at the door, caught DC Gregg's eye. 'Read him his rights will you, Constable? I'm going to have a chat with the DCI.'

Halfway down the second flight of stairs, McLean's concerned musing was interrupted by a loud shout from an open doorway. He bustled down and stuck his head into another bedroom, larger even than the ones he had seen already. It was different, too, though he couldn't quite work out how. The bed was as big as all the others, and doors led off to what looked like an en-suite bathroom and a dressing room. One wall was dominated by two tall windows that looked out on to the blackness of the back lane behind the building. Between them, an antique dressing table much like the one in his grandmother's bedroom was heaped with heavy-looking academic books, a spiral-bound notepad open in suggestion of study. Detective Sergeant Ritchie stood with her back pressed against the edge of the table, pushed there no doubt by the strident tones of the woman making all the noise.

'This is an outrage. Have you any idea who I am? Who I know? You can't just break down my door in the dead of night.'

'Running a brothel is against the law, ma'am. As is living off immoral earnings. Does the taxman even know about this?' Ritchie gestured towards the open notebook, then noticed McLean standing in the doorway. 'Ah, sir. I wonder if you could explain the situation to Miss Marchmont here. She doesn't seem to want to listen to me.'

'Sir? About bloody time I spoke to someone in charge.' The woman whirled around, mouth open to tear McLean off a strip. He braced himself, seeing the fury in her eyes even as he noticed her sensible clothing, thin face hung with straight black hair. There was something hauntingly familiar about her eyes, but he couldn't for the life of him think where he might have met her before.

'I . . .' Her voice died as a puzzled frown spread across her face. Or maybe it wasn't puzzlement but something else. Fear perhaps. Whatever it was, the woman's anger seemed to leach away like air from an old party balloon.

'Miss Marchmont, is it?' McLean strove to sound conciliatory even as he racked his brain trying to work out where he knew her from. Certainly the name meant nothing to him. She didn't reply, giving instead the faintest of nods.

'We're acting on good information that this house is being used as a brothel. I have a warrant to search the premises for evidence to that effect, and given what is going on in the basement I don't think I need to justify my actions any further.'

Marchmont let her head droop forward, as if the muscles in her slender neck had grown too tired to take the weight any more. Her long black hair slid across her features like a stage curtain. 'You've got it all wrong.'

Something about her words, the way she spoke, made McLean believe her. It wasn't a happy thought, the ramifications all too easy to imagine.

'I'll be the judge of that,' he said, and at the same time realised what it was about the room that had been bothering him. Not that the bed was made, or that Miss Marchmont had clearly been discovered in here alone. It was the smell. The rest of the house reeked of sex, of cheap aftershave and booze. But this room smelled like a room in a house this old should. Like the spare rooms in his own house that he rarely had any need to visit. Not a place anyone spent much time.

He walked to the dressing table and picked up the notebook. Miss Marchmont's handwriting was neat but tightly packed, difficult to read. The words weren't any kind of book-keeping, though, nor a tally of names and addresses. McLean put the notebook down and picked up one of the heavy leather-bound books. On the outside it claimed to be a manual of corporate law, and a quick flick through the densely printed pages within showed that it wasn't lying. He put it back down again, a sinking weight dragging in his gut. Turning around to face Miss Marchmont, he saw her hand covering her stomach, as if protecting herself against this invasion of her privacy. Her face was a white mask, emotionless and unreadable, her eyes locked on him, peering from behind that curtain of straight black hair, and for a moment he thought he knew where he had seen her before. Then she dropped her hand to her side, shook her hair from her face and pulled herself upright, and the moment was gone.

'You won't find anything untoward here. None of my guests are doing anything illegal.'

'And yet you're not – how shall I put it – joining in?'

The hand went up to the stomach again, the ghost of a smile appearing on Marchmont's lips. 'What can I say?

13

These parties take a lot of organising, but this evening I really wasn't feeling up to it. Didn't want to put everyone off just because I'm a bit under the weather, so I let them get on with it. We're all friends, after all.'

'Think we might have a problem, Jo.'

McLean found DCI Dexter in the kitchen, at the back of the house on the ground floor. It looked surprisingly like the kitchen of any large, modern house; the sort of thing you'd probably find in the pages of a glossy lifestyle magazine. It was bright and shiny and didn't feel all that homely to him compared with the lived-in warmth and omnipresent cat hairs of his own kitchen, but at least the coffee machine worked.

'You're telling me, Tony. We had it on good authority this place was operating as a brothel, but now I'm beginning to have my doubts.'

McLean pulled out a tall wooden stool and sat down at a long breakfast bar. Dexter was leaning against the other side of the counter, cradling a mug in both hands.

'It's got to be, though. I mean, I may be new to things here, but the last time I checked, a house where more than one sex worker was trading counted as a brothel. OK, a lot of the customers here are claiming they never paid for anything, but that's not meant to matter.'

'Not meant to. No.' Dexter took a long swill of coffee, then placed the mug down on the perfectly clean work surface. 'Bloody stupid law if you ask me. I wish people didn't buy and sell sex at all, but I'm a realist. It happens and my job's making sure nobody gets hurt. It'd be much easier to do that if these women could all club together and run things themselves, but the law says no. So here we are, busting open a brothel and turfing a bunch of sex workers out on to the street where no one can keep an eye on the sick bastards abusing them.'

'At least we get a few more names and photos for the records.' It wasn't really any consolation at all, but McLean didn't know what else to say.

'That's the thing though, Tony. All those women in the hall there. Not a single one of them's on our database. Far as I can tell we've never seen any of the men before either.'

Without thinking, McLean reached out and took up the mug. It was still half-full, the dark liquid warm but bitter. Jo Dexter liked her coffee black and strong.

'What are you saying?'

'I don't know. You know as well as I do that you can't have a brothel without sex workers. What if none of these women are?'

McLean looked around the room again, taking in the decor. The counter Dexter was leaning against housed a large gas hob and a small preparation sink. The worktop was polished granite and oiled wood. The rest of the kitchen units were stylish, the built in appliances all top names. Half of the room was taken up with a dining area that he could imagine young professionals chatting around while they sipped chilled Pinot Noir or ridiculously strong craft beers, waiting for their hostess to serve up something that had probably been prepared by a local restaurant but which she'd pretend she had slaved for hours cooking. It was, in short, a designer kitchen. Not the sort of place a dozen working girls might use to reheat their pizza, or as a retreat from the steady flow of johns through the front door.

'Do we know who actually owns the house?' he asked. Dexter gave him a stare that said quite clearly just how much of an idiot she thought him.

'I wasn't born yesterday. And if you'd been paying attention at the briefing you'd know anyway.' She snatched back the mug and downed the coffee in one, grimacing at the taste.

'The notes just said it was rented. Who owns it? And who's paying the rent?'

'It's owned by a letting company. Sanderson Holdings. Probably part of some pension fund or something. Name on the tenancy agreement's Heather Marchmont.'

McLean recalled the young woman alone upstairs, her strange familiarity. 'Aye, I just met her. Not sure what to make of her, really.'

'How so?' Dexter raised a quizzical eyebrow, dragging the other one up with it into a comical frown.

'Well, she's up there in her room all on her own, fully dressed, working on something that looks a lot more like contract law than running a brothel while all around her there's people . . .' McLean tailed off, not quite sure how to describe the myriad ways in which the people they had found had been pleasuring themselves and each other. Not quite sure how they could have got something so simple as a raid on a brothel so spectacularly wrong. 'I think we need to get her out of here and into an interview room. Quick as. Is it possible this really is a private house? These people are all just here having sex with their wives and girlfriends? I don't know, some kind of swingers' club?'

Dexter's look of incredulity changed as her gaze shifted from McLean to a space just behind him. He turned to see

DC Gregg standing in the doorway. She had her airwave set in one hand, an electronic PDA in the other.

'Think I might have something, sir, ma'am,' she said.

'Is it proof these women are sex workers? Because if it is I'll kiss you.' DCI Dexter crossed the room with alarming speed, bearing down on the hapless detective constable like a seagull spying a poke of chips. Gregg backed away, out into the hallway.

'No, ma'am. Sorry.'

Dexter stopped almost as quickly as she had started. 'What is it then?'

'It's one of the ... um ... clients?' Gregg held up her PDA even though the tiny text on the screen was impossible to read. 'We got a hit from the PNC.'

Judging by the noises coming from the front hall, the women the police had found in the building had mostly recovered from the shock of the raid and were now moving into the angry stage. The sooner they were taken to the station and processed the better, really. Except, having met Miss Marchmont, McLean had a horrible feeling that wasn't going to go as well as planned. He ignored them anyway, following DC Gregg as she led them up the stairs and back to the room where Mr John Smith was getting fully dressed. A bored uniform PC watched from the doorway and stood to one side to let them in. Smith was pulling on shiny black leather shoes and looked up as they entered.

'Did you really think we wouldn't find out, John?' DCI Dexter asked.

'Who're you?'

'See, that's what the N in PNC stands for, isn't it?

National. That's National as in the whole of the United Kingdom. Not just Scotland. You're a long way from home now, aren't you?'

'Who is this?' Smith turned his attention to McLean. 'What is this?'

'This, Mr Smith, is my boss, Detective Chief Inspector Dexter. You'd do well to answer her questions. Just bear in mind we probably already know the answers.'

Smith switched his attention back to Dexter, his head sweeping up and down as he appraised her, the slightest of sneers forming on his face. McLean watched and started to understand. It hadn't been there before, when it had just been DC Gregg and him conducting the interview. There the woman had clearly been the underling, in her proper place. Now, presented with the senior officer conducting the entire operation and finding out that it wasn't a man, Smith's true colours were beginning to show. How was it he'd been found? With two women? The man probably thought one was too few to be worth bothering about. What a wonderful specimen of unrepentant misogyny.

'Why didn't you tell us you were on the sex offenders' register, Mr Smith? Did you think we might miss a little thing like that?' Judging by Dexter's tone, she'd got the measure of the man too. He opened his mouth to speak, then shut it again, shoulders slumping.

'There's the small matter of forgetting to check in with the local constabulary when you moved here too. That detail slip your mind?' Dexter nodded at the uniform constable. 'Get him down to the van. Sooner we get this lot all processed, the sooner we can all go home and get some kip.'

She stood to one side as the PC produced cuffs that were decidedly not fluffy, ordered Mr Smith to stand, put his hands behind his back. By the way the man complied, McLean guessed it wasn't the first time he'd been through the routine. He was almost out of the door, pushed rather than led by the constable, when Dexter stopped him with a light touch to one arm.

'Thanks, by the way,' she said, receiving a puzzled scowl in return.

'What for?'

'For being here. I was beginning to worry we'd cocked up, if you'll excuse the bad pun. Finding you's enough to justify the raid, even if we can't pin anything on anyone else.'

# 4

Dawn's early light was pinking the cloudy sky as McLean pushed open the back door and walked through into his kitchen. The familiar smells comforted him, the warmth from the Aga a welcoming embrace after the chill outside. Mrs McCutcheon's cat stared up from her usual spot in the middle of the big wooden table, her head bobbing up and down a couple of times as she tasted the air, decided he wasn't an intruder worth bothering about.

'Morning to you too.' He dumped his case down on a chair, heaved open the stove top and put the kettle on to boil. It was a reflex action, the thing you did as soon as you got in from a long shift, but no sooner had he started fishing around for mug, teabag and the ever-optimistic biscuit than McLean realised just how tired he was. They'd made a start on processing all the people in the New Town brothel, and with each new identity confirmed so the mood in the SCU had darkened. They'd been acting on good information, raided what had all the hallmarks of a brothel, found a house with a dozen bedrooms all occupied by men and women engaged in sexual acts of varying degrees of perversion. And yet none of the women they'd identified so far were sex workers, not by any stretched definition. There was no evidence any had taken payment, and they all appeared to be gainfully employed in more traditional walks of life. If it hadn't been for John Smith, they'd be screwed.

McLean smiled at the bad joke, poured boiling water on to the teabag and stared out the window at the garden beginning to extract itself from the darkness. Even with Mr Smith they were on dodgy ground, although it was unlikely anyone would complain too loudly that their swingers' party had been disrupted. He didn't much fancy the job of breaking the news to the Deputy Chief Constable, though. A lot of man hours had gone into the operation, a lot of overtime, a lot of expense. All for nothing. No wonder Jo Dexter was back on the cigarettes.

Clasping a mug of tea as much for the warmth as anything, he headed out of the kitchen, across the hallway to the front door. He scooped up a pile of mail, the fruits of at least two days' deliveries if the weight of them meant anything. Moving back to the SCU had been a mixed blessing. It got him out of the way of the newly promoted Detective Superintendent Brooks and Detective Chief Inspector Spence, marking their new territory like badly trained spaniels. But it also meant working odd shifts and further disrupting his already meagre sleep patterns. McLean couldn't remember a time when he hadn't felt weary, put upon and generally fed up.

It was still too dark to see properly in the hallway, so he took the pile of letters back to the kitchen. Leafing through the plastic-wrapped catalogues, offers of credit cards and other junk, he didn't really expect anything interesting. It was months since the last postcard from Emma and he found it increasingly hard to remember her face. How long had she been gone now? Eighteen months? Two years? McLean had almost given up hope that she would ever come back. And even if she did, could they pick up where they'd left off?

The shrill jangling of his mobile phone cut through the kitchen silence. DC – no, of course, Detective Sergeant – MacBride had programmed different ringtones for various regular callers, not that McLean ever remembered who was who. This was just the generic ringtone though, and a glance at the number on the screen didn't help. Five in the morning was a bit antisocial, too, but then it might have been desperation rather than rudeness. He thumbed the button, held the phone up to his ear.

'McLean.'

'Tony? Is that you?'

For a second McLean thought it was Emma calling, but only because he'd been thinking of her. It was a young woman's voice, but not the right young woman. Familiar, even if he couldn't quite place the name.

'Um . . . Yes.'

'I'm so sorry. Ringing so early and all that. Just didn't know where to turn. It's—'

'Rachel?' McLean finally made the connection, risked a quick look at the screen. It was a mobile number, but not international. 'You're in the UK?'

'I'm in Edinburgh, actually. Didn't know what to do. Jen's away at some big fashion event, won't be back for a week.'

'Slow down a bit, Rae. Are you OK? Is Phil OK?' McLean was trained not to jump to conclusions, but he couldn't help worrying when his best friend's wife rang up out of the blue. Even more so given she was supposed to be in San Francisco.

'Phil?' There was a bit of a pause, the line hissing slightly. 'No, Phil's fine. He's off on a field trip in New Mexico. I just couldn't . . . I needed to get away.'

McLean pulled out a chair, sat down at the kitchen table. Mrs McCutcheon's cat stood up, stretched, and then presented her head to be scratched. When had he last talked to Phil? He couldn't remember. So much for being best friends. Perhaps oldest friends was a better way of describing things.

'Where are you right now, Rae? Do you need a place to stay?' The words were out before he'd even considered the implications of the offer.

'I'm at Waverley Station at the moment. Are you sure? It won't be for long, honest. Just 'til Jenny gets back.'

'It's a big old house; there's plenty of room.' McLean was still trying to remember the last time he'd spoken to either of them or to Jenny, Phil's sister. Then it all started to fall into place.

'Aren't you expecting a baby soon?' he asked.

'Don't worry. It's a couple of months yet. That's why I came back, though. Couldn't bear the thought of my baby being born in America.'

McLean couldn't think why. Phil was on a senior professor's salary and presumably had a healthcare plan to go with it. He knew better than to ask, though.

'You want me to come and fetch you?' He looked up at the kitchen window, saw grey clouds as the light leached into the morning. What he really wanted was to crawl into bed and get some sleep. That seemed a distant prospect now.

'No. Thanks. I'll get a taxi.' Rachel paused for a moment before adding, 'If you're sure you don't mind.'

'If I did, I'd have said. I'll air out one of the spare bedrooms. Get yourself over here as quick as you can, and you can tell me what's going on face to face.'

*

It didn't take long for Rachel to arrive. At that time of the morning the traffic was very light, and if she'd phoned him from the station then finding a taxi wouldn't have been hard. McLean had bustled upstairs, thrown open a window in his grandmother's old room, checked the bed was made and then gone back down to the kitchen. In the back of his mind he was aware that he'd not slept in close on twenty-four hours, that he'd have to be back at work by one at the latest. He tried phoning Phil, but it went straight to a message, confirming what Rachel had said. His friend was away on a field trip and would be out of communication until the end of the month.

The crunch of car tyres on gravel startled him awake. He shook away the fatigue that had seen him half dozing at the table, clambered to weary feet. He reached the front door just as the taxi was turning away, leaving a small figure alone on the drive, only a rucksack for luggage.

'Rae. Hi. Here, let me get that.' He picked up the bag and ushered his guest into the hall. He didn't know her all that well, if he was being honest with himself. She'd come into Phil's life just a couple of years back, tied him down where so many others had tried and failed. McLean had been best man at the wedding, and in the run-up to that he'd spent plenty of time in the future Mrs Jenkins' company – or at least talking to her on the phone as she made sure every detail was taken care of – but no sooner had they come back from honeymoon than Phil had landed the job in California. This wasn't how he'd imagined their first reunion since then would go.

'I'd forgotten how big this place was.' Rachel stood in the middle of the hall, staring up to the round skylight so high above. She was shorter than McLean remembered, or was he confusing her with Emma? No, most likely it was the pronounced bulge of her pregnancy making her seem small in comparison. A couple of months away, she had said on the phone. He was no expert, but it looked more like a couple of weeks to him.

'Kettle's on, if you'd like a cup of tea. Or I can show you your room, let you get settled in. I tried calling Phil—'

It happened so quickly he didn't know how to react. One moment Rachel was standing a couple of paces away, the next she had enveloped him in a fierce hug, sobs racking her body as she buried her head in his shoulder. Not quite sure what else to do, McLean held her gently, waiting for the moment to pass. It took a long time, but eventually she stopped crying, stood away. In the growing light, he could see her face was puffy, eyes red from tears. Flecks of grey peppered her shoulder-length red hair and crease lines ran across her forehead. She looked as tired as he felt.

'Sorry.' She sniffed, ran the back of her hand under her nose like a teenager. 'I just didn't know where to turn.'

'Well, you're here now and you can stay as long as you need. But seriously, Rae, what's up? If I didn't know better I'd say you were running away from your husband.'

'I know. It's just, I don't know. It's not been easy. California should've been a dream, but it just didn't work out. They promised there'd be a job for me in the department, but I think they just said that to get us over there. It was always Phil they wanted. It was bad enough to begin with, but when this happened . . .' She patted her bulge. 'Let's just say neither of us really had that planned.'

It started to make a kind of sense. McLean knew his old

friend, the permanent adolescent. Phil might have been a brilliant scientist, but he wasn't exactly the most mature of people. How would he have coped with impending fatherhood? Not well, at least not until he really had to. And as had been the case ever since they'd first met, it would be McLean's job to hold the fort in the meantime. Ah well. It wasn't as if he had anything better to do with his spare time.

'Come on, Rae. Let's get that cuppa. Everything looks better after you've had some tea.'

# 5

He doesn't know what makes him stop.

Perhaps it's the way she's dressed: not tarted up like some cheap whore, and not hiding behind androgynous feminist camouflage either. He's seen both before, hopeful thumb out, scrap of cardboard with some distant destination scrawled on it in heavy black biro. Girls young enough to be his daughter, selling themselves for a few miles of road, or scowling at the capitalist scum who so clearly represents the system they would smash down. Not seeing – or refusing to admit – the irony in their begging for his help.

But this one is different.

She has hair a shade of dirty blonde, tied up in a tight ponytail and wedged under a sensible hat. She's wearing a woollen coat, tidy and expensive. Her skirt is tweed and cut unfashionably long. How far up her calves her dark brown leather boots go, he can't see, but they are built for walking, not beckoning. She's not as young as he first thought, either. Still youthful, but there's a far-off gaze in her eyes, a look of world-weariness that comes with the years. Her smile is friendly enough, as she leans to the window, reaches for the door handle.

'Trying to get to Edinburgh, aye?' Her voice is soft, almost hypnotic, a delightful Highlands burr. She has a scent about her that reminds him of happier times.

'Looks like you're in luck then. Headed there myself.'

'You're so kind. Room for my brother too?'

How could he have not noticed the man? He's standing right behind her, holding a dark leather bag; a Gladstone bag, isn't that what they call them? Together, it's obvious they're brother and sister. Same hair colour, same high cheekbones and narrow nose, same skin texture, same smile, same tidy, expensive, slightly archaic clothing. He wouldn't normally pick up one hitchhiker, let alone two, but there's something about this pair that makes him trust them. What could possibly go wrong?

'Aye, go on then.'

# 6

Lunch had long been and gone before McLean finally made it in to work. All the officers involved in the raid would be coming in late today, but the early shift should have been busy dealing with the interviews, processing the men and women they'd arrested the night before. Even so, an almost empty main SCU room was not what he expected to find, but when he walked in there were only a couple of uniform constables manning the phones and DCI Dexter staring thoughtfully at a whiteboard covered in scribbles.

'Afternoon,' he said as she turned to face him. 'Where is everyone?'

Dexter spread her arms wide. 'My wonderful team? I sent most of them home. Bugger all point moping around here.'

'What about the people we arrested? Who's processing them?'

'All done. All released. Well, apart from Mr Smith. Naughty little Mr Smith. We'll keep him a wee bit longer, let him sweat before we go and talk to him.'

McLean fancied he heard an edge of hysteria in Jo Dexter's voice. Fair enough; she'd not had any more sleep than the rest of them, probably less even than the couple of hours he'd managed to grab between Rachel showing up and his alarm going off. There was more to it than that, though; the DCI was almost legendary for her ability to survive on coffee and cigarettes.

'Everything OK, ma'am?'

'Don't you start "ma'am-ing" me, Tony. Bad enough I get it from the uniforms. Makes me feel like my mother.' Dexter slumped against the nearest desk. 'But since you ask, no. Very little is OK. The expression "clusterfuck" springs to mind. Probably just as well you only just got in, otherwise you'd have had to endure the DCC's wrath as well.'

McLean rested his backside against a chair. 'He was here? The deputy chief?'

'Seems one of the men we arrested last night knows enough people in high places. There were lawyers circling almost before we'd got anyone into the cells. We couldn't hold anyone.'

'Hang on a minute. A dozen men using an illegal brothel? One call to the DCC and they all get to go home with a slap on the wrists?'

'Illegal brothel's a tautology, Tony. No such thing as a legal one.'

'You know what I mean, Jo. How could we just let them go? And the sex workers as well?'

'If they'd actually been sex workers, we'd maybe have a leg to stand on. But they weren't. Not a single bloody one of them has so much as a hint of a record. Hell, they've all got jobs, boyfriends – husbands, some of them. Most of their men were there with them. Just not in the same rooms, if you get my meaning.'

McLean recalled the sinking feeling from the night before. With Rachel turning up unannounced, he had forgotten the nagging doubt. Now it came back even stronger.

'So what you're saying is we raided someone's swingers' party? It was a private house?'

Dexter grimaced, tapped her fingers against the edge of the desk in a rapidly accelerating drum roll, but otherwise said nothing.

'Christ. How the hell did we get that so wrong?'

'Because it was a fucking brothel last week, that's how. You sat in on the briefings, Tony. You saw the reports, the intel. We knew who was in there, who was working and who was using them. Should have been a textbook raid, and what do we turn up? Sweet fuck all except for a sicko on the register who just forgot to tell us he was in town.'

Dexter pushed herself away from the desk, all jittery nerves and pent-up energy. McLean could only guess at how much of a dressing-down she'd had from the deputy chief constable. All they needed now was for the press to get hold of the story.

'The press. Why were they there last night?'

'Eh?' Dexter had been fishing around in her jacket pockets and came out with a packet of cigarettes.

'I thought one of our lot had tipped them off, but what if it wasn't us?'

'I have no idea what you're going on about.'

'You said it yourself, Jo. Should have been a textbook raid. We knew it was a brothel, only when we turn up there it's actually a private house being used for swingers' parties? I don't buy it. Someone tipped them off. Not enough time to shut it down completely, so they did the next best thing and tipped the press off too, so we'd look even more stupid than usual.'

Dexter stared at him. She'd taken out one of the cigarettes and was tapping it absent-mindedly against the packet, spinning it round with each tap.

'And I thought my mind was twisted.' She shook her head as if trying to dislodge the idea. 'Fuck this for a game of soldiers. I need a fag.'

'There's someone in reception asking to see you, sir.'

McLean was on his way back to his temporary office in the SCU when Detective Constable Sandy Gregg waylaid him. He had been hanging out with DCI Dexter in the clear plastic bus shelter that had been set up around the back of the building for all the smokers, but the steady stream of officers nipping out for a quick cigarette had made discussing the not-a-brothel case almost impossible. He didn't much fancy having to dig out a fresh suit either, or sacrifice his lungs to the tobacco gods, so he had made his excuses and left before she had lit up her third, showing no sign of going back in any time soon.

'Any idea who? Only I'm fairly busy.'

'Sorry, sir. Just got handed the message by the duty sergeant. Said he'd tried your phone a couple of times but got no answer.'

McLean pulled his mobile out, stared at the blank screen. No doubt a couple of missed calls and voicemails would appear in due course. 'Guess I'd better go and see who it is then.'

It hadn't been designed that way, but the small waiting area just off from the main reception had a glass partition which meant that officers approaching from the business side of the building could see who was in there without themselves being seen. McLean didn't like looking at the people waiting there; it felt too much like the observation booths off the interview rooms, reminded him of watching a suspect sweat as they waited to be interrogated. There were two people sitting patiently, one of whom he recognised immediately. Short and round, Clarice Saunders ran a charity that helped sex workers who wanted to leave the industry. They had crossed paths before, when he'd last worked in the SCU, and while most of his colleagues thought she was an annoying busybody, he had a grudging respect for her stubborn tenacity.

'Someone to see me, apparently.' McLean tapped on the door of the reception booth, startling the uniform sergeant who had been leaning back in his chair, nose deep in a book.

'Sorry, sir. Yes. Came in about twenty minutes ago. Tried your phone, but . . .' As if on cue, McLean's mobile chimed in his pocket. Message received.

'Miss Saunders I know. What's she want?'

The sergeant scrabbled around with the rosters, managing to tip a pile of paperwork to the floor in a show of professionalism that suggested he would be more suited to a career in plain clothes. After a moment, he managed to retrieve the relevant pages, swivelling them round on his clipboard before handing them over.

'No idea, sir. Last night's raid'd be my guess.'

McLean turned back towards the reception area, unsure whether he had the energy for a bout with the formidable Ms Saunders. No point putting it off, though; she'd only be back again. He tried to hide the sigh that wanted to escape, maybe even managed it.

'Guess I'd better go talk to her then.'

'Miss Saunders. Sorry to keep you waiting. I only just got the message you were looking for me.'

Clarice Saunders snapped to attention as soon as she saw him. Her face had been relaxed, but the well-practised scowl slid into place swiftly. She stood up, not actually increasing her height by much, and puffed out her ample chest. McLean got the impression she was readying herself for a rant, and cut in before she could get started.

'Come through, please. It's not very comfortable in here.'

He led Saunders through the security door and along to the nicer interview room; the one with a window you could see through and a heating system that worked. It was normally used for people who genuinely were helping the police with their enquiries. That and storing boxes of Lothian and Borders Police headed notepaper that no one had found a use for yet.

'Can I get you a coffee or anything?' He pulled out a chair for her. McLean wasn't quite sure whether there should be another officer present. Perhaps he should have called DS Ritchie in.

'No, thanks. I've had what you call coffee in here before. Took me days to get the taste out of my mouth.'

'Umm . . . OK.' McLean took the seat across the table. 'What's this about then?'

'It's about the house you raided last night, Detective Inspector. It's about the women you've had locked up in the cells for hours. They've done nothing wrong, you know. It's the men—'

'I'm aware of your views on the law regarding prostitution, Ms Saunders. You might be surprised to find that I agree with you. On most of it, at least.' McLean once more interrupted Saunders before she could get fully into her stride. The tone of her voice was hectoring, but then he suspected she sounded like that even when she was in a good mood. He'd hoped to have surprised her by being reasonable, but clearly she wasn't having any of it today.

'Don't try to deny it. I have reliable sources. It's a shame no one spoke to me or my organisation in advance. We could have solved all this amicably, I'm sure.'

'Actually I wasn't going to deny anything. You might find it hard to believe, but I have a lot of time for the work you do. And as for the women? Well, we let them all go as soon as we'd spoken to them. The men too.'

A moment's pause, and then Saunders put on her best outraged voice. 'You've done what?'

'We let them go. Had to; they'd done nothing wrong. Well, not in the eyes of the law, anyway. Sixteen women engaged in varied consensual sexual practices with a dozen or so men, and not a single one of them was a sex worker, registered or otherwise.'

Saunders stared at him, her mouth hanging slightly open in disbelief. What had she really come here for?

'How come you thought that house was being run as a brothel?' McLean asked. 'Do you know more about it than you're letting on?'

Saunders started to speak. Then something stopped her.

There was a moment's pause as she gathered her thoughts, shook her head.

'Don't catch me out that easily. You know how our organisation works, Inspector. Sex workers won't talk to me if they think I'm just going to pass their details on to the police.'

'I wasn't going to ask for details . . .' McLean stopped speaking. That was exactly what he had been going to ask. Time to try a different tack. 'Look. I understand where you're coming from. I'm not really interested in harassing women trying to make a living that way. Much rather point them in the direction of organisations like yours than lock them up or fine them or whatever. But you know the law as well as I do. Two or more sex workers working out of the same building makes it a brothel, and that's against the law.'

'Except you said none of them were sex workers. So this was, in fact, a private party in a private house. I imagine there are a few red faces in the station today.'

McLean couldn't help noticing the triumph in Saunders' voice as she spoke. It was matched by an expression on her face all too easy to read. There was no way she was going to help him out of this embarrassing situation. A shame, really, since a favour given was a favour owed as far as he was concerned.

'Let's just say we're as surprised by the way things turned out as you are. Leave it at that.' He stood up, and Saunders did the same reflexively. 'But as I said, we've not taken any sex workers into custody, so there's really no need for you to be here. Rest assured, I'll be passing your contact details on to anyone I think could use them.'

# 7

McLean wasn't sure which he preferred, the office he had been given at the SCU or the tiny little boxroom back at his old station. This one was bigger, and the window didn't look out directly on to a stone wall just a few feet away. On the other hand, his old office was out of the way, which meant he wasn't often interrupted there by people passing. And for all its tendency to be too hot in summer and too cold in winter, at least his old office window hadn't leaked. This one did, especially when the wind was in the northeast, throwing cold rain at the glass wall like a suburban dad with a pressure washer. The carpet tiles showed evidence of storms past in archaeological rings spreading out from the grey aluminium frame, and everything smelled of mould. Then again, this office was big enough both for the desk and a couple of extra chairs. You could even see some floor, dubious carpet stains and all. And it wasn't piled to the ceiling with paperwork needing his immediate attention. At least not yet.

The chair behind his desk was comfortable, too. He leaned back in it, resisting the urge to put his feet up. Outside, the sky was taking on the colour of a week-old bruise as the evening progressed towards night. Once again the day seemed to have slipped away far too quickly.

Flicking on his laptop screen, McLean checked his emails. He scrolled down through endless admin junk and invitations to training sessions, deleted anything that looked like he'd just been copied in as an arse-covering exercise and shuffled all the important stuff into various subfolders where he could safely forget about it until people either came and found him or picked up the phone. Paper trail be damned, email really was the invention of the devil. He reached for his mobile phone, lying on the desk in front of him. He'd been intending to put it in his pocket, switch off the computer and go home, possibly via the curry shop, but as his fingers brushed the metal casing the screen lit up and the phone began to ring. A glance at the clock showed it was late for a social call, but then the name appearing on the screen wasn't exactly someone he would ever consider socialising with. No point trying to avoid it; part of him had known this was coming sooner or later. He picked up the handset, thumbed the screen to accept.

'Ms Dalgliesh. What an unexpected pleasure.'

'You're all heart, Inspector. How's the heid?'

McLean reached instinctively for his temple, even though the injury he'd sustained there had long since healed. As much as he disliked the reporter, he couldn't ignore the fact that she'd saved his life.

'Fine. I take it this isn't a social call, though.'

'Well. No' exactly. I was hoping you might be able to give me a wee bit of a heads-up. Heard you were back in Vice, aye?'

'We call it the Sexual Crimes Unit, actually. But yes, I'm part of that team.' McLean tried not to sigh; he knew where this was going.

'So you'll have been part of the wee raid the other night then. The knocking shop in the New Town? Only, way I hear it, wasn't a knocking shop after all. Just a bunch of weirdos and their wee sex club. Must be a few red faces in the department the now. Mebbe red faces all round, come to think of it.' Dalgliesh chuckled at her own joke.

McLean didn't answer right away. He leaned back again in his chair, staring at the stained ceiling tiles, and let the silence lengthen. It wasn't surprising that the reporter had heard about the raid, of course. It wasn't even surprising that she'd come to him for information, given their history. But he couldn't help remembering the car parked up the street from the New Town terrace house and the assumption he'd made that it was journalists inside. They'd taken everyone out the back, loading them into vans with blacked-out windows so that no one would be identifiable, but he couldn't remember if anyone had actually approached the hacks to ask them what they were doing.

'You're very well informed, Ms Dalgliesh,' he said eventually.

'Is that a roundabout way of telling me I'm right?'

'It wasn't meant to be, but you are. We'll be having a press conference tomorrow, anyway.' He sat forward again, picked up a pen and wrote 'Press Conference?' on the nearest scrap of paper he could find. 'At least be putting out a press release, anyway.'

'What about the cock-up? You admitting to that too?'

'Let's just say we're not entirely convinced it was a cock-up, OK?'

'Go on.' Dalgliesh's voice dripped with intrigue and McLean knew he had her hooked.

'Well, your lot knew something was up, right? Otherwise why send a couple of paps out to get juicy photos?'

'Our lot?'

'Come on, Dalgliesh. I saw them myself. Parked up the road with a long lens, waiting for us to parade a bunch of people out through the front door. Someone tipped you off, and told you it'd be worth your while too. So who were you expecting to see?'

This time the silence came from the other end of the line, the reporter no doubt weighing up the cons of giving away too much information about her sources against the pros of a possibly even more interesting story. McLean knew how to be patient.

'You're right we had a tip-off,' Dalgliesh said finally. 'Normally reliable source. Not the police, before you ask. Told us it would be worth our while keeping an eye on the house. Don't suppose you found anyone famous in there with their troosers down?'

'Always looking for the story, eh? No. Sadly no one famous. No politicians, no captains of industry or public figures. Just a bunch of ordinary people with unusual sexual appetites. It wasn't a brothel and they weren't breaking any laws, so we've not charged any of them. Which begs a question, don't you think?'

'It does?' Dalgliesh feigned uninterest well, but McLean knew her better than that.

'Go speak to your source, ask them what they thought you were going to find. We had good intel there was a brothel running out of that house; you had a reliable source tell you there was some salacious news to be had from our raid. Looks like we've both been played for fools here. The real question you should be asking is why.'

\*

The last gloaming light of the evening painted the trees in shadow as McLean piloted his little Alfa up the drive. On the passenger seat beside him a bag of takeaway curry leaned against a half-dozen bottles of beer; the rest of the night taken care of. It was only when he stepped out of the car, saw the light from the kitchen window spilling on to the back lawn, that he remembered his house guest. He hauled the curry and beer out, trying to work out if there was enough to eat for two, if Rachel was vegetarian. A small part of him wondered why he'd agreed to let her stay, but it was a tiny voice he'd long since grown accustomed to ignoring.

Mrs McCutcheon's cat looked up at him as he entered the kitchen, sniffing the air to see what he'd brought her this time. Almost certainly not enough curry for three, perhaps he could phone for something. He put the bag down on the table, was reaching for the handset when Rachel came in from the hallway.

'Thought I heard something. Phil said you worked ridiculous hours, Tony. I never really believed him, though.'

'Comes with the territory, I'm afraid. As does forgetfulness.' McLean waved hand and phone in the general direction of the takeaway. 'I only bought the one curry, but there should be enough for us to share. I can phone for something else if you'd rather.'

Rachel eyed the bag, a hungry expression on her face. McLean had told her to treat the place like her own, but he'd not noticed much food disappearing from the fridge or the cupboards. Not that there was much to disappear, mind you, but he wasn't sure she'd eaten much more than a few slices of toast since she'd shown up at his door. He had the impression she'd not been out of the house either, almost as if she were hiding from the world, not just her husband. Who he would have to try phoning again, as he had done every day since Rachel had arrived. How long could a man go on a field trip for and not check his phone?

He found plates, divided up the meal into two surprisingly large portions, poured a beer and offered it to his guest.

'No alcohol for baby, thanks.' Rachel patted her bulge as she pulled out a chair and settled into it heavily.

'Of course. Sorry.' He put the glass down on the table. 'Can I get you something else?'

'It's OK. Thanks. I'll have some tea when I've eaten.' She picked up a fork and started on her curry. Despite her obvious hunger, she took small bites, he noticed, chewing each mouthful slowly. He was more used to wolfing down his food as quickly as he could; eating was a necessity these days, hardly a pleasure. Still, he tried to match her pace.

'This is very good,' Rachel said after a while. 'Shame I've not got much room to spare.' She put her fork down on a plate still half-full of food. Mrs McCutcheon's cat wouldn't go wanting after all.

'Probably the least healthy lifestyle I could have, eating curries or Chinese most evenings, or whatever's left in the station canteen. There never seems to be time to cook anything, though, and it's a pain anyway, making something just for one.'

'Yeah. I guess it is.' Rachel had been looking at him, but now her stare unfocused, as if she was seeing something miles off.

'You spoken to Phil today?'

She started at the question, a guilty look flitting across

her face. 'I left a message. He's still not back from the desert, obviously. You'd think he'd have a bit more concern for his wife so close to . . .' She patted her belly. 'Well, you know.'

McLean didn't need years of police training and experience interviewing suspects to see the lie. Best not to call it, at least not now.

'I spoke to Jen, though. She's going to be home in a few days. Said she'd drop by as soon as she can, take me off your hands.' She paused before adding, 'If that's OK?'

'Her taking you away, or you staying until she does?' McLean smiled as he asked, hoping to convey that he meant it as a joke. Rachel's frown suggested he'd missed the mark.

'Look, Rae. You're my best friend's wife. You can stay here as long as you want. I've plenty of space. But sooner or later Phil's going to call me back. I'll have to tell him what's going on, you know?'

Rachel went back to staring into the middle distance again, silent for a while before finally looking straight at him. 'I know, Tony. It's just . . . Well, it's not easy. I don't really know where to start.'

McLean pushed the last of his curry around the plate before deciding that he didn't really have the appetite for it any more. Mrs McCutcheon's cat was going to be very well fed indeed. He got up, filled the kettle and put it on the Aga to boil, all the while aware of Rachel's dark, round eyes following him. He found a mug, dropped a teabag into it, added boiling water, then realised he couldn't remember how Rachel liked her tea. In the end he opted for putting the mug down in front of her, fetching the milk bottle from the fridge. There was sugar in a bowl in the middle of the table; she could help herself.

'Stay as long as you need to,' he said eventually. 'And if Jen's not got a room she can spare, don't worry about it.'

Rachel's relief spread like a warm glow across her face, tears glistening in the corners of her eyes. 'You mean it?'

'Sure. It's not as if I've a full house, after all.'

# 8

'You're a very kind man, you know that?'

He doesn't really understand how he has got here. For a moment he can't even tell where here is, then the details begin to filter through. The grey, pebble-dashed concrete screened with wire mesh as if the building might just slough off its outer skin at any moment. The dull, lifeless eyes of the windows, empty, abandoned rooms behind. The tarmac, rippled and cracked by endless cycles of hot summer sun and bitter winter chill. The shiny pewter-grey bonnet of his car through a windscreen spattered with a thousand dead insect bodies. Slowly, as if his thoughts are wading through warm treacle, he begins to see where he is. What he can't understand is how he came to be here. The last thing he remembers is . . . what? Driving. A woman standing at the side of the road, thumb out. A Gladstone bag.

'It would have taken us an age to walk all the way here.'

The voice registers. She's sitting beside him in the passenger seat. As he looks around at her, he notices for the first time that his hands are still on the steering wheel as if the car has only just this moment stopped. Ten to two like they teach in advanced driving. He wants to lift them off, but it's as if they're glued in place. As if he is merging with the car, becoming one with the machine.

'—' He opens his mouth to speak, but no sound comes

out. Whether it's his voice that fails, or the thickness of the air choking away all sound, he can't tell. The woman sitting beside him reaches across, places a hand on his thigh, fingertips caressing the inside in an unmistakably sensual way. He tries to move, but cannot.

'Shh.' The sound is like a snake slithering through autumn leaves, and with it the hand becomes more intimate. More searching. He should stop her, he knows. This isn't right, isn't necessary. But he cannot move, can only stare at her pale blue eyes, her mischievous smile. He knows this is wrong, but he is only a man. And it's not as if he has forced this upon her. Quite the opposite.

'No good deed should go without reward,' she says, and the scent of her swells in the confines of the car until he is struggling to breathe. As she leans towards him, breaks eye contact, his head slumps back against the car seat. He can't stop the stuttered gasps that escape from his throat, the hammering of his heart and the building pressure. His sight dims, eyes losing focus as he stares out the window at the rough concrete wall, oblivious to everything. Almost everything.

When the explosion comes, it is not in his loins but in his head. A wave of bright white that he rides to oblivion. And with that last dying surge he sees a face in the rear-view mirror. Remembers the other passenger. The brother, sitting quietly in the back. Watching.

# 9

'Well, Mr Smith. It would seem you've been telling us lies.'

The interview room smelled of unwashed male. John Smith had already been up in front of the Sheriff Court, refused bail and remanded in custody, but in the days that had followed he didn't appear to have washed. Either that or it was his natural odour. McLean wrinkled his nose, trying not to breathe too much. He was only sitting in on this interview; the actual grilling was being done by DCI Dexter. Her involvement spoke volumes as to how much pressure the whole Sexual Crimes Unit was under to rescue something, however small, from the debacle that had been the brothel raid.

'Seems you've spent a bit of time inside.' Dexter had been pacing the room, clasping a folder in her hand. Now she opened it up as if she needed to consult the list of convictions written inside. Admittedly it wasn't short, but there was a certain amount of repetition that made it easy enough to memorise.

'Where do you actually buy Rohypnol these days? You don't strike me as the kind of guy who could fool a doctor into prescribing it.'

'I would caution you not to answer that, Mr Smith.'

Smith's solicitor had moved his chair a little further away from his client the moment he'd sat down, as if he too found the smell difficult to live with. He was a small man, but fat, bulging out of his ill-fitting suit and sweating even though the airless interview room wasn't particularly warm. Pretty much all he'd done so far was identify himself, complain about his client being denied bail, and then tell him not to answer each question as it was asked. He needn't have bothered. Smith said nothing, just sat on his side of the table, one hand clasped in the other, both resting in his lap. To a casual observer he appeared calm, but McLean knew one or two tells when he saw them. Every time Dexter asked a question, the muscles in Smith's jaw would tense, twitching at the side of his neck slightly as he bit down the urge to answer. The effort of keeping his expression slack was beginning to tell, too; his blink rate had increased noticeably in the past ten minutes.

And then there was the smell.

'Charge sheet lists half a dozen accusations against you that never played out. What's the betting you've notched a fair few more than that on your belt, eh?'

This time Smith looked up at Dexter briefly, before dropping his gaze back down to the table.

'And then there's poor old Eileen Dornan. You couldn't have known she was already taking the stuff regularly. One tablet just wasn't enough, was it? And she remembered what you'd done to her. Clever enough to get herself tested, too. Not that it did her much good, poor soul.'

That got another look, the slightest questioning cock of the head.

'What? You didn't know? No, of course you didn't. She was just another conquest, after all. And I guess you were inside at the time.' Dexter dropped the folder down on to the table, leaning over it so her face was close to Smith's. Or as close as was safe.

'She took an overdose. That's what happened. Inquest said suicide, but if I had my way it'd be down on the sheets as murder.'

Smith opened his mouth to say something, but his solicitor butted in.

'My client agreed to this interview in an attempt to clear up what appears to be a simple misunderstanding that has seen him deprived of his liberty and unable to continue his work. If all you're going to do is bring up his past . . .' He looked up at Dexter, then across to McLean. Beside him, Smith closed his mouth slowly, settling back down into his chair as he did so.

'Doesn't matter anyway. Except maybe to Eileen's family and friends.' Dexter resumed her pacing. 'What does matter is the Sexual Offences Act and the sex offenders' register. You're on it, Mr Smith, and yet you didn't think it worthwhile telling us you'd moved to town. You know what that means, don't you, John?'

Smith said nothing, just stared at his hands, but the twitching in his jaw showed the battle inside.

'My client has already explained and apologised for his oversight—'

'You didn't much enjoy being inside, did you, John?' McLean pitched his voice low, keeping his tone reasonable in contrast to Dexter's aggression. Smith didn't react at first, but then slowly lifted his head.

'Nobody likes a rapist, but criminals are an odd bunch. They have this strange, warped kind of moral code. They really don't like sex offenders, and they tend to be very direct in letting you know how they feel, don't they?'

The nod was almost imperceptible, but it was there. McLean pressed on.

'I'm guessing they did . . . things to you. Made you do . . . things.' He laid extra emphasis on 'things', seeing the flinch grow with each repetition.

'What do you want?' Smith's voice was little more than a whisper.

'Mr Smith. I really must—'

'The house where we found you, the party, the women. Who organised all that? How did you get invited? Can't see you as the sort of man who'd set that all up himself.'

Smith's expression changed from blank slackness to worry in a slow reflection of the thought processes churning in his brain. This was the point where he'd either clam up, go back to staring at his hands and end up back in prison as soon as the paperwork was dealt with. Or he might just open up and shed a little light on their mysterious brothel-that-wasn't.

'I would caution you not to answer that, Mr Smith.'

'I . . . I can't.' Smith dropped his head, exhaling in a long, low sigh. Closed his mouth tight and would say no more.

'Dammit. I thought we had him for a moment.'

Outside the interview room, McLean watched as John Smith was led back down to the cells by a couple of uniform PCs. Both were large, burly men; he'd made sure of that. The solicitor had already gone, pleading an appointment clearly far more important than keeping a serial rapist out of prison.

'We've still got time. He's not going anywhere in a hurry.'

'Unless the bastard manages to secure bail. His legal

team have already called for a second hearing.' Dexter leaned against the wall, hands shoved deep into the pockets on the front of her long jacket. McLean knew there was a packet of cigarettes in there that was occupying most of her attention. So much for trying to quit.

'You reckon he'll get it this time?'

'They'll put a tag on him, set him loose. Mark my words. It's cheaper than keeping him on remand. Or more profitable for someone, at least.'

McLean raised an eyebrow at that. Dexter was getting cynical in her old age.

'Well, if he's tagged we can follow him. Might get us further than the good cop bad cop routine anyway.'

'If he even knows anything. Slimy little shit. What was he doing in that house?' Dexter held up a hand before McLean could start his reply. 'And I don't mean what was he actually doing when you found him. I saw the two he was with. No, I mean how did he come to be there? Who does he know? What kind of person invites someone on the register to a swingers' party?'

'What about the tenant, Miss Marchmont? You talked to her yet?'

'Briefly. Really didn't help that she's a lawyer.' Dexter almost spat the word out. 'Damn them all and their scaly hides.'

'A lawyer?' McLean remembered the books in Marchmont's bedroom. 'Think she knows Mr Smith's friendly weeble there?' He nodded in the direction of the interview room, recently vacated by the fat solicitor.

'Nah, she's corporate. No' someone you'd have come across in court. Still, makes life difficult for us.'

'You think she'll take it further? I mean, I don't imagine going public's going to help her career much. She's either running a brothel or has eclectic sexual peccadilloes. Either way it's as embarrassing for her as it is for us.'

'I wish I had your faith in human nature, Tony.' Dexter scowled, as if McLean's ignorance on matters of sexual adventurism was a personal insult. 'Still doesn't hide the fact that we fucked up, though. How the hell did that happen? We had solid intel that was a brothel.' She kicked away from the wall. 'Fuck it, I'm off for a cigarette. You want one?'

McLean shook his head. He knew it was an invitation to keep on discussing the case, but he didn't much feel like following his boss out into the cold car park. 'I'll head back up to the office, go over the logs, make sure we're not missing something.'

'You do that, Tony. I'll catch up with you later.'

Dexter headed off in the direction of the smoking shed but McLean stood for a moment in the corridor. It was quiet here, away from the bustle of the rest of the building. The door to the interview room was still open, and he stepped back inside, closed the door. It still smelled of unwashed bodies, but the aroma was dissipating, sucked out by the quiet ventilation fan. No window in here, of course. Not like the interview room where he'd met Clarice Saunders. What had brought her to the station? She'd been sure they'd raided a brothel, had been keen to protect the sex workers they'd arrested. But they hadn't arrested any; the women had all been professionals of a different kind. Lawyers, for instance. That couldn't have been who Saunders was referring to, surely?

Still trying to make sense of it all, McLean left the interview room and climbed up the stairs to the SCU offices. Open plan, most of the desks spread haphazardly around the large room were unoccupied, but a familiar figure sat at one. She looked up as the door banged shut behind him, offered a weary smile. He still didn't quite understand why DS Ritchie had asked to be transferred over to the unit with him but he was grateful nonetheless.

'Afternoon, sir. I was about to give you a call.' Ritchie's voice cracked slightly as she spoke. Tired as everyone else on the case.

'You were? Anything important?'

'Just wanted to arrange a time to go over the interviews. Might as well try and make something of them, eh?' She hefted a thick wodge of papers, let them fall back to the desk with a dull thud. 'Fancy giving me a hand?'

McLean picked up the first sheet of the pile, scanned the poorly typed transcript of an interview with a woman called Theresa Gardiner. From what he could gather she was twenty-six, lived in Cramond, ran her own IT consultancy and had a thing for leather. Not your typical streetwalker then.

'We got Heather Marchmont's interview in here?' he asked.

Ritchie's eyebrow shot up. Or at least the skin above her eye wrinkled and arched; the hair of her eyebrows had never really grown back after it had been burned off in the fire she'd pulled him from a couple of years earlier.

'Oh God. Her.' She shuffled through the papers. 'Should be here somewhere. Why?'

'Well, it's her house. At least she's the tenant, pays the rent. Got to assume she's involved in organising the party.'

53

Ritchie fished out the relevant transcript and handed it over. It was thinner than most. 'We didn't get much out of her, to be honest. She was . . . weird.'

McLean said nothing, hoping Ritchie would explain herself. The detective sergeant just fell silent, staring into the middle distance as if reliving some experience she'd rather not. He flicked through the transcript, finding little useful information. Difficult to get a tone of voice from written words, but he could almost hear the terseness in Marchmont's answers. As soon as she'd identified her profession as lawyer, the interview had come to a stop, even though she hadn't actually threatened any legal action.

'We should go and talk to her.' He handed the transcript back to Ritchie. It took her a moment to realise that was what he was doing, and when she took it, something like fear slid across her features for the briefest of moments.

'We?'

'Well, I can hardly go talk to her on my own now, can I?' McLean checked the clock hanging on the wall over the entrance. The afternoon was gone, rolling into evening, which probably explained the empty desks. 'Sort something out, will you? We'll go to her. Home or office, I don't mind which.' He paused a moment, remembering the terrace house and its dungeon. 'Maybe office would be best.'

## 10

McLean wasn't sure what the owner of his local curry shop was called. Not that he didn't speak to the staff who served him, one of whom was almost undoubtedly the man in charge. It was just that there were so many of them, and they came and went with such frequency, he never quite managed to pin a name to a face with enough certainty to make it worth the risk of getting it wrong. His visits were frequent but short-lived, so there wasn't much chance for in-depth conversation anyway. Still, it was nice to see a familiar face on his way home from work, perhaps not every day but more often than was healthy. It wasn't often that the familiar face was on the same side of the serving counter as him, though.

'Never really saw the attraction of curry myself. Hurts going in, hurts even more coming out. Where's the fun in that, aye?'

McLean turned around from the counter where he had been about to place his order, not really surprised to find Jo Dalgliesh sitting on the plastic bench against the far wall. She was wearing her long leather overcoat despite the heat, and a soft canvas bag beside her hung open to reveal the tools of her trade – notebooks, pens, digital recorder, camera and cigarettes.

'Seems an odd place to come for your tea if you don't like curries.'

'Aye, well. Work'll take youse all sorts of places you don't much like. Got any recommendations for something that won't take the skin off the roof of my mouth?'

McLean was tempted to suggest a phaal, but thought better of it. 'You a veggie?'

'Fuck off.'

'Just asking. No need to get nasty. I'd recommend the chicken korma then. Nice and creamy. Only you're not here for a curry, are you?'

'No' really. Might try it and see what keeps bringing you back, mind. Anyone wanted to kidnap you it'd be a piece of piss. Station, home, here. Maybe the Chinese down the road a ways once in a while. You're an easy man to track, McLean.'

'Was there something you actually wanted to speak to me about, Dalgliesh? Only it's been a long day and I'd really like it to end soon.'

'Aye, don't get your panties all in a heech. I wanted to talk to you about that wee raid that went tits up. Or tits oot, depending on your point of view.'

McLean didn't laugh at the pathetic joke, and neither did Dalgliesh. He could see that she was skirting around the real issue, which made him suspect she wanted something. If she'd been about to put the knife in then she'd have been far more insufferable.

'Suit yourself.' The reporter closed the notebook she'd been writing in and dropped it into her bag, pulled the whole thing closed and hung it over her shoulder as she spoke. 'Wasn't my story to start with, and you know us lot don't exactly play well together, but I found out who the source was, went and had a wee chat. Only they made like they'd never heard of the place. Never talked to nobody. Didn't know nothing.'

'Someone got to them?'

'That much seems pretty obvious. Just can't work out who. Or why. I mean, she . . . the contact's no' exactly important. Least I didn't think so.'

'You sure you got the right person?'

Dalgliesh gave McLean a scowl, but drew short of telling him to fuck off again. The last one had drawn angry looks from the man behind the counter.

'OK. OK. I didn't mean to question your journalistic prowess. So your contact's been leaned on. Isn't the first time, won't be the last.'

'Aye, but it's interesting. Way I hear it, you had good intel there was a brothel in that house. High class, mind. Catering to folk with money and strange fetishes. Pretty much tallies with what we heard too, along with when you lot were going to raid the place. Only when you turn up there's no working girls to be found. Makes you think.'

'You reckon it's a cover-up? They knew we were coming and that was the only way to explain the more esoteric equipment we found there?' McLean recalled the dungeon and a naked man stuck in his cage, another shackled to a table by his intimate parts. He'd wondered the same thing himself immediately after the raid. Put it down to paranoia on account of too little sleep. 'Seems a bit far-fetched, doesn't it? You'd need some serious organisation to pull something like that off. And at short notice too.'

'Aye, I ken that. Something doesn't smell right, mind. And I'm no' meaning your curry.' Dalgliesh nodded in the direction of the counter, where a bag had just been brought through from the kitchen beyond. McLean didn't recall ordering anything, but then they knew him well enough now that he didn't really have to.

'You reckon there's a story in it. And you want my help.' The penny dropped.

'No' sure at the moment, but I'm digging. There's something going on I can't see, and I don't like that. But I'll find out what it is.'

McLean paid for his curry, picked up the bag. 'Got to run before this gets cold,' he said. 'But if I can help, I will.'

'You will?' Dalgliesh looked genuinely surprised.

'Sure. If it means you're not writing stories about how incompetent we are.'

Dalgliesh's words were still weighing on his mind as McLean stepped through into the kitchen, dumped the bag and its precious contents on to the table. Mrs McCutcheon's cat looked up at him from the tattered rug in front of the Aga, checking the aroma to decide whether she was going to be well fed again. The darkness outside and the fact she wasn't sitting in the middle of the table where she usually waited for him suggested that autumn was on its way out now. Certainly there was a chill to the air after what had been a long, warm and muggy spell of weather. He wasn't entirely sure where the seasons went, where the years went for that matter. Time lost all meaning when each day was much the same as the last.

The daily routine included a trip to the front door to see what the postman had brought. These last few days Rachel had sifted through the mail, piling it on the wooden chest that sat in the porch by the front door. McLean couldn't for the life of him think why. No one knew she was here, not even her husband if the lack of response to his many messages was anything to go by. It was unlikely any of the letters would be for her.

Low noise spilled out from a half-open door as he walked across the hall; the television he so rarely had time or inclination to watch. He shuffled through the pile of junk mail and bills, hoping there might be a postcard but knowing it was unlikely. He couldn't remember how long it was since Emma's last card, which suggested it was too long. Had she grown bored of writing them? Was she even still on her travels? He found it hard to picture her, the image in his mind half the spiky-haired, energetic whirlwind of chaos he had first met, half the quiet, intense woman she had become after spending months in a coma.

Shaking his head to dispel the thought, he pushed open the library door. The television sat on an antique table in front of one of the bookcases on the other side of the room, placed so it could be easily viewed from the sofa. Rachel lay propped up on cushions and draped with a heavy blanket against the cold. McLean was about to tell her that she should have lit the fire when he realised that she was fast asleep, the remote control lying on the floor beside her outstretched hand. He retrieved it, stared at the flickering images for a moment and then switched the television off. He should probably have woken her, suggested she go upstairs to bed, but she looked so peaceful laid out on the sofa he hadn't the heart to disturb her.

Back in the kitchen, Mrs McCutcheon's cat had abandoned the Aga and was up on the table, sniffing at the bag of curry.

'There's plenty for everyone. Just be patient.' McLean found a plate and a beer, scooped half of the food on to the one and poured the other into a glass. The kitchen was warm but the rest of the house had a chill about it. Soon he'd have to venture down into the basement and fire up the old boiler. Not that it actually heated the place, but the gurgling noises it made through the ancient cast-iron radiators reminded him of his childhood and happier times.

Normally after eating he would have gone through to the library. Perhaps listened to some music while he read through the work that had followed him home. Knowing Rachel was asleep in there, McLean lingered over his meal instead, listening to the quiet tock of the clock on the kitchen wall, the soft noises of the Aga and the hum of the fridge. The quiet was something he savoured, a chance to think. He might have done some work, but it was late and it would still be there in the morning.

'There you go. Just don't be sick like the last time.' He scraped some curry and rice into the cat's bowl, keeping enough back for Rachel should she wake hungry. It was unlikely; she hardly seemed to eat anything and always complained that the baby left her no room for food anyway. A couple of months, she had said, but McLean didn't believe that any more now than he had when she'd first arrived. It was surprising the airline had let her fly home.

The light was still on and the library door hanging half-open as he climbed the stairs to bed, so the voice behind him as he opened his bedroom door gave McLean more of a fright than was reasonable.

'You turned off the telly.' Rachel appeared from the shadows like a ghost, still draped in her blanket.

'Thought you were asleep.'

'I was. Sorry. Just get so tired sometimes.' Rachel winced, a hand going to her stomach. 'Little bugger never gives me much peace. I can't remember the last time I slept more than an hour straight.'

'Not long now, I guess. You hear from Phil yet?'

Rachel's expression was answer enough.

'He'll be in touch, Rae. Just give him time. I can't imagine this is easy for either of you.' McLean stifled a yawn, risked a glance at his bed in the room beyond the open door.

'You have the smallest room in the house.' Rachel leaned past him, not quite crossing the threshold, but peering in nonetheless. 'I'd have thought you'd have the biggest.'

'This is where I grew up. It was always my room. Seems, I don't know, a bit weird moving into my gran's room or one of the spare rooms. Comfy enough where I am.'

Rachel stepped back, a fleeting smile on her face. 'You're a strange man, Tony. A good man, but strange.' She leaned forward and kissed him lightly on the cheek. 'Sleep well.'

And then she turned away, the darkness swallowing her as if she were no more than a dream.

'I don't rent out rooms to just anyone, you know.'

She eyes the pair of them suspiciously. Turning up on her doorstep first thing is not good, even if they have the reference. True, they're well dressed, but that doesn't mean as much as it used to. Look at the luggage, that's more of an indication if she's any judge. Too much and they're staying longer than they've any right to. Not enough and they're up to no good. These two don't have much, but it errs on the right side. And they're well dressed. And they have a reference from . . . Well, she knows better than to question them.

'I'm sure you run a very proper establishment, Mrs . . .'

'Prendergast. And it's Miss. There are rules if you want to stay here. I'm not running a bawdy house, you know.'

The girl smiles slightly at this. It's not an unkind smile, but something in it prickles the back of Miss Prendergast's neck.

'We won't be staying long. Just a little unfinished business to attend to in the capital.'

'And you just want the one room?'

'As long as it has two beds. I love my brother dearly, but it's a long time since last we had to share.'

The young woman smiles again, fixing Miss Prendergast with a stare that is pure innocence. There is no harm in her at all, it says. She can be trusted, as can her brother.

'Of course, of course. I have just the room, if you'll follow me.'

She leads them up the stairs, pausing at the first floor.
The front room here has two single beds in it, a good view
out over the road. They'll be comfortable in there, this
strange brother and sister. But before she can take out the
key, a hand touches hers, stops her.

'Higher up?' It is the young man, the first time she has
heard him speak. His accent is like his sister's, cultured,
polite, a lilt of Western Highlands about it.

'You don't mind the stairs?'

'We are both of us young, Miss Prendergast. We'll manage. And I like to be able to look down.'

She considers a moment, then takes them up two more
flights of stairs. The room is in the roof, walls sloping
down to the floor. Two narrow beds have their heads to
the gable, a single shaft of sunlight lying across them from
the narrow roof window. It smells of stale air and dust; no
one has been up here in a while.

'This is perfect.' The young woman pushes past her,
boots clumping noisily on the bare wooden floorboards. It
is not a big room, so the inspection doesn't take long, ending with her sitting heavily on the end of one of the beds.
If she notices the cloud of dust billowing up from the covers, she doesn't mention it.

Miss Prendergast clears her throat. 'There's no visitors
after nine p.m., no food to be consumed in the room. The
bathroom is across the landing there; please do not use all
the hot water. And I'll need a week's rent in advance.'

The young woman's smile flickers momentarily, then
she rises to her feet, walks back to where Miss Prendergast

stands just inside the doorway. Before she knows what's happening, the young woman has taken both her hands, holding them together as if in prayer. She brings them up to her breast slowly, all the while staring deep into Miss Prendergast's eyes. There is a scent about her that is hard to place. It evokes spring, memories of childhood.

'Are you sure that's really necessary?'

She has run this guest house for years, along with her sister before Esme died. Now it's just her, but she knows the rules. She has never let a lodger stay without the first week's rent in advance. And yet these two seem so trustworthy; they are surely honest people. She doesn't need to bother about money just now. And besides, they're taking a room she's not rented out in a decade. More. And they have that reference. Almost family. What harm can come of it?

'I'll just give you your key then.' Miss Prendergast extricates her hands from the young woman's hold, pulls a single heavy key from the pocket of her cardigan and hands it over.

'I lock the front door at eleven sharp. If you're not back by then you'll have to take your chances I'm still awake.'

The young woman takes the key from her unresisting fingers, and there's that smile again. 'Don't you worry about us. We'll be as quiet as church mice. You won't even know we're here.'

'Hope you don't mind me calling you in on this one, Tony. Thought you might be a bit more use than that idiot Carter.'

McLean climbed out of his car as Detective Chief Inspector Jayne McIntyre approached. It was perhaps the only silver lining in the shuffling of seats that had followed Detective Superintendent Duguid's retirement that McIntyre had been promoted to DCI. She should have been Deputy Chief Constable by now, but that particular career path had been cut short by an incident involving an investigative journalist and a punch on the nose. It only made McLean respect her more.

'What's the situation? You said something about a body?' Reckon there's foul play?'

'That's kind of what I wanted you here to help with. It's unusual, I'll give you that much. Probably best if you see for yourself first.'

They were on the top storey of the car park at the back of the St James Centre, looked down upon by the empty windows of New St Andrew's House. The only other cars here were either police or forensics, except for the familiar British racing green and mud Jaguar of the City Pathologist, McLean's own rather incongruous red Alfa Romeo GTV and an anonymous silver-grey repmobile that seemed to be the centre of attention.

'It's all private parking up here.' McIntyre led him over

towards the throng of white-suited Scene of Crime and medical staff. 'Doesn't get used much now the offices are closed.'

McLean looked up at the brutalist concrete architecture surrounding him. If memory served it was all due to be knocked down soon, replaced with expensive apartments, designer shops and a boutique hotel. But for now it was clad in what looked like giant chicken-wire mesh, the empty windows reflecting grey clouds and the threat of rain.

'Who found the body?'

'Security guard was doing the rounds first thing. Noticed the car had been parked up for a while and went to see if everything was OK. He called it in.'

'Guess I'd better have a look then. Do I need to get suited up?'

'Probably for the best. You know what forensics are like. And if it does turn out to be suspicious . . .' McIntyre left the sentence hanging as McLean found first the correct SOC van, then a spare boiler suit and overshoes. He struggled into them, taking the opportunity to observe the scene. A spiral concrete ramp brought the cars up from the street below, and judging by the arrows painted on the cracked tarmac, that was the only way they could get out again, too. Pedestrians could either fight their way through traffic or use a doorway at the opposite end of the car park that he expected would lead on to ill-lit stairs smelling strongly of vomit and piss. There were CCTV cameras at both ends, which meant a slightly greater chance of there being some video footage than if they'd not been there. But only slightly. Up this high, there should have been grand views over the city's rooftops towards the Firth of Forth and

Fife beyond, but a high parapet cut off most of them. The looming bulk of the empty office block dominated everything, staring down on the scene in silent judgement. It had been empty for years now, which was a pity. Otherwise someone might have seen something.

The registration plate of the car suggested that it was nearly new, the road grime down its sides that it had covered a fair few miles in its short life. A Peugeot estate, it was exactly the sort of vehicle a travelling salesman might use. McLean approached from the back, peering in through the glass to see a load space filled with a jumble of cardboard boxes, back seats empty save for a dark suit jacket. The driver's door was open, two white-suited figures kneeling beside it as they studied the body inside. One looked around as he approached, his frown morphing into a smile of recognition.

'Tony. It's been a while. I thought you were chasing down prostitutes these days.' Angus Cadwallader let out a low groan as he clambered to his feet. Beside him, his assistant Tracy just looked over her shoulder and nodded a greeting.

'It's always good to diversify, Angus. What have we got here?'

'Something you don't see every day. I'll give you that much.' Cadwallader stepped aside to give McLean room. As he approached, he could see the back of a man's head, short-cropped greying hair, white shirt. He appeared to be sitting with the car seat tilted back too far to be comfortable for driving, and he was staring straight ahead through the windscreen as if the empty office block was the most fascinating thing in the world. He didn't recognise the man's face; hadn't expected to. It was slack, eyes open, mouth too. A thin smear of drool glistened on his stubble-flecked chin and McLean followed it down with his gaze until he finally noticed the man's lap.

'Dear God. Is that . . .?'

'Yes, Tony. It is. Like I said, not something you see every day.' Cadwallader leaned in, one arm on the open car door for support. Beside him, Tracy was busy with a swab taking samples. Not a task she could have been relishing much. McLean really didn't want to get any closer than he already was.

One of the driver's arms lay between his thigh and the gearstick, the other fallen down no doubt when the door had been opened. His crotch was exposed, trousers unbuttoned, flies zipped down to reveal a painfully swollen erection, black with clotted blood.

'Should that not, you know, go down? I mean, he is dead, right?'

'Very dead, yes.' Cadwallader stood up again, allowing Tracy space to back away. 'And it's unusual but not impossible. The position he's lying in is probably restricting blood flow, plus we don't know exactly where his right hand was before the door was opened. I'll know more once we've got him back to the mortuary, but right now I can't even tell you what killed him.'

McLean looked up at the faceless buildings, across the car park to the cityscape beyond, over to his little red Alfa parked a good distance away from the bustle of the investigation, anywhere but down at the dead man and his unfortunate condition. There was an obvious joke that no one had made. No grizzled old sergeant who'd seen it all, saying the unsayable to break the tension. He forced himself to look back down at the dead man, see the scene beyond the most obvious, distracting, detail.

The inside of the car was clean, the passenger seat empty. He could see no sign of rubbish, no scrumpled up chip pokes or greasy burger bags. The car had its own Sat-Nav inbuilt, probably a hands-free set-up for a mobile too. Looking around, McLean could see no sign of a phone and there were no round sucker-rings on the inside of the windscreen.

'I know that look. What are you thinking?' McIntyre approached from the other side of the car. She had pulled on her own white suit, dark hair spilling out around the hood.

'I'm not sure. Has anyone looked at his jacket or been through the glove box?'

'Don't think anyone's opened any of the other doors. Why?'

'Well, I'm no expert, but I'd have said if you were going to . . .' McLean nodded downwards. 'You know. Pull one off. You'd need some kind of stimulation. But there's nothing here. No magazines, no photographs, no phone. He hasn't even got a handkerchief or anything to wipe up the mess.'

'Maybe he gets off on abandoned concrete buildings?'

McLean smiled briefly, said nothing.

'What are you suggesting then?' McIntyre asked after a moment's pause. 'He wasn't alone?'

'Well, it makes sense, sort of. If he picked up a hitch-hiker, maybe. And she was . . .'

'I never had you down as a prude, Tony. Working Vice I'd have thought you'd seen it all.'

'Ha. Yes. It just doesn't feel right, not with him lying here. Sorry. The whole set-up's just too complex for my liking.'

'What's complex about it?' McIntyre leaned on the car roof, her hands conducting the conversation. 'He picks someone up. Maybe a hitchhiker like you said, maybe a prozzie for sex. Brings them up here – could be a she, could be a he, I try not to be judgemental. He's getting a blowjob when his heart gives out. She, or he, realises what's happened, panics, runs off. End of story.'

McLean wasn't so sure. Something didn't add up; he just couldn't put his finger on it.

'You done here, sir? Only we'd like to, you know, get him out of there.'

He stood aside to let the technicians move the body. It took a moment to work out the best way to shift him, but eventually they had him laid out on a folding gurney, ready to be wheeled to the waiting ambulance. His condition was all the more apparent, causing a moment's awkwardness as a technician tried to close the body bag. Cadwallader leaned forward, pressing the tumescence down with gloved fingers as he pulled up the zipper.

'Well, at least he died happy.'


'His name's Eric Parker. Fifty-six years old. Works for a packaging company called Boxing Clever. His card says Senior Marketing Director, but he's basically a sales rep.'

McLean leaned against a desk in the CID room, listening as Detective Sergeant Stuart MacBride brought their small team up to speed. Promotion had gone some way towards easing MacBride's irritation at the job. He was more relaxed than McLean had seen him in months, and he'd also given up trying to conceal the jagged scar on his forehead. Where once he'd grown his hair long at the front like a throwback to the early eighties, now it was cut military short.

'Do we know what he was doing in that car park?'

'You mean apart from wanking himself to death?'

A nervous ripple of laughter spread out around the small team. Apart from MacBride, and McIntyre herself, they were all new to McLean. Strange how things could change in a few short months, how the old hierarchies could be thrown into disarray by a couple of retirements and a few choice promotions.

'Seriously though, the company has offices on Queen Street. They use the top of the multi-storey for parking. There's a few other companies use that level too, but it tends to be empty at the weekend.'

'Do we know where he'd been?' McLean asked.

'Not yet, sir. I'm trying to arrange a meeting with his boss this afternoon. Should be able to put together his last known movements after I've talked to his colleagues.'

'What about the post-mortem? When's that scheduled?' McLean glanced up at the clock above the door. Lunchtime, and breakfast had been a long, long time ago. What were the chances of making it in and out of the canteen without being spotted by either Brooks or Spence? Not good, given the detective superintendent's fondness for pies.

'They're going to try and get it done this afternoon. I'm guessing it'll be later, though. We're still not sure whether there's foul play here or it's all just an unfortunate accident.' MacBride flipped the lid on his tablet computer closed. Briefing over.

'OK. You speak to Parker's boss, find out what he was up to, who he was. The usual stuff. I'll check in with Angus about the PM later. If it turns out he just had a heart attack then at least we've covered the bases.'

McLean hoped that it was as simple as that. A lonely man finding some executive relief in an empty car park. He also knew that he was kidding himself if he thought it would be an easy case. McIntyre wouldn't have called him in if she'd thought it was, and there were other problems with the scene. For all that the police and forensics experts had joked about the man pleasuring himself to death, there was very little evidence to suggest that was what he'd been doing. No, this one was going to be complicated.

'One other thing, Stuart.' He caught the detective sergeant just before he left the room.

'Sir?'

'CCTV footage. Have we got the tapes?' Not that it was tapes any more. Everything was in the cloud these days.

'Wasn't sure it would be necessary, sir. Don't want to waste resources watching hours of cars going up and down the ramp.'

McLean raised an eyebrow at that. Time was MacBride wouldn't have given a thought for the cost. Investigate first, worry about the budget later. How a little bit of authority could change a person.

'Get on to the car park people anyway, aye? We probably won't have to watch any of it, but I'd rather they didn't record over anything that might be important.'

*

72

McLean was halfway to the back door when a familiar voice called out from an open doorway.

'You back, sir? Didn't think Vice would keep you long.'

Stepping backwards, he ducked into the room as the familiar form of Detective Sergeant Laird unfolded himself from a chair. A case file lay open on the desk in front of him, pages splayed as if he had been working through it meticulously. The newspaper on the floor and the warm aroma of coffee gave the lie to the carefully constructed ruse.

'Just helping Jayne out. If anyone asks, I'm not here. Plenty to be getting on with over at HQ.'

'Ah yes, the priapic salesman. I heard.'

'Course you did, Bob. There's nothing gets past you. What's that you're pretending to work on?' McLean pointed at the open folder.

'Pretending?' Grumpy Bob feigned a hurt expression. 'Actually it's a cold case. Got a whole stack of them to go through, see if I can prioritise them.'

'Jesus, who'd you piss off? And prioritise them for what?'

'The why's because someone in head office thinks it's a good idea to reopen the Cold Case Unit. Reckon Dagwood will be running it once he's got bored of going to the golf course every day. As to the who . . .' Grumpy Bob looked up at the doorway. McLean turned to see DCI Spence standing just outside.

'What the fuck are you doing here, McLean?'

'Afternoon, Mike. How's life on the top floor treating you?'

'You do know you're supposed to address a senior officer as "sir"?'

'And yet with some people I just can't bring myself to do so. Something to do with it being a sign of respect, I think.'

Spence held McLean's gaze for a moment before backing down, turning his attention on Grumpy Bob.

'You done with those files yet, Sergeant?'

'Pretty much, sir. Just going through this last one. Headland House. Don't know if you remember it? Might've been before your time.'

'I don't really care. Just tell me whether you think it's worth reopening. The DCC's going to be in later this afternoon and I promised him this lot would be sorted by then.'

'I'll have it finished in half an hour, sir. Don't you worry.' Grumpy Bob picked up the folder, shuffling the pages back together and giving McLean a none-too-subtle wink.

'You still here, McLean?' Spence turned on the heel of his well-polished shoe, quite deliberately knocking shoulders as he headed for the door. McLean resisted the urge to mutter 'arsehole' under his breath as the detective chief inspector marched out of the room. It would only end in tears and tantrums.

'Headland House?' he asked when he was sure Spence was gone. 'That was the upmarket knocking shop that got raided in the early nineties, right?'

Grumpy Bob held up the folder. 'The same. You know it?'

'One of my first ops. I was still in uniform then. Thought the case was closed.'

'Oh, the raid was. But that was only ever half of the story. There was that wee lass who was found there. Never got to the bottom of who'd taken her there. Reading through this, it looks like no one really tried.'

74

McLean was about to say something, a memory long forgotten coming to the surface, but the shrill electronic bell of his mobile distracted him. Peering at the screen showed that DCI Dexter was trying to get a hold of him. Fair enough; there was still the less than successful brothel raid that needed explaining to the powers that be, and they could only put it off for so long.

'Do us a favour, Bob. Get me a copy of that file, could you? Only don't tell anyone I asked for it, OK?'

'No problem. I'll get Sandy Gregg to bring it over. She's shuttling back and forth between CID and Vice almost as much as you.' Grumpy Bob closed up the folder. 'Any particular reason why you're interested in it?'

McLean paused before answering. Partly it was just his natural curiosity getting the better of him, but he couldn't deny the similarities between Headland House and the New Town terrace they had just recently raided. Except that for all the excesses he'd witnessed that night, there had been no children involved. And there had been no doubt Headland House was being used as a brothel.

'Nostalgia, maybe?' He shook his head, knowing it was a lie. 'And that wee girl you mentioned? I was the one who found her. Christ, I've not thought about it in years. Always wondered what had happened to her.'

# 13

He hasn't seen this many uniforms since Police College, out at Tulliallan. Not that it's been all that long since he graduated. His first raid, and from the look of things it's been a jackpot.

Headland House sits, as its name implies, on a headland in Newhaven, overlooking the Forth. Time was this would have been a good neighbourhood, a couple of miles from the urban sprawl of the New Town. The sort of place wealthy financiers and merchants used to live once. It's not quite so fancy now, the houses faded and sorry-looking. Even Headland House itself is ramshackle. Hardly the sort of place you'd expect to find a high-class brothel.

From what he can gather, it all started with a tip-off. That's how these things usually go. Someone at the briefing said something about surveillance, what they could expect to find, but he'd not really been listening by then. Too nervous. Too excited. Probably for the best he's been left outside to keep gawkers at bay. Not that there are many at this time of night.

He watches as they take the johns out, recognising a couple of faces who won't find this easy to live down. Some go arguing, some hang their heads. One or two look around as if expecting paparazzi, but the press are mercifully distant. After the men, it's the turn of the prostitutes. He can't help noticing how young they look, and it's not as if he's all that old himself. Some of these girls are barely old enough to be out of school.

'You there. McLean, isn't it?'

He looks up to see the old sergeant, Guthrie McManus, wandering in his direction.

'Sir.'

'Christ, but this is going to leave a lot of people with very red faces.'

'It is?'

'Too fucking right it is. You see anyone you know in that lot?' The sergeant waved in the direction of the van being used to transfer a dozen embarrassed men back to the station.

'One or two. I think my local MP was one. Won't be getting my vote come the election. Not that he got it the last time, mind you.'

'That'll be your MP who plays golf with the Chief Constable once a week. And there's judges, lawyers, a couple of bankers. Thank fuck the press didn't get wind of this. Don't know how long we can keep a lid on it, mind.'

He's not entirely sure why they should, but he's not so green as to even think of saying it. Instead he looks up at the house, rising into the dawn-pinked sky. Lights are on in most of the windows, the occasional glimpse of policemen in silhouette as they collect evidence. He's not sure what they're going to need it for; they were caught with their trousers down, after all.

'What's that?' Movement in an upper window, still dark. He strains to see.

'Eh? What're you on about?' Sergeant McManus stamps his feet against the chill.

'Up there, sir. Could have sworn I saw someone in the top window.'

'Well, you've better eyes than me, laddie. Still, best go tell his nibs about it. Might be we've missed one.'

The house is full of plain clothes and uniform police. Most are milling around a large entrance hall like the one at his gran's house; a few clustered around the bottom of the stairs. One of them, tall, thin, ginger-haired, plain clothes, sees him and beckons him over.

'Aren't you meant to be outside keeping the scene secure?'

'Sorry, sir. Thought I saw something, someone, moving around up in the attic. Only there's no lights on up there. Sergeant McManus told me to come tell you about it.'

'Guthrie sent you in? Ah well. Get upstairs and have a look then. Just don't move anything around without asking first.'

He scurries away before the detective sergeant can shout at him. Duguid has a reputation, he's heard. Going to be a DI soon, and then who knows?

The house is on three floors, rooms getting progressively smaller the higher he goes. Police are everywhere, looking under beds, opening closets, tapping floorboards as if there might be hidden lairs below. If he'd not been told otherwise, he'd have taken it for a run-down old hotel, and that's probably how it appears on the accounts. Renting out rooms by the hour to the city's wealthy elite; just no mention of the additional services included in the price.

No one seems to be paying attention to the narrow door off the top landing. Perhaps not many police officers grew up in big houses like this one, but he did, and he knows

78

where the servants' quarters would have been back in the days when people still had servants. The staircase leads up into the attic, and he climbs it slowly, listening for any noise above the racket of the officers below, sniffing the air with its curious sweet scent. The walls up here are plain, a corridor running the length of the roof, with windows at either end and doorways opening on to what he knows will be tiny rooms tucked into the eaves.

The first has a pair of narrow beds that look recently slept in, a tiny wooden chest of drawers between them and nothing else. The sweet smell is stronger here, rich like flowers and honey. He sniffs, trying to place it, but it fades quickly and is gone.

The next room is even more sparsely furnished; just a single painted chair. The third room is a little bigger than the previous two, and has a metal grate built across it, making a cage of the far side. Against one wall a heap of mouldy blankets look like they've been chewed by whatever dog lived in this place long ago. The same dog that drank from the chipped tin bowl of water on the floor. Except that the bowl's full of pale yellow liquid, the stench quite different from the sweet smell in the first room.

And then his eyes adjust to the pale light seeping in through the grimy window. There is a cupboard built into the eaves, doors opening on to a space too small for anything except boxes.

Or a little girl.

# 14

McLean weaved his car through the early morning traffic, stifling a yawn with the back of his hand. He hadn't slept well, despite being dead on his feet from far too many late nights. Rachel wasn't a bad house guest, as these things went, but he always felt slightly ill at ease when there was someone else about. He'd lived alone too long; it was a strain having constantly to think about what he was doing. The lack of contact from Phil was troubling, too. It wasn't like his old friend.

At least the car was working well, even if he felt a pang of guilt every time he took it out. The Alfa was more than forty years old. It should have been a weekend plaything, polished and cherished and taken to shows, not a daily driver in a busy city. And yet there was never time to look for something more sensible. Perhaps he could ask Ritchie to sort something out; she liked cars. But then that would have been a gross misuse of police resources. And it wasn't as if he had time for playthings anyway; wouldn't have known what to do with a free weekend.

The latest in a long line of red lights turned green and he dropped the clutch, getting an enthusiastic chirp from the tyres as they struggled to grip the tarmac. It would be hard to find something modern that was anything like as much fun to drive, it was true. Then again, most of the time he was just shuttling between home, his station and

HQ anyway. An awkward slow triangle that was surely not doing the finely tuned Italian engineering any good at all.

The roads cleared a bit as he approached the outskirts to the west of the city, running in the opposite direction to the bulk of the rush hour traffic. McLean took the back roads, crossing the bypass which looked like a long, narrow car park, and headed for a small compound just past the airport. The forensic services had their large labs there, and it was where Eric Parker's car had been taken for analysis after the priapic salesman's body had been removed to the city mortuary. He could probably have waited for the report; it wasn't as if the car was likely to yield much evidence. But the thought of going back to his office – either of his offices – made the weariness even worse. Better to be doing things, and killing time until the post-mortem. And if he was being completely honest with himself, avoiding the miasma of despondency that had settled over the SCU in the wake of the botched raid.

'I can't believe you're using her for work.'

Amanda Parsons must have been passing by as he arrived. Either that or she spent her days staring out of a window that looked on to the car park; there was no other way she could have known he was coming. As McLean locked the door, she had already trotted down the steps and was running a hand over the car's wing.

'And a good morning to you too,' he said, smiling. The forensic scientist glared at him.

'I'm not joking, Tony. This car should be for special occasions, not Edinburgh rush hour. Get yourself a cheap runabout for that.'

McLean just nodded his head once in agreement. Her words mirrored his own thoughts on the matter, after all.

'When I get some free time, I'll do that,' he said. 'Meantime, I was hoping you might have had a chance to look at the repmobile you brought in.'

Parsons gave the Alfa a last, loving pat on the bonnet. 'As a matter of fact, I have. Why don't you come around to the garage and take a wee look.'

She set off across the compound towards a modern building with half a dozen roller doors in the front. Most were closed against the chill autumn breeze whistling in off the Forth, but one was open high enough to walk inside. The salesman's car was up on a lift and McLean waited while it was slowly brought back down to earth, keeping his distance as he had learned was best to do when dealing with forensic scientists.

'You could do worse than getting yourself one of these,' Parsons said as she snapped on a pair of latex gloves, handing another set to McLean.

'Peugeot estate? Isn't that, I don't know, a little staid?'

'Maybe, aye. It's anonymous, though. Great for stake-outs.'

McLean didn't have the heart to tell her how long it had been since last he'd sat in a car on a stake-out. Mostly they used pool cars for that sort of thing, and constables.

'It's probably a bit big. I'd be better off with a Mini or something.'

Parsons sniffed, as if she didn't think much of that suggestion.

'What about forensics?' He tried to drag the conversation back to the actual reason he was out here. 'Has this car yielded any useful secrets?'

'That depends on what you consider useful.' Parsons opened the driver's door, then fetched an inspection lamp from a nearby workbench, picking up a couple of pairs of yellow-lensed safety spectacles at the same time. McLean slid his pair on as she directed the UV lamp at the footwell.

'This car's not all that old. Just a few months, but it's racked up some miles. Your Mr Parker was a busy man.'

'He travelled all over Scotland, apparently. Last trip took in Thurso and Inverness. Have to hope he liked driving.'

'Aye, well. Most of the car's pretty clean, but obviously this bit's had his feet in and out of it a lot. We found plenty of mud, some small gravel stones. No food, though, which is unusual. I'd have expected a sales rep to eat on the go. Crisps, bits of bread and cheese, chocolate. You know what it's like.' Parsons clicked off the light then pulled off her safety spectacles.

'I'd hate for you to run that lamp over my car,' McLean said, although in truth mostly what she'd find would be spilled coffee.

'Maybe later.' Parsons smiled, then frowned. 'The other thing we didn't find was any bodily fluids. No blood, no semen. Not even any bogeys.'

'You make it sound like that's a bad thing.'

'Well, it is, isn't it? You saw him sitting in here, all swollen and stiff. You'd expect something to get on the seats if nothing else.'

McLean looked again into the footwell, trying not to remember the last time he'd seen the car, when it had still been occupied. 'Have you been through the rest of it?'

'Everything's over there.' Parsons waved her gloved hand in the direction of a table towards the back of the garage. A pile of cardboard boxes were stacked neatly on one side, dark blue jacket laid out alongside them. Beside it, a heavy black leather bag, battered around the edges from much use, stood open, contents arranged in neat little piles. McLean looked over it all briefly.

'He have a mobile on him?'

Parsons pointed to a chunky-looking old-fashioned handset lying beside the bag. Not exactly the smartest of phones. 'It was in his jacket pocket. There's hands-free built into the car. Charging cable was in the bag.'

McLean picked up the phone, clicked it on. The screen was too small to show much more than a signal strength meter and basic text messages. 'You didn't find any pornographic material then.'

'Nope. Not a thing. The most erotic thing he had was a copy of yesterday's *Daily Telegraph*, and even that was in the bag there. We've not had a look at his laptop, mind. But it was packed away.' Parsons reached over the table and picked up a hefty computer bag.

'So he's all alone in the car park, tackle out but not looking at anything stimulating. And from what you're saying about the state of the carpet, he wasn't a habitual . . .' McLean trailed off.

'Wanker?' Parsons offered. The smirk made her look even younger than she was. When had the forensic services started employing teenagers?

'Quite. So it looks like he wasn't pleasuring himself, which would suggest maybe he wasn't alone. Someone was doing it for him.'

Parsons put the computer bag down, went off to the workbench at the back of the garage, returned with a clear plastic evidence bag. McLean took it from her, holding it up to the light to see what was inside. A thin coil of pale gold twisted around in a perfect circle.

'Found that on the passenger seat headrest, tucked in where it meets the top of the seat. I think Mr Parker was mostly grey, wasn't he? And he didn't have that much hair to start with. I'll be sending that off to the labs as soon as I'm done here. Might get some DNA off it if we're lucky.'

'How long do you reckon it's been in there?'

'Well, the car's new. I doubt more than a half-dozen people have ever been inside it.' Parsons took back the evidence bag with its single strand of blonde hair. 'Given where I found this, though, it can't have been there for very long. A week tops.'

'Mr Parker picked up a passenger then.'

'Unless his wife is a blonde, or his boss. Looks that way, yes.'

'It's called priapism, after the Greek god Priapus. Quite uncommon as a cause of death, not seen much at all now we don't hang people.'

McLean stood in the cool stillness of the examination theatre, deep in the bowels of the city mortuary. Laid out on the stainless steel table, Eric Parker looked even more uncomfortable than he had done sitting in his car. Perhaps it was the lack of clothes, or the horrible mottled colour his most prominent feature had taken on as the blood within had curdled and set. Angus Cadwallader stood on the other side of the table, a gleam in his eye McLean knew all too well. There was nothing like an unusual case to get the pathologist all fired up. Fortunately his assistant, Tracy, was on hand to curb his enthusiasm.

'Is this . . .' McLean gestured towards the erection. 'Is this what killed him?'

'Patience, Tony. We've only just begun that voyage of discovery.' Cadwallader flexed his fingers, working them deeper into his white latex gloves. 'Got to wait for Tom, too. You know as well as I do that we have to have everything witnessed these days.'

As if on cue, the theatre doors banged open and Doctor MacPhail strode in. He looked as dishevelled as ever; McLean didn't think he'd ever seen the man tidy.

'Sorry I'm late. Did I miss anything?' He approached the examination table, then did a double-take as he saw the cadaver laid out. 'The memo, obviously. Post-mortem priapism if I'm not mistaken. Not seen one outside of a textbook.'

McLean resisted the urge to ask how he could be sure if he'd never seen one before, but the phrase 'in the flesh' felt somehow inappropriate to the moment. He was keen to get the examination over and done with too. Apparently Cadwallader was also anxious to press on, adjusting the microphone that dangled over the body before beginning his examination.

'Subject is male, Caucasian, late fifties. Appears to be in generally good condition for his age. Maybe a little over-weight.' He worked his way from toes up to head, pausing only briefly at the groin. McLean watched the process, horrified by the casual intimacy of it and yet equally fascin-ated. At least up until the point where the pathologist reached for the scalpel. He wasn't squeamish really; it wasn't possible to be after what he'd seen in twenty years of police work, but something about the parting of dead

86

flesh always unsettled him. For a while at least, his shoes and the polished floor of the examination theatre were quite fascinating enough.

'Ah. Interesting. Yes. That would make a certain sense.'

McLean looked back up to see Cadwallader peering at something that looked suspiciously like a heart.

'Cause of death?' he asked.

'Probably. Looks like he didn't have the strongest of hearts to start with, but this is a mess.' Cadwallader passed the organ to his assistant, who placed it in a plastic carton, then on to a set of scales. Weight noted, it joined a number of other organs which she would soon be putting back prior to sewing up poor Mr Eric Parker with her neat stitches.

'What about . . . You know?' McLean nodded at the still tumescent penis.

'That. Yes.' Cadwallader grinned. 'I was saving the best till last.' He turned his attention to Doctor MacPhail. 'What do you make of it, Tom?'

MacPhail had perched himself on a stool by the bench that lined one side of the theatre, close enough to observe the procedure but far enough away not to get underfoot. He shrugged. 'I'm just here to witness, Angus. Not meant to comment, remember?'

'Of course. Well.' Cadwallader manhandled the member, peering closer than McLean would have felt comfortable doing. 'I had a half-decent look at the crime scene, obviously, but there was the small matter of trousers in the way. Not to mention the steering wheel. Thought I saw something back there, but here . . .' He paused a moment. 'Yes. Tracy, a swab, please.'

McLean stepped back from the examination again. He'd known Cadwallader long enough to tell the difference between theatre and genuine fascination. Best to let the man get on with his job. It didn't take long.

'Get that off to the labs for DNA analysis, will you, Tracy?' Cadwallader dropped the swab into a sterile sample bottle. His assistant rolled her eyes just slightly, but enough for McLean to see and share a smile. It was an open secret that Doctor Cadwallader and Doctor Sharp were somewhat more than senior pathologist and assistant, and despite their disparate ages, they made a good couple.

'What have you found?' McLean asked.

'I'll need to take some photos, send them off to someone who knows a bit more about these things than I do. But I think these are bite marks.' Cadwallader held the dead man's swollen member in one hand and pointed at its base with the other. Given the mat of wiry hair and the mottled blues and reds of the skin, McLean was hard pressed to see anything at all, but then he wasn't the expert.

'I see a picture forming here,' he said. 'Seems like our man really wasn't alone when he died.'

'It's beginning to look like that.' Cadwallader stepped away from the body, peeling off his latex gloves and dumping them in a nearby bin. 'My best guess is someone was giving him head when his heart gave out. Probably came as quite a shock to whoever was performing the – ah, act. Hence the teeth marks. We should get DNA from the saliva if we're lucky. Not quite sure what you're going to do with it, mind. But that's your job, not mine.'

'What about his condition, though? Is that normal? You know, if someone has a heart attack while . . .' McLean left the words unsaid, not quite sure why he found discussing it so embarrassing.

'Normal? No. But it happens. Given how he was sitting, it might just be that the blood couldn't get back out again once his heart stopped. Or he might have been on some medication we don't know about. Might even have popped a little blue pill to put himself in the mood. We'll know a bit more once the toxicology results come back.'

'But there's nothing to suggest foul play. Just an unfortunate coincidence.'

Cadwallader paused a while before answering. 'If you'd found him in his bed, I don't think this would be more than a footnote in a medical journal. It's possible, probable even, that the excitement of arousal was too much for his heart, but that's not the same as intent. No, Tony. I don't think there's any foul play here.'

## 15

McLean sat in his Alfa, staring out the window at the cityscape as a squall of rain spattered the grey concrete. He wasn't quite sure why he'd come here after the post-mortem rather than heading straight to the police station to brief McIntyre. Maybe it was because the image of the dead man, Eric Parker, wasn't an easy one to dispel from his mind. Bodies were like that sometimes. Mostly he could compartmentalise, think about them abstractly as a part of the job then forget about them when he went home, or at least when he went home and stopped think-ing about the job. But every so often a case would get under his skin and he could feel this one going that way. There was something not right about it, quite apart from the fact that someone had been with Parker when he'd died and then run off without telling anyone. Had the salesman been with a sex worker? A rent boy? Anything was possible, really; they knew depressingly little about the man.

Pulling his phone out of his pocket, McLean thumbed the speed dial numbers, waited for the call to connect.

'Morning, sir. What can I do for you?'

Detective Sergeant MacBride sounded much more grown up than the fresh-faced DC that McLean had first met just a few short years ago. Promotion suited him, and only idiots like DCI Spence would refuse to admit that Stuart had been doing the job better than most sergeants for a long time already.

'Eric Parker. You interviewed his boss yet?'

'Couldn't see him yesterday, sir. He's been at some overseas conference. Due back in town later this afternoon. Thought I'd go see him tomorrow morning. Unless you want me to go earlier. You want to come along?'

He knew he should say no, let MacBride get on with the investigation. The detective sergeant was quite capable, and it wasn't as if McLean didn't have plenty of other cases to work on. Then again, if he didn't go he'd just have to read the report later.

'Drop me a text with the time, will you, Stuart? I'll swing by the station tomorrow morning. I've got a nasty feeling this isn't going to be as easy as we'd like.' He told MacBride about the forensics and post-mortem, the evidence of a third party at the scene. 'I don't suppose we've got anything on CCTV?'

'Haven't had a chance to review it yet, sir. I told them not to delete anything, but it's all electronic. No tapes.'

'I'm at the scene at the moment. I'll drop by the offices and have a word.'

'You're at the scene?' McLean could sense the question 'why?' forming in MacBride's mind, but the detective sergeant managed to suppress asking it.

'Just trying to get my head around the post-mortem results, work out what exactly Parker was doing and why. It's quieter here than back at HQ, and no chance of bumping into Spence or Brooks either. See you tomorrow then.' He hung up and went back to staring out through the window, the view blurred by drizzle fast turning into cold rain.

Not sure who he was trying to fool, MacBride or himself. Going to the forensic labs, the mortuary and now here; they were all just ways of avoiding either of his offices and the problems waiting for him. If he was being honest, McLean envied MacBride just a little. Sergeants had paperwork to do, for sure, but it was nothing compared to the nonsense inspectors put up with, and they had only a fraction of the responsibility when things went wrong. How bad would it be even higher up the food chain? He hoped he never found out. Meantime he'd stick to what he did best, solving puzzles by getting out there and asking questions.

Firing up the engine, McLean took a last look around the wet car park where Eric Parker had met his sticky end, then slipped the car into gear and headed off for the exit ramp.

'Wasn't expecting anyone so soon. Just got off the phone with some detective laddie. MacBurnie or something?'

It had taken McLean longer than expected to find the control centre for the multi-storey car park, tucked away in the basement level in a little concrete bunker built to survive a nuclear holocaust. The tiny office smelled of stale sweat and even staler cigarette smoke, the latter oozing off one of the two security guards whose den this most clearly was. Two small tables pressed into service as desks, two cheap chairs not designed for sitting in for any length of time, the rest of the room was taken up with filing cabinets and shelves loaded with bulging folders. Quite how a car park could generate so much paperwork, McLean wasn't sure, but then he had no idea how his own line of work did either.

'You've still got the tapes, though?' He scanned the room for any sign of recording equipment, seeing none.

'No one uses tapes any more, aye?' The second of the two security guards was younger than his colleague and was presumably responsible for the other dominant smell. He looked like he worked out, or at least hung around in the gym taking steroids. His jacket hung over the back of his seat, the better to show an upper body two sizes too big for the shirt he was wearing. Sweat sheened his face even though it wasn't particularly warm, slicking his short black hair to his scalp.

'Figure of speech. I know it's all on hard drive, or somewhere in the cloud. Thing is, can I see it? The two cameras up on the private parking level.'

'Aye, sure. C'mon. I'll show you.' The younger security guard stood up to a squealing of metal chair legs on concrete floor. He grabbed his jacket, flinging it over one shoulder as he pushed through the narrow gap between the older guard and McLean, headed out the door.

'No room in there for the monitors. We keep it all over here.' The guard indicated a man-sized grey metal panel set into a wall of concrete slabs behind a couple of parked cars. It looked like an access hatch for the services to the building above, but when opened revealed a surprisingly large, dark and warm room. A couple of fluorescent tubes buzzed in the high ceiling, but most of the light came from a bank of CCTV monitors relaying feed from all the car park levels, the stairwells and the entrance and exit gates.

A third security guard looked round from the screens as he heard them enter. 'Who's this?' he asked, nodding in McLean's direction.

'Polis. Come to see the video from the top level. Where they found that bloke died of a stiffy.'

'Oh. Right. Wasn't expecting anybody till tomorrow.' The third guard sniffed, scratched at his armpit and then reached for a grubby computer keyboard. He tapped at it with two fingers, occasionally doing something with a mouse that might once have been white. The main screen in front of him cycled through a few different views before settling on one of the car park level McLean had not long left. The view showed no cars at all.

'This is the evening before we found your man there. Not been many people using that level since the accountants moved out.' The security guard tapped a few more commands and the screen split, now showing the view from the other end of the level, complete with the same timestamp.

'You got his number plate there?'

McLean dug out his notebook, flipping the pages until he found the notes he'd scribbled down, wishing all the while that MacBride was with him. The detective sergeant had a knack for remembering important details.

'Was it you who found him?' he asked.

'Nah, that was Pete. He's not working today. I can tell you when the car arrived, though. Number plate recognition logs everyone in and out.'

McLean found the number, read it out and watched as the guard typed it in. Modern technology certainly made his job a lot easier, but he couldn't help finding it a bit scary.

'Here we go. Came into the car park at eight fifteen in the evening. Should be able to bring that up on the cameras.' The guard tapped a few more commands, shuffling the image forward until the timestamp matched the arrival of the car. McLean watched as the seconds ticked forward, the time taken to get from the entrance, up the spiral ramp and on to the top level. The image wasn't brilliant, jumping and flickering, the colour balance different between the two cameras. After a moment the car appeared at the top of the ramp, but it passed out of view in a couple of stuttering jumps. Its bonnet appeared in the second camera's view, then disappeared again, the actual parking spot not covered by either camera.

'Is that it?'

'Aye. Sorry. One of those cameras got knocked a while back. Pointing in the wrong direction. I put in a request to maintenance, but . . .' The security guard shrugged.

'What about the stairwells?'

The guard looked at him as if he were mad. 'Not up there. Down on the lower levels where the shops are, aye.'

McLean peered at the static screen, wondering whether he could justify having someone sift through all the video footage in the vague hope of catching sight of someone who may or may not have fled the scene of something that wasn't really a crime. Put like that he couldn't see Brooks being happy at the expense incurred.

'What about the entrance, where the cars come in? You've got NPR cameras. Do you record the footage as well?'

'See where you're coming from. Aye, I can do you something.' The guard tabbed through a series of screens until he brought up one showing the entrance barrier and ticket machine. The image was a bit clearer here, the lighting designed to make the number plate recognition software's job a bit easier. They watched as the dark silver-grey Peugeot turned in from the street outside. It paused a while, and McLean thought he could see an arm reach out from the driver's side window and tap at the ticket machine. The overhead lighting shone in a bright line across the windscreen, obscuring the view inside. The hand withdrew, a short pause, and then the car moved forward, out of shot.

'Could you see if there was anyone in there with him?'

The guard shook his head. 'Sorry, mate. Too much reflection.'

So much for that idea. McLean glanced at his watch, wondered just how much more time he could spend on this. None, if he was being honest. It was time to get back to the station and face whatever shitstorm was waiting for him there.

'Well, thanks for trying anyway.' He started towards the door, then had a thought. 'See that last footage, at the entrance? You couldn't get me a copy of it, could you? I'll see if our forensics people can't do something with it.'

'Sure.' The guard nodded. 'Just don't get your hopes up.'

# 16

The shrill electronic screeching of his phone broke McLean's concentration as he was parking the Alfa in the station. He was trying not to scratch a shiny clean, top-spec Jaguar that had to belong to newly promoted Detective Superintendent Brooks. It must have been in the contract that you had to buy a Jag or a Range Rover when you made a certain grade; all the senior officers had one or the other. Yet another reason to avoid promotion as long as he could.

He fiddled the handset out of his pocket as he killed the engine. The screen told him only that the call was from overseas. Chances were it was someone trying to persuade him he'd been in a no-fault accident and could make a claim for compensation, but it was also just possible it was a call he'd been waiting for.

'Yes?'

'Tony? Hey, it's Phil here. What the fuck's going on? Where's Rae?'

'She's fine, Phil. She came back to Edinburgh. Says she couldn't face having her child in America.'

'I tried talking to her, Tony. You know that. I tried.'

McLean looked at his watch. Just past noon here, which meant it was very early morning in San Francisco. 'We've both left messages, Phil. We've both been trying to get hold of you for well over a week now. Can you really not get a signal in New Mexico?'

'Both of you? She's with you now, is she? Just the two of you in that big old house of yours.'

McLean hadn't noticed it at first, but now he caught the edge in his old friend's voice. It was too long since last they'd been to the pub together, staggered back to one or the other's flat and got stuck into a bottle of whisky. He'd forgotten the signs, but now he could tell that Phil had been drinking, and probably for quite some time.

'Look, Phil. You need to come back to Edinburgh. You can't be half a world away when your wife's about to have a baby.'

'M'at the airport, Tony. Flight to Frisco's in a couple of hours. I'll have to grab some stuff from the apartment, get the first flight home I can. If they let me board. Jesus.' Phil said something else, but he also must have pulled the phone away from his mouth as he did so, the words lost in an indistinct noise. McLean strained his ears to hear the background sounds, looking for confirmation that his friend was indeed where he said he was, and not propped up in the corner of some downtown bar. Sure enough a tannoy announced the imminent departure of a flight to Los Angeles, and then Phil was talking again.

'Is she OK, Rae? You're looking after her, right?'

'She's fine. Don't worry about her. She'll get the best care too, when the time comes. And you'd better be here with her when it does.'

'Why'd she come to you, Tony? Why'd she not come to me? I was only gone a week or two.' Phil was slurring his words badly now. Any minute and he was going to drop the phone.

'She came to me because Jenny's out of town.'

'Jenny?'

'Her sister, remember? Look, Phil. If your flight's really in a couple of hours you need to sober up. Get some strong black coffee and—'

But whatever McLean's advice was going to be he never managed to give it. There was a brief cry of 'Oh shit!' and then the line went dead.

He was still debating whether or not he should try to phone Phil back as he pushed his way through the door into the station. It was the same as it had ever been, and yet strangely different. So much had changed in just a few short months: Duguid retiring, Brooks getting his job, the move back to the SCU. McLean couldn't quite decide whether that had been Duguid's idea or a nudge from the new detective superintendent. It didn't really matter as long as it kept him out of the way. It had surprised him when DS Ritchie had followed him over, but it was always nice to see a friendly face.

'Afternoon, sir. Wasn't expecting to see you today.'

McLean looked up. DS MacBride was somewhat incongruously dressed in a grey T-shirt and sweatpants, in-ear headphones dangling from their cords around his chest. The scar on his forehead was a livid, shiny red mark against his pale skin and short-cropped ginger hair.

'Going for a run?' It was a stupid question, and got McLean the withering look it deserved.

'Perils of being a sergeant.' MacBride patted his flat belly. 'Too much sitting around on my arse. My trousers are beginning to get a bit tight.'

McLean laughed. 'Well, don't overdo it. I've a feeling we're going to need your well-honed detective skills on this case.'

MacBride frowned, his scar creasing into even more of a lightning bolt. 'That bad?'

'Worse. I'm just going to tell the boss about it. She around?'

'She was in the CID room last I saw her. I'll come with you, it'll save time.'

'And miss your run?'

'I'm not really a running kind of person, sir. Might go down the gym later.' MacBride fell in beside him and they walked up to the CID room in companionable silence. McLean saw a few people he recognised on the way, nodded greetings to some of them, but most of the faces in the station seemed new, and young. A fresh influx of recruits, or more spare officers shipped over from the west to upset the genteel Edinburgh folk with their rough Glasgow ways? He couldn't tell.

They found DCI McIntyre in the CID room as promised, but by the look of the folders wedged under one arm she was on her way out.

'Ah, Tony. I was going to give you a call.' Her smile turned into a frown as she noticed MacBride in his running kit. 'What on earth are you wearing, Stuart? The marathon's not for months yet.'

MacBride opened his mouth to answer, paused, then shut it again. So he was learning. McLean slapped him gently on the arm by way of encouragement.

'I had an update on Eric Parker. Thought I'd come over and tell you rather than putting it in a report or waiting for the next briefing.'

'And anything that keeps you away from the SCU at the moment's a good excuse? I heard there was a bit of a fuck-up. Didn't realise it was that bad.' McIntyre disentangled the folders from under her arm and handed them to Mac-Bride. 'Here, make yourself useful, will you?'

'Seems Parker wasn't alone in the car, and he almost certainly wasn't alone when he died.' McLean relayed the information he had gleaned from forensics and the post-mortem. McIntyre listened without interruption, and MacBride put the folders down on the edge of the nearest desk, paying attention even though McLean had already told him most of it on the phone. There weren't many other detectives in the CID room, but by the time McLean was finished they were all silent, listening in. No one said anything for a long while, then McIntyre sighed, pinching the bridge of her nose in an all too familiar indication of despair.

'I knew I shouldn't have got you involved, Tony. Things always get complicated when you start digging.'

For a moment McLean was taken in. Not unlike Mac-Bride, he opened his mouth ready to argue his case. Then he remembered who he was talking to. This wasn't Duguid or even Brooks.

'Almost had me there, Jayne.'

'I'm losing my touch, clearly. Seriously though, how do we want to take this forward?'

'Treat it as a suspicious death, obviously. Might be a help if people stopped referring to him as the priapic salesman, for a start. We'll have a meeting with his boss soon as he's back from his trip. We know he had no family, so I think we need to start compiling a list of all Parker's contacts in the last week, try and speak to as many as possible. And we need to track his movements over the twenty-four hours before he was found. We can run his registration number through the traffic system, see where he's been and cross-check that with where he was meant to be.'

'What about the DNA?' McIntyre asked.

'It'll take time, and it might not lead anywhere. They only found one hair in the car and Christ only knows what Angus will get from the swab he took. Best get to work on tracing Parker's movements first, then we can slot the DNA evidence into the mix if it's any use.'

'Umm, one question, sir?' MacBride fidgeted with his hands as if he wasn't quite sure what to do with them.

'Yes?'

'Angus . . . The pathologist put cause of death as heart attack, right?'

'That was the ultimate cause, yes. He had a weak heart.'

'So chances are this wasn't, you know, deliberate.'

McLean realised what the problem was; MacBride didn't have his tablet computer with him. Without his favourite prop he didn't know what to do with his hands.

'Suspicious doesn't necessarily mean murder, if that's what you're getting at. We still have to investigate. You know that.'

'Yes, of course.' MacBride shifted uncomfortably, like a little boy who's wet his pants and doesn't want teacher to know. 'It's just . . . Well, it seems most likely Parker picked up a hitchhiker. Maybe got a little more than he was expecting by way of thanks. His heart gives out at the excitement and she panics and legs it.'

'Your point, Stuart?' McIntyre asked. McLean couldn't help remembering this was exactly the scenario she had offered at the beginning of the investigation.

'Well, it's just we're getting hung up on the weirdness. The stiffy and the single incriminating hair. Don't get me wrong, if someone was with him when he died, we need to find them and talk to them if we can. But is it really that high priority it needs a DI and a DCI on it?'

What a change a few months and a bit of responsibility could make. McLean could hardly believe this was the same detective who was ready to quit and get a nine-to-five job in finance back in the spring. It was good to see; losing MacBride would have been a blow, and not just to him. And, of course, he was right. Mostly.

'We've a dead body on our hands, so at the very least an inspector needs to be involved.' McLean saw MacBride take a breath, ready to argue his point. Cut him off before he could get started. 'Don't worry, Stuart. I agree with you. Most likely there's a simple, rational explanation, and we don't want to go blowing the department budget chasing shadows.'

'You want to take lead on this, Tony?' McIntyre asked. 'Even with your work at the SCU?'

McLean wanted nothing more than to say no, but he was too far in now. Handing over to someone else would be even more difficult than just running with it.

'You want to pass it over to DI Carter?'

McIntyre made a face. 'Fuck, no. I'll square it with Brooks. You can break the good news to Jo Dexter.'

'You just can't keep away from the place, can you, McLean?'

Heading back to his car, mind distracted by the Eric Parker investigation, McLean had momentarily forgotten he was on enemy territory now. Detective Chief Inspector

Spence was the unwelcome reminder, springing up the stairs towards him like a badly controlled puppet. He was a thin man, counterpoint to Detective Superintendent Brooks who would have given Billy Bunter a run for his money in a who-ate-all-the-pies competition. Little and Large, they were known as, mostly behind their backs. Sometimes they made a good team, but more often they seemed to act like a couple of old women.

'Was I meant to be, Mike? I've still got an office here, you know.'

Spence scowled at the use of his first name. Stopping one step below McLean put him almost face to face. 'I thought you were working out of HQ these days. Watching kiddie porn with Jo Dexter or whatever it is you do all day. Certainly not gathering good intel, if your most recent cock-up's anything to go by.'

McLean wasn't really surprised that the brothel raid was the talk of the town. Nothing like wallowing in someone else's misfortune. Spence's attitude was something he could have done without, though.

'If you'd ever had to deal with the sick fucks who get off on that kind of thing you wouldn't use that term, Mike. It's not porn. Call it what it is. Child abuse.'

Spence blanched. Clearly he wasn't used to being answered back to. He tried to retort with aggression, but lacked the skill of Duguid, or even Brooks. 'You'd think you'd know a punishment when you saw one. Everyone knows the SCU's for losers.'

'Maybe you missed the memo when we stopped being Lothian and Borders and started being Police Scotland, Mike, but we go wherever our skills are needed.' McLean put extra emphasis on the noun, then paused a moment before adding: 'Of course, maybe this station's the only place your particular skills are of any use.'

A nervous tic pulsed at the corner of Spence's eye. His floppy, greying hair and skeletal face lent him the air of an old man, almost cadaverous even though he was only two years McLean's senior. Given their parallel career paths, they should have been friends or at the very least amicable, but for some reason the DCI seemed to take offence at McLean's general existence.

'Don't think your lack of respect isn't noticed and commented on, McLean.' He pushed past. McLean anticipated the shoulder, twisting out of the way so that Spence missed and stumbled on the step as he went. He half expected another rant, but the DCI didn't look back or say anything more. Just another bear with a sore head.

'He's been walking around like he's got a stick of whittled ginger up his arse all week, sir. Reckon he's starting to realise what a useless bag of meat Carter really is.' Grumpy Bob stood at the bottom of the stairs, no doubt having just witnessed the whole exchange. McLean jogged down the last few steps to meet him.

'That's worse than usual? Can't say as I really noticed.'

'Aye, well, you're no' here that much. How's life treating you over in Vice?'

'Could be better, Bob. And don't pretend you've no idea what I'm talking about.'

Grumpy Bob said nothing, just tilted his head slightly in confirmation.

'Be seeing a bit more of me now, anyway. Looks like I'm going to be the lead on the Eric Parker case.'

'Parker?' Grumpy Bob's face creased into a puzzled frown. 'Oh, right. The priapic salesman. How's that going?'

'Best not to ask or you might get roped in.'

'Got to be better than setting up this cold case unit. I thought we were finally shot of Dagwood, but he's back here pretty much every day, sticking his nose in where it's not needed. That's probably another reason why Spence is a bit on edge.'

'He here now? Dagwood, that is?' McLean peered around the hallway nervously.

'No, he's away to his golf. I've just spent the last two hours with him, though. Not sure what I did to deserve that.'

'I'm sure you'll be richly rewarded in the afterlife.' McLean slapped his old friend on the arm, noticed that the smile it elicited was only half-hearted. Was it really that bad here?

'You didn't manage to get me a copy of the Headland House report, by the way?' he added.

'Ach. Knew there was something else I was meant to be doing. I'll get a copy printed up soon as. Not that it'll do you much good.'

'No?'

'There's a fair bit missing, and what's there's been redacted, far as I can tell. To be honest I'm not sure why Dagwood even added it to the list. It's not as if they'll let him reopen it.'

'They?' McLean had to ask the question, even though he had a fairly good idea who Grumpy Bob was talking about. He'd recognised a few faces coming out of the house all those years ago. Establishment figures, powerful people.

Most of them would be dead by now, it was true. But enough of them weren't. And enough favours were owed by the younger men who were now in charge. 'I guess you're right, Bob. If even half the rumours I've heard are true, then exposing that mess to the light of day won't end well.'

# 17

Everyone is silent as he carries her down the stairs. All eyes are on him, he can feel them burning his skin, but no one says a word. The whole house is unnaturally quiet, as if it is holding its breath, waiting to see what happens next.

She is tiny, the girl. Stick-thin and unkempt. She hasn't spoken, just stared at him with those deep black eyes as he unlocked the cage, hunkered down and tried his best friendly face to reassure her he wasn't a threat. It had taken a while to coax her out of the cupboard under the eaves, clearly her safe space. She hadn't shown fear, so much as wariness, a fierce intelligence in her gaze as if she knew perfectly well what was going on. Only when she had satisfied herself he posed no threat had she emerged from her bolt-hole, walked over to him and flung her bony arms around his neck, allowed herself to be carried down from the attic.

He never had any brothers or sisters, doesn't really know much about children either. At a guess he'd say she was eight or nine, but she's so thin she could well be older. She smells unwashed, her black hair tangled and matted in places, and she returns the stares of all the other officers with such intensity that one by one they turn away. He can only wonder what they will say to him once this is over.

'What the fu—?' Detective Sergeant Duguid has just enough sense to stop himself from swearing in front of her. His scowl suggests this is a complication he would rather not have.

'I found her up in the attic, sir. Looks like there were others up there too, and recently. Don't know where they've gone, but the place is empty now.' He goes to put her down, but she clings fiercely to his neck.

'What's your name, pet?' Duguid takes a step closer, bends down so he is at eye level with the girl and tries to put on a conciliatory tone. It's clearly not something he is used to doing, and she clings harder, turning her face away. He shifts his focus up. 'She speak to you?'

'No, sir. Hasn't said a word.'

Duguid frowns, turns to another plain clothes officer. 'Get on the phone to social services. We need a team here soonest. And put some bodies on the room where she was found, I don't want anyone going in there again until the forensics boys have had a chance to see it.'

The team sets about following its orders like a well oiled machine. There is something in the air, almost like a sense of relief. As if they had known this was going to happen but none of them wanted to be in the spotlight. He can't understand that.

'What do you want me to do, sir?' He hefts the girl in his arms slightly. Thin though she is, her weight is beginning to tell, but she won't let him put her down.

'You, McLean?' DS Duguid cocks his head to one side at the question. 'Better find yourself somewhere quiet to sit down. Social services will be a while, and it doesn't look like your new friend's going to let anyone else take her away.'

## 18

The offices of MacFarlane and Dodds, Solicitors and Notaries Public, were housed in a modern, glass-fronted building in Fountainbridge, overlooking the Union Canal where it terminated at Lochrin Basin. McLean could remember the area from his student days, when the railway marshalling yards and McEwan's brewery had been there, semi-derelict slum tenements waiting for the long-promised redevelopment money to appear. It had taken a couple of generations to come, but slowly the place was being dragged out of the mire into a form of respectability.

'Miss Marchmont is expecting you, Detective Inspector. I'll show you to the conference room and let her know you've arrived.'

The receptionist was all efficiency and charm, offering coffee and pointing out the location of the toilets as she led him and DS Ritchie along a corridor of identical frosted glass doors interspersed with frosted glass walls. Only individual name plates gave any clue as to what went on in the rooms beyond. The one at the far end read 'Conference 1' and the door opened on to a compact room dominated by a large table, around which were arranged too many chairs. A sideboard under the window already held a tray with cups, a large cafetière of coffee and a plate of expensive-looking biscuits.

'Please help yourself.' The receptionist bustled over to the tray, plunging the filter on the cafetière. 'Or if you'd prefer tea?'

'No, coffee's fine,' McLean said, then looked to Ritchie for confirmation.

'Aye, coffee's fine for me.'

'I'll away and tell Miss Marchmont you're here, then.'

'Thank you.' McLean waited until the receptionist was at the door, then added: 'One thing. I forgot Miss Marchmont's position in the company. What is it she actually does here?'

The receptionist looked a little surprised at the question. 'She's head of Corporate Law, Inspector. One of the partners.'

'Of course. Sorry. Brain's not what it used to be.'

'Comes to us all.' The receptionist smiled and left the room.

'What was that about, sir?' Ritchie asked. She had already helped herself to coffee and biscuits, he noticed.

'Exactly what I asked. Miss Marchmont's file just says she's a lawyer who works for this firm. Helps to know if she's a junior intern or the senior partner, wouldn't you say?'

'Guess so. To be honest I'm not really sure why we're here at all.'

'Call it damage limitation. I'm here to apologise for our mistake, but I also want to make sure it really was a mistake, if you see what I mean.'

Ritchie opened her mouth to answer, but the door opened before she could speak. They both turned to see the woman who walked in.

McLean had met her before, but that had been in the

hurly-burly of the raid. People were never at their best in that sort of situation, and he remembered Miss Marchmont's angry bluster turning to confusion. But he also remembered how she'd been found alone in her room, not participating in the party. How she'd claimed not to be feeling well. Hardly surprising given how thin she was. Dressed in a charcoal-grey business suit, her clothes hung off her like she'd borrowed them from her dad, and her face, framed with straight, shoulder-length, jet-black hair, was narrow. She wore no make-up, as far as he could tell, and looked like she really didn't need to. Her skin was flawless and so pale she must never have seen the sun.

A flicker of something indefinable crossed her face as she saw him. It was as if a light had suddenly switched off inside her, an instant shutting down. For a second she had appeared open, ready to talk. No sooner had she cast her eyes on him than she had closed up completely. And he was certain it was him, not Ritchie. It had been the same back at the house, and once again he felt he knew her from somewhere, that she knew him too. He couldn't for the life of him think where they could have met, though. It wasn't as if he frequented the Edinburgh swingers' scene. Or had that much to do with corporate law either. Perhaps the easiest way to find out would be to ask.

'Miss Marchmont. Thank you for giving us your time. I'm—'

'Detective Inspector McLean. I know. And this must be Detective Sergeant Ritchie. I've heard a lot about you. Both of you.'

McLean knew a leading comment when he saw one.

Ritchie was wise enough not to say anything either. It led to an awkward pause before Marchmont continued.

'I see Janice has given you coffee. Perhaps we can get straight to the point then? Only I've a busy day ahead of me.' She pulled out a chair and sat down. McLean did the same, noting that she'd not offered a handshake.

'I'm really here to apologise on behalf of Police Scotland and the SCU for the raid,' he said. 'We were acting on what we thought was good intelligence.'

'SCU?' Marchmont interrupted.

'The Sexual Crimes Unit. We deal with prostitution, trafficking, child sexual abuse, the list is depressingly endless.'

'I'm sure it is, Detective Inspector. But what was going on in my house was not a crime, so it would seem your intelligence wasn't up to much at all. I don't suppose you'll tell me who spoke to you.'

'It's not that simple, I'm afraid. We gather intelligence from many different sources before embarking on any operation. I can assure you we're re-evaluating those sources, though.' McLean could hardly believe the words coming out of his mouth. When had he turned into Spence? Marchmont must have seen it too, as the faintest of smiles creased the corners of her eyes. It didn't last.

'Nevertheless, your actions caused a great deal of embarrassment to my friends.'

'I am sorry for that. If it helps, their details have not been kept on file. And we managed to keep the press at bay. No one has been charged. Except for Mr Smith, of course.'

'Mr Smith?'

'You know. Your friend from London? The one we found looking a bit lost while the two ladies he was with enjoyed their own company?'

There was that fleeting smile again, and with it something else. 'I don't believe I know a Mr Smith, Inspector,' she said. 'At least not one who comes to my parties. He might have been a guest of one of the others, but that's really not meant to happen. At the very least they should have let me know beforehand. Contrary to what you might think, we don't all just jump into bed with any stranger who comes calling. Tell me, what has this Mr Smith done?'

McLean couldn't tell if Marchmont was lying or not. She seemed genuine in her ignorance, but there was an edge to her voice that hadn't been there before.

'Three years for statutory rape, for one thing. Not telling us he was in town for another.'

'Are you suggesting—'

'I'm not suggesting anything, Miss Marchmont. Mr Smith's only illegal action was a failure to report in under the Sexual Offences Act. He's on the register, so he should have let us know as soon as he moved to the city. He didn't. We found him at your place by chance. We weren't looking for him. In some ways you've done us all a favour.'

A frown creased Marchmont's brow, not quite anger, more concern. 'He shouldn't have been there. I would never have let him in.'

'If you'd known?' Ritchie asked the question, Marchmont turning her attention on the detective sergeant for the first time, giving McLean more of a profile view of her face. There was something else about her that he couldn't quite put his finger on, something about the way she was responding to their questions. He'd been so preoccupied with trying to work out how he knew her that he'd not been paying attention to her almost flawless performance. But it was there nonetheless. She was acting, lying. Hiding something.

'Quite so. You might find our little get-togethers strange, but all the people in my house when you raided it are friends. People I've known a long time. Some of them lovers.' Marchmont lingered on this last word for a while, her eyes misting over as if she were remembering nights of passion. She shuddered gently before continuing. 'As I said before, I'd never let a stranger in without being introduced to them first. Getting to know them, getting to know all about them. This Mr Smith? He sounds like a monster. I have no idea how he came to be in my home.'

And there it was, the slightest of tells. The hand to the stomach was less easy to notice as she was sitting down, but McLean had interviewed enough people, suspects and witnesses alike, to know when he was being lied to.

'I've met a few in my time, and that is one screwed-up individual.'

DS Ritchie peered over the steering wheel, checking the traffic before easing the little Alfa Romeo out into the stream heading east towards Lothian Road. McLean had given her the keys when they'd met up at HQ before coming over to interview Marchmont; she was much better at driving than him, more mechanically sympathetic, and he liked being able to think without having to focus on the road ahead.

'Each to their own, Kirsty. And that screwed-up individual is being very understanding, given how we raided her house and carted off all her friends to the station for questioning. She could kick up far more of a fuss if she wanted to.'

'Aye, and have her dirty wee secret all over the press.'

McLean said nothing for a while. He was still trying to piece together how he could possibly know Heather Marchmont. She was too young to be an old school or university acquaintance, and he certainly didn't move in the same circles as her. Not given her nocturnal antics.

'What do we know about her? Apart from her sexual proclivities, that is?'

'How do you do that, sir?'

McLean glanced over at Ritchie. 'Do what?'

'Act like it's perfectly normal to have a bunch of people come round to your house and fuck each other. I mean, Christ's sake, "sexual proclivities"? Could you be any less judgemental?'

'I can never remember whether it's a genius who can hold two contradictory ideas in his head at the same time or a madman. Never found it that hard to do myself, so I guess it could be either.'

Ritchie executed a perfect double declutch downshift, putting the Alfa into the roundabout perhaps a little more aggressively than was strictly necessary. McLean felt himself pushed back into the seat as she accelerated away. Maybe it wasn't such a good idea to wind her up when she was driving his car.

'Look, so she has an interesting sex life. Not sure what that says about her, or what it says about us that we find it uncomfortable to even talk about it. The thing is, what gets her going is of little interest to me at the moment. I want to know her background. Where she comes from. How long she's been working at that law firm. What she did before. We know where she lives, but is she an Edinburgh native? Where did she study law? Who is she?'

'You think she's hiding something?'

McLean laughed. 'A great many things, how she knows John Smith not the least of them. Look, I know Jo's writing this whole escapade off as an embarrassing mistake, but I'm still not convinced. I've been over the files. There was a brothel working out of that house the week before we raided it. If I was a betting man I'd lay good odds the sex party's a cover.'

Ritchie slowed down, only partly because the speed limit had dropped to thirty. She was concentrating on the road, but giving him sideways glances as if trying to work out whether he was joking or not.

'And you think Marchmont's involved? In a brothel? Isn't that, I don't know, a bit unlikely? She's a partner in an international law firm. Hardly your typical Madam.'

Put like that, McLean had to admit she had a point. Perhaps he was chasing shadows, desperately trying to find a reason for what was quite clearly a monumental cock-up. Better perhaps to put it behind him, accept the black mark on his record and move on.

'Aye, you're probably right,' he said even as he knew she was wrong.

'It's all come as something of a shock. Eric is . . . was, well, he was Eric. I still can't really believe he's gone.'

The second interview of the day, only this time McLean was accompanied by DS MacBride. The offices of Boxing Clever were in sharp contrast to those of MacFarlane and Dodds. They occupied a couple of storeys of an old seventies concrete monstrosity of a building, just off the top end of Leith Walk. The place reeked of damp cardboard and sweat, and the coffee they had been brought in stained mugs tasted like it had been made a couple of days earlier, possibly a couple of weeks.

'Can you tell me what he was working on?' McLean asked.

'Eric? He was in charge of sales for the northern sector.' The Chief Operations Officer, as he had introduced himself, was a thin man called Donald Hutcheson. He was younger than Parker, but stooped like a man twice his age. His phone rang constantly, a medley of different ringtones that he mostly ignored. Just occasionally he would glance at the screen, thumb the call to message and slip the phone back into his jacket pocket, only for it to go off again seconds later.

'That would be everything north of the Highland Line?' MacBride had his tablet computer back, and tapped away at it with one merry finger.

'Everything north of Hadrian's Wall if I'm being honest. North of the English Channel, even. Our operations . . . We're not the biggest company in the packaging sector.'

'So what was he doing the day he parked up in the multi-storey?'

'It's most odd. Don't really know why he parked there at all. We don't use it much since most of our operations moved out to Loanhead. That's where we manufacture most of our products. We'll be moving offices out there just as soon as we can get out of the lease on this place.'

'But he'd been out on the road before . . . beforehand?' McLean steered the interview back to the topic.

'What? Oh. Yes. He'd been up in Inverness. We've a lot of small manufacturing clients up there.'

'Did you speak to him about the trip? Did he call you on the way back?' As if to underline the question, Hutcheson's phone rang again, yet another different ringtone. It couldn't have been important, as he didn't even bother to look at the screen.

'He did, yes. Mobile signal's not much cop on the A9, but he checked in at Perth. He'd made a couple of sales, had a few potentials to follow up.' Hutcheson's face dropped. 'Damn. I'll have to get on to that.'

'Did he call you on that phone?' MacBride pointed at the jacket pocket as it erupted into another electronic ditty. This time Hutcheson pulled out the handset, thumbed the screen until the noise died.

'This? Yes. Everybody calls me on this. Couldn't live without it.'

'So there'll be a log of the time. When he was in Perth?'

'I guess so. Why?'

'We're just trying to trace Mr Parker's movements. Things like phone call histories help to narrow it down.'

'Oh. Right. You know how to get that sort of information off it, then?' Hutcheson passed the phone across the table. MacBride tapped at the screen a few times, then tapped something into the screen of his tablet before handing the phone back. Almost as soon as Hutcheson took it, the ringing started up again. He peered at the screen, frowning slightly. 'Ah, now this one I have to take. Sorry.'

Before they could say anything he had stood up and darted from the room, talking hurriedly.

'Popular man,' MacBride said.

'Looks like he's heading for a heart attack if he's not careful.' McLean realised as he said it just how insensitive the comment was. Fortunately Hutcheson wasn't within earshot. 'What time did Parker call from Perth?'

MacBride tilted the tablet so McLean could see his notes. 'Half-five in the afternoon. Fits in with the rest of his schedule.'

'Half-five? But he didn't arrive at the car park until nearly half-eight. It's hardly an hour from Perth to Edinburgh. What was he doing that kept him busy for two hours?'

McLean leaned back in his seat, hearing the muffled tones of Hutcheson's important conversation just beyond the half-closed door to the office. 'We've still got Parker's phone, right?'

'Mike Simpson in IT forensics was having a look at it.'

'He'll presumably be able to bring up the call log. Like you did just now?'

'Once he's got past the password. I'll need to ask if anyone here knows what it is. You want me to see if I can trace where it's been? Where Parker went between half-five and half-eight?'

'You can do that?' McLean had hoped, but he knew he was not technology's master so much as its dim-witted servant.

'Possibly. It'll take time, though.'

Meaning money. Overtime and a dwindling budget. How

much could they justify spending on a man who appeared to have died of natural causes? McLean suspected the answer was going to be not a lot.

'Leave it for now, OK? But keep the options open. I've a nasty feeling we're not done with Eric Parker quite yet.'

# 19

'Wee birdie tells me you went to see Heather Marchmont this morning. What the hell was that about?'

McLean hunched over a keyboard at one of the dozen or more empty desks in the SCU main office, and looked up in surprise at the question. DCI Dexter stood in the open doorway, silhouetted by the sun low in the evening sky as it shone through the windows behind her. He didn't need to see her to know who it was, but the tone of her voice wasn't as friendly as he might have hoped.

'I thought we agreed at the briefing I'd speak to her. Thought given the circumstances it would be better to go to her rather than dragging her into the station.'

'Better you hadn't gone at all. Least not without me.'

'But—'

'Ah, forget it, Tony.' Dexter came into the room and McLean could see her face was creased with weariness. She stooped more than usual, her shoulders slumped as if the whole world was weighing her down. 'You're right. We agreed. But that was before I had the DCC breathing down my neck, as good as ordering me to sweep the whole sorry affair under the carpet.'

'He said that?' McLean swivelled his chair around as Dexter pulled out one from the next desk and dropped into it. A quick glance around the room showed they were alone.

'He's no' that stupid, but I can take a hint. Especially one that comes with a threat of calling in Professional Standards. Your giving Miss Marchmont the third degree isn't going to be all that helpful. No' if she makes a formal complaint.'

'Credit me with some intelligence, Jo. I hardly gave her the third degree. More like an abject apology. I was just typing up my report now.' McLean pointed at the screen and keyboard in front of him.

'Oh aye? You not like that office we gave you then?'

'It's fine. Just easier to do it here. Ritchie wrote it up, I've been checking it over before signing it off. Beats doing the overtime rosters.'

'Talking of Ritchie, where is she?' Dexter looked around the room, apparently only just noticing that it was empty.

'Shift end. And she had to leave anyway; her boyfriend's in town for the week.'

'The priest? That still on?' Dexter shook her head in disbelief.

'Seems to be. Poor sod's still recovering from his run-in with that psycho back in the spring. Reckon it'll be a while before he can walk properly. He seems to be a hit with the bishop, though. Spends most of his time in St Andrews these days.'

'Just as well they don't need any sergeants in Fife then, or we'd be a detective down.'

'Don't even suggest it. She's all the team I've got left. MacBride's busy keeping on the right side of Brooks, Grumpy Bob's cruising towards his retirement.'

'It's not all bad. You've still got Sandy Gregg.' Dexter gave him a wicked smile. 'Now why don't you finish that report in the morning. No' as if it's going to be read by anyone tonight. Go home. Get some rest.'

McLean swivelled his chair back so he was facing the screen again. 'Think I'd be happier knowing this was done and dusted. It shouldn't take long. Just squaring what Marchmont said with the statements we took from everyone on the night. You know she wasn't taking part?'

'When a senior officer tells you to go home and get some rest, Tony, you should . . . what?' Dexter had launched into her scolding before McLean had finished speaking, his words taking a while to sink in.

'She wasn't taking part. In the sex. We found her in her room alone, working on some legal case with all that grunting and groaning going on all around her.'

'But she gave a statement?'

'Aye, so did everyone in the place. I'd say she was making it up, but I saw her there and she really wasn't dressed for the party. She said she wasn't in the mood, felt a bit sick or something. It could have been a lie, but to be honest I don't see why she'd bother. She admitted to organising the whole thing, just didn't feel like getting it on when it started.'

'And she didn't cancel the whole thing?' Dexter shook her head. 'Sounds to me like someone else was pulling the strings then.'

'The thought had occurred to me. And there's the small matter of Mr Smith too.'

'Oh aye? What about him?'

'Well, she says she doesn't know him, doesn't know who invited him. She gave a very good impression of being angry that he was there.'

'But you don't buy it.'

'I don't buy any of it. It just doesn't stack up. It's too complicated. Too off the wall, even. I mean, I'm sure there's a swingers' scene in Edinburgh, same as any other city where there's men and women with too much time on their hands and an underdeveloped sense of prudishness. But I'd bet good money if we'd raided the place a week earlier we'd have found working girls in there, and paying clients. Somehow they found out we were coming, and the party was a last-minute cover-up. A way to explain away all the sex toys.'

'Which would make Miss Marchmont what? The Madam? She's a corporate lawyer with a top city law firm. One whose senior partner regularly plays squash with the Deputy Chief Constable.' Dexter shook her head slowly. 'You're seeing conspiracies everywhere, Tony. I'd love for them to be true, believe me. I'm the one getting it in the neck for this fuck-up, after all. No one would be happier than me to go back to the DCC and the Procurator Fiscal, tell them we were right all along. But we weren't. We got it wrong. End of story.' She stood up, pushed the chair back under the desk where it had come from, placed a hand on McLean's shoulder. 'Give it up. Go home and have some of that very fine whisky you keep hidden away in your library. We'll wrap this all up at the briefing tomorrow.'

McLean said nothing, just held Dexter's gaze long enough for her to be sure he'd got the message, nodded to show he was going to do as he was told. She shrugged, turned away and left the room. For long moments after she'd gone, he just stared out through the open door, the window beyond and into the falling evening sky, wondering why it was that nothing was ever easy.

And how the hell Jo Dexter knew about the whisky in his library.

An unfamiliar car greeted him, parked on the gravel outside the house as McLean drove in through the front gates. For the briefest of moments he wondered whether it was Emma returned, but it was a while since he'd even had a postcard from her. This car was quite new too. Emma's old rust and blue Peugeot must surely have died by now, but he didn't imagine she'd have much money for a brand-new one.

The mystery was solved as soon as he stepped into the small utility room that led off the kitchen to the back door. Peals of laughter filled the air, and he could see Rachel sitting at the big wooden table, clutching a mug of tea. Another woman stood with her back to him, her shoulder-length blonde hair glowing in the light from the ceiling lamp, but it was her clothing that gave her away. Rachel's older sister, Jenny, ran a vintage and second-hand clothes shop on Nicholson Street, and liked to wear the merchandise. She'd helped him identify the dress found on the body of a young woman, walled up in the basement of an old mansion house out Sighthill way. That had been a couple of years ago, and he'd not seen her since Phil and Rachel's wedding.

'Tony. You're home.' Rachel spotted him and struggled to get out of her chair.

'Don't get up on my account,' he said as he stepped into the room. Jenny turned to face him, much closer than was perhaps comfortable.

'Tony. Hi. It's been a while.' For an awkward moment he

thought she was going to hug him, but she settled for a light peck on the cheek. She looked well, he couldn't help noticing. Younger than he remembered her from their first meeting, but then she'd been under a great deal of stress then.

'How's Chloe?' The flicker of surprise in Jenny's eyes confirmed that he'd got her daughter's name right. Hard not to, given what she'd been through because of him. What he'd saved her from.

'She's fine. Off at university in Aberdeen of all places. Studying materials science. I'm not even sure I know what that is.'

McLean looked around the kitchen for signs that anyone had eaten. He'd picked up enough takeaway for two this time, and now they were three. The bag hung heavy in his hand, so he hefted it on to the table.

'Oh, I almost forgot. I spoke to Phil. He's on his way back to Edinburgh. Should arrive tomorrow if he managed to get on the plane.'

'Drunk, was he?' Rachel asked. Her smile at his return and the joy of seeing her sister had evaporated at his words. McLean felt a certain guilt at that, but it was something that had to be addressed.

'He'd been drinking, yes. I told him to get some black coffee and sort himself out. I've not heard anything since, so I have to assume they let him on the flight.'

'Either that or he's under a table at the airport. Christ, if I'd known he was such a drunkard I'd never have married him. Bad enough seeing Dad go that way.' Rachel slumped back into her chair, peered into her mug.

'Phil's not a drunkard, Rae. Sure he likes a drink now

and then, but who doesn't?' McLean had been going to get himself a beer from the fridge, but in the light of how the conversation was turning, he opted for putting the kettle on instead.

'Anyone who drinks himself into a stupor every night is a drunkard in my book. You making tea?' She held up her mug, indicating that it was in need of a refill. McLean took it from her, turned to Jenny.

'You want one?'

'Yeah, why not?' She pulled out a chair and sat herself down, leaving McLean the only one standing. The two sisters sitting so comfortably either side of his kitchen table made him feel like a stranger in his own home, and it was only then that he noticed Mrs McCutcheon's cat was nowhere to be seen. Not the only one feeling put upon then.

'Have you heard from Emma recently? Rae was saying she went off a while back.'

McLean studied Jenny's face, looking for any sign of ulterior motive in the question. It appeared to be genuine.

'Had a postcard a couple months ago. From New Zealand. Some place called Te Anau on the South Island.'

'What on earth's she doing there?'

'I gave up asking a long time ago. Besides, she's not got a phone with her. At least not one I've got the number for. And she's never anywhere long enough for me to write. I get the feeling her quest might be coming to an end, but that's probably just wishful thinking.' He tried to suppress the bitterness in his voice, wondering where it had come from.

'Her quest?' Jenny asked.

'It's something to do with her being in a coma for six

months, losing her memory and all that. She needed to get away, to travel around the world. I can understand why. I mean, if I'd been helpless like that, lost even, I'd want to take control. Do something wild and different.'

Jenny said nothing in reply, so McLean busied himself with making tea and passing out mugs. It was uncomfortable talking about Emma, but not for the reason he expected. She seldom came up in conversation at work these days, just the occasional question when he met one of her old colleagues from forensics at a crime scene. He'd managed to convince himself she would be coming back soon. That was enough, and he'd fallen into the trap of believing it, accepting her absence as normal in the process. Talking about her forced him to confront the truth: she'd been gone eighteen months now and the postcards were coming more and more infrequently. He genuinely had no idea where she was or whether she would ever return.

'But I'm sure she'll be back when she's ready.' He shifted the curry from the table to the counter, pulled out a seat and sank into it.

'I'm sure she will.' Jenny reached out and patted his hand in an oddly motherly gesture. McLean covered his growing unease by taking a sip of his tea, burning his lip on the scalding liquid. Not a problem he ever had with beer.

'How about you then, Jenny? Successful trip?'

'Can't complain. I picked up a lot of stock from an online retailer who's gone bust. Which brings up a rather difficult topic.'

McLean couldn't help noticing that Jenny looked away from him, across the table to her sister as she spoke. He'd interviewed enough people in his time to know who she was talking about, and he wasn't so stupid as to not know why.

'That flat of yours above the shop isn't very big, is it? And I'm guessing if you've just bought a load of stock you need somewhere to store it all?'

'I knew you'd understand. I'd be happy to have Rae staying any other time, but . . .' She trailed off.

'I've more than enough room, and I doubt you'd have been able to put up Phil as well.'

'Phil . . . ? Ah, yes.' Jenny looked at her sister again. Rachel was studying her mug of tea intently, but looked up sharply at her husband's name.

'He's coming here . . . Of course he's coming here. Where else would he go?'

'He's my oldest friend, Rae. And he's going through a bit of a rough patch right now.' McLean picked up his own mug of tea, put it back down again. He'd kill for a beer. 'There's room enough for everyone.'

# 20

'There you go. All sorted. If you'd just sign this form here, sir?'

McLean wasn't sure what he thought about tagging and releasing offenders considered low risk to the community. It was meant to save money and relieve some of the pressure on the prisons, but he couldn't help thinking it was just another way of hiving off public services to the private sector. Someone making a profit out of justice felt wrong to him, even if he wasn't exactly sure why. On the other hand, with a GPS-enabled tracker around his ankle, John Smith would be easy enough to find, and if he tried to do a runner before his trial they'd know about it.

'Chafes a bit. How am I meant to get it off?' The man rolled down his trouser leg, trying to hide the ankle bracelet and its heavy electronic package. His tight-hemmed jeans wouldn't easily stretch, which meant getting undressed that evening would be an interesting challenge for him.

'You're very funny.' McLean sniffed the air and tried not to grimace. John Smith's flat might have been a nice place to live, a high-floor apartment in a modern development overlooking the Firth of Forth. It must have cost a bit in rent, but the landlord would be making a loss, even if he kept the deposit. The place was grubby, the furniture stained and the carpet didn't look like it had seen a vacuum cleaner in months. Whatever he was, Mr Smith was not house-proud.

Still, this was his home, and the terms of his bail meant he'd be seeing rather more of it than he was perhaps used to. Maybe he'd use some of that time to tidy up a bit.

McLean addressed the technician who had attached the tag to Smith's leg, now tinkering with a small black box of electronics set up by the phone. 'We all good to go?'

'Aye. The base station's linked up an' running. He moves more'n a hundred yards from here and we'll know about it. He tries to tamper with the box or the tag we'll know about it even quicker.'

'A hundred yards?' Smith pulled at his jeans, forcing the tracker down to his foot but still not managing to get the fabric over. 'That's a bloody joke. How'm I supposed to do my shopping? How'm I going to go to work?'

'Thought you said you worked from home.'

'Yeah, well. Still got to meet clients, you know.'

'I suggest you arrange for them to come here, then. Only don't forget to let us know they're coming. You probably won't get much business from them if we stop and frisk them when they leave.'

'What? You're going to be watching the place even with all this shit here?' Smith threw an arm wide, indicating the black box of tricks that would monitor his every move and report it back to them, via the private company operating the system. The technician finished stashing his tools away, snapped the latches closed on his hard plastic tool case and stood up.

'That's me finished. I'll leave youse to it, aye.'

McLean nodded, watched the man leave. As he closed the front door, DS Ritchie appeared from the other end of the room.

'Place is clean, sir. Well, there's nothing here shouldn't be.' She ran a finger over the back of one of the chairs clustered around a dining table piled high with empty pizza boxes and lad mags. 'Not sure "clean" is the right word for it.'

'This is a fucking disgrace.' Smith had given up with trying to get his trouser leg down. Now he stalked across his living room to where Ritchie stood. 'You can't go rifling through my stuff. That's personal.'

'You'd prefer to spend the time until your trial in Saughton, Mr Smith? Only I've heard the inmates there don't much like rapists. Don't much like the English either.' The detective sergeant stood her ground, staring the man down. McLean readied himself, not so much to go to her aid as to intervene should she decide to break Smith's arm.

'I think it's time we left, Sergeant,' he said after a moment's silence. 'Mr Smith will want a little time to adjust to his new circumstances.'

'Sir.' Ritchie nodded, stepped past Smith and joined McLean near the front door to the apartment. Smith watched, a mixture of anger and disbelief painted across his face.

'Wait. You can't leave me like this.' He hopped theatrically, pulling up his tagged ankle where his jeans were rucked up his shin. 'How'm I supposed to get undressed?'

'That's entirely up to you, Mr Smith,' McLean said. 'I'd maybe suggest you try a pair of scissors.'


'Heard a rumour you were in the building, sir. Got a little something for you.'

McLean looked up from his desk, his old desk in his tiny

old office back at his old station, to see Grumpy Bob standing in the doorway. There was no point in the detective sergeant coming in. Hardly enough room to swing a very small kitten, and no extra chairs. Some of the piles of folders and box files had been there since McLean had first been allocated the space. He had no idea what was in them, but they were like old friends now.

'Anything interesting?' He dropped the page he'd been squinting at back on to the pile. Amazing how so much paperwork could accumulate even when he was working for another unit in another station. Most of it seemed to be marked for the attention of a certain Detective Inspector Carter, so how it had ended up here he could only guess.

'Just a copy of the Headland House file. You said you wanted a look. I don't reckon the DCC will reopen it, though, no matter how much Duguid wants to.' Grumpy Bob reached over the desk and handed McLean the folder. It was surprisingly slim; he'd have expected box loads of stuff.

'Is that it?'

'Pretty much. Apparently there was more, but it was lost in the records fire, back in 'ninety-five. This is all the stuff that was on the computer.'

McLean flicked open the folder, scanned the first page, then closed it again. 'Thanks, Bob. I'll have a look at it later.' He wasn't entirely sure why he'd asked to see the folder. Pure curiosity, perhaps, or the fact that it had come up, sparked a memory, an itch he just had to scratch. Or maybe it was the coincidence, an old brothel raid case coming to his attention just at the same time the new brothel raid case had gone spectacularly wrong. There were parallels. Well, not exactly parallels, more like echoes from the past.

'Just keep it to yourself, aye?' Grumpy Bob nodded at the plain folder, and only then did McLean notice it wasn't an official one. 'Wouldn't want anyone asking how you came by it.'

'Seriously?' He opened the top drawer of the desk and slid the folder in. 'Why would anyone care?'

'Put it this way sir. I don't often get calls from the DCC. Not on my direct line. He tends to go through my bosses' boss, if you know what I mean.'

'He called you on this? Why?'

'Oh, he mentioned a couple of the other cases we're considering, but I wasn't born yesterday. Could tell this was the one he was really interested in. I got the impression from the conversation that someone even higher up the food chain had been bending his ear. He was very keen the case not be reopened. To be honest, I don't think there's enough left to reopen it anyway. Most of the folk arrested are dead or good as.'

McLean closed the desk drawer, wondered whether or not to lock it. There was something else bothering him about the whole situation, and the knowledge that something was being actively suppressed only made him more curious. 'What was the actual unsolved crime, anyway? Not as if we didn't catch everyone with their pants down.'

'It was the girl,' Grumpy Bob said. 'The one you found in the attic. Aye, your name's in the report, sir. Only they never found out what she was doing there, who'd abducted her or what they were planning to do with her. They never even found out who she was.'

Newhaven hadn't changed a great deal since that day, twenty years earlier. Creeping signs of redevelopment, tidying up the ramshackle houses; a few of the worst examples of sixties architecture had been replaced with more modern housing that wasn't really much of an improvement. The biggest change, as far as McLean could see, was that the houses that had once looked out on to the Firth of Forth now had an unrivalled view of the modern tower blocks that budded out of the reclaimed land west of Leith Docks like so many glass and concrete mushrooms. John Smith lived in one of those flats, which just about summed up the whole situation as far as he was concerned.

Headland House was still there, but it looked like it had been converted into apartments. McLean parked across the street, listening to the tick, tick of cooling metal as his car fell silent. He really shouldn't have been here; there were far more important things to worry about. But he couldn't help thinking about the place, the raid that should have been the talk of the city but which fizzled away with barely a mention in the press, the unnamed little girl he'd found locked up in a cage in the attic.

What had happened to her? She'd be what, thirty now? Older? Christ, where did the years go?

He shook his head even though there was no one about to see. The folder Grumpy Bob had given him lay on the passenger seat, but he didn't pick it up to read immediately, just sat there staring at the old building as the trees swayed in the breeze coming in off the Forth. So much going on, at work and at home. Sometimes he envied Emma. How easy it would have been to have just headed off into the wild with her, travelled the world. He had no real ties to Edinburgh any more. Just a job he was more compelled to do than actually enjoyed, a social life that revolved around takeaway food and Mrs McCutcheon's cat. Not much to show for twenty years and more of service.

With a sigh, he took up the folder, flicked it open and scanned the pages. It was sparse, mostly photocopies of heavily redacted notebooks, a couple of witness statements. There was no mention of the girl beyond that she had been found and delivered to social services for rehousing. There were no arrest forms, no details of preparations for court. There wasn't even any record of what had been sent to the Procurator Fiscal, let alone the outcome of any trial. McLean cast his mind back, trying to remember anything of the case at all beyond the raid and finding the young girl. He'd been selected for the fast track not long afterwards, sent up to Aberdeen and then over to Strathclyde to try and cram two years of beat work into six months. Then they'd made him a detective. At the time he'd assumed it was a reward for his diligence. Now it didn't seem quite so innocent. What better way to get the awkward young constable out of the picture than swamp him with so much work he never had time to ask any questions?

The phone squawking away in his jacket pocket interrupted his trip down foggy memory lane. He pulled it out, expecting a call, but it was only a reminder that there was a wrap-up briefing for the brothel raid scheduled for half an hour's time. That was something he would love to miss, but there was no getting away from it. At least they should be drawing a line under the case and hopefully moving on. He shuffled the papers back into their folder and tucked it under the passenger seat out of the way of prying eyes. No wiser for having looked at it, and good luck to Duguid if he thought there was a cold case in there to pursue. Firing the engine back into life, he took one last look at the imposing bulk of Headland House, then headed back to the station and his fate.

'Well, I won't say this is the happiest of briefings, but at least we can say we did our best.'

The SCU offices were almost full for a change, the collected officers involved in the brothel raid assembled for the wrap party. The mood was sombre; nobody liked a fuck-up at the best of times, and this was a spectacular one. It didn't help that Stevie Robinson, the Deputy Chief Constable, had come down from his office to watch over proceedings. He hadn't said anything, which probably made things worse. DCI Dexter wasn't letting him cramp her style, though.

'On the plus side, we've all still got our jobs. And it's no' as if we didn't salvage something from this debacle. Bless you, John Smith.' Dexter raised her coffee mug in a mock toast. A dozen or so other mugs were held aloft and a low murmur of 'John Smith' echoed around the room. It was that kind of day.

'There'll be an investigation into what went wrong, of course. But it's going to be internal. No one from the complaints nosing around and making us all feel dirty.'

That got a murmur of surprised cheer out of the crowd,

short lived, but there nonetheless. McLean looked out across the room of faces, some he knew well, some hardly at all.

'But there's no getting past the fact we fucked up. I'm no' looking to blame anyone. We're all in it together and all that pish. But let's not make a habit if it, aye?' Dexter paused a moment, as if waiting for the class to say 'No, Miss, sorry, Miss'. They didn't, so she continued. 'Now there's plenty else for us to be getting on with. Someone's been carving his initials in the faces of working girls down on Leith Docks. Going to have to put a stop to that. And there's been too many reports of flashers in Holyrood Park for my liking. Looks like someone's building up to something. Let's stop it before it starts.'

The meeting carried on in similar fashion, a collective sigh of relief at the light reprimand over the brothel raid fiasco helping to lift the mood and inject a sense of purpose. McLean admired Dexter for her ability to motivate her team; far better than Duguid's veiled threats and temper, or Brooks' shouting. He wasn't so wet behind the ears as to believe it could be that easy, of course. There were always repercussions. Finally Dexter wound things up, sending them all off on their various tasks, and the room swiftly emptied. No one wanted to be stuck in there with the DCC, which was perhaps understandable. Even DS Ritchie just glanced nervously past him, then nodded at McLean before scurrying out.

'Tony, a word.' McLean had hung back, knowing this was coming. He was second in command, after all, and the cock-up had been squarely on his watch. He turned to where Dexter and Robinson were standing.

'Ma'am. Sir.'

'This has all been a bit of an embarrassment.' The DCC bounced lightly on his heels, hands behind his back headmaster-style as he spoke. McLean had only met him a few times before; he was a Strathclyde Region man, shipped over from the west coast when all the local constabularies had merged into Police Scotland. For a Weegie copper, he wasn't too bad by all accounts. It didn't help to be on his wrong side, though.

'That may be the understatement of the year, sir.'

'Call me Stevie, please. None of this "sir" nonsense, Tony. We're not in the army.'

McLean resisted the urge to say 'could've fooled me'. It was refreshing to meet a senior officer who didn't immediately pull rank, but he'd also seen the way the DCC stood silently at the back of the room, watching, appraising. He'd need a bit more than first names before he felt he could trust the man.

'Thank fuck for that.' Jo Dexter lowered the tone, as ever. 'Never was one for uniforms. Still, we are where we are, and the important thing is to make sure we don't get here again, right?'

McLean had an inkling of where this was going. Too much to hope that he was wrong. 'I'm still not quite sure how we got things so spectacularly wrong. It should come up in the case review, though.'

'Aye, about that—' Dexter started to speak, but was interrupted by Robinson.

'I want you to run the investigation, Tony. Shouldn't take long. Find out where the wires got crossed. If we got the intel from a CHIS, then we need to re-evaluate using them. That sort of thing. Only keep it low key. The fewer people in the loop the better, you understand?' He gave McLean what he no doubt thought was a friendly pat on the arm.

'You'll have a report on your desk by the end of the week, sir,' McLean said, and wondered whether he could stomach the whitewash he was being asked for.

'Call me Stevie. Please.' The DCC smiled at him like a shark. 'I look forward to reading it.'

# 21

It takes a long time for the woman from social services to arrive.

He sits quietly in a corner of the entrance hall, watching as the swarms of police, plain clothes and uniform, slowly subside. The discovery of the little girl is like a kick up the backside to what was a lacklustre effort beforehand. Every so often he catches a snippet of conversation, angry voices as if the extra work is somehow his fault. He can see the way they look at him, but can't understand why. It's not as if he's done anything wrong.

The girl smells. He has no idea when last she washed, but it's likely weeks rather than days. Her clothes feel dirty, her hair is matted, but he can't put her down, can't push her away. She clings to him as if he were a rock in the middle of a raging torrent, her head buried into his shoulder. He has tried talking to her, but she won't answer. It's hardly surprising. Who knows what traumas she has suffered in a place like this?

'This the wee girl, aye?'

He looks up to see a woman standing in front of him, half bending down to peer at the child. She has a friendly face, but careworn and tired. An ID card hangs from a lanyard around her neck, the photograph showing a woman with a lot less grey in her hair.

'Social services?' he asks, trying to gently ease the girl's grip from around his neck.

The woman nods once. 'You must be PC McLean. I'm Dot.'

'Dot?'

'Aye, just Dot.'

Something about Dot's voice must be trustworthy, as the girl finally stops trying to burrow her head into his neck, turns round to look at her. He can see something crawling around in her hair. A spider perhaps.

'Well, you're a bonnie wee thing, aren't you?' Dot crouches down so that she is on the same eye level. 'Bet you're hungry, though. You look hungry.'

The girl nods, very slightly. She acts more like a toddler than a child her size, doesn't seem to want to speak. Maybe she can't speak, if she's been locked up in this place all her life, used as a plaything for the sick old men they found when they raided the house. There's a special place in hell for people like that, and he doesn't even believe in hell.

'Have ice cream?'

The words are so quiet he almost doesn't hear them. Dot's ears are clearly better tuned to the voices of small children.

'Ice cream? I'd have thought so. What's your favourite flavour?'

The girl doesn't answer, but she carefully detaches herself from him, climbs down off the bench he's been sitting on and fixes him with a very serious expression before nodding once in thanks. 'Ice cream,' she says and points at Dot.

He reaches towards her head, the small insect crawling in her hair. She flinches visibly, even though he has moved as slowly as he can. What has been done to this poor little girl to make her so afraid? And so compliant? Despite the fear in her eyes, she stays stock-still as he teases the bug out, drops it into the palm of his other hand and shows it to her.

'You go with Dot now. She'll look after you. Make sure the bad men don't hurt you any more.'

The little girl relaxes slightly when she sees what he has done, realises what he has not. She reaches up and takes Dot's outstretched hand, allows herself to be led away. He watches her go, across the hall to the open front door, her head twisted around and haunted, dark eyes fixed on him until she is finally gone. He makes a mental note to keep an eye on her progress, check that she's OK.

He will never see her again.

# 22

The office still smelled damp and mouldy as McLean slumped wearily into his chair. Whilst he'd been away someone had come in and dumped a pile of paperwork in the middle of his desk. He pulled the top sheet towards him, half expecting it to be meant for newly promoted and utterly useless Detective Inspector Carter even though he was based on the other side of the city, but it was mostly a series of short transcripts of the interviews with the women in the brothel raid. Not sex workers, he had to remind himself. Just women who liked to have sex with men they hardly knew. For fun, not money. What was missing from their lives that they sought solace in such an unusual place? Was there anything wrong with their lives at all?

Shaking away the thought, he shuffled the transcripts together and put them in a pile that would soon enough morph into a report for the DCC. Call-me-Stevie. Like they were best pals. This was the same DCC who had shut the investigation down, the one who played squash with the senior partner at MacFarlane and Dodds. The one who had threatened to have Professional Standards come in and stick their noses into everything the SCU was doing if they continued to pursue the investigation. And now he wanted a report into where it had all gone wrong. Not hard to see where that would lead, and McLean was the one tasked with delivering the names.

'Bloody marvellous.' He rubbed at his face with tired hands, looked around the office for something to take his mind off the problem, at least for now. Had he been back at his old station, he'd have been able to spend a happy half-hour or more tracking down Carter and explaining to him exactly what he could do with his paperwork, but there wasn't really any excuse to drive over there right now. There was the small matter of the report folder hidden under the passenger seat of the Alfa, though.

McLean pulled out his phone, thumbed through the names in the address book until he found the one he was looking for. There wasn't really any good reason why he should have this number, except that he was a policeman and so naturally nosey. He paused for a moment, then hit the dial button. It rang four times before the call was picked up.

'Hello, Duguid residence.' The voice was pure Morningside, even though McLean knew ex-Detective Superintendent and Mrs Duguid lived in Prestonfield. He'd met Mrs Duguid exactly once in his entire career, but he had no doubt she knew all about him.

'Very sorry to disturb you. It's Detective Inspector McLean here. I was wondering if I could speak to your husband.'

There was a distinct pause before Mrs Duguid answered. 'Charles? He's not here. It's Tony, isn't it?'

He was surprised that she would know that. How dreadful a detective he was, what a complete pain in the arse, and many other similar complaints, yes. But his first name?

'Yes, it is. You couldn't let him know I called, could you? Or tell me where he is?'

'Och, it's no secret. He's away at the golf. Goes there every afternoon. I'm not sure if he plays much, or just likes to get out of the house. I don't think retirement's really suiting him, you know.'

McLean chatted for a while longer, or rather listened politely, muttering the occasional 'aye' as Mrs Duguid blethered on. He finally managed to end the conversation by pretending someone had walked into his office needing something urgent, but not before finding out which particular golf club Duguid was a member of. His ear burned as he took the handset away from it, whether from the pressure of keeping it held there for so long, or from embarrassment he couldn't be sure. He had an address, though, and a mobile phone number he was fairly certain he shouldn't have been given. He stared at it for a while, trying to decide whether to call or not. Better perhaps to talk face to face, much as he didn't like the ex-detective superintendent. Scooping up his phone and jacket, he headed for the door. Paperwork and the DCC's report could wait.

The little red Alfa Romeo looked very much out of place in the car park at Priestfield Golf Club. McLean found a space between two massive four by fours, far too shiny to have ever been further off the road than the neatly raked gravel on which they stood. At least his car was presentable; it should have been after the amount of money he'd spent having it restored. He was going to have to give it a wash sometime soon, though, or more likely find someone to do it for him. He knew some of the senior detectives took theirs to the police maintenance garage, but it was an abuse of the service for one thing and he didn't trust the mechanics not to take her for a spin while he was away either. Life really would be a lot easier with a new car.

The club house was a white-rendered art deco affair, tucked behind the detached bungalows of this leafy suburb and overlooked by the grey volcanic mass of Arthur's Seat. McLean had never been all that interested in sport, golf perhaps least of all, but he remembered coming here once with Phil and a couple of other students just out of curiosity, after dark, drunk, quite probably having already been thrown out of all the local pubs. It was only a short walk from the flat in East Preston Street, after all. Hopefully the management would have forgotten that incident, a good twenty-five years earlier. He doubted he looked like that young, fresh-faced student these days.

A middle-aged lady in a stern tweed skirt and sensible shoes gave him a look of disapproval as he entered the entrance hall.

'Can I help you, young man?' The accent and clipped tones went with the outfit, and for a moment McLean worried that perhaps his youthful misdemeanour hadn't been forgotten after all.

'I was looking for Detective Sup— Charles Duguid. His wife told me he was here.'

The woman's expression turned even sterner, if that were possible. 'If he's here, he'll be in the bar. I don't think I've ever seen him swing a club.' She pointed towards a dark wooden door on the far side of the hall. McLean nodded his thanks and started towards it.

'You can't go in there. It's members only.'

Stopping mid-stride, he pulled out his warrant card and

handed it over. 'It's police business. I just need to have a word with him.'

The woman peered at the card for a moment, then retrieved a pair of wire-rimmed spectacles from beneath her sensible cashmere sweater, where they had been nestling between her breasts on a fine silver chain. 'McLean, McLean. The name rings a bell. How would I know your name? Are you a golfer?'

'Not really, no.' McLean tugged back his card, trying to imagine this woman twenty-five years younger. It was possible she might have been club secretary or something similar then. He seemed to recall a rather tweedy young woman threatening to call the police on them as they dicked about on the eighteenth green in the dark. Bloody students.

'It's no matter. You'll have to sign in.' She walked briskly to the reception desk and pulled open a leather-bound book. McLean followed her, found a pen and scribbled his name down. Three rows above, he recognised the spidery scrawl of the ex-detective superintendent, and no time in the column to suggest he'd left. That much at least was helpful.

'Sign out when you leave,' the stern woman said as he headed for the door to the members' bar. 'And don't let me catch you out on the eighteenth.'

The members' bar had a certain welcoming dark opulence about it, all wooden panelling and polished oak floorboards. A bar dominated one wall, but there was no sign of a barman at the moment, just light spilling out from an open door and the occasional clatter of kitchen noises.

Dotted around the room, comfortable leather armchairs circled small tables or sat off on their own for a little privacy. A long metal-framed window gave a view of the golf course and Arthur's Seat beyond, and at the far end of the room a small fire crackled cheerily in a massive fireplace. At first McLean thought there was no one about, but then he noticed a hand resting on the arm of a high-backed chair, facing the fire. A small glass sat on an occasional table beside the chair, empty now but presumably once filled with single malt whisky. He hadn't made much noise entering the room, but even so the chair's occupant struggled to turn around and a familiar face appeared.

'I wondered who'd be the first to come here looking for me. Never thought it would be you, McLean.'

Retired Detective Superintendent Charles Duguid looked far more relaxed than McLean could ever remember him being. His straggly, thinning grey hair was neatly trimmed and combed, his face fuller for a few months of proper eating. He was wearing a suit, but unlike the ill-fitting shiny outfits he had worn while working, now he had taken a leaf out of the stern club secretary's book and was dressed in well-tailored tweed.

'I phoned your home, sir. Your wife said I'd find you here.'

Duguid's brow wrinkled at this news, as if he felt he'd been somehow betrayed. He reached for his glass, picked it up, realised it was empty and put it back down again.

'You don't have to call me sir any more. I retired, remember.'

'Sorry, I just can't ever see myself calling you Charles, sir.'

Duguid shook his head. 'Bloody public school boys. You're all the same.' He hauled himself up out of the chair, grabbed the glass and headed for the bar. McLean followed, and by the time both of them had reached it, a barman had appeared, as if by magic.

'Another, please. Better make it a double.' He looked at McLean. 'You'll be working, I expect.'

In all the years he'd known the man, McLean didn't think Duguid had ever offered to buy him a drink. He wasn't even sure if this was an offer, but it was the closest to one he'd seen.

'Let me get that,' he said. 'I'm the one who's disturbed your peaceful afternoon.'

Duguid looked like he was going to argue, then just shrugged his acceptance. McLean paid for the drink, ordered a coffee for himself, then waited until both arrived. It was an awkward silence, neither of them wanting to talk while the barman was in earshot. McLean knew that he was out of order even speaking to his old boss like this, and no doubt Duguid did too.

Finally the drinks arrived and the barman sloped back off to the kitchens or wherever it was he had been lurking. Duguid poured a generous measure of water into his whisky, sniffed it and then took a sip before speaking.

'So what's this all about then?'

McLean had considered warming up first, getting the detective superintendent to talk about his plans going forward, maybe a bit about golf. In the end it was easier just to jump straight on in. 'Headland House.'

The members' bar hadn't exactly been noisy before-hand, but the silence that descended upon it was like a blanket being thrown over the world. Even the hum of the drinks refrigerator behind the bar seemed to dull down to nothing, the air taking on a still quality more reminiscent of the wide open moorland of the Pentland Hills just before a thunderstorm broke.

'I think we'd better go and sit down.' Duguid's voice was low, both in volume and tone. He took up his whisky and headed back to his chair by the fire. Only once they were both seated did he speak again.

'You've been talking to Grumpy Bob, I see. I'll have to ask him to be a bit more circumspect in the future, if he wants to have something more than ballroom dancing to do after he retires.'

'I was there, sir. I remember the raid. I found the girl.'

Duguid frowned, as if casting his mind back that far was painful. 'Yes. Yes, you were, weren't you? Snotty-faced little PC fresh out of training and you thought you knew better than anyone else even then.'

It was a typical Dagwood insult, but curiously half-hearted. As if he knew he ought to be saying something snide but couldn't quite muster the energy.

'It should have been the making of my career, that case.' Duguid took another sip of his whisky, savoured it a while before continuing. 'Big bust like that, a few notable scalps. And your wee girl, that made it newsworthy. But I bet you can't remember what happened, who got sent down and for how long.'

'I was just a beat cop. Fresh out of training like you said. I went where they sent me. Spent a few months up in Grampian region on some strange exchange programme they had running back then. It's all a bit of a blur.'

Duguid let out a snort that was part laugh, part disbelief. 'You took the fast track option, what did you expect? Not a lot of new recruits got offered that, back then. Had to be something special.'

'Special? Felt more like a punishment. I always meant to check in on the little girl, see how she was doing. Never had the chance.'

'Aye, well. They'd never have told you where she went anyway. No one came forward to claim her, so she went into care. Social services found her a foster family, I heard. I think it might have been in Glasgow, further west maybe. Never found out the name. I asked, of course, but I was told it was best it was kept secret.'

McLean couldn't exactly say how he knew, but he was certain Duguid was holding back. Perhaps working with the man for so long had given him some kind of sixth sense. Either that or retirement had robbed the superintendent of some of his subtlety. The thought brought a wry smile to McLean's face.

'What about the house?' he asked. 'Surely the tenant or the owner must have been prosecuted? I mean I know we were a bit lenient on brothels back then, but child abduction? Didn't anyone even try to find out why she was there? What they were going to do to her?'

'Course we bloody did. What, you think no one knew how to run an investigation before you came along?'

McLean bit back the obvious retort. It had all too often been that way with Duguid before, and there was no great reason the superintendent needed to even talk to him, let alone about the case.

'There was no owner, at least none we could find. You

wouldn't think it possible, but the last person on the deeds died a hundred years ago and nobody could find any living relatives. The prozzies were all hired in for a party, apparently. From what I recall most of them were horrified when they found out what was going on upstairs. Likewise the johns. None of them had any links to the house apart from being in there when we raided it. We couldn't pin the girl's abduction on them. Well, that's not strictly true. We could have prosecuted every last one of them, but we didn't. And you know why?'

McLean suspected that he did, for much the same reason that they weren't looking any more closely into the goings-on in the New Town terrace house where Heather Marchmont lived and her friends indulged in their sad sexual perversions.

'We could have found out who was behind it all.' Duguid carried on as if he hadn't noticed McLean's lack of answer. 'It would have taken time and cost a lot of money, sure. But the clues were there.'

'Only you were told to stop looking.'

'Oh, it was more subtle than that. But aye. Made pretty clear to me that if I carried on the way I was going it wouldn't be just me out on my ear. My DI and DCI were in the firing line. Left a bitter taste, that did.' Duguid picked up his glass again, but instead of a sip, he threw the whole lot back in one gulp, as if trying to wash away the sourness of the years. 'So why are you interested in digging up old dirt?'

'I'm not really sure. You heard about our brothel raid?'

Duguid nodded. 'Typical clusterfuck by the sound of things. I thought better of Jo Dexter, mind.'

'Well, it's partly that, partly just Grumpy Bob mention-ing the case. Brought back a few memories and . . .' He tailed off, unsure how to voice his suspicions without sounding like some paranoid conspiracy theorist.

'And someone told you to leave it. Maybe suggested it wouldn't be good for your career, or Dexter's, if you kept rocking the boat?'

'Something like that.'

Duguid hauled himself out of his chair, one long-fingered hand smoothing his hair back, the other picking up the empty whisky glass.

'Well, my advice to you would be to do what they say. Let it lie.' He walked across the empty members' room, put the glass down on the bar top. McLean followed, knowing the interview was over.

'Thank you, sir. I'll consider it.'

Duguid laughed, a sound so unusual it took McLean a moment to realise the superintendent wasn't having a seiz-ure. 'Aye. Like fuck you will, McLean,' he said, then stalked out of the room.

## 23

The house was quiet when he finally made it home; no little black car, which suggested Jenny wasn't visiting her
sister. McLean wasn't quite sure whether he was relieved at
that or not. He didn't mind having people staying in the
house; it was big enough for a small army and with just him
and Mrs McCutcheon's cat it could get quite lonely at times.
But part of him enjoyed the solitude, and the melancholy
with it.

An empty kitchen greeted him, only the quiet gurgle of
the Aga interrupting the silence. He dumped his case down
on the table, along with the Headland House report file. He
stared at it a moment, then picked it back up again, carried it
through to the library. His grandmother's antique pedestal
desk – he still couldn't really think of it as his, much like the
rest of the house – had a locking central drawer, and more
importantly he had the key. He slipped the report inside
away from prying eyes, locking it up as he heard a creak on
the stairs. Moments later Rachel appeared at the door.

'You're home,' she said in a tone of voice that asked
'what time do you think this is to be traipsing in?' McLean
remembered all too well being scolded by his grandmother;
it was something else to get it from someone almost ten
years his junior.

'How's your day been?' he asked, pocketing the key as he
crossed the room.

'Dull. Frustrating. Phil should have been here by now.'

'You've spoken to him?' McLean had to admit that he'd forgotten about the conversation more than twenty-four hours ago, his friend drunk in Los Angeles Airport waiting for his flight. It shouldn't have taken that long to get to Edinburgh.

'I'm sure there's a perfectly reasonable explanation.' He pulled out his phone, flicked through the contact numbers until he found the one he was looking for. It went straight to message so he ended the call. 'Probably on his way here now.'

'Aye, right.' Rachel began to say something, then clutched at her stomach. 'Ow. Little bugger's kicking up a fuss.'

'Here, come and sit down.' McLean took her arm, led her to the sofa.

'Why'd I have to pick Phil when there's gentlemen like you around, Tony?' It was spoken as a jest, he could see the tired smile in her eyes as she said it, but something about the words was deeply discomfiting. He wasn't really sure what to say.

'I guess I was taken?'

'Was? You don't think Emma's coming back?'

McLean was saved from answering by the noise of a car on the drive outside. 'You expecting Jenny over?' he asked, but Rachel just shook her head, a worried frown spreading up from her eyes. He left her in the library, went across the hall and opened the front door, just in time to see a taxi heading off down the drive and a familiar figure standing in front of him.

'Took your time, Phil. What happened? They throw you off the flight?'

McLean regretted the poor attempt at humour as soon as he saw his old friend properly. Phil looked haggard, there was no other word for it. He'd always been an annoyingly skinny fellow, despite a diet consisting mainly of beer and curry, but now his clothes hung off him as if he'd borrowed them from a much larger man. His hair was unkempt, no change there, but the dark brown was shot with grey streaks that most certainly hadn't been there two years ago. Mostly though it was the hangdog expression, the slouched shoulders and the general aura of a man whose world has just lost its bottom. McLean had seen homeless people with more lust for life.

'Had a spot of bother at Heathrow. I'd have called, only they took my phone. Is Rae—?'

But whatever Phil had wondered about his wife was lost in the noise as she burst out through the door, moving far more quickly than a woman in her condition should have been able to. With a loud cry that was part rage, part relief, she burst through the door, crossed the gravel to where he was standing and started thumping him on the chest with tiny, impotent fists. For his part, Phil just stood there and took it, the look on his face suggesting he felt he deserved far worse. McLean stood back and let the unhappy reunion unfold on his driveway as Rachel berated her husband for every fault any man ever had. Finally she ran out of steam, her anger evaporating in the cool evening air. She took a step back and looked at him properly.

'What happened to you? You look like shit.' She wrinkled her nose. 'Smell like shit too.'

'Perhaps we could have this conversation inside?'

McLean said before the argument started up again. 'Maybe over some food and a glass of beer?'

'You wouldn't believe the nightmare it's been getting home.'

They were sitting at the kitchen table, McLean's carry-out for two split between the three of them. Rachel hardly took anything, which was just as well, really, since Phil had fallen on the food like a man who'd not eaten in months. The two of them were on opposite sides of the table. McLean didn't need a degree in psychology to feel the simmering tension.

'You said something about them taking your phone.' He took a sip of beer, noticing Phil's glass was empty again, Rachel's water barely touched. 'Who took it? Why?'

'Ah, I'd missed that. The detective inspector's incisive mind.' Phil waggled his fork in the air in McLean's general direction. 'Bloody customs and excise or whatever they call themselves these days. I was strip-searched, Tony. For fuck's sake. What's this country coming to?'

'You were . . . why?' McLean couldn't help notice Rachel stifling a laugh, had to admit that in any other circumstances he would probably have joined her. He knew Phil, though, and this was as serious as he'd ever been.

'They never said. Just stopped me as I was going through the "Nothing to Declare" door and hauled me off to a little room in the back end of Terminal Five. It was fucking terrifying, let me tell you. They went through everything, spread it all around this great big table. Clothes and all. Ran some kind of sensor over it. Fuck me, there was this one woman, short hair, built like a fucking rugby player. Hands like a brickie's. And there was me in nothing but my undies.

Christ, I thought she was going to pull on the rubber gloves and go in without any lube.'

Phil shuddered at the memory, and serious though the story was, McLean had to go to the fridge to fetch another beer for his friend, otherwise he was going to burst out laughing. By the time he'd brought it back, popped it open with the bottle opener lying on the table and poured it into Phil's glass, he'd composed himself enough to speak.

'Mistaken identity?'

'That's what they said.' Phil took a long gulp, downing about a third of his drink in one go. 'Wouldn't tell me who they thought I was, though. And by the time I'd packed everything back in my bags, I realised my phone was gone. They took it away, trying to find all my dirty secrets. No way I was going to ask for it back, only it had all my contact numbers on it, so I couldn't call anyone. Missed my connecting flight, didn't I? And was there anything like an apology? Any offer to pay for the extra fare? Like fuck there was.'

'I'll see if I can get someone to ask some questions. Maybe we can find out who they thought you were.' McLean pushed the last of his congealing curry around his plate, then decided he'd had quite enough. As if she had read his mind, Mrs McCutcheon's cat clattered in through the cat flap and sauntered into the kitchen. Silence fell on the room as she sniffed the air, looked askance at Rachel and Phil, then wandered off towards the main body of the house. McLean stared at her departure, tail tip twitching from side to side as she went, then turned back to face his friends. This time he couldn't help but laugh, and it didn't take long for Rachel to start. After a moment staring between them, mouth open, Phil joined in, and for a moment, just a moment, everything was fine.

'You ever get that feeling where you know you've done something really stupid, but you can't think how to get out of the situation?'

Late night and the library windows were black mirrors, hiding the outside world from view. McLean sat in his favourite armchair, tasting the last of his small glass of whisky. Phil sprawled on the sofa like a teenager, red-eyed but awake as his body fought against California time. Rachel had long since taken herself to bed, muttering dark words about how useless her husband was, but McLean hoped he could feel a slight thawing in her frosty reception.

'Pretty much every day,' he said in response to his friend's question. 'Sometimes more than once.'

Phil managed a weary smile. 'The whole America thing seemed like such a good idea at the time. It only took a few weeks of actually living the dream to realise I was wrong, though. Maybe I should have packed it all in then.'

McLean suppressed the urge to glance at his watch, sensing a late night when all he really wanted was to get some sleep. There were times Phil had stayed up into the wee small hours just to keep him company, though. Back when Kirsty had died and all he'd wanted to do was follow her. It's what friends did, helped each other out no matter how inconvenient that might be.

'Why didn't you?'

'You know me, Tony. Never been one to quit easily. Or ask for help, come to think of it.'

'So what's the plan? You know you can stay here as long

as you want, but you're going to be a father soon. A child needs stability in its life.'

Phil grimaced. 'I know. I just need a bit of time to get my head straight.'

'Well, don't leave it too long, eh? Baby's going to be here any time now.'

'Nah. Couple months, surely.'

'That's what Rae told me when she got here a couple of weeks back, and I didn't believe her either. Reckon the first thing you need to do tomorrow is get her seen by a doctor. Get yourselves registered on the system again. You can use this address if you need to.' McLean put his glass down on the table beside his chair.

'I'll do that. If Rae'll talk to me.'

'She will. Give her time. She was worried about you, you know?'

'She was?' Phil looked genuinely surprised.

McLean stifled a yawn. 'Yup.'

Phil looked up at the clock. 'Here, it's late. You don't need to stay up just to keep me company.'

'You sure?' McLean levered himself out of the chair, trying not to groan like an old man as he did so. 'I really need to get some sleep. Long day tomorrow.'

'Yeah, I'm fine. I'll just kip here. Not sure if I'll be able to sleep anyway.' Phil sunk deeper into the sofa, trying his best to hide the shiver that ran through him.

'Rae's in Gran's old room. The bed's big enough for the both of you.'

'Don't think I can face that right now. She's got a temper on her, you know.' Phil smiled to himself. 'Probably why I love her.'

McLean sighed. Too much to hope for a swift and easy reconciliation. 'Well, there's plenty other rooms. You'll find blankets in the big cupboard on the landing if you really want the sofa. But you're going to have to start talking to her soon.'

## 24

The phone rang as he was driving into work, singing an urgent, unknown tone at him. No hands-free in the Alfa, so McLean pulled over on to a double yellow line, grabbed the handset and thumbed accept just before it switched to voicemail.

'McLean.'

'Detective Inspector McLean?' A woman's voice, familiar although he couldn't immediately place it. He tried to remember who he'd given his card to recently. This number didn't tend to attract junk calls from bogus insurance claims specialists or people offering to fix a non-existent fault in his computer.

'Yes. Who's this?'

'Miss Marchmont, Heather Marchmont.' The voice was hesitant, as if the woman on the other end wasn't entirely sure who she was or why she was calling. Even so, as she said her name McLean recognised the voice from their interview. He remembered her face, how he was sure he'd met her before but couldn't put his finger on when, and he also remembered the half-hearted bollocking he'd got from Jo Dexter about going to see her in the first place.

'Hello, Miss Marchmont. What can I do for you?'

There was a pause, and through the windscreen McLean noticed a traffic warden striding up the road towards him.

He fished in his jacket pocket for his warrant card, just in case he needed it.

'It's . . . It's complicated. Not something I can really talk about on the phone. Could we meet somewhere?'

The traffic warden was coming closer now, bending her head forward to get a better view of him whilst at the same time pulling out her electronic PDA to check his registration number. He really didn't need a run-in with traffic control right now.

'Did you have anywhere in mind? I'm a bit busy first thing, but I could probably meet around eleven.'

Miss Marchmont let out a quiet, startled 'Oh', as if she'd been expecting him to put up more of a fight. 'There's a place just around the corner from my house? Wee cafe just down the hill?'

McLean glanced briefly at the screen; it was a mobile number, but that didn't mean she wasn't at home. He'd noticed the cafe a couple of times before.

'I know it, yes.'

'Eleven then. I'll buy you coffee,' she said, and hung up. McLean saw the traffic warden bending down to peer in through the passenger door window, a frown on her face as she looked to the information on the screen of her PDA and then back at him. He smiled, held up the phone and waggled it around by way of explanation. Dropped it on to the seat behind him, checked his mirror and pulled away from the kerb. It was only as he was slowing for the next roundabout that he realised he had no idea what Marchmont wanted to talk to him about. Whatever it was, he'd almost certainly get it in the neck from Call-me-Stevie, the

Deputy Chief Constable, if he ever found out. He should call her back from the station, cancel or arrange a more official meeting. But he knew there was no way he would ever do that.

Stepping into the cafe, McLean didn't expect Miss Marchmont to be there already, but she must have seen him coming. She stood up a little too quickly from a table near the back as he entered the room, waved to get his attention. She was dressed less formally than when he'd met her at the office, baggy jumper over tatty jeans and calf-length brown leather boots. Her hair was tied back too, which only helped to accentuate her skeletal thinness and too-prominent cheekbones. That face he knew from somewhere but just couldn't say where.

'Thanks for coming. Can I get you a coffee? The cake here's delicious.' She offered no hand to shake, and McLean couldn't help wondering how she would know about the cake. She couldn't possibly have been the shape she was if she'd ever eaten any.

'Just a coffee's fine, thanks. Got to watch the weight.' He patted his stomach, realised what he was doing and stopped. Marchmont ordered and then led him back to her table. Judging by the notebook, phone and laptop she had been here a while.

'Can't seem to concentrate in that house at the moment,' she said by way of explanation as she tidied the paraphernalia of work into a large, soft leather bag beside her chair, leaving only a slim smartphone beside her empty espresso cup. 'And if I go into the office, I just get pestered by the boss. He thinks I work too hard.'

'That would be your boss who plays squash once a week with my boss?'

'The same. I think they maybe went to school together? I picked that up somewhere. One a career policeman, the other a top lawyer. There's a certain symmetry.'

McLean didn't doubt there was more to it than that. 'Did you speak to him? Your boss, that is? Ask him to have a word?'

Something like anger flashed across Marchmont's face, but only fleetingly. 'God, no. I just want the whole thing to go away. He knows about the parties anyway. Probably been to a lot more than me. He was the one introduced me to the scene.'

And there it was, the elephant in the room. Difficult to talk to this young woman without remembering the people he'd found in her terrace house in various states of undress, the dungeon room with its sado-masochist equipment. The smell of sweat and semen and other, less pleasant things.

'I get the feeling that's not what you wanted to talk to me about, though,' McLean said.

Marchmont stared at him, her dark, haunted eyes unblinking.

'I wanted to thank you, really,' she said after he'd broken eye contact, unable to cope with her stare.

'You did? For what?'

'The raid. It was a wake-up call. You mix with a certain type of people for long enough, you forget that you're not the same as them. I was losing myself in that lifestyle and hating myself for it. Then you come along and break it all up.'

'But you hadn't done anything wrong. We had to let

everyone go. Well, except Smith, and even he's out with a GPS tag on his leg until we can get a trial date.'

That angry frown flitted across Marchmont's face again at the mention of the name, softening after a moment. No wonder she was a corporate lawyer; with a poker face that bad she'd have been lost in court.

'In the eyes of the law we hadn't done anything wrong, it's true. I guess some of my guests were married and so technically being unfaithful, but that's hardly a crime these days. And besides, most of their other halves were either watching or participating with someone else. That's kind of how it works.'

'You don't sound so happy about it.' McLean wondered how much he owed this woman. She'd bought him a coffee, so he'd talk to her for that long. Then again, he'd invaded the privacy of her home on what had turned out to be false information, so he probably owed her a bit more sympathy than that. And of course he couldn't help feeling there was something more to the botched raid, some deeper story, more sinister. At least she'd come to him, and if the shit hit the fan he had the phone records to prove it.

'Like I said. Wake-up call. First the raid, then you coming to the office. It made me realise I've been coasting, relying on others too much. It's time to stop that.'

'At the risk of seeming rude, what has it got to do with me?'

'I'm a lawyer, Inspector. OK, I may be a corporate lawyer, but I know criminal law as well as anyone. You're being made to clear up this mess, make the embarrassment go away. My boss to your boss to you. Am I right?'

'I probably shouldn't be discussing it with anyone out-side the SCU, but that's pretty much how it goes, yes.'

'It must be horrible, dealing with brutality day in and day out.'

'It certainly gives you a unique perspective on people. Let's put it that way.'

Marchmont shook her head, just the slightest of move-ments as if she were trying to dislodge an image from her mind. 'People can be . . . cruel. And selfish when it comes to satisfying their desires. I thought the scene I was in . . . The people . . . They were better than that. It was about sharing, consent, fun. I'm not so sure now.'

'I've always thought that as long as no one gets hurt—' McLean was interrupted by Marchmont's phone rattling silently on the table between them. A number flashed up, an Edinburgh code but he couldn't quite read it upside down. She looked around the cafe nerv-ously, stared out the window at the cars parked across the road. Then, before he could say anything, she had snatched up the phone, rejected the call, blanking the screen from view.

'I have to go. The office.' She waved the unanswered phone once, then dropped it into the bag on the floor beside her. McLean stood up as she grabbed her coat from the back of her chair, threw it over her arm.

'Well, I guess I ought to be at work too. Thank you, though. For the coffee.' It seemed a rather trite thing to say, given that his drink had not yet arrived. Marchmont didn't seem to have noticed.

'You're welcome, Inspector. We must do this again some time. I'll call you, if you don't mind?'

There was a question in her voice, but Marchmont didn't wait for an answer. With another quick look around the cafe, she marched out just as a bemused waitress appeared from the serving counter.

'Your coffee, sir?'

A half-hour later, and after a fruitless search for spaces in the station car park, McLean left his Alfa slotted carefully between two crowd control Transits, hoping they weren't due anywhere for an hour or so. Most of the riot squad drivers were well trained and conscientious enough, but the vans were so heavily armoured it was almost impossible to know where the edges were. He'd seen one knock over a lamp post once, taking a corner just too tightly. What one might do to his fragile little car didn't really bear thinking about.

The route from the back door up to the CID room was mercifully clear of senior detectives, and the room itself was remarkably devoid of life too. He located DS MacBride's desk and was in the process of writing a note on a Post-it when he saw the whiteboard. Close by the detective sergeant's desk, it had been commandeered for the Eric Parker case; the one McLean was supposed to be lead investigator on. He'd let it slip, too distracted by other things, but MacBride had been busy. There were half a dozen names under Parker's, some scored through, a couple with question marks by them. DNA was underlined twice and circled in red. Another line of enquiry suggested Mike Simpson in the forensic IT department had Parker's phone and was working on it. Good to see things were moving on without him.

'Wasn't expecting to see you here, sir.'

McLean spun round, sending a twinge through his hip as his foot caught on the stained carpet tile. DS MacBride stood just inside the doorway as a line of detectives filed in behind him. He recognised a few of them, some even smiled or nodded a greeting, and then a less friendly figure pushed his way in.

'What are you doing dawdling in the doorway, MacBride? Oh. It's you.' Detective Inspector Carter held McLean's old position of junior DI in the station, having somehow managed to wangle a promotion when Brooks and Spence each took a step up the ladder. McLean had never thought much of him as a detective constable, let alone sergeant, and by all accounts his move to inspector had not been an unconditional success.

'Morning, Carter. Keeping busy?'

Carter just stared at him for a moment, then lumbered off to shout at some of the constables. McLean gave MacBride what he hoped was a sympathetic look. 'I'd be surprised if he makes it to the end of the year.'

'End of the year? End of the month would be a miracle. Never thought I'd want to see old Dagwood back, but things here are getting ridiculous.'

'Well, maybe it would help if people didn't keep on filing his paperwork in my office, you know? I'm sure it was very funny when whoever it was first thought of it, but I'm not there half the time, which means people are going to start missing their overtime payments.'

'You know what this lot are like, though, sir. Once they get an idea in their heads.'

'Aye, I remember paying the bills.' McLean turned back

to the whiteboard. 'How're you getting on with Parker?'

'Early days yet. Still waiting on the DNA. Even a match between the hair and the saliva would be a start. Be a while before we can do a trawl through the database, though.'

'What about the phone?'

'Mike's having a look at it. He's also going over the car's GPS, seeing where it was and when. Should have a map soon. Not much else we can do right now.'

'OK. Keep me in the loop then.' McLean paused a while, unsure whether he should be asking the question. Unsure even how to phrase it. 'There is one thing you could do for me, though. If you've a minute or two spare.'

MacBride gave him a look that suggested he was heartily sick of being asked, but he didn't say no.

'Was wondering if you could do a background check on someone. But keep it quiet. Don't want to ring any alarm bells.'

'How deep do you want to go?'

'Not deep. Just basic background would be fine. I don't think there'll be anything too unusual, but I've got a nasty suspicion I'm being set up for a fall again, and I'd like to have a bit of ammunition if I need to fight back.'

MacBride held up his omnipresent tablet computer, tapped at the screen a couple of times, his interest clearly piqued. 'Does he have a name, this person?'

'She, actually. And yes. It's Heather Marchmont.'

# 25

She's never really liked this place. It's too high up, battered by the endless gales that scream in off the North Sea. Sure, the view's nice on a good day, but there's too few of those to make it worthwhile. Mostly it's the haar coming in off the Forth and smothering everything in a thick blanket of white, or the rain splattering against the thin glass windows, or the wind howling around the poorly fitting frames. The neighbours aren't so bad, at least in the main. Not noisy like some places she's lived, though she'd be hard pushed to know if they were over the constant whistling of the wind. But mostly she hates this place because it's a trap. Four floors up, right at the end of the line, one door in. No escape.

But that hardly matters. She's Big Tam's girl, after all. No one's going to mess her around even if he is away in Saughton right now. A hollow laugh slips out as she thinks about him in his cell. Big Tam's girl. Aye, that'll be right. If only he knew the half of it. Why does she stick with him anyway? Just about the only thing he's good for is keeping the low-lifes off her back, giving her some kind of status in this shithole of a suburb. And what does she have to give him in return? Too much, that's what. Expects her to work the streets when there's good money to be earned in the rich part of town. No imagination, just fists. She could do much better. Will do much better.

Another hollow laugh shakes her empty belly. He's away, and not just for a wee while either. Nothing to keep her here except these concrete walls. She could just leave. Pack up a few things and go. OK, she's not as young as she was, but she's still got her looks. She kicked the habit too, not like so many of the other girls she's met over the years. And there's those rich folk who'll pay good money for someone with her particular skills. She couldn't stay in Edinburgh, but there's other places, other fetishes.

The knock on the door is so sudden, so abrupt, she almost cries out in alarm. She looks through the peephole to see a man and a woman, standing side by side as if they've never been apart. They look like they might be Jehovah's Witnesses; no one else would come a-knocking at this hour, up here at the end of the world. They don't seem to be a threat, so she opens the door just enough to poke her head through the gap.

'If it's about God, you've just missed him.' The joke's old and lame, but she makes it anyway. The young woman cocks her head to one side like a dog, confused. The young man says nothing, just stands beside her like he's made of stone.

'Look, I'm no' interested in saving my soul, aye?' She relaxes a little, the sense of threat leaching away. And that's when it all starts to fall apart.

'You've been a naughty girl, Stacey.' The woman takes a step forward, forces the door open. She steps into the hallway as if she owns it.

'I . . . I don't know what you mean.'

'Shh.' The woman reaches up, puts a slim finger to Stacey's lips. Her touch is strangely comforting, reminding

Stacey of her mother, even though this woman is younger than her. She yields to its gentle pressure, stepping backwards as the two of them come into the hall. Looking at them it is clear they are twins. He is heavier-set, but they have the same muddy blonde hair, the same shape to their faces, the same dead eyes.

'We know what you did, and why you did it.' The woman takes her by the hand, clasping it to her breast as if it's a gesture she has seen perhaps in a film. Something she feels she should do without truly understanding why. Stacey can't stop staring at those eyes.

'This house. It's so mean-spirited. It's not a home. Why do you live like this?'

'It's not so bad. Once you know your place.'

'Oh but it is. And your place isn't here, Stacey.' The woman moves down the short corridor towards the bathroom and the bedrooms as if she knows where she's going. Hand still firmly clutched, Stacey can do nothing but follow. She is confused. Not scared, at least not yet, but somehow unable to think straight.

'You've done such great work for us. People ask for you by name, you know?'

The woman pushes through to the main bedroom, still dragging Stacey by her hand. She goes straight to the wardrobe as if she already knows where it is, what it contains.

'Such pretty clothes. Can I try them on?' Without waiting for permission, she pulls something out, holds it up to herself for size. Stacey cannot stop her, though looking round she sees that the other twin has followed them into the room.

'Oh, this is nice. Here, hold it for me.' The woman

shoves a shiny black figure-hugging dress into Stacey's hands, then starts to undress in front of her. She wears staid clothes, as if she belongs to an earlier century. Long tweed skirt and cashmere sweater over a heavy cotton blouse, woollen stockings up to her knees, soft leather boots. She peels off the layers with surprising enthusiasm, revealing pale white skin flecked all over with livid red scars. No inhibitions whatsoever. Stacey can only stare as the woman takes back the dress, pulls it on with surprising dexterity, smoothing the soft material over her figure. It fits well, hugs her like a second skin, not damaged like the one she wears underneath.

'Who are you? What do you want?'

'Sweet, sweet Stacey. You know who we are and you know what we want.' The woman wearing her clothes reaches out and takes Stacey's hands in hers, pulls her close. She smells of the soft rubber of the dress, shampoo and something else, a scent that Stacey can't place. It's intoxicating, though, and bewildering. She can't move of her own free will, can't resist or pull away or do anything as the woman leans in, and kisses her firmly on the lips, pushes through with a tongue that tastes of childhood. Her legs give and she sinks slowly down until she is sitting on the bed. When the woman breaks away it is as if she takes something with her.

'Iain, my clothes. I think I'll keep these on for now.' She twirls in the dress like a little girl who has been raiding her mother's wardrobe. Stacey just sits and watches as the man dutifully picks up the discarded garments, folds them neatly and stows them away in his bag. When he's done he simply nods to her, turns and leaves the room.

'You know what to do, Stacey.' The woman bends down, gives her a brief kiss, less intimate this time. A smile that almost reaches her eyes. And then she too is gone.

# 26

'It was a tip-off, wasn't it? That's what started the whole thing, right?'

McLean nursed a cup of unpleasant canteen coffee, his half-eaten lunch congealing on the plate in front of him. Across the table, DS Ritchie had polished off her salad and was shining a juicy red apple on her sleeve. She took a thoughtful bite, chewed a bit before answering.

'Pretty much. Anonymous mobile phone call telling us to have a look at the address. The SCU don't normally pay too much heed to that sort of thing, apparently, but the same place came up in an interview with a sex worker picked up for soliciting on the street a couple of months earlier. Seems she tried to offer information in exchange for a caution. Not sure why nobody looked into it then.'

'That's right.' McLean remembered reading the file before going to Dexter about sanctioning the raid. 'What was her name again? Charlene something?'

'Stacey Craig. She was a bit of a regular a few years back, but seemed to have seen the error of her ways.' Ritchie intoned the last few words like a judge handing down sentence. 'We've locked up her boyfriend a couple of times too. A bit too free with his fists. Can't see why Stacey stayed with him, really.'

'Sometimes people mistake attention for love.' McLean waited for Ritchie to take another bite of her apple. She certainly seemed to have picked the better lunch. His lasagne had been cold in the middle, the chips soft and flaccid. His stomach rumbled and he wondered whether he shouldn't have taken Marchmont up on her offer of cake earlier. There was no way he was going to chance his luck with the chocolate stodge on offer in the station canteen. 'Do we know the boyfriend's name? If he's inside and what for?'

'Not sure. I can check.'

'Thanks. And get an address for this Stacey Craig too. But don't put it in the report. Or her name.'

Ritchie stopped mid-bite, took the apple away from her mouth. 'Don't put it in?'

'Not yet. Maybe not at all.'

'What do you want the address for then?'

'I think we ought to go and pay her a visit.' McLean stood up, motioned for Ritchie to stay sitting when she went to do the same. 'Don't rush your lunch. Half an hour's fine. I need to make a call anyway. Think there's someone we might invite along.'

He was on his way back to his office, in search of a little privacy, when his phone went. McLean stared at the number on the screen, trying to work out if he recognised it, but all he could tell was that it was a mobile number. He half thought about letting it go to voicemail; if it was important they'd leave a message, and if not he'd have saved himself ten minutes getting annoyed with a telesales operative in a call centre halfway around the world. But then again, they usually came through as ID withheld. Reluctantly, he thumbed accept, held the handset up to his ear.

'McLean.'

'Going to have to work on your telephone manner, Tony. Is that any way to greet an old friend?'

McLean pushed through his office door, slumped into his chair. No matter how often he programmed her number into his address book, or more accurately got MacBride to do it for him, somehow she always managed to catch him out. 'A very good afternoon to you too, Ms Dalgliesh.'

'Aye, well, it would be if I weren't stuck on a train to Inverness. Bastard paper wouldn't even pay for first class, either.'

'Inverness? What on earth are you going there for?' McLean could hear the rattling of the train in the background now, a few muffled voices.

'Fuck knows. Some controversial art installation is all the editor told me. Problem with cutting half the reporting staff is those of us left have to cover everything. Johnny says Inverness, Inverness it is.'

'And you thought you'd just phone and chat? I'm flattered you should think of me, but I've work to do.'

'Aye, very funny. You and everyone else. I've a list of folk to call long as my arm. No point wasting my time staring at mountains, is there?'

'So what's so important you couldn't wait to share it?' McLean settled back in his seat, lifted a foot on to his desk.

'What I was telling you about the other day. Over at your curry place. That karma was delish, by the way. Thanks for that.'

'Korma.' McLean remembered the incident, tried to remember what Dalgliesh had been telling him. 'Remind me what you said again?'

Dalgliesh made a noise that might have been annoyance,

or might have been her signalling to the catering trolley that she needed tea. 'You ever heard of the Beggar's Benison?' she asked eventually.

'The secret society? Bunch of aristocrats and wealthy merchants playing at being debauched and evil, mostly in Anstruther of all places. Drinking and whoring was their thing, I think. They started off in the mid-1700s and petered out at the start of the Victorian era, when prudery became more fashionable.'

'See, that's what I like about you, Tony. Any other copper wouldn't have had a clue, but you're a font of useless knowledge.'

'Is that meant to be a compliment?'

'Take it how you want to. Thing is, there were lots of those societies around back then. Hellfire Clubs all over the place. That's what happens when you've a wealthy elite with too much money and time on their hands.'

'Is this going anywhere, Dalgliesh? Only I've an important meeting I don't want to miss.'

'Christ. Someone got up the wrong side of the bed this morning.' Dalgliesh coughed, long and loud and bubbly. 'And you're not the one who's no' had a fag since Edinburgh.'

'OK. OK. Beggar's Benison. Hellfire Club. Secret societies in the eighteenth century. What of them?'

'Well, like you said, they kind of went out of fashion when the Victorians invented prudery. But what if they never went away, eh? What if they just went underground? Got good at keeping themselves hidden, protecting themselves. A couple hundred years is a long time to develop a sophisticated network, wouldn't you say?'

'I'd say you and reason were beginning to part company, if I was being honest.'

'Aye, you're all heart yourself, Inspector.' Dalgliesh made a noise that McLean hoped could only be heard through the phone. He imagined her sitting at a four-seat table in her train carriage, notebooks and other detritus spread all around her, fellow passengers looking on in growing horror at her antics.

'I'm just not sure where you're going with this. You reckon the brothel raid had something to do with Beggar's Benison? I'm a detective. I'm going to need something a bit more concrete than that.' He was going to add, 'Save the conspiracy theories for your books,' but decided against it. Dalgliesh was being uncharacteristically kind to the police at the moment and he didn't want to be known as the officer who had brought that détente to an end.

'I'm working on it. You'll see. Already found some interesting links between your friend—'

McLean listened to silence, then took the phone from his ear and looked at the screen: 'Call Failed'. He dialled the number Dalgliesh had been using, but it went straight to a generic voicemail message. For a moment he entertained the idea of a train crash or some other disaster, but it was clear enough what had really happened. Phone reception only got worse the further north you went. And besides, Dalgliesh sounded like she was on a wild goose chase, and happy with it. Far better she kept distracted that way. It stopped her from noticing what a rubbish job the police were doing.

He cut the call without leaving a message, then thumbed through the address book until he found the number he'd been intending to ring. There were far more important things to worry about than Jo Dalgliesh and her lunatic ideas.

In the end it took rather longer to organise things than McLean would have hoped. Mostly he had been searching around for an unmarked pool car, since it turned out that Stacey Craig lived in a council block in Muirhouse and there was no way he was taking his Alfa anywhere near the place. A cluster of high-rise tower blocks overlooking the Forth, the area was struggling to claw its way out of the mire of decades of underinvestment and badly planned housing policy. McLean found it hard to blame the feral youth who roamed the streets; it wasn't their fault life had dealt them the shitty end of the stick. He still wasn't going to trust his car to them, though.

The address Ritchie had found took them to a low-rise housing block overlooking a strip of dual carriageway that seemed to go to nowhere, as if the town planners had intended building a way to escape the place but had run out of enthusiasm. Or money. Or both. Across the road, a gang of young men were loafing around in front of a pharmacy, its windows covered with steel shutters. McLean glanced at his watch; it was possible that it was closing time, he supposed. More likely the shutters were a permanent feature.

'And I thought Torry was bad.' Ritchie peered out of the window, craning her neck to see the tops of the tower blocks, looming up into the late afternoon sky.

McLean looked at his watch again. 'Hope we don't have to hang around here long. The locals can spot a cop at a hundred yards.'

'Why're we waiting anyway?' Ritchie asked. 'Sooner we get this over with the better, surely.'

'I called for some back-up. Unless I'm much mistaken that should be it arriving now.'

McLean opened his door and clambered out as a beaten-up little Vauxhall Astra pulled in to the kerb just ahead of them. It looked far more in keeping with the rest of the vehicles parked nearby than their conspicuously clean and new Ford. A familiar figure stepped out, short but determined, looked first up at the housing block they were visiting, then over towards him.

'This is most unusual, you know, Inspector,' Clarice Saunders said as he and Ritchie joined her at the entrance to the block. 'I generally try to keep you lot at arm's length when I'm dealing with . . . well . . .'

'Shall we go in then? Before too many people see us?'

The interior of the building lived up to the lack of promise of its exterior. The individual flats were accessed from a series of wide balconies that wound around the building, and a chill wind blew through the grey concrete tunnels. The lifts worked, which was something of a miracle, but the smell emanating from them was unlike anything McLean had ever encountered before. Saunders didn't seem to notice, stepping inside and hitting the button for the top floor without a word.

Stacey Craig lived right at the northern end of the building. The balcony gave a great view out across the Forth to Fife, but the wind was enough to drive even the most hardened fan of the picturesque indoors. McLean shivered as he waited for the doorbell to be answered, although Ritchie and Saunders seemed to be made of sterner stuff. Either

184

that or the coats they'd remembered to bring were wind-proof, unlike his lightweight summer jacket.

'Aye? Whit ye want?' Stacey Craig barely looked at them as she opened the door. No chain, McLean noticed. Perhaps up here, at the end of the world, it was unlikely someone would try and rob her. Or maybe they had so often there was nothing left to take. Judging by how little she was wearing, they'd stolen most of her clothes some time ago.

'A word, if we may?' he asked. He had his warrant card in his hand, but didn't show it. No need to cause alarm if he could avoid it.

Stacey looked up slowly, her eyes struggling to focus. Her head swivelled from side to side like it was being remotely controlled.

'You polis?' she asked eventually.

'We're not here to arrest you, Miss Craig. We just want to ask you a couple of questions.' Ritchie took a step forward, and Craig stepped back into her hallway. She didn't close the door on them, though.

'Youse had better come in then. Cold oot there.'

By the time the three of them had entered the hall and McLean had shut the door behind them, Craig had wandered off towards the living room. She was definitely on something, even if he couldn't immediately tell what. He just hoped she was lucid enough to give him some useful information.

The living room was sparsely furnished, a tiny television shoved into one corner, table piled with rubbish, a couple of armchairs that had somehow escaped the seventies, and a saggy sofa. Craig slumped on to this, didn't bother offering a seat to McLean and Saunders. Ritchie hung back in the doorway.

'I'll make us all a cup of tea, will I?' It was code for have a snoop around while the suspect was otherwise occupied, but McLean reckoned Craig would hardly notice.

'You feeling OK, Stacey?' Saunders settled into one of the armchairs, leaning forward to get a closer look at the young woman. Craig stared at the wall above a small electric fire, then slowly focused.

'I know you, don't I?'

'You've been to my clinic before, remember? I'm Clarice.' She reached out and took one of Craig's hands, cradling it between both of hers. The touch seemed to waken the woman.

'Aye. The clinic.' She turned slowly to face McLean. 'Who's he then?'

McLean took one look at the other armchair with its impressive collection of stains and decided that squatting down was a better option. His hip protested, but he did his best to ignore it.

'My name's Tony McLean, Stacey. I'm a detective.'

'What, like Columbo?' For some reason this seemed to amuse the young woman.

'A bit, I suppose. Only I haven't got the trench coat and I can't stand cigars.'

'What you here for then? You looking for favours?' Craig tried to sit up and shift her blouse off her shoulders at the same time, failed at both and gave up, slumping back into the cushions on the sofa.

'Not of that kind, no.' The pain in McLean's hip made it hard to concentrate, and there was something in the air that clouded his head a little too. He sniffed, but there was no telltale smell of hash. He shook his head to try and clear it.

'I wanted to ask you about the house in the New Town. The one that was being used as a brothel. You said you'd worked there, was that right?'

'Posh party, that was. Lots of money. Some gentlemen with very particular needs.' Stacey slurred out the word 'particular' as if it had more syllables than she'd been expecting.

McLean couldn't take the pain in his hip any more. Inwardly cursing the old injury that caused it, he stood up. 'Have you worked there before?'

'You grew tall.' Craig's head tipped back as she looked up at him. And then she started to laugh, just gently at first, but soon her whole body was convulsing in uncontrollable hysterics.

'What's happening?' Clarice Saunders leapt to her feet at the same time as McLean moved forwards.

'Ritchie, get in here.' He grabbed Craig's arms, pulling her upright. The woman was still laughing, but now there was panic in the sounds bubbling from her, spittle beginning to foam around the edges of her mouth. Her eyes had gone very wide, locking on to him with a sudden fear as the laughter turned into choking. Choking turned to seizure.

'Come on, Stacey. Stay with me.' McLean heard Ritchie behind him calling for an ambulance, but all his attention was on the young woman. He had taken her hands in his, and now she grasped him with a ferocious tightness. What were you supposed to do with someone having a fit? All that training and he couldn't for the life of him remember.

187

And then Ritchie was kneeling beside him, pushing Saunders out of the way, calmly taking over. 'Ambulance is coming, sir. ETA ten minutes.'

He looked at the woman, convulsing on the sofa. The foam around her mouth was flecked with red now. Would she even last that long?

## 27

'I'm sorry for dragging you into this, Miss Saunders. I never imagined . . .' McLean ran a weary hand through his hair. The past hour had been a nightmare of trying to keep Stacey Craig alive, then watching helplessly as the paramedics took over. They had arrived in just eight minutes, but it had taken a lot longer to stabilise her enough to get her moved to the hospital.

'It's not the first time I've seen someone overdose, Inspector.' Saunders shook her head slowly. 'I wish it was, but it's not. Won't be the last time either, I dare say.'

'We'll make this place secure. Keep the local youth from helping themselves to her stuff while she's away. I've got one of the local community liaison officers on the way. We'll do our best.'

'You think she's coming back? From that?'

'We can hope. She's more of a chance than if we'd not paid her a visit. That's for sure.'

'You're a good man, Inspector.' Saunders patted him on the arm. 'Pity there's so few of you about.'

He watched her go, headed back to her car and then the sanctuary she ran for women like Stacey Craig. She could be a right pain in the arse sometimes, but he had a grudging respect for Clarice Saunders. Not many would go out of their way to try and help the sort of people she did.

'We all done here, sir?' DS Ritchie appeared from the

kitchen as Saunders left. She'd found a towel and was drying her hands, having carefully scrubbed away the blood and phlegm.

'Just waiting on the local boys to turn up. Shouldn't be long now.' He glanced at his watch, long past Ritchie's shift end. Ah well, he'd swing the overtime for her. Except there was more to it than that, of course. 'You were meeting Daniel this evening, weren't you?'

Ritchie shrugged. 'He's used to me being late. I'll give him a call and let him know I'll be on my way soon.'

She took out her phone, tapped the screen a couple of times and moved off across the living room for a little privacy. McLean left her to her chat, headed out into the hallway and then on to the other rooms in the apartment. It wasn't big, but it was spacious by city centre standards. One of the few things they'd got right when putting up these concrete monstrosities in the fifties. The kitchen had enough space for a small dining table as well as a standard range of units and a cooker. One door led into it from the hall, another from the living room. Down a short corridor, he found two bedrooms and a shared bathroom. They were all shabby, the furniture old, the carpets stained, but there was a basic tidiness about the place at odds with his initial thoughts about Stacey Craig. He had her painted as an addict prostituting herself to pay for her habit. Her record sheet showed a few charges for possession, but nothing major and nothing recent either. He stood in the bathroom, looking at the cracked bath, the mould growing in the grouting between the tiles, the limescale on the shower curtain. A medicine cabinet hung over the basin, but it had nothing stronger in it than aspirin and a couple of ladies' razors. Even the toilet cistern held only water. The only thing of any note was a pregnancy test kit, unopened and collecting dust on top of the cabinet. He didn't want to judge, but he didn't have Craig pegged as the motherly type. Maybe it was insurance.

'Looking for anything in particular?' McLean turned to see Ritchie in the corridor.

'Her stash. If she's got one. Thought she was on something when we arrived, but it might have been a precursor to the seizure, I suppose.'

'I had a look around before. Couldn't see anything obvious. She's used in the past, but maybe she's gone straight.'

McLean moved from the bathroom to the first bedroom. The double bed was made, the closet closed. Just a few clothes thrown over the back of the wooden chair to mess the place up. He picked up the book lying on the bedside table, surprised to find a collection of Scottish poetry. There was nothing on the other side of the bed.

'Boyfriend's inside, isn't he?' he asked as Ritchie hovered in the doorway.

'Aye, bloke called called Tam Roberts. Nasty piece of work by all accounts. Used to beat her up if she didn't go out to work. He's two years into an eight-year stretch for armed robbery. Reckon she's well shot of him.'

'And yet she's still working. We picked her up off the street the last time, didn't we? That's pretty desperate.'

'Does make you wonder. There's this too.' Ritchie pointed towards the second bedroom door and McLean followed her down the short corridor. The room was bigger than the first, no doubt intended to be the master bedroom, but that bit further from the bathroom. The window looked north towards a darkening sky, the lights of the tower blocks spoiling what might otherwise have been quite a view. A large hanging cupboard dominated the far wall, cheap chipped brown veneer like much of the rest of Stacey Craig's furniture. Ritchie walked over and opened it up, pulled out a dress that looked something like a pervert's idea of a schoolgirl's uniform. She draped it over the bed and McLean saw the material shine oddly under the cheap overhead light. He reached out and touched the fabric, recoiling as his fingers squeaked against the surface.

'It's latex,' Ritchie said, her freckles darkening against her pale Aberdonian skin. She pulled out another outfit, this one black and shiny, hanging from her hand like the discarded skin of some human-shaped reptile. 'She's got dozens of outfits in here. All good quality. None of this stuff comes cheap. I'd say these were her working clothes, wouldn't you?'

McLean peered into the wardrobe and saw what Ritchie meant. It was an impressive collection, even if he didn't want to know how she knew its value.

'You think she was entertaining clients here?' He looked around the rest of the room. Not the sort of place for that kind of business.

Ritchie put the outfits back in the wardrobe, smoothing them down carefully before closing the door again. 'Not here, no. And these aren't street clothes either. This is for a much more select clientele. Much more upmarket.'

Home was a welcome sight, but far later into the evening than he had anticipated. McLean found himself silently relieved that Jenny's little black car wasn't parked on the driveway, but that still meant he had to deal with Phil and Rachel. He could no more have turned either of them away than chop off his own foot, but that didn't mean the small kernel of resentment wasn't there, deep down. And just occasionally it was preferable to spend the evening alone and let the stress of the day wash away in the silence.

Mrs McCutcheon's cat looked up at him from her place in front of the Aga as he stepped into the kitchen and dumped his case down on a chair. A teapot, mugs and a couple of dirty plates lay on the table where someone had eaten a meal and not cleared up afterwards. Trying hard not to sigh, he carried them over to the dishwasher, noticing as he did so that the sink was filled with unwashed pots and pans. Flashbacks to the years he'd spent living with Phil in the flat in Newington, first as a student, then as a trainee police officer. No wonder Rachel had walked out.

'Going to have to lay down some house rules, I think,' he muttered to no one in particular. Mrs McCutcheon's cat just looked at him with an expression that clearly said 'aye, right'.

Noise from the television spilled out of the library into the hall as he went to the front door in search of post. It had been picked up and placed on the wooden chest, the usual round of fliers, offers of loans at extortionate interest rates and catalogues addressed to his grandmother. He flicked through them all, hoping for a postcard from Emma, but finding none.

'You're back. I'd forgotten the ridiculous hours you work, Tony. Makes being a scientist look sane.'

McLean turned around to see Phil standing in the library

doorway. He was dressed in pretty much the same clothes he'd been wearing when he arrived, scruffy jeans torn at one knee, T-shirt for a band who had split up almost twenty years ago, bare feet. He hadn't shaved, but he looked a lot more relaxed. Amazing what a good night's sleep and a couple of meals could do.

'We had a bit of an emergency. I wasn't planning on being this late.'

'Nah, this is early for me. I'm still on California time.' Phil scratched at his stubbly chin. 'Think Rae's over the jet lag, though. She spent most of the day talking babies with Jen.'

'Jenny was here?' McLean scooped up the pile of mail, headed back towards the kitchen and the paper recycling bin. Phil followed him, leaving the library door ajar.

'Yup. She was asking after you. Reckon the two of you would make a sweet couple.'

McLean felt the tips of his ears redden and wondered why. He'd missed Phil's bluntness, but normally his crude suggestions had no effect.

'Surprised you haven't found the beer yet.' He changed the subject perhaps a little too obviously, dumped the unwanted mail in the bin and then extracted two bottles from the fridge.

'What makes you think I haven't?' Phil accepted one of the bottles, taking a moment to study the label.

'Well, there's the same number in here as there was yesterday, for one thing.' McLean found glasses and a bottle opener. He should probably have looked for something to eat as well, but it was late and all he really wanted was a beer and his bed.

'Good point. I guess I'm just losing my touch. Old age and all that.'

'Or maybe it's the responsibilities of parenthood finally sinking in.'

Phil said nothing to that, opened his beer and poured it into his glass. He took a thoughtful sip.

'She doing OK, Rachel?' McLean asked, nodding his head in the direction of the hall and the library beyond.

'Yeah. Sort of.' Phil pulled out a chair and slumped into it. 'She still scowls at me whenever I come into the room, but I think she's more or less forgiven me for being completely useless. Don't think I'll be joining her in your gran's old bed any time soon, but then that's probably a good thing.'

'Can't be long now. Reckon you can cope not being the centre of attention?'

Phil smiled at the joke. 'Sure it won't cramp my style. And I can always rely on Uncle Tony to help out in a crisis.'

'Sounds about right. Winding up other people's kids and then giving them back is about all I'm fit for. The amount of shit I deal with on the average day, I don't think I could bear to bring a child into the world.'

Phil leaned forward, elbows on the table, glass held lightly between both hands. For a moment it could have been any time in the past twenty years, the two of them chatting over a beer.

'Work that bad, is it?'

'I try to leave it at the office, but working at the SCU, well, I thought the murderers and drug dealers were the worst humanity had to give, but throw sex into the mix . . .'

The silence hung heavy for a while, just the muted strains

of the television coming in through the open kitchen door. McLean was grateful to his old friend for not pushing the subject; Phil had always been good at that.

'I've a meeting with my old head of department at the uni tomorrow,' he said after a while.

'You have?'

'Yeah. Gave him a call when I woke up this morning. This afternoon, I should say. Hoping he's got a job for me.'

'You're coming back? To Edinburgh?'

'Ah, the sharply honed detective skills at play.' Phil laughed. 'Yeah, I'm coming back. California was fun, but it's no place to raise a kid. And we've no network out there, no friends to call on in an emergency. Back here Rae's got Jen and all her old chums. I've still got a few I've not burned my bridges with completely.'

McLean leaned back in his chair, slowly beginning to relax. It wasn't until Phil started recounting his plans that he realised how on edge he'd been not knowing what his old friend was going to do.

'Well, I hope it goes well tomorrow. It'll be good having someone I can go to the pub with who isn't a copper for a change.'

Phil opened his mouth to make a sarcastic comment, as he always did when McLean mentioned his lack of drinking buddies, but the silence was shattered by a piercing scream. McLean was on his feet and heading for the kitchen door almost instantly, but Phil was way ahead of him. Together they rushed to the library as another wail rent the air.

Rachel lay on the sofa, doubled up and clutching at her belly. Her face was contorted in agony and she let out another powerful scream as Phil dashed across the room to be by her side. At his touch, she grabbed him hard around the wrist, pulling him close, shouting in his ear.

'Jesus, it hurts. It's not supposed to hurt yet. Why does it hurt? What's happening?'

Transfixed, Phil could only look around, a curious, helpless pleading in his eyes. McLean already had his phone out, calling the second ambulance of the evening. So much for a quiet night to rest and unwind.

## 28

'She's going to be fine. The baby should be OK too. Doctor's just induced her, so hopefully it won't be long now.'

McLean stood in the waiting area at the Royal Infirmary, only half listening to the nurse in charge of the maternity ward. It was fully dark outside, heading towards midnight, and he had an early start tomorrow.

'It's unusual to miss, though. Normally we'd expect the GP to pick up high blood pressure, any other indicators. And they go over it at prenatal.'

There was no mistaking the hectoring tones, but his slow brain had a hard time working out why he should be told off.

'She's only just got back from the US. Maybe they covered it there, I don't know. What's wrong with her?'

'Pre-eclampsia. What did you think it was?' The nurse shook her head as if he was the biggest idiot in the world. 'Never mind. You can go and be with her for the birth, if you want. I know some fathers like to, others don't.'

Realisation dawned. 'I'm not the father. Sorry. She's just staying with me. You'll need to talk to him.' McLean turned and pointed to where Phil was laid out across three plastic chairs, sleeping like a baby.

The nurse looked at him as if he'd just spat in her eye, then stalked off to wake Phil. McLean pulled out his phone to check the time, sensed a commotion off to one side before he heard the noise.

'Oh my God! Tony! Is she all right?'

Jenny Spiers looked like she'd scrambled out of bed half-asleep, thrown on the first clothes she could find, and dashed out the door without a thought for anything else. Given that McLean had phoned her from his car as he followed the ambulance from his house to the hospital, this was very likely the case.

'She's going to be fine, Jen.' He repeated what had been just told to him, without the scolding. Watched as her face dropped in horror.

'Oh my God! Mum had that with Rae. It almost killed her.' She started towards the corridor behind him, no doubt determined to find her sister and check for herself. McLean stopped her, holding on to her arms as gently as he could. She stiffened at his touch, then relaxed a little.

'Let's leave her to the professionals, shall we?' He looked around, saw that Phil was no longer on his chairs or indeed anywhere to be seen. 'She'll be good. Phil's going to be with her all the way.'

'That's supposed to reassure me, is it?'

'Well, he is a biologist.' McLean let go, dropped his hands to his sides. 'Here, let's see if we can't find some coffee in this place. I've a feeling it's going to be a long night.'

The canteen was closed, along with all the little gift shops and the newsagents in the main foyer of the hospital. They ended up back at the maternity ward waiting room with little plastic cups of foul-tasting vending machine coffee, but at least the walk around the hospital had calmed Jenny's nerves. By the time they settled into the hard plastic seats, McLean had learned more than he ever really wanted to know about childbirth, and in particular both Rachel's and Chloe Spiers'. He had spent enough time in hospitals to know that Rachel was going to be fine; there was a way nurses talked to you when they wanted to prepare you for the worst, and McLean's earlier conversation hadn't been one of those ones he dreaded. The fact that Phil was still missing was a good sign too, but Jenny was a worrier and the best way to help her cope with it was to let her talk.

'It's normally a problem with older mums, though oddly enough teenage mums can get it too. Rae's at the young end of old, if you see what I mean.'

McLean nodded, but only because it seemed the right moment in the conversation to do so. Weariness was dragging at him, making his thoughts sluggish. There had been another vending machine, next to the one dispensing coffee, filled with chocolate bars, packets of crisps and all manner of other healthy treats. He was beginning to wish he'd bought a couple, beginning to wish he hadn't skipped supper.

'You're not really listening to me any more, are you, Tony?' Jenny's change in tone alerted him to the question, otherwise he might simply have nodded in agreement.

'What? Oh. Sorry. Sort of listening. It's been a long day, though, and I've got to be up in—' He looked at his watch. '—About four hours.'

'So why are you even here? You didn't need to come. I mean, it's very good of you and everything, but you don't have to be the world's dad.'

McLean leaned his head back until it hit the wall behind him, fiddled with his now-empty coffee cup, stared at the notices pinned up everywhere giving advice, reminding people not to smoke or use their mobile phones. Finally he looked at Jenny, sitting beside him. She was attractive, attracted to him, almost an older version of her sister, only her hair was blonde shot with grey where Rachel was a redhead. Crow's feet wrinkled away from the edges of her eyes, giving her the air of someone who had spent most of her life smiling. Without her mask of make-up he could see the tiny imperfections in her skin: a mole on one cheek, a thin scar close to one eye that doubtless had an interesting story behind it.

'I guess I just feel like I have to be doing things, helping people, always on the go. If I stop, then I start having to think.'

'Is that why you always bring your work home?' Jenny must have seen his frown. 'Rae told me, but I've seen the case files on your desk sometimes, or tidied away in the kitchen.'

'Just don't look inside any of them, OK? And please don't tell my boss.'

'Confidential, are they?'

'Kind of. Sensitive information and that kind of thing. Mostly though you're likely to come across a photograph you won't be able to forget in a while. Especially the work I'm doing at the moment.'

Jenny put a hand on his arm, her touch warm through the thin fabric of his jacket. 'I can't begin to imagine what that must be like. Don't want to, if I'm being honest.'

'Very wise.' McLean was about to say more, but the doors at the far end of the waiting area swung open and Phil staggered through. His face was white and he looked about as lively as a reanimated corpse. For a moment

McLean thought something must have gone wrong, that Rachel was in trouble. Jenny must have sensed it too, as he felt her hand tighten around his arm, her other hand join it as she leaned in close to him. Then he saw the idiot grin on his old friend's face.

'Bloody hell, Tony. It's a boy!'

# 29

'You never were all that good at keeping things low key, were you, Tony?'

He'd managed to get the morning briefing put back a couple of hours, but McLean still felt like he hadn't slept in a week. It had taken an hour to get out of the hospital, leaving the increasingly bubbly Phil behind with his wife and their newborn son. Jenny had promised to deliver Phil home just as soon as he was ready to leave and McLean had managed to get to his bed a little before four in the morning, only to be woken by the alarm at six. Driving across town to the SCU offices had been a nightmare of near misses, and not for the first time he remembered his police training and the advice about never driving while tired.

'That's a bit unfair, isn't it? We've not exactly splashed the news across the front page.' He stifled a yawn with the back of his hand, feeling itchy stubble on his cheeks where the razor had missed.

'No' the nationals, but the local rag's picked it up.' Jo Dexter tossed a folded tabloid across the table to him. McLean opened it, seeing the article halfway down page three beneath a smiling young woman with bared breasts. 'Muirhouse Call Girl In Drug Coma Shock!' Not the snap piest of headlines, and neither was the reporter anyone he'd heard of. Scanning the article, they seemed to be well enough informed, though, if a bit lurid in their speculation. At least his and Ritchie's names were missing from the report. Clarice Saunders got a mention, along with her charity, so maybe she'd been speaking to the press.

'It's hardly the *Daily Record*. And this stuff about heroin cut with rat poison is bollocks. We don't know what she was on yet, or if she was on anything. Could just as easily have been a seizure.'

'Aye, well, you'll need to speak to the doctors about that. And have a word with your wee friend Clarice.' Dexter managed to put a sneer into the name that would have done Hannibal Lecter proud. 'I've had the DCC in my office twice this morning asking what's going on. You did know he wanted this tidied away nice and quiet, aye?'

'He came to your office? Didn't summon you to the third floor?'

Dexter smiled. 'Aye, I noticed that too.'

'You think he has something to do with this?' Ritchie asked.

'I don't even know what "this" is, but he's being leaned on by someone. I know Stevie of old; he's not bent. Well, no' that bent.'

'But he was the one who wanted a report into the brothel raid.'

'A report, Tony. Not an investigation. Going off to talk to this wifey.' Dexter peered down at the sheaf of papers in front of her. 'Stacey Craig? That wasn't part of the deal.'

McLean opened his mouth to complain, then his sleep-deprived brain caught up with him and he closed it again.

'Look, I know you were just being thorough. Check the sources, see where the mistake was made. I get that. But it's not what the high heidyins want. They're prepared to take this one on the chin. Don't push that.'

'I'll have the report done by the end of the week.' McLean looked across to Ritchie, sitting alongside him. 'That OK?'

'Have it done by the end of the day if all you want's a whitewash.'

'See, I knew you were smart.' Dexter smiled again, less like a shark this time.

'We'll still need to talk to the doctors, though, about Craig.' McLean rubbed at his eyes, but that only seemed to make the grittiness worse.

'We do?' Ritchie asked.

'It doesn't need to go in the report. I'd not name Craig at all if we can get away with it. Just put in enough detail to keep the top brass happy. If we're bandying about names, let's put John Smith front and centre. He's the only positive to come out of the whole fiasco, so might as well make the most of him. But we do need to know about Craig. Who she is, where she worked, what's caused this.' He pointed at the newspaper, still lying in the middle of the table.

'You sure about that, Tony?' Dexter asked, an edge to her voice he hadn't often heard.

'For us, yes. We've been played, Jo. Looks like we might still be. I want to know why, if only so I can keep one step ahead of the game.'

The phone call came as he was heading back to his office after the briefing. McLean looked at the name on the screen for three rings, trying to decide whether to answer or not.

He thumbed accept just before the fourth would have sent the call to voicemail.

'Miss Marchmont, what an unexpected pleasure.' He ducked into an empty room, closing the door behind him.

'I didn't know you felt that way, Inspector.' Marchmont let out a little laugh, bordering on the edge of hysteria.

'A turn of phrase. Is there something I can do for you?'

'I heard the news this morning. The woman in Muirhouse?'

McLean leaned against a table, trying not to squeeze the phone too hard against his ear. 'You know her?'

Marchmont's voice wavered with uncertainty. 'She's still alive?'

'It's touch and go. Lucky we were there when it happened or she'd certainly be dead. How do you know her, Miss Marchmont? Muirhouse isn't exactly your patch.'

There was a pause, and for a moment McLean wondered whether she had hung up. But the line was still open, a gentle hiss in his ear confirming it for him. He looked around the room, only just noticing the whiteboards scribbled with notes from an old investigation, the desks pushed into one corner waiting for the next major incident, the banks of elderly computers stacked up against the far wall. For an instant he thought there was someone else in the room, spun around to see who it was, but he was alone.

'Are you still there, Miss Marchmont?' he asked finally.

'Sorry. Yes.' Marchmont's voice came across slightly muffled, as if she were trying not to be overheard. 'Look, I can't really speak on the phone. Could we maybe meet again? The same place as before? I'll buy you lunch.'

McLean's stomach took that moment to remind him with a loud grumble that he'd fed it only coffee and a couple of stale biscuits since getting up that morning. He'd not exactly managed to eat much the night before either, which might have explained his light head and the difficulty he was having concentrating.

'OK. Same place as last time.' He glanced at his watch. 'Half-twelve?'

'I'll be there,' Marchmont said, and hung up.

'There you are, sir. Thought you'd gone to your office.'

McLean almost dropped his phone as he stepped out of the empty incident room to find DS Ritchie heading up the corridor towards him.

'Just got a call, needed somewhere quiet to answer it.' He juggled the handset, all too aware that the corridor was empty apart from the two of them, and tucked away in a quiet part of the building as well. Ritchie raised a hairless eyebrow but said nothing else.

'Were you looking for me for anything in particular, or just missing my company?'

'Ha. No.' Ritchie's face creased into a broad smile at his terrible joke, which brightened the room. Not enough smiling these days. 'I just got off the phone myself, actually. With the hospital.' The smile disappeared as quickly as it had come. 'Prognosis isn't good for Craig. The seizure cut off the oxygen supply to part of her brain. Basically she's had a massive stroke and they'll be surprised if she ever wakes up again.'

'Any idea what caused it?'

'Not drugs. Well, not anything they'd normally screen

for. She'd certainly not injected anything anywhere they could find. Still waiting on some blood tests, but I think she just got unlucky.'

'And us too, it would seem.' McLean saw the frown begin to form on Ritchie's face. 'Was that too harsh? I know she doesn't deserve what's happened to her, it's just I really don't like coincidences.'

'You think someone got to her before she could speak to us? Is that not just a little paranoid?' Ritchie paused a moment, then added 'Sir?' for good measure.

'Probably. Doesn't help that I'm tired and hungry. Didn't get much sleep last night, or food for that matter.'

'I heard, yes. How's Rachel doing? Phil too for that matter?'

'I'm not sure, really. They were fine last night. I guess I'll get an update when I get home.'

'They're still at your place then?' Ritchie did the thing with her hairless eyebrow again. 'That's going to be interesting, bringing a baby into the house.'

'Hadn't given it much thought, to be honest. Shouldn't be for too long, though. Phil's looking for a job, and he only rented out his old place. They've just got to give the tenants a couple of months' notice to move back in.' Even as he said it McLean could see the future mapped out in screaming babies, dirty nappies and tired, grumpy parents. And all happening under his roof. Well, it wasn't as if he spent much time at home anyway.

'You're too nice, you know that? People take advantage of you.'

'Ach, it's only Phil and Rachel. I was best man at their wedding. Couldn't see them on the street.'

'I rest my case.' Ritchie pulled out her phone, checked the time. 'Reckon I'm going to grab a bite to eat and then get cracking on this report for the DCC. You want to try the delights of the canteen again? That lasagne you had last time looked delicious.'

McLean laughed at the joke. 'Think I'll give it a miss, thanks. And anyway I've got a lunch meeting scheduled.'

'You have? Who with?'

'Heather Marchmont, of all people. That was her on the phone just now.' He jerked his thumb over his shoulder, indicating the door into the empty incident room. Ritchie's hairless eyebrow shot up again.

'Marchmont? Isn't she . . . ? Is that wise?'

'Probably not. It's not the first time she's contacted me since we interviewed her, though. I get the feeling she's trying to tell me something, but every time she starts, she loses her nerve.'

'You sure she doesn't just fancy you?'

McLean felt the tips of his ears burn, and for some reason the image of Ritchie expertly handling the erotic clothing they'd found in the spare bedroom in Stacey Craig's Muirhouse flat sprang into his mind, making them burn even hotter.

'Why don't you come along? ' The suggestion was out of his mouth before his tired brain caught up with the implications. But then, why shouldn't she come along? If anything, another officer should have been present at all their meetings.

Ritchie hesitated for all of two seconds. 'OK,' she said. 'I'll just go and grab my coat.'

*

'You brought your partner, Inspector. I'm not sure that was part of the deal.'

Miss Marchmont had taken her favourite table to the back of the cafe and was reading a printed sheaf of papers, making notes on a spiral-bound notebook, when he and Ritchie arrived. Her startled look on seeing the detective sergeant softened as they approached, a rare smile spreading over her face.

'It's all right. I won't make you pay for her lunch. We just both need to be somewhere afterwards. Thought it would be easier if she came along. You've met before.'

'It's Detective Sergeant Ritchie, isn't it?' Marchmont held out a slim hand, and Ritchie shook it, holding on perhaps a little longer than was necessary. McLean watched the two of them, not quite sure what it was he was seeing pass between them. Eventually Marchmont broke the contact.

'Come, have a seat. They do a very good salad here, if that's your thing. Would you like some wine? I'm not drinking at the moment myself.' Her hand moved almost involuntarily to her flat stomach. 'Health reasons.'

McLean couldn't help but notice that Marchmont's behaviour was different to their previous meetings. She was more like the partner in a prestigious law firm, not the slightly nervous young woman struggling to come to terms with something he couldn't quite understand. And yet even with the veneer of professionalism, she was still worried. He could see by the way she constantly looked to the window. The seat she had chosen was perhaps the best in the whole cafe for watching everyone come and go without being seen herself. They ordered salad, declined the offer of a glass of wine, and chatted of inconsequential things in a manner that might have been pleasant in any other circumstances. And all the while they skirted around the real reason they were here. Finally, when the coffee came and the waitress had gone off to serve another customer, McLean could wait no longer.

'You told me on the phone you knew Stacey Craig.'

Marchmont had been joking with Ritchie about the ridiculousness of something called Hipsters, which McLean thought were a kind of trouser but which seemed to be something to do with young men who grew very bushy beards and took themselves too seriously. She stiffened at his words, as if they were a rebuke. Ritchie looked at him askance too, her scowl clearly signalling her annoyance at the interruption.

'I asked about her,' Marchmont said after a moment's pause. Her eyes darted once more to the window.

'But you wouldn't have done that if you hadn't met her. Or at least knew of her. You do know what she did for a living?'

'Oh my dear Inspector. You have no idea.'

'She was part of your circle, though, Heather?' Ritchie asked the question; the two women had been on first-name terms almost from the start of the lunch. McLean assumed the detective sergeant was just playing good cop, but the ease with which she navigated the conversation suggested something more.

Marchmont picked up her tiny espresso cup, went to take a sip only to discover it was empty. Sighing, she put it back down again.

'Sort of. I mean, yes, she came to one or two parties.' Marchmont stared off into the distance, lost in memories.

'I met her a couple of years back, when that brute of a boyfriend of hers was sentenced. We were both going through difficult patches then, discovered we weren't all that different, really. She's been my friend ever since.'

'You know she—'

'Was a sex worker?' Marchmont cut across McLean's question. 'Yes. With the emphasis on was. Past tense. She was a drug addict too. Once, when she was younger. But she got over it. Not many do. Maybe that's what attracted me to her. We're both survivors.'

McLean almost saw her then, the person he was certain he'd met sometime in the distant past. An inkling at least. Before he could pin it down, though, Ritchie spoke and the moment was gone.

'I saw some of her clothes. Beautiful. They must have cost a fortune.'

'She always did have an eye for quality. And she had the figure to carry them off, too.'

'Where did she get her money from, if she wasn't working?'

'I don't really know. I guess Big Tam might have left some around. I bought her some of those outfits myself.'

'You think she might have been doing a bit of high-class escort work?' Ritchie asked. 'Only that doesn't square up with us finding her working the streets down Leith way.'

'She was on the streets? When?' Marchmont snapped up straight again, eyes bright with surprise and a hint of anger. 'She'd given up that life. She wasn't doing that any more. She promised me . . .'

'We picked her up a couple of months ago,' McLean said.

'Stacey? Are you sure? But I—' Marchmont seemed

212

genuinely surprised. 'But that makes no sense. Why would she? She hated that . . .' She picked up the glass of water, looked at it and then from Ritchie to McLean. 'Oh.'

'Miss Marchmont . . . Heather. We're not here to arrest you. We're not even suggesting you had anything to do with this.' McLean put his hand flat on the table top in a gesture of conciliation. 'You called me, remember? You've been trying to tell me something for a while now. I'm guessing it's something to do with the raid, what was really going on in your house that night. More than that, probably. I'd really like to know what it is.'

Marchmont looked at him, her head cocked slightly to one side in a manner McLean found disturbingly familiar. Where had he seen that quizzical expression before?

'You really don't remember me, do you?' She shook her head. 'Of course not. Why would you?'

'I don't understand. Have we met before? I mean, you look familiar, but—'

McLean was cut off by the trilling of Marchmont's phone, lying on the table in front of her. Once more she looked at the screen, tapped to reject the call. 'I'm sorry. I have to go.'

She stood up quickly, her chair scraping back on the floor with a horrible screech. McLean struggled to stand more quietly, but Ritchie just stayed where she was.

'It was nice meeting you again, perhaps another time,' Marchmont said, placing a hand lightly on Ritchie's shoulder, then turned to McLean. 'I'm sorry to keep running out on you like this, Inspector . . . Tony. I really was shocked to hear about Stacey. Even more so to hear she was working the streets. That's not the woman I know.'

McLean finally extricated himself from his chair, catching it before it toppled backwards on to the floor, but Marchmont had already gone, striding swiftly across the cafe and out through the door without a backwards glance. He looked down at Ritchie, who just shrugged, then back to the window and the street outside.

'Guess I'm paying for lunch then.'

# 30

'I don't want to even try and work out what's going on in her head.'

McLean drove his Alfa slowly through the city centre, navigating the route out towards Little France and the Royal Infirmary. DS Ritchie sat in the passenger seat, staring at nothing in particular. They had left the cafe soon after Marchmont, saying nothing about the lunch and its abrupt ending until they were in the relative privacy of the car.

'She's a troubled soul. I'll give you that much. I can't help thinking she's playing me like a fish, though.' McLean braked sharply to avoid being hit by a bus that had pulled out without indicating. The driver stuck his hand out the window and gave a thumbs up of thanks.

'Why do you put up with it then, sir? If you know that's what she's doing?'

He said nothing for a while. Partly because he needed to think about the answer, partly because the roundabout at the top of Leith Walk was something of a free-for-all and needed all his concentration to negotiate safely.

'You heard what she said about me not remembering her?'

Ritchie nodded, McLean barely catching the movement out of the corner of his eye as he dropped a couple of gears and accelerated briskly past a dawdling truck.

'Well, it's true. Ever since I first saw her, when we raided her house, I've not been able to shake the feeling I know her from somewhere. I just can't think where.'

'Well, she's a regular on the Edinburgh swingers' scene. You could have met her there, if there's something you're not telling the rest of us.'

It was as well McLean knew Ritchie was teasing, otherwise he might have crashed the car.

'You seem particularly well informed about these things, Sergeant. Is there something I should know?'

It was Ritchie's turn for an embarrassed silence, but only a short one. 'Do you know who it was phoned her?' She changed the subject rather awkwardly.

'No. Same thing happened the last time. We were chatting away quite happily, then a call comes in, Edinburgh number, and she ups and leaves. You saw how she was looking out the window too, as if she thought she was being watched.'

Ritchie nodded. 'Classic paranoid behaviour, though they do say just because you're paranoid it doesn't mean you're not being watched.' She pulled out her phone, tapped the screen for a speed dial number and leafed through her paper notebook while the call connected. McLean concentrated on the road as they crossed North Bridge.

'Control? Aye, Detective Sergeant Ritchie here. Can you run me a phone number?' Ritchie rattled off a string of digits scribbled down in her notebook. The traffic opened up a bit, and McLean was able to speed up, a rare line of green lights keeping things moving. They passed Jenny Spiers' shop and he craned his neck to see if it was open.

Chances were Jenny herself would be at the hospital with her sister. Unless they'd discharged Rachel already? How long did they keep new mothers in these days? He had to admit he had no idea.

'You sure?' Ritchie noted something down on her pad. 'Sorry, of course you are. Aye. Thanks.' She ended the call, slipped the phone back into her pocket.

'That was the number on Marchmont's phone? I never managed to see all of it.'

'I've always been good at reading things upside down. And remembering numbers too. Not something people do much now, with everything stored on their phones.'

'So whose is it then?'

'It's one of a sequence assigned to her office, MacFarlane and Dodds. Not the main switchboard number, mind, but it's not so unusual to be getting a call from them, I suppose.' Ritchie drew a line across the page of her notebook, folded it closed and shoved it back in her bag.

'She didn't answer it, though. Not this time, not the last time either.' McLean turned on to East Preston Street, glancing up at the scaffolding that still clung to the facade of his old tenement block like ivy on a dying tree. Another legal nightmare to deal with; maybe he should ask Miss Marchmont to look into it for him. Then again maybe not.

'And there's the fact that she hasn't put the number in her contacts list. You'd think a modern girl would have done that.' Ritchie leaned back in her seat, enjoying the ride. The traffic freed up some more as they approached Cameron Toll and headed out on the Old Dalkeith Road, early afternoon clearly a good time to negotiate Edinburgh's suburbs.

'Unless she doesn't want people knowing that number.'

'Or we could just be getting as paranoid as she is. The life she leads – the double life, I should say – it's not really all that healthy.'

'You seem very knowledgeable about it, Kirsty.'

Ritchie laughed. 'There you go again, sir. Skirting around the subject. Why don't you just out and ask me?'

'Your private life's not really any of my business.' McLean felt the tips of his ears burning again and wondered why. It wasn't as if they didn't deal with sex and the myriad ways people found to satisfy their urges on a daily basis.

'I'd argue you're wrong there, but it's not important. I worked Vice a while up in Aberdeen before I transferred down here. Met some interesting people, learned a lot about their lifestyle. Edinburgh's no different, really, and most of the time it's pretty harmless, at least physically. Mentally it can fuck you up a bit. You saw what they were up to in Marchmont's house. Nobody was getting hurt who didn't want to be, and far as I can tell everyone was there by choice. It can get lonely in the city, surrounded by so many strangers. Some people go to church, some join gyms, some support a football team and some like to dress up in rubber outfits and have sex with people they hardly know.'

'Each to their own, I suppose.' McLean slowed down as they approached the hospital, looking for the entrance to the car park.

'Except that it leaves a bad taste in the mouth.' Ritchie paused a bit before laughing. 'Sorry, poor choice of words. What I meant was it's all rather distasteful, a bit seedy, not spoken about. No one judges you if you work out, or pray on Sunday. Well, not really. But sex is another matter altogether. Those folk we found in Marchmont's house, they're bankers, entrepreneurs, lawyers even. I imagine they'd bend over backwards to stop their colleagues from finding out about what they get up to on their weekends.'

'You think there's blackmail going on?'

Ritchie shook her head. 'I don't know. Probably. Maybe some mutual support too. Guess it's a bit like the masons, only with your trousers off rather than one leg rolled up to the knee.'

McLean smiled at the image. 'And what does that make Marchmont? Grand High Poobah?'

'Nah, I reckon it's like she told you at the off. She wants to get out, just doesn't really know how. Nothing so lonely as an orgy, after all.'

McLean spotted the sign for the car park and joined the queue of cars at the entrance. He wanted it to be that simple, but he was too old, too cynical, to believe there wasn't more to Heather Marchmont than that.

He knew the intensive care unit at the Western General Hospital well, but McLean hadn't often visited the one at the Royal Infirmary. Not since they'd moved the whole hospital from its old site overlooking the Meadows out to this purpose-built modern complex at Little France. He didn't know any of the nurses either, which meant the familiar face of Doctor Caroline Wheeler was a welcome relief after twenty minutes of searching for the right place.

'Stacey Craig. A sad case indeed.' Doctor Wheeler shook her head as she spoke. She looked as tired as McLean felt, but then he didn't think he'd ever seen her looking anything other than careworn.

'The prognosis isn't good, I'd heard,' DS Ritchie said.

'There's damage to her brainstem and most of her higher cortical areas have been starved of oxygen. She'll never wake up. In many ways it would have been kinder if she'd not been found. Without paramedic intervention she'd have just slipped away peacefully.' Doctor Wheeler led them down a wide, well-lit corridor as she spoke, pushing through double doors into the ICU ward. Stacey Craig lay on white sheets, head propped up on thick pillows, plugged into a collection of machines that kept her alive.

'Any idea what caused it?' McLean asked. He didn't approach the bed, didn't want to get too close. If he was being honest with himself, he hadn't really wanted to come here at all; it was just an excuse to get out of the station.

'Could have been any number of things, but it's most likely an embolism of some form. The brain's amazingly fragile if you attack it from the inside.'

'She was acting strangely just before it happened. I thought she might have been on drugs or something.'

'Well, we didn't find anything in her bloodstream.' Doctor Wheeler went to the end of the bed, picked up the chart and leafed through the pages. 'Nope. Clean. If she was incoherent then she might have been having a TIA, a mini-stroke if you will. They can sometimes be a precursor to something bigger.'

'What will happen to her now?' Ritchie asked. She too

had hung back at the door, unwilling to commit fully to the room with its softly beeping machines and smell of antiseptic.

'That depends on how her condition progresses. We've stabilised her, but like I said, the damage to her brain is too severe. It's highly unlikely she'll ever wake up, and if by some miracle she did I'd be very surprised if she was able to communicate. Do you know if she has any family?'

'We're working on that. She lived alone and her ex is in prison.'

'Well, keep me in the loop.' Doctor Wheeler put the chart back on the end of the bed, stared at the comatose figure for a few seconds. 'It's not as if we can do anything more for her, but it helps if there's someone out there to make the decisions.'

She didn't say what decisions those were, and McLean didn't need to ask. He'd been here before; there was only one way out.

'You got a minute to spare? Only I thought I might drop in on Rachel, see how she's getting on.'

McLean still didn't know his way around the Royal Infirmary, but he'd spotted a sign advertising the maternity ward as they were trying to find their way back to the main entrance and the car park. Ritchie gave him a non-committal shrug of the shoulders.

'Only thing I had planned for today was writing up the report on the brothel raid, but that's not going to take me too long.'

They wandered up a couple more corridors before they finally found the maternity ward. McLean didn't know where to begin looking for Rachel and was starting to feel a bit foolish when a familiar voice piped up behind him.

'Hi, Tony. Didn't think we'd be seeing you here any time soon.'

He turned to see Jenny Spiers standing by the unmanned reception desk. How he'd managed to miss her he couldn't have said.

'Jenny. Hi. We were here on business. Just thought I'd drop in and see how Rae's doing. It was a bit of a drama last night.'

'You could say that.'

McLean noticed Jenny giving Ritchie the eye. 'You've not met Detective Sergeant Ritchie?'

'No, I don't think I have. Hi. Jenny Spiers. I'm Rachel's sister.' Jenny held out her hand and Ritchie took it.

'Pleased to meet you, though if I'm being honest, I'm not really sure what I'm doing here. I've never met Rachel either.'

'Tony keeping you all to himself, is he?' Jenny laughed, perhaps a little too forcefully. 'Come on. It's this way.'

They followed her through to a large ward, filled with mothers and their newly born infants. Some of the beds had curtains drawn around them for a bit of privacy and a few worried-looking fathers sat beside their significant others. Rachel's bed was near the door. She was asleep when Jenny approached, but she woke quickly.

'Thought you were going home, Jen . . . Oh, Tony. Hi.' Rachel's face lit up as she saw him standing in the doorway. She craned her neck to see who was behind him, but Ritchie ducked to one side.

'I'll just . . . I'll wait outside. Me and babies don't really

. . . I'll just sit here.' She hurried over to the other side of the corridor where a couple of chairs sat underneath a noticeboard.

'Coward,' McLean mouthed, then stepped into the ward. While his back had been turned, Jenny had crossed the floor and scooped an impossibly tiny child out of a small cot beside Rachel's bed.

'Tony, meet Tony,' she said, presenting the bundle. McLean peered at something that looked a lot like a miniature version of Winston Churchill. Or possibly Peter Lorre. Then Jenny's words sunk in.

'Sorry, what?'

'We decided ages ago,' Rachel said. 'If he was a boy he'd be Anthony. Tony for short. If he'd been a girl, well, we were thinking maybe Gladys after Mum, but that's an old person's name. So it's probably for the best he was a boy.'

'Here. Why don't you hold him.' Jenny offered up the baby and McLean took him with some trepidation. He'd not had a great deal of experience with babies, wasn't entirely sure how he was supposed to support this one. Something about keeping the head up. Or should he be cradling him in the crook of his arm?

'Men! You're all the same. Bloody useless. Here, give him back.' Jenny rolled her eyes at him as she retrieved the infant and carefully handed him over to his mother. Rachel immediately started to stroke his nose and tweak his chin, babbling inanities that nevertheless seemed to entrance young Tony.

'I really only dropped by because I was here anyway. Police business. Just wanted to make sure you were OK.'

'We're fine. Thanks for checking.' Rachel gave him a

weary smile that reminded him of just how little sleep he'd managed to get in the past twenty-four hours. 'Now get back to your sleuthing, or whatever it is you do with your days.'

Bloody police. Who the fuck do they think they are? Getting on his back like that when he's done nothing wrong.

He limps around the sparsely furnished flat, the tag around his ankle chafing at his skin, dragging him down. Some break this has turned out to be, and he wasn't even doing anything wrong. Not really. He'd only just arrived. Well, maybe a couple of weeks. But that stupid fucking register. If it hadn't been for that whore and her bloody drug dependency he'd never even have been on it in the first place.

He bangs through to the kitchen, fills the coffee machine up with water, stabs at the button a half-dozen times until it springs into life. Why does everything have to fight him? A scramble to find a mug, pulling one out of the sink and rinsing it at least partly clean before the dark brown liquid starts to drip from the spout. Christ, but he'd give anything for a decent cup of coffee. Why did he even agree to come to this godforsaken shithole of a city? Athens of the North. What a fucking joke. He's been to Athens and it's warm there. The sun shines.

A buzzing in the hallway like a swarm of flies on acid. Why can't they leave him alone? He takes a deep swig of coffee, then spits it out on to the plates and mugs in the sink. Fucking washing-up liquid. The taste numbs his lips like cheap perfume. A Rohypnol kiss.

The buzzer again. Why can't they just all fuck off? He's

got better things to do than talk to the filth again. But a part of him knows the more he ignores them the more they'll hound him. Best get it over and done with.

The letting agent is a right precious bastard; there's got to be at least a dozen locks and chains on the door, and that's after he's jabbed at the intercom button to let them in off the street. No point talking to whoever's there; only the fuzz know where he lives. No one else would be interested in talking to him. Work's dried right up since the police started hassling his clients. Wankers. He can hear them on the stairs. Voices, well, one voice anyway. A woman talking to someone else. Makes sense. Coppers always come in pairs, the bastards. It's probably that posh-sounding git and his ginger bint. The one with no eyebrows. Fucking jocks. Why can't they just leave him alone?

Leave it, John. Don't let them see they're winding you up. Don't let them wind you up, for fuck's sake.

He listens as they slowly climb the stairs, waits until he knows they're on the landing. Puts on his biggest fake smile and opens the door to let them in.

It's not who he was expecting. Sure it's a man and a woman, but she's definitely in charge. Not ginger either. Dirty blonde, maybe a bit old for his tastes, but she's a looker.

'You've been a naughty boy, Mr Smith.' Her voice is soft, teasing, the faintest hint of a lisp to it, unless that's some odd jock accent. She brushes past him, entering the flat whether he likes it or not. The scent of her lingers in the air. Not a perfume as such, at least not one he's familiar with. It's something wilder that excites him even as it puts him on edge.

'Can you do that? Just walk in like that?' He had opened

the door angry, but in control of it. Now he's bewildered. She doesn't answer his question, but her partner follows her into the hall, forcing him back towards the kitchen. He's a glum fellow, head down, dressed in a tweed suit. His hair's the same colour as hers, though, and when he looks up, there's an undeniable similarity between the two of them. That's odd. Since when did the police start sending out brother and sister teams? Twins?

'You kept a secret from us, Mr Smith. We don't like it when that happens.'

'What're you talking about, secrets? I only forgot to sign in when I got here. It's not as if—'

The slap isn't hard, but the suddenness of it brings tears to his eyes, sends a shock through his body.

'I want to know who invited you to the party. Who told you where it was happening and how to get in?'

'I don't know what—'

This time the slap is more of a punch, rattling his teeth. He's about to give as good as he gets, never had a problem with dishing it out to a woman if she deserved it and this one's right up there. Only there's the man standing behind him, her brother or whatever the fuck he is. He hasn't said a word yet, and that's somehow even more scary than if he was shouting. Fear's not something John's used to. Not something he deals with well.

'Thought I told you lot to leave me alone. I've got my tag on, went through all your bastard procedures.'

'Oh, we're not the police, John.' She smiles at him and the hallway seems to darken, turn cold. 'At least, not the kind of police you're used to dealing with.'

## 32

'We're not going back to HQ, are we?'

McLean had handed his keys to Ritchie, letting her drive while he made a couple of calls. She drove the little Alfa much more smoothly than he did, coaxing it around the corners with a perfect balance of throttle and steering that suggested she'd spent some time on a racetrack somewhere in her past. Yet more he didn't know about her.

'Not just yet, no. I want to have a word with Craig's ex, Tam Roberts. Someone's going to have to tell him what's happened, and since we were there at the time . . .' He knew it was a poor excuse. Ritchie didn't say anything, but he could tell she was thinking the same thing.

'He in Saughton?' she asked after a while.

'Yup. I just let them know we're coming.'

'We should really leave it to Family Liaison, you know.' Ritchie blipped the accelerator, nipping in front of a bus as it came round the roundabout. The manoeuvre was safe enough, but she got a toot of the horn for her troubles anyway. She took her hand off the steering wheel just long enough to give the bus driver an unladylike gesture, then sped off in the direction of Liberton Brae and the bypass.

'I don't think they teach that at Tulliallan,' McLean said.

'Nah, it's more of a rally thing. But I mean it, sir. We shouldn't be chasing this like it's an ongoing investigation, really. Not when the DCC and Jo Dexter have both told us not to.'

'If it makes you feel better, I can always say I ordered you to come with me. Anyway, this isn't part of the brothel raid report. We were present at Stacey Craig's—' he was about to say death, but stopped himself '—incident. We need to find her next of kin to inform them of her condition. Roberts is the closest we've got, so it makes sense to go and tell him.'

'And if you just happen to ask him a few questions while you're at it . . .' Ritchie left the sentence hanging. McLean knew she didn't believe him, any more than he believed himself.

'What do we know about Roberts?' he asked.

'Not a lot more than I already told you. I could do with MacBride's little computer thing. Way I hear it, he's doing eight years for armed robbery. Bit of a hard man by all accounts, but not exactly Mensa material. Him and his gang got caught because one of them posted selfies on Facebook with the getaway car in the background.' Ritchie grinned at some internal joke, dropped a gear and accelerated on to the bypass. 'Always nice when the criminals do our job for us.'

McLean didn't like visiting Saughton Prison. There was a smell to it, or a feeling, he couldn't quite say what it was. Not the obvious reason that it was full of people who hated what he stood for, nor the sullen looks of the overworked prison officers. There was something else that hung over the place, sucking the life out of anyone who spent too long there.

'Big Tam Roberts, aye?' The duty warden looked at McLean's warrant card, even though he'd seen it plenty of times before.

'Yes. I've some bad news for him. Thought I'd deliver it in person.'

'You're all heart, Inspector. I'll bring him to interview room two. One's still a bit of a mess after . . . Well, it's no matter.' The warden took back the visitor book McLean and Ritchie had just signed, handed them their passes and then left through a back door that needed a heavy, old-fashioned key to unlock.

'Charming fellow,' Ritchie said.

'Ach, he's all right. You should see them when they're pissed off with us.' He set off down the corridor in the direction of the interview rooms. A foetid smell hung around the door to number one; he could only imagine what had happened in there. Number two was fine, if a little spartan. A plain table, three chairs, no window.

'Nice place.' Ritchie pulled out a chair and sat down. McLean paced for the five minutes it took for Roberts to arrive. He was escorted in by two hefty-looking wardens, hands cuffed behind his back even though he was a thin and weedy man. Big Tam was clearly an ironic nickname, though appearances could be deceptive of course. McLean's first reaction was one of surprise; Stacey Craig could surely have done better than this.

'Thomas Roberts?' McLean asked as the wardens shoved the man down into his seat. They left the cuffs on him, stood either side of the chair.

'Aye, who the fuck are you?'

'Detective Inspector McLean. And this is my colleague,

Detective Sergeant Ritchie. We're with the SCU. You know what that is?'

Roberts' moronic stare showed eloquently that he didn't, but his eyes lingered perhaps longer on Ritchie than was polite.

'Fuckin' polis. Thought I could smell filth.' He spat on the floor and one of the wardens twitched. McLean was impressed at the man's self-control; he'd have belted the prisoner if he'd been in the same position.

'The SCU is the Sexual Crimes Unit. We investigate crimes of a sexual nature, as you might imagine. Things like prostitution, pimping, sex trafficking, child abuse of a sexual nature. Means I get to meet scum like you.'

Roberts squinted across the table at McLean as if someone had stolen his spectacles, or he was trying to squeeze out a particularly reticent fart. 'Whit the fuck youse on aboot? I ain't no fuckin' paedo.'

'No. No, you're not. You're in for armed robbery. That went well, didn't it? Right up until your idiot mate went and bragged about it on the internet.'

Roberts made to lunge forwards, but the two wardens standing behind him were quicker, restraining him before he could do anything more than rise a few inches off his seat. He struggled a bit, but only half-heartedly, allowing himself to be pushed back down before shrugging his shoulders and shaking his head in a pathetic show of rebellion. McLean waited until he was done before continuing.

'Anyway. That's not what I'm here to talk about. No, this is more what you'd call a condolence visit.'

Roberts gave him that piggy stare of incomprehension again, so McLean pressed on.

'Stacey Craig. You know her?'

'Stace is my bird, aye. What's it to youse?'

'She had a stroke last night. She's in the Royal Infirmary in a coma. Doctors say she won't wake up.'

Roberts stared at him, silent as the wheels in his brain moved slowly around, processing the information.

'The fuck?' he said eventually.

'She had a stroke. You know what that is? Blood clot in the brain, stops the oxygen getting to the thinking bits.'

'Aye, I'm not stupid. I ken what a stroke is. My nan had one, but she was ninety. Stace is just . . . Aw man. What the fuck?'

'She have any family, Stacey? Anyone we should be getting in touch with? Other than yourself, that is.'

Roberts shook his head. 'Naw. Her folks're long gone. She's a friend lives in the New Town. Posh lass, but she's no family. Just me.'

McLean was almost fooled by the show of remorse. 'You were never married, though.'

'Fuck would I want to do that for?'

'You tell me. You lived with Stacey for long enough. I guess marrying her wasn't what it was about. More a bit of control. Maybe you knew the life she lived, the sort of people she mixed with. Maybe you forced her to it sometimes, when you couldn't be arsed working yourself.'

'I've got to sit here and take this shit?' Roberts looked up at the two wardens. Neither of them said anything.

'Doesn't really matter.' McLean continued as if Roberts had said nothing. 'You knew what she was doing, and you knew who she was working for, when she wasn't working for you. I'd like to know their names.'

Roberts barked out an angry laugh. 'Why the fuck would I tell you something like that, pig?'

McLean leaned back in his uncomfortable chair, looked around the tiny interview room before answering. 'Let me see now. Your parole hearing's in what? Two months? I can't sway the board in your favour. Wouldn't even if I could. But a word in the right ear would mean no one would even bother listening to you. Easy enough to make a note in my diary, do the same every year. You'd be stuck here serving the rest of your term. The full term. No getting out on licence early.'

Roberts creased his forehead in an attempt to squeeze out a thought; thinking wasn't something he was used to doing, clearly.

'What you mean? You threatening me, copper? Coz when I'm out I'll come find you.'

'Now that is a threat. It's also exactly the sort of thing the parole board would be just delighted to hear. Shows you've developed a sense of moral judgement, maybe come to see the error of your ways and you want to turn over a new leaf. Start afresh.'

'You taking the piss?' The furrows on Roberts' brow were deep, his skin turning a dark shade of red as his temper rose. McLean couldn't for the life of him imagine what Stacey Craig had seen in the man. Fists she couldn't easily get away from, most probably

'Why did she stay with you, Mr Roberts? She could have done much better for herself. Way I see it, she was doing better for herself without you. And yet she kept on coming back. What was it you gave her she couldn't get anywhere else? I'm guessing it wasn't witty banter.'

'"Mr Roberts". Aye, I like that. Shows a bit of respect.'

Roberts leaned forwards, slowly this time. McLean saw the wardens tense to catch him before he could do anything violent, but with his hands cuffed behind his back, McLean knew the odds were in his favour should there be a tussle.

'I'll tell youse why Stace stayed with me. Sure, that was her place and she knew it, but she knew she'd be fucked out there without someone strong to protect her too. She mixed with a dangerous crowd, and I don't mean folk like me an' the boys. We just robbed a couple of trucks full of cash. Naebody got hurt. These people'd no' think twice about killing you just coz you said the wrong thing.'

Finally they were getting somewhere. 'And you could protect her? That's why she stayed with you? Must've been hard for her you being in here then.'

'Aye, she was scared all right. Why'd you think she was walking the streets? She didn't need the money. She wanted to get arrested. Thought it was safer inside, but you just sent her home with a caution.'

'What was she scared of? What had she seen?'

Roberts slumped back in his chair, shook his head. 'No' a fuckin' scooby. Last time I saw her was about a month ago. Came in here for a visit. First one since I got caught. Wanted to know if I had any contacts on the outside. No' really sure why or what for. She wasn't making much sense.'

'She was scared for her life?'

'Aye, that might've been it.' Roberts strained to think again, the effort making him look severely constipated.

'So who was threatening her? She must have told you.'

'She wouldn't tell me. I told youse, she wasn't making much sense.'

McLean looked at Roberts, studying his features as the

piggy-eyed little man stared back. There was some native cunning in there, sure, but not enough to lie about this. Not enough to try and use the knowledge to his advantage. He really didn't know who or what had scared his girlfriend into a coma.

'Well then, looks like we're done here. Thank you, officers.' McLean stood, nodding to the two wardens, who bent down as one and took Roberts by the arms. He let himself be led from the room, pausing only at the door to look back.

'She's no' waking up? Is that what they're saying?' It was the first sign of any emotion other than anger McLean had seen in the man.

'I'm afraid so. I'm sorry. She didn't deserve that.'

'I'll fucking kill them.' Roberts' threat was all the more convincing for it being delivered in a flat monotone. 'See when I get out of here. I'll find out who they are and I'll kill every last fucking one of them.'

'Jesus wept, Tony. Can you no' just leave it alone for a minute? You're like a wee boy picking at his scabs.'

DCI Dexter had been sneaking a crafty cigarette out the back of the station when McLean and Ritchie returned from Saughton. Too much to hope that she didn't know exactly where he'd been all day, or even that she might have gone home already. The afternoon was over, turning into a warm autumn evening in which it would have been pleasant to have spent some time outside, maybe in a pub garden with fine ale and good company. The glass bus shelter provided for the station's die-hard smokers was perhaps not so pleasant.

'What were you even doing at the hospital? Ritchie

spoke to the doctors on the phone this morning. That was all you needed to know for the report, surely.'

Dexter stubbed one cigarette out into the sand-filled bucket that served as an ashtray, fished out the packet and lit up another.

'You're driving me to an early grave, you know?' She waved the packet in the air. 'Before you came back to the SCU I'd quit. Well, nearly.'

'I'm sorry, Jo. But you know me. Someone tells me to wrap things up neatly, then I immediately start asking why. There's something going on here. You know it as well as I do. It was bad enough when we were just trying to put the lid on an embarrassing cock-up, but now a woman's good as dead and I'm not convinced it's a coincidence.'

Dexter stared at him a moment, then let out a long cloud of smoke before switching her gaze to Ritchie. 'You buy any of this, Sergeant?'

'Don't really know, ma'am. I just do what I'm told.' A half-smile played across her lips as if she'd just thought of something funny. 'I do know it stinks. Not sure what of, though.'

'You've got her well trained, Tony. I'll give you that much.' Dexter ground out her cigarette even though it still had an inch and a half to go. 'Foul habit. And I'm no' going to cover for you again. If the DCC finds out you visited Saughton this afternoon you'll be busted down to constable and working traffic before the end of the week.'

'Just trying to be thorough, Jo.'

'Well, stop it. For once in your godawful life do what you're told and sweep this whole sorry mess under the carpet.'

McLean must have sighed more loudly than he'd meant to. Either that or Dexter was just having a really bad day. Before he could take another step towards the back door into the station, she stopped him with a surprisingly firm hand to the chest.

'Not now. Tomorrow. It's past shift time anyway and I heard you were up all night having babies.' Dexter's stern face softened a little and she let her hand fall to her side. 'Go home, the both of you. Get some kip. We'll sort out this mess in the morning.'

## 33

Early morning after a surprisingly good night's sleep and McLean found himself in his old station at his old desk leafing through piles of old paperwork that surely couldn't have been all that important if they'd been allowed to sit there unattended for a couple of days. He was pleased to see there were fewer of DI Carter's case files in the heap, which meant that the message was starting to filter through. It had been the same when he was first promoted to inspector; the lower ranks deliberately making life difficult for him by mis-filing or just making sure nothing was straightforward. Perhaps it was character forming, some kind of initiation rite above and beyond the hoops he had to jump through before he could even be considered for the post. Either way he couldn't help thinking it was a bloody stupid waste of everyone's time.

A knock on the open door interrupted his musings. McLean looked up to see DS MacBride standing in the doorway, his tablet computer under one arm, a slim brown folder in his hand.

'Heard a rumour you were in today, sir. Thought you'd be at the SCU.'

'I'm a bit persona non grata there at the moment, Stuart. Went slightly off-script yesterday. Thought I'd put in some hours here, catch up on the Parker case and generally keep out of the way of Jo Dexter.' McLean knew that

MacBride would already have heard. His great skill was communication after all. There wasn't much went on he didn't know about, the only difference between him and the older sergeants being he didn't then tend to pass on the gossip.

'You'll be pleased to hear we've got some preliminary DNA results in then, sir. On Parker himself and the hair the forensics labs found in the car. The labs are fairly sure it's the same person. Female. No matches in the database yet, but we've not had the full profile to run.'

McLean leaned back in his chair, trying to remember all the details of the case. It had only been a couple of days since he'd last discussed it with MacBride, but a lot had happened in between.

'So it looks like he probably picked up a hitchhiker with blonde hair. Most likely in Perthshire if the phone records are anything to go by. Brings her down to Edinburgh and she shows her appreciation in an intimate way. Too intimate for Eric Parker, as it turns out. He has a heart attack. She legs it. Can't say as I blame her, really.'

'The final report from the post-mortem's here too, sir.' MacBride placed the slim folder on McLean's desk, on top of the pile of case files that should have gone to DI Carter. 'No evidence of foul play. It really does look like Parker's heart gave out.'

McLean picked up the folder, opened it and let his eyes glide over the text within. He closed it and put it back down again quickly. He hadn't been taking any of it in, just needed a prop while his mind worked away.

'I don't like loose ends, you know that.'

MacBride had the decency not to answer.

'But we can't really waste any more time looking for this mysterious woman if there's no evidence of foul play. Write it up, put a note on file to run the full DNA when we've got it. I guess poor old Eric Parker will have to go in the unaccounted file.'

'Well, at least he died happy.' MacBride swiped at the screen of his tablet computer, tapped in a note. McLean thought about taking him to task for his flippancy, then remembered he'd said exactly the same thing back at the car park when they'd found the dead body.

'You have a chance to look into that other matter?' he asked instead.

MacBride fished around in his jacket pocket, pulling out a folded A4 printout. 'I did a bit of searching, like you asked. Not much out there. She doesn't seem to use social media at all, and there's not much press coverage mentioning her. I'll dig a bit deeper when I've got a moment free.'

'Thanks. I'll have a look at it once I've got all these squared away.' McLean hefted the pile of paperwork on his desk, then pointed at the stack under the Eric Parker report. 'Those you can drop off in DI Carter's office on your way back to the CID room.'

McLean waited until MacBride was gone before unfolding the sheet of paper the detective sergeant had left him. He knew he should have been working through the overtime rosters and all the other important but equally dull bureaucratic nonsense that seemed to multiply with each new management review, but he also knew it would still be there if he ignored it for half an hour. The enigmatic Miss Marchmont was far more interesting.

Except that there was precious little information in the printout MacBride had left him. She was a junior partner at MacFarlane and Dodds, specialising in Corporate Law. That much he already knew. She had studied law at Glasgow, then spent a couple of years in the US and Japan before ending up in Edinburgh, working for the firm that had eventually made her a partner. There was virtually nothing about her early life, no information about her parents or where she had been raised. All the other information MacBride had gleaned pointed to someone plain to the point of anonymity; nothing on Facebook or Twitter, not even an indiscreet teenage MySpace account lurking in the deep archives. She was really quite the cypher. McLean folded the sheet of paper back up and tucked it into his jacket pocket. He'd hoped a background check on Marchmont would have given him some clue as to what her game was, but if anything it had just made things even less clear.

No sooner had he pulled his hand away from his pocket than his phone began to buzz. He fished it out, saw Grumpy Bob's name appear on the screen, thumbed accept.

'What's up, Bob?' In the background he could hear a hubbub, most probably the CID room downstairs, although normally that was a hive of inactivity at this time of day. Then the noise muffled, as if Grumpy Bob were shielding the handset.

'Not good things, sir. Sorry to be the bringer of bad tidings, but the DCC just arrived with Jo Dexter and headed straight for Brooks' office. I expect you'll be getting a summons any moment now.'

As if on cue, the phone half-buried under paperwork on McLean's desk started to bleep weakly.

'Sounds like that's them now. Thanks for the heads-up, Bob. I reckon I know what this is about. Do me a favour though, will you?'

'Aye?'

'If you see Stuart about, tell him he's not seen me today. Might be better if you can find something he's meant to be doing on the other side of town.'

'Detective Sergeant MacBride? Sure I heard him say he was going to be checking up on a reported sighting of that missing teenager over Cramond way. Headed out first thing and I don't expect to see him much before shift end.' Grumpy Bob had clearly taken his hand away from the phone as he spoke, the muffled background sound of busyness returning with a vengeance. He'd raised his voice too. No doubt MacBride was with him and would soon be departing by the back door.

'Thanks, Bob. I'll let you know how I get on. May be my last chance to buy you a beer.'

He hung up as the phone on his desk started ringing again. There was a screen that was supposed to show the number of the extension calling within the building, but it had given up the ghost. McLean ignored it, squeezed out from around his desk and went off in search of whatever trouble he was in now.

Detective Superintendent Brooks had yet to discover the benefits of an open-door policy, which meant that McLean had to knock before entering. He stood outside the door for a moment, listening to the low murmur of voices within. At least nobody was shouting, not yet.

'Enter!' Brooks' low baritone barked out the command. McLean put on his best innocent schoolboy face, took a deep breath and went in.

'I was told you were looking for me, sir,' he said before anyone else could speak. Jo Dexter and Stevie Robinson were sitting on one side of the small conference table by the large window wall of the office, DCI Spence on the other side. Brooks himself was at his desk, staring at the screen of his mobile phone which was doubtless telling him that his call to McLean had been rejected. He didn't look up as he spoke.

'About bloody time. We've been phoning you for the last half-hour.'

'You have?' McLean feigned innocence with the skill of a man who's spent a lifetime observing others trying to do the same. Brooks ignored the comment, finally meeting his eye.

'What's your relationship with Heather Marchmont?'

The question threw McLean, at least momentarily. He'd been expecting a bollocking for visiting Stacey Craig and then her boyfriend in Saughton.

'I'm sorry, I don't quite understand the question.'

'Should be easy enough, McLean. How long have you been seeing this woman?'

'Ah, now. That's a different question. Might I ask why you want to know?'

'I'd have thought that would have been obvious, wouldn't it? We get information her house is being used as a brothel, only when we raid it we find it's nothing of the sort. Then it turns out you've been fucking her all along.'

'Is this some kind of joke? I'd never met the woman before the night we raided the place.' McLean looked around the room. Most eyes were on him, except for Dexter, who was picking at her yellow fingernails and finding her hands fascinating.

'Why don't you have a seat, Tony.' The DCC gestured to a chair at the table opposite where he was sitting. Figuring it unwise to disobey, McLean sat down, leaned back and folded his arms.

'You've been seen with Marchmont on several different occasions. Most frequently at a cafe in Stockbridge just around the corner from her home. The same home that we raided, is that not correct?'

McLean looked around the small collection of senior officers. There was no real reason for Spence to be there except that he was Brooks' lickspittle. Jo Dexter seemed to be as embarrassed about the whole thing as he was angry about it. The DCC, Call-me-Stevie, had a smug paternal expression on his face that suggested he knew exactly what was going on. That left just Brooks himself to do all the talking. Quite why he was involved at all McLean wasn't sure, but the absence of anyone from Professional Standards hadn't gone unnoticed. No summary execution, this; there was something more being played.

'I've met Miss Marchmont a couple of times, yes. We interviewed her first during the raid, then again not long after. Well, I say interview, but it was more of an apology. After what happened at her house I felt that was the least we owed her.'

'And then what? True romance blossomed between the two of you?' Brooks made a noise like a fat man spitting into a bucket. 'You expect us to believe that?'

'If you'd let me finish, sir.' McLean kept his voice as calm as he could. 'Miss Marchmont contacted me the day after our interview. She requested a meeting, informal. I got the impression there was something she wanted to tell me. About the raid.'

'And did she?' the DCC asked.

'No, sir.'

'So why did you call her? Why arrange another meeting?'

'I didn't. I've only ever met her when she has called me. I'm only interested in hearing what she wants to say about the raid. Nothing else.'

'Likely bloody story.' Brooks rumbled away like a spoiled child who's had his toys taken from him.

'Now, now, John. There's no need for that. If Tony says there's nothing more to this, then I'm inclined to believe him.' Call-me-Stevie silenced the detective superintendent with a hand not quite slapped, but placed firmly on the table. He leaned forward, dragging everyone's attention to him. 'There is however a small matter of propriety to consider.'

Always a 'but' in there. McLean looked up, meeting the DCC's eyes; a far more calculating intelligence than Brooks, or even Spence. The two of them just hated him, but Robinson was something else entirely.

'Propriety?' he asked, although he had some inkling as to what was coming.

'See it from my perspective, Tony. An important and expensive SCU operation goes spectacularly tits up. It happens from time to time, and we try to smooth things over, but the lead investigator seems reluctant to accept that it was just a simple error. Maybe he's trying to cover his own arse, or maybe he's trying to divert attention from something a bit more sinister. I don't know. Either way, it's suspicious when that same investigator appears to be engaged in some kind of relationship with a key suspect in the initial investigation, wouldn't you say?'

McLean decided it was best not to. Besides, his brain was having a hard time keeping up with Robinson's convoluted reasoning, trying to work out what the DCC's angle might be. Just as well he'd managed to get some quality sleep the night before; if he'd faced this inquisition yesterday God only knew what he'd have made of it.

'It's no matter. As you've pointed out, Miss Marchmont could have raised a serious complaint against us, but for whatever reason she has chosen not to. I for one think it wise not to rock that boat, which is why I asked you to wind up the case as quickly as possible. You've done that now, haven't you?'

McLean thought about the questions hanging over Stacey Craig's unfortunate condition, the things he'd learned from his conversation with Tam Roberts.

'Detective Sergeant Ritchie has been preparing it this morning, sir. All I need to do is sign it off and the case is closed.'

'Then that can be your last act as a member of the SCU team.' Robinson smiled like a headmaster doling out detentions.

'My last?' McLean asked.

'You what?' Jo Dexter said at the same time.

'You're a good detective, Tony. Thorough. Some might say dogged. But this affair with Marchmont, it's very ill-advised. I can't leave you in the SCU, not with that hanging over you. Better to move you somewhere that keen mind and hunger for the truth is well suited.'

McLean knew a back-handed compliment when he saw one. He also had a horrible feeling he knew what the DCC was going to say next. There was a terrible logic to it.

'We've been setting up a new unit. Should really be a DCI in charge, but I'm sure you're up to the job. Play your cards right and you could see promotion in a few months. You'll be working with Detective Sergeant Laird on a day-to-day basis, and we're drafting in some retired detectives to do the rest of the work.'

'The Cold Case Unit.'

'That's the one. I think it'll be perfectly suited to your skills, Tony.' Robinson grinned again as he delivered the coup de grâce. 'And you'll get to work with your old friend Charles Duguid again.'

'They can't do this. How am I meant to run a fucking investigation if they keep reassigning all my team?'

The inquisition had broken up quickly after the DCC's announcement. McLean had just been glad to get out of the room, wanting some time to think his way through what had happened. He wasn't surprised when Dexter had followed him out, asking for directions to the smoking hut even though she knew perfectly well where it was. She hadn't said anything all the way through the station, but let rip as soon as they were outside.

'I'm sure you'll find someone. I heard Brooks was quite keen to find Carter somewhere he could shine.'

'Don't you fucking start. Carter's a useless streak of piss and you know it.' Dexter lit a cigarette, drew in deeply, calmed down a little as the nicotine hit. 'You know it's your own stupid fault. You wouldn't let it lie.'

McLean tried to stand upwind to avoid the worst of the smoke. There were a couple of uniform constables in the hut, but they were puffing as quickly as possible to get their fix and away from the obviously agitated senior officer. Jo Dexter had something of a reputation, even away from her own station. McLean knew it was mostly just bluster.

'I know. Sorry. But there's more to it than just me seeing how far I could push that report into an investigation. I'm still not sure why they want it all swept away. And don't tell me it's because admitting we made a mistake is too embarrassing for the suits. I don't buy it. If that was the case I'd be hung out to dry. No, there's something else going on here.'

'Why'd you have to go and see her, anyway? You that desperate for a shag?'

'Oh come on. You don't believe all that shite, do you? I've met the woman four times, and three of those times Ritchie was with me. She lives in the house we raided on false information. Why the hell wouldn't I talk to her if I'm trying to find out how that happened?'

'You – what? Ritchie was with you?' Dexter had been about to take another drag, but now she held the cigarette, glowing end down, halfway towards her open mouth. 'Why didn't you say so? In there?' She flicked her head backwards to indicate the bulk of the station and the office of Detective Superintendent Brooks in particular.

'Credit me with some intelligence, Jo. Someone's been spreading malicious rumours. If Ritchie was implicated, she'd have been in there with me, and there'd have been a union rep too. She wasn't, so I'm not going to get her involved unless I really have to.'

'That's very . . . noble. But don't you think you're being a touch paranoid?'

McLean watched the two constables squeeze out the back entrance to the smokers' shelter to avoid having to make eye contact with either him or Dexter. 'Not really, no. This feels very much like someone doesn't want me digging any deeper into the brothel raid and will do whatever they can to stop me. Looks like it's worked, too. Now who do we know who was very keen to have it all tidied away and forgotten about?'

Dexter shook her head, dropped her cigarette to the ground and stood on it to put it out. 'Now I know you're paranoid. The DCC? For fuck's sake, Tony. He's no' bent. Stevie can be a bit of an arse at times, but he's one of the good guys.'

'So you keep saying. And I guess he didn't sack me, so I've that much to thank him for. If it'd just been Brooks, he'd have called in Professional Standards on me. I'd be suspended and under a full investigation right now. As it is, I have to work with Dagwood. Not sure which I'd have preferred, to be honest.'

Dexter patted McLean on the arm. 'Ach, you'll be fine. And Stevie's right about one thing; guddling about in old cases is something you'll be a natural at. No, it's me who's come off worst here. I'm down an inspector and the only one going spare's a waste of space.'

'Why not ask your new pal Stevie if he can get Ritchie a temporary promotion?' The idea came to McLean almost as he spoke it, but he could see it take root in Dexter's brain just by the expression that spread across her face.

'Now there's an idea. And I could maybe pinch one of the more competent detective sergeants from Brooks' team too.' She slapped McLean on the arm again, harder this time. 'I like your thinking, Tony. Now give us a lift in that wee sports car of yours. We can head over to HQ and tell Ritchie the good news in person.'

# 34

McLean looked around the office he'd been assigned on joining the SCU. It wasn't much to write home about, what with the mouldy carpet tiles and interesting collection of ceiling stains. The desk had seen better days, probably sometime before Margaret Thatcher rose to power, and he suspected most of the furniture was there only because nobody else wanted it. He'd not been using the room long, had only been back at the SCU for a few months and spent half of that shuttling back and forth between this and his tiny little broom cupboard at his old station. But it was a place where he'd found peace and quiet, a place where he'd managed to think. He was going to miss it.

'I can't believe they took you off the unit, sir. I mean, just because . . .' DS Ritchie stood in the doorway, a slim folder clasped in one hand. No, not DS, acting DI. McLean smiled at the thought that at least something good had come of the whole fiasco.

'Office politics, Kirsty. You'd better get used to it now you're playing with the big kids.'

Ritchie raised an invisible eyebrow at the joke. Or maybe it was because he'd used her first name. McLean couldn't explain it, even to himself, but he'd often had trouble with that. Now they were both the same rank it felt more natural.

'That the final report on the brothel raid?' He nodded at the folder Ritchie was carrying.

'Aye, for what it's worth.' She waved it about unconvincingly, then handed it to him. 'Just need a signature and then it all goes away.'

'Why do I get the feeling you don't believe that?'

'Guess I've been hanging around with you too long, sir ... Tony.' Ritchie handed over the folder. He took it, opened it up, saw a slim sheaf of papers, the text double-spaced. He folded it back up again and dropped it on to the desk.

'You deserve the promotion. Probably would have happened a while ago if you hadn't got sick. I just hope it gets changed from acting to permanent quickly. You don't need me to tell you to tread carefully, though. At least for a while. I expect upstairs will be keeping an eye out to see what happens next.'

'I'll be as good as gold. It's going to be strange, not having you around, mind.'

'I'm only over at the old station, you know. I'm not retiring just yet.' McLean lifted the box he'd been filling with all the important files he needed to keep, placed it on the chair by the door. It wasn't very full, or particularly heavy.

'Aye, I know. It's just all a bit sudden and a bit brutal, if I'm being honest.'

'Brutal? How so?'

'You know the cold case squad's a dead end, right? And making you work with Dagwood, too.'

'Ach, he's not so bad.' McLean couldn't quite believe he was saying it. 'And technically I'll be his boss. That could be interesting. Grumpy Bob's the one I worry about; he's going to get all the work to do and that's not really his style.'

'No. I guess not.' Ritchie pointed at the report she'd brought in. 'I'll leave that with you. Don't think there's any great rush to sign it, except for maybe drawing a line under this whole sorry business.'

McLean fished in his jacket pocket for a pen, opened up the folder again. 'I'll sign it right now. Can't imagine you've put anything in there I wouldn't endorse.' He scribbled his signature on the top page in the space provided, closed the folder and handed it back.

'I'll give you good odds that's not the last we'll hear of it all, though.'

He caught a familiar whiff of tobacco smoke on the breeze as he was loading the last cardboard box into the back of the little Alfa Romeo. Not Dexter's brand of cigarette, this was something rougher. Taken from a packet and rolled into a crisp Rizla paper. No filter if he was any judge.

'Heard a rumour you'd had the boot. Wouldn't have believed it if I wasnae seeing it with my own eyes.'

McLean closed the boot with a dull metal clang, turned to see Jo Dalgliesh standing a few yards off.

'Just a move from one department to another. It's not like I'm being fired.'

'Is it no'?' Dalgliesh cocked her head to one side. 'Coz it sure looks like it from where I'm standing.'

'Were you after something? Only I've got to head across town. Lots to do.'

'Aye, setting up Dagwood's cold case squad. How's that working for you?'

'Look, Dalgliesh. I get it. You've heard the news and you've dropped round to let me know how well informed you are. Great. I'm happy for you. Now I've got better things to do than stand around in a car park trading insults. Especially when that car park's overlooked by most of the senior police officers in Edinburgh.'

'All right, all right. No need to get yersel' all wound up.' Dalgliesh looked up at the glass facade of the building, gave a little wave. 'I wanted to have a wee chat about something of mutual interest, if you get my meaning. The wee stooshie that's got you in all this bother.'

'The case is closed. I signed off the final report just a half-hour ago. We raided a house thinking it was being used as a brothel. Turned out we were wrong. Egg on face, apologies all round, end of story.'

'You sayin' that coz you believe it, or for them up there?' Dalgliesh flicked her head in the direction of the building.

'Can they not be the same thing?'

'Ha. You don't mean that, Tony. Not if you're half the detective I've heard people say you are.' Dalgliesh shoved her hands in the pockets of her faded leather coat, scuffed her foot against the cracked tarmac as if trying to make her mind up about something. Like a teenager summoning the courage to ask someone she fancied out on a date. 'Tell you what. I ken you can't talk here. No' to me anyways. But if you want to know something might be important to you, then I'm going to be getting myself a coffee in half an hour or so. You know the place. You've been there a lot recently.'

And without another word, she turned and sauntered off.

*

McLean half expected to see Heather Marchmont at her usual table as he entered the cafe a half-hour later. Failing that, perhaps Dalgliesh would be sitting in the same place. As it was, neither of them were anywhere to be seen. It wouldn't be the first time the reporter had played a practical joke on him, so he reckoned he might as well make the most of it.

'Coffee and a slice of that chocolate cake, please.' He pointed through the glass counter to the first in a row of fine-looking cakes and pastries. The cafe wasn't busy; late-morning would be the lull after the rush of takeouts as people headed to their work and before the rush of customers looking for some lunch. He picked a table by the window, watching the traffic and people walking by, until a light cough distracted him.

'Oh, thanks.' He leaned back in his chair as the waitress placed coffee and cake on the table. He didn't recognise her, but then he was hardly a regular. The trail of whatever perfume she was wearing sparked a memory, but before he could place it the front door clattered open and Dalgliesh stumbled in, looked around until she saw him and slouched over.

'Bloody hell, I needed this.' She slumped down in the chair opposite, reached over and helped herself to McLean's coffee. Grimaced. 'Christ, do you no' take sugar?'

'I thought you said half an hour.' McLean looked back to the serving counter where the waitress was staring at Dalgliesh with an oddly hostile expression on her face. He indicated as best he could for her to bring more coffee, then turned back just in time to see the reporter tucking into his cake.

'Sorry. Had an important phone call I couldnae ignore.'

'Someone high up, then.'

'Aye. No' quite the big boss man, but I was left in no doubt as to where the message was coming from.'

'And the message itself?'

Dalgliesh shovelled more cake into her mouth, crumbs sticking to her bristly moustache and in her cracked lips. 'What makes you think that's any of your business?'

'I'm a policeman, remember? Everything is my business.'

Dalgliesh swallowed, washed the cake down with an unladylike slurp of coffee before speaking again. 'Aye, fair point. It's sort of to do with you anyway.'

'Why is it I find that both unsurprising and alarming at the same time?'

'Ha ha. You're all heart, Inspector. Or should I say Chief Inspector?'

'Not yet. Not ever if I have any say in the matter.'

'Oh aye? I'd've thought you'd prefer it being higher up the pole.'

'Not really. The more senior you get, the more time you spend managing people and the less time solving cases. I really can't be arsed with the bureaucracy, if I'm being honest.'

'A man after my own scaly heart.' Dalgliesh finished McLean's coffee just as the waitress appeared with another cup and a second slice of cake. 'Couldn't get a refill, could I, love?'

The waitress scowled, but went away for more.

'What is it you wanted to say to me, Dalgliesh?' McLean asked as soon as they were alone again. He took up his own coffee before she could grab it, savoured the aroma and sipped delicately. Watching the reporter devour the first slice of cake like a hyena at a rotting carcass had quite spoiled his appetite, though.

'Your new girlfriend, the dominatrix lawyer, and her band of kinky pals. Soon as I start looking into them and my editor's giving me ridiculous assignments. Whale sighting off Aberdeen? Off you go. Gangs of illegal immigrants being used as berry pickers in Tayside? Oh, that's right up Dalgliesh's street. Art installation in Inverness? Fuck off. They even sent me to the fucking football. Oh, 'scuse my language.' Dalgliesh almost blushed as the waitress returned with a coffee pot, refilled her mug and offered milk from a jug in her other hand. 'Cheers.'

'Are you sure you're not just being paranoid?' McLean asked.

'Of course I'm being bloody paranoid. I'm a journalist. It's part of the job description. Sure, I might get sent to look into something outside my usual field from time to time. Money's tight in this business, so you do everything you can. And even a byline on the sports page is a byline. But every time I make a call about Marchmont? Even when I started asking about the tip-off for your raid? No, I know when I'm being steered away from something. Then I get a call from senior management asking me about my pension arrangements? Aye, too right.'

'So you've not got anywhere? Still chasing after your secret society angle?'

Dalgliesh grimaced. 'You know how to rub it in, aye? What a fucking waste of time that's been.'

'No secret society, then? No sinister band of dirty old men pulling the strings, making people disappear without trace, turning perfectly innocent brothels into free-for-all swingers' parties?'

'You going to eat that cake?' Dalgliesh didn't wait for an answer before grabbing the plate and sliding it noisily over to her side of the table. Any hope that eating would have slowed her answer to his questions was forlorn.

'See. I thought I was on to something wi' the Benison. Stuff like that never really goes away.'

She shoved a heavy forkful of cake into her mouth, chewed a little, then started talking again, waving the fork around for emphasis. 'And there's remnants of it all around, if you just look. Those swingers you get so excited about, aye? There's a wee secret society if ever I saw one. There's connections, favours given, misdemeanours overlooked. Your mate Dagwood's beloved Masons're another. You scratch my back I'll scratch yours, you know the form. Hell, there may even be some overlap between the two, but there's nothing systematic about it. There's no great organisation sitting behind the scenes, pulling all the strings. Every time I found a link, it only went so far before I hit a dead end. Everything's connected, sure, but no' in any meaningful way.'

Dalgliesh swallowed heavily, then took a long swig of coffee to wash it all down.

'How do you mean, everything's connected?'

'Edinburgh's a small wee place. See, if I tried hard enough I'd be able to find links between you and Miss Marchmont that neither of you know anything about. Friends of friends of friends, that sort of thing. Imagine if you could tap into that, know all that without having to do all the digging. That'd give you some power, eh?'

'I don't—'

'You wouldn't need to blackmail people, just find out which of their friends owes you a favour. Or maybe who they owe a favour to. Who's seen someone doing something they'd be embarrassed about, maybe when they were younger and more stupid, aye? A word here, a nudge there. Or if things got really bad then maybe a threat. You might even use people to recruit their friends to your cause without them even knowing there was a cause.'

'But—'

'See, something like Marchmont's wee sex club, now that's going to be embarrassing if it comes out. You've got obvious leverage there. But what if it went further than that? Maybe catering to less harmless desires? What if there were people out there who got off on hurting wee kids? Or killing tramps? Or, I don't know.' Dalgliesh was in her element now, the fork stabbing dangerously in McLean's direction as she emphasised each possibility.

'But how would you do that? Who could do that? Why would anyone do that?'

She shook her head. 'That's the point, right? No one could. No one does. It's just patterns forming out of complexity. Stare at the dots for long enough and you'll see whatever's on your mind. Mix in a healthy dose of journalist's paranoia and boom! You've got a conspiracy theory. One born every day.' She put the fork down on the empty plate, pushed it away from her. 'Thanks for the cake.'

'So what you're telling me is there's no conspiracy at all?'

Dalgliesh wiped her face with a napkin, smearing chocolatey cream across her cheek in the process. 'That's no' what I'm saying at all, Inspector. Quite the reverse. It's all one big conspiracy. Just there's naebody pulling all the strings.'

# 35

'Afternoon, sir. Didn't think you'd be showing up today. Thought you might have some time off between jobs.'

Grumpy Bob greeted McLean from his familiar feet-up-on-the-desk position, newspaper spread across his legs. The room given over to the new Cold Case Unit was surprisingly large, considering the size of the team occupying it. Even on a late autumn afternoon it was dark, though, tucked away in a back corner of the building, below street level and with windows that looked out on to concrete light wells. This was the remains of the old station knocked down to allow the construction of the seventies concrete monstrosity above them. Down below the polished wooden floorboards were more dungeon-like levels where the archives were stored in old windowless cells.

'Not sure I'd know what to do with time off, Bob. And I rather got the feeling HQ would be pleased to see the back of me. Not sure what I've done wrong, but that never stopped them before.'

'Ah well. Their loss is our gain.' Grumpy Bob lifted his paper off his lap and his feet off the desk in one swift move that showed remarkable agility for a man of his advancing years. Or at least a great deal of practice. He stood up and walked over to a desk on the other side of the room, where a stack of official-looking brown folders awaited. 'Our first batch of cases. I was going to give them to Duguid to review, but he's not in today.'

'I'd better get stuck in then. Anything interesting?'

'If you mean Headland House, then no. The Procurator Fiscal's office didn't think there was enough evidence to make it worthwhile. Least, I assume that's why they rejected it. Said as much about a couple dozen others I put their way, too.'

McLean picked up the first folder in the pile, opened it up and read the front page of the report. Nineteen seventy-six. A desiccated body found up on the Pentland Hills. Initially thought to be a prank by students at the university, stealing an Egyptian mummy from the National Museum and staking it out on the moors during the summer heatwave. Only the museum found its missing mummy soon afterwards, and a post-mortem on the body showed it had died much more recently than the last of the pharaohs.

'Christ, I was barely out of nappies when this happened.'

'Now there's an image to savour in my retirement.'

McLean spun round to see Detective Superintendent Duguid standing in the doorway. Ex-Superintendent, if he was being correct. He was dressed in the same tweed suit McLean had seen him wearing at the golf club, and carried a heavy leather briefcase which he clunked down on the nearest desk.

'Heard a rumour you'd been reassigned to this team, McLean. Thought it was someone's idea of a joke. Or maybe an attempt to get me to stick to retirement. Who've they put in charge of this dead-end place anyway?'

McLean dropped the Pentland Mummy case file back on to the desk. 'That would be me.'

It was worth it just to see the look on Duguid's face. A mixture of surprise and despair and anger in equal proportions. He reached out a long-fingered hand towards his briefcase, and for a moment McLean thought he was going to pick it up, turn around and leave. Instead he just let out a heavy sigh, popped the catches and pulled out a stack of yet more files.

'Well, it could have been worse, I suppose. At least your knack for causing trouble won't be too much bother down here. There's a few more cases I thought might be worth considering.' Duguid took a moment to look around the room. 'If we've got anyone to help us, that is.'

McLean picked up the stack of folders and leafed through them.

'You won't find Headland House in there either. More's the pity. Seems there's still people with enough influence alive who're worried what might happen if we open that particular can of worms. Besides, no one was killed on that one. Our remit's unsolved murders, is it not?'

McLean put the folders back down again, felt the heat spread through the edges of his ears. Was he that easily read? Duguid was right, though.

'Very well.' He went back to the first file he'd opened. 'The Pentland Mummy it is.'

'Jesus. How much more of this stuff is there?'

Late afternoon and McLean was beginning to reappraise his estimation of the size of the room they'd been given. Where once it had been a nice airy open space, albeit a little on the gloomy side, now it was piled high with damp-smelling cardboard boxes newly arrived from the archives and evidence stores down below them. The Pentland Mummy case might have been put on ice almost forty years earlier, but nothing had been thrown away. Neither had it been digitised or, apparently, indexed. The stark contrast with the lack of records for the Headland House investigation hadn't gone unnoticed.

'You're the one who chose it, McLean. Could have told you going for something pre-eighties would be a mistake but I suspect you wouldn't have listened.' Despite his words, McLean couldn't help but hear an unexpected note of glee in Duguid's voice. He'd spent most of the afternoon going through boxes of dusty notebooks, occasionally snorting in surprise or laughter, or asking either McLean or Grumpy Bob if they remembered such-and-such a sergeant or Chief Inspector somebody. Grumpy Bob would occasionally nod, laugh or grimace, but McLean felt like the new kid at school who knows nobody and doesn't have a clue what they're all talking about.

'That's the last load, sir.' The uniform constable who had been ferrying back and forth from the evidence stores in the deep basement handed McLean a clipboard with a manifest attached. He scribbled his signature on the bottom sheet before handing it back.

'What about forensics? Did they keep any samples for DNA analysis?'

'Not sure, sir. I can check. They'd be over at the city mortuary, I'd guess.'

'Thanks. Do that, will you?' McLean checked his watch,

past shift change for those who worked shifts. 'It can wait until tomorrow, though.'

The constable nodded once, then scuttled off. McLean opened up the last box to be delivered, seeing a stack of Blue Peters neatly tied up with string. Each would be filled with notes typed on old-fashioned mechanical typewriters. He could smell the carbon paper used to make copies, imagined he could see the banks of typists – all young women, of course – hammering away at their keyboards, the air heavy with smoke from the detectives' cigarettes.

'You do realise that pretty much anyone who had anything to do with this case is dead, right?' Duguid dropped a thick folder back into the box he'd been rifling through, picked up another and then discarded it again. 'Including the murderer.'

'Do you want to tell that poor constable he's to take all this lot back again?' McLean indicated the stacks of boxes, tempted to do just that.

'It's your call, McLean. I'm just here to give you the benefit of my many years' experience. Most of which is telling me this is a waste of time, even if I am getting paid.'

'Well, we can waste some more time on it tomorrow. Reckon we should call it a day now.'

The number on his phone screen wasn't one he recognised, although the code showed that whoever was dialling was in Edinburgh. McLean paused on his way to the car, wondering whether to take it or not. If it was important they'd leave a message, and it was probably only someone trying to sell him something. He thumbed the screen to accept the call anyway, guddling in his pocket for his car keys.

'McLean.'

'Detective Inspector McLean? Police Scotland CID?'

Technically, yes. 'Who is this?' he asked.

'Oh, I'm sorry. Yes. I'm Johnny. Johnny Bairstow. I work with Jo Dalgliesh. Well, I'm her editor to be precise.'

McLean stopped as he was about to put the key in the lock. There weren't many reasons why this man would be phoning him and not Dalgliesh herself. 'How can I help you, Mr Bairstow?'

'Help me?' The man on the end of the line seemed confused, as if that hadn't been his intention all along. 'Oh. No. Not me. Though it's possible you might be able to help Jo. I understand you had a meeting with her this morning?'

Something about the way the question was phrased put McLean on edge. Was this the senior editor who had been sending Dalgliesh out on inappropriate assignments; the one who had been leaned on by the paper's rich, powerful and influential proprietor?

'Can you not ask her that?'

'Umm . . . Not exactly, no. I know she went to a cafe; I'm just trying to find out where.'

'Is she trying to claim it on expenses? Only I paid for the coffee and cake.'

'No, no. It's not that at all. I'm sorry, Inspector. It's a bit of a shock, really. Cake, you say. Well, it's possible, I suppose.'

'What's possible? What are you going on about?' McLean unlocked the car and opened the door.

266

'She had a bit of a turn in the office this afternoon. Started . . . well, it looked like she was having a fit. Foaming at the mouth. I've never seen anything like it.'

McLean dropped into the driver's seat, slammed the door and shoved the key in the ignition. 'Is she OK? Where is she now?'

'The paramedics came, gave her some horrible-looking injection. She's been taken to the Western General. She's in intensive care.'

'Did they say what it was?' He started the car, revving the engine perhaps a little too enthusiastically.

'They thought it was an allergic reaction to something she ate. Anaphylactic shock. That's why I wanted to find out what she'd eaten.'

'I'm on my way to the hospital now. I'll call you back when I've spoken to the doctors.'

'Umm . . . Is that necessary? If you could just tell me—'

'Goodbye, Mr Bairstow. I'll call you back.' McLean ended the call, dropped the phone on the passenger seat and slotted the car into gear, startling a couple of constables as he exited the car park at speed.

Unlike the Royal Infirmary on the eastern outskirts of town, McLean knew the Western General well. His grandmother had spent eighteen months here, plugged into life support in the intensive care ward. Emma had been here too, and now Jo Dalgliesh. True, he'd never had much more than contempt for the journalist, muting into a grudging acceptance in the past few months, but she didn't deserve this.

He walked swiftly down familiar corridors, his presence

unquestioned by the nurses he passed. Most of them knew him by sight, if not by name, and he'd learned over the years that you could get away with almost anything if you acted like you were supposed to be doing it. Only when he reached the corridor that opened on to the intensive care ward did someone actually speak to him.

'Inspector McLean. Tony. It's been a while. I didn't expect to see you here.'

Jeannie Robertson was one of the senior nurses on the ICU. She'd looked after his grandmother, even come to her funeral. They'd exchanged words for eighteen months, then another six whilst Emma had been in the same ward, but he'd not seen her for what . . . over a year now?

'Not somewhere I'd really choose to visit often.' He tried a reassuring smile, got a tired one in return.

'Here on business, I take it?'

'Alas, yes. Jo Dalgliesh, the journalist. She was brought in this afternoon?'

'Ah . . . her. The allergic reaction. People don't realise just how serious that can be, and how rapid. Still, you'd think she'd at least have been carrying an EpiPen on her.'

'To be honest, I didn't even know she was allergic to anything. Not that it would have come up in conversation. How is she?'

'It's not good, I'm afraid. You know how anaphylaxis works, right?'

'Swelling, constriction of the airways, that sort of thing?'

'Exactly. And it can come on in minutes. Quicker even. If you can't administer epinephrine, you've got to make sure they can breathe. The paramedics got to your friend quickly, but she was already unconscious. We don't know if there's been damage to her brain. They've got her in an induced coma at the moment. Going to bring her out slowly tomorrow, or maybe the next day.'

McLean had been looking towards the ward doors, but he turned away. Not much point trying to talk to Dalgliesh right now.

'Any idea what caused it?'

'Probably something she ate. That's the most usual trigger for symptoms this severe. If I had to hazard a guess, I'd say nuts, given what came out of her stomach. Either that or chocolate. You'd think she'd have known better, though.'

McLean turned back towards the ward. Not quite sure why he was so indecisive. 'Can I see her?'

'Sure. Just don't prop the door open with the fire extinguisher like you used to, OK?'

'I won't. Thanks, Jeannie.'

She smiled again, a slight tilt of the head, then walked away. McLean went to the ICU ward doors, peered in through the glass. It was all too hauntingly familiar, just different faces in the beds. Pushing through, he found Dalgliesh in the one nearest the entrance. She reminded him curiously of Stacey Craig, sunken into crisp white pillows as if they were trying to ingest her. Tubes and wires connected her to monitors, an IV drip plugged into one arm. For a moment he imagined they were sucking the life out of her, rather than working to put it back. He shuddered at the unwanted memory that idea brought; a man slowly drained of his vital blood, staring blindly at a dark iron cross on the ceiling.

'What the hell happened to you?' McLean spoke the words quietly, even though nobody else in the room would be disturbed by him. Dalgliesh didn't reply, and all he could do was stare at her, wondering what the answer might be.

Trying not to think about her tucking into two slices of chocolate and walnut cake, both of them intended for him.

## 36

Light spilled from the house, illuminating the front drive and the little black car that sat by the front door. McLean parked up in front of the old coach house, converted into garages long ago. From there he could see more light painting yellow squares on the lawn and illuminating the trees that surrounded the garden. It made a change to come home to light and company. After having just spent half an hour in the intensive care ward staring at the comatose figure of Jo Dalgliesh, it was probably what he needed. Even if part of him longed for a quiet room, a long dram and his thoughts.

The kitchen table was a mess of supermarket carrier bags, some unpacked, some still spilling out their contents. A case of cheap lager had been opened and a couple of tins were missing. The rest would be all but undrinkable, even when all the flavour had been chilled out of them. In the warmth of the kitchen they would be utterly disgusting. McLean was appalled to think that his real-ale-drinking friend could have been so corrupted by such a short time in the USA.

'Oh, Tony. You're home. Did you just get in? Only I didn't hear your car.' Jenny Spiers walked into the kitchen carrying a stack of plates. She dumped them down on the table before turning to the Aga. Steam billowed out of the oven door as she opened it and retrieved a plate of what looked suspiciously like sausage rolls. The smell wafted over, making McLean's stomach gurgle in hungry anticipation. He'd not stopped off for a carry-out this evening, figuring there'd be something in the house, even if it was only stale corn flakes. It looked like he'd struck lucky.

'You can't hear anything outside once you've got the music on.' Strains of something poppy he didn't recognise were filtering through from the hall. 'I take it Rae's home with the wee bairn?'

'She is, yes. And Chloe's down from university. Wanted to see her new cousin. She's very excited about it. They're all in the library.' Jenny straightened up from where she had been arranging sausage rolls on to a plate, a sudden look of worry on her face. 'I hope you don't mind.'

'Mind? Why would I?' McLean caught a flash of movement from the corner of his eye, looked down to see Mrs McCutcheon's cat slinking in from the hall. She stopped just long enough to give him the kind of accusing, reproachful stare only cats can, then scuttled off for the back door. The clatter of the cat flap was her final condemnation.

'Why don't you come through? I reckon Rae'll be heading for bed soon and Phil will want everyone to wet the baby's head, as it were.'

'If it's with that pish, I think I'd rather have a cup of tea.' McLean waved in the general direction of the cans of warm lager.

'Ah, no. Chloe brought that. I think she thinks it's cool? Either that or she's just doing it to piss off her mother.'

'Mum, where's those sausage rolls? I'm fair starving here – oh.' The voice echoed up the short corridor from the hall as Chloe Spiers came through to the kitchen in search of food, her final expression of surprise at the realisation her mother wasn't alone. McLean might have uttered the same word himself. He remembered Chloe as a sixteen-year-old girl, small for her age, though not lacking in self-confidence. His most abiding memory was of finding her alone and scared, chained up to the wall of a basement room in an abandoned, semi-derelict mansion on the outskirts of the city. It had been too dark for her to see the body laid out on the floor beside her, the preserved remains of another young woman sacrificed to the insane lusts and greed of a half-dozen men some sixty years before, but Chloe had maintained the dead woman had spoken to her, and McLean believed her.

'You grew up,' he said, realising as he did just how stupid he must sound. It was true, though; Chloe was a very striking young woman now, shades of her mother and aunt in her features, but sharpened by her youth. She appeared to have given up on the vintage clothing, adopting the standard skinny jeans and tour T-shirt uniform of a university undergrad.

'Er . . . Hi?' She gave him a nervous little wave, seeming to shrink under his gaze. McLean wasn't sure who was more embarrassed, Chloe or him.

'Here. Take these through to your uncle Phil. I swear he could eat his own bodyweight and not put on an ounce of fat.' Jenny came to the rescue, thrusting the plate of sausage rolls into Chloe's arms and shooing her out of the kitchen. Only once her daughter was gone did she turn her attention back to McLean.

'She gets a bit nervous whenever, you know . . .'

'I can imagine. It's not something anyone should have to

go through.' He wasn't sure what else to say. He might have been the one to find Chloe before she could come to the same grisly fate as her companion in the cellar, but he was also the reason she'd been abducted in the first place.

'Come on.' Jenny broke the silence that had fallen over the kitchen. 'Better hurry or there'll be no food left.'

Much later, sitting at the kitchen table with a mug of tea and staring blankly at the mound of plates, pans and oven trays Jenny had washed up and stacked neatly to drain, McLean had to admit that the evening had been more enjoyable than he was expecting. Rachel had been radiant but tired, milking the new-mum angle for all it was worth before heading to an early bed with an already sleeping Tony Junior. Phil was his usual self, amusing and annoying in equal measure, but McLean had to admit he'd missed his old friend's company. Chloe slowly relaxed, helped perhaps by a few cans of the unspeakably foul lager she insisted was fine despite all attempts to convince her otherwise. For a while the house had felt warm and alive, a place to live rather than a place to exist. Now, with Jenny and her daughter gone, Phil passed out on the couch and Rachel and the baby apparently sound asleep upstairs, he could finally enjoy a moment of contemplative quiet. Finally think about Jo Dalgliesh and her sudden allergic reaction.

A clatter at the back door broke the comfortable silence and Mrs McCutcheon's cat stalked in. She sniffed the air as if trying to decide whether the noisy people were still there or not, then leapt gracefully on to the table and presented her head to be stroked. McLean scratched her behind the ears, earning an unexpected bout of purring as his reward.

Looking over to the corner by the door, where the food and water bowls lived, he saw the real reason for the sudden show of affection.

'It's always food with you, isn't it?' He got up, found the cat food bag and filled the bowl, then went back to the table and his mug of tea. His phone sat on the wooden table top in front of him, screen showing that it was probably past time he went to bed. He considered phoning the hospital, asking for an update on Dalgliesh's condition. Strange how times changed; just a few years earlier and he would have been raising a toast to her demise. Now he had to admit to feeling concern for the journalist. And not just because the food that had almost certainly been the cause of her reaction had been intended for him. Bloody stupid of her to eat it, really. The walnuts had been quite clearly visible, pressed into the chocolate cream icing on the top of the cake.

Now he thought about it, he'd seen Dalgliesh eat similar things before. The fact that she didn't carry an EpiPen around with her suggested allergies weren't something she normally encountered.

And the cake had been intended for him. Come to think of it, he hadn't even ordered the second slice. The waitress had brought it without him asking. He tried to picture her, tried to remember the faces of any of the serving staff in the cafe. He'd not been there enough times to really be sure, but he was fairly certain she was new. And surly. He remembered her now. Perhaps he should have a word with her.

The phone was in his hand before he'd even considered what he was doing. Too late to call, but he could always text. A short message, an excuse to visit the cafe, or was there more to it? McLean's thumb hovered over the send icon, as he looked once more around the kitchen. Mrs McCutcheon's cat had finished eating and was now cleaning herself by the Aga. She stopped as if she had felt his gaze fall on her, stared back to say it was none of her business what idiot stuff he got up to, then went back to her grooming.

The phone buzzed in his hand, so unexpected he almost dropped it. The words on the screen confused him; a reply before he'd sent his own request. He'd been about to delete his message unsent, but somehow it had gone out anyway.

*Meet for coffee? 8 a.m. Usual place.*

An electronic glitch, or his subconscious at work? He couldn't say, but there was the evidence in front of him.

*OK. C U there.*

Either way the die was cast.

## 37

There was no sign of the surly waitress when McLean entered the cafe early the next morning. It was possible – probable, even – that she worked a different shift. Likely that there was nothing to his suspicion about the cake Dalgliesh had eaten. A far more rational explanation was that he was tired, overworked and letting his paranoia get away with him. The reporter could have reacted to anything, even an insect bite. And yet he couldn't shake the feeling there was something suspicious about the whole incident. Too much coincidence for his liking.

Marchmont wasn't about either, so he ordered a coffee and sat down at her usual table. No cake this time.

'There was another young woman serving in here, yesterday late morning,' he said to the waitress when she brought him his coffee. She looked momentarily surprised.

'Yesterday morning? No, it was just me, and Elaine over on the counter.' She looked round and McLean followed her gaze to the short, grey-haired lady operating the till and doling out cake. Neither of them looked remotely like the surly woman who had served him.

'You sure? Youngish, a bit taller than you, straw-blonde hair?'

'I think I ought to know. I own this place after all.'

The door clattered open and Heather Marchmont walked in. McLean watched her features change as she scanned the room; face blank until she saw him, then lighting up in a wide smile. The waitress – owner, he corrected himself – was still hovering by the table.

'Sorry,' he said to her. 'I must have got myself mixed up. Can I get another coffee for my friend?'

'Of course. The usual, Heather?' The waitress smiled as Marchmont approached.

'Thanks, Sue.' She shrugged off her coat as McLean stood and pulled out a chair for her. The waitress headed back to the counter and the coffee machine.

'I wasn't sure if you'd come,' he said once they had both sat down.

'After your mysterious text at midnight? Of course I was going to come. I'm intrigued to hear what the Sexual Crimes Unit wants from me now.' Marchmont had a way of emphasising the word 'sexual' that was entirely deliberate.

'Actually I'm not with the SCU any more. I'm heading up a new unit, looking at old unsolved murders and other serious crimes.'

'You are? When did this happen?'

McLean studied Marchmont's face for signs that her surprise was feigned. She was always difficult to read, but he wasn't convinced she hadn't known.

'Yesterday. It's sort of a promotion, but it's also a punishment.' He told her about the meeting with Brooks and the DCC. Marchmont showed little emotion as he recounted the tale, but she fidgeted with her bag, clearly suppressing the urge to get her phone out and check it for messages.

'Why are you telling me this?'

'Because I was set up and you were part of that. Either

knowingly or not, it's not all that important to me. I just want to know why.'

Marchmont sat silent for a while. The waitress came over with her coffee, lingered for perhaps a moment longer than was necessary before heading back to the counter. McLean took a sip from his own cup, happy enough to wait. It was good coffee, too, with a rich aroma that measured up to the flavour for a change. Noticing it, he realised he couldn't smell any perfume in the air. She'd worn a peculiar scent before, hadn't she? Or had that been someone else?

'It's . . . complicated.' Marchmont's answer cut through his musing, the moment lost.

'It always is.'

'The house you raided. The house where I live now. I've not been there very long.'

'And the parties?'

'That was the first. The first one since I moved in, anyway.' Marchmont dropped her gaze as she spoke, her words coming out in a low monotone. Almost as if she were afraid of being overheard, or lip-read.

'So what was going on there before?'

'I think you know that already, don't you?'

McLean leaned forward, put his elbows on the table. Close up, he still couldn't smell that perfume. Perhaps she wasn't wearing it today. Or maybe it wasn't hers at all.

'You're damage limitation. That's what you do, isn't it?'

A thin smile, a tilt of the head. 'I'm a corporate lawyer.'

'So MacFarlane and Dodds are part of this?'

'Not the firm, no. Some of the people there, probably. I don't really know. Same as some of the police, the judiciary, politicians. There's no "this" in the way you're thinking. Like I said, it's more complicated than that.'

'But someone told you to move into that house. Someone organised that party for the same night we were scheduled to raid the place. That had to have happened pretty much as soon as we knew about it.'

'Oh, there've been parties before. But it's not always like the one you raided. Sometimes there's sex workers there, paying guests. I first met Stacey at one of those.' Marchmont was fidgeting again, glancing occasionally at the window. Every so often her hand would leave the coffee cup, go to her stomach, not quite touch it before she realised what she was doing and went back to the cup. He had thought it a tell before, the little nervous tic that showed when she was lying, but now he wasn't so sure. She wasn't telling all the truth, but what she was telling wasn't a lie.

'You were the one who called us, weren't you? The anonymous tip-off.'

'I . . . I thought it would protect Stacey. When she talked. And I wanted out, same as she did. We were going to get away together. Only there is no out. I should know that by now, of all people.'

McLean reached across the table, put a hand over Marchmont's to stop her fidgeting. She startled at the touch, looked straight at him, and for an instant he almost remembered where he had seen her before.

'Why should you know that, Heather? What makes you so different?'

'I can't say.' She pulled her hand away from him, stood up. 'I'm sorry. I should never have involved you in this at all. I have to go.'

'I can help you, you know. If someone's leaning on you I can . . .' McLean stopped talking, unsure what he could do. Marchmont gave him a weary smile again.

'I know you think you can, Tony, but you can't. It's too late. Best you leave it alone. I'm not the only damage limitation in play here.'

'Christ, I used to think I was a bit slow in the morning. What time do you call this to come slinking in?'

McLean glanced at his watch. He'd not been expecting anyone to be in the Cold Case Unit room yet. Grumpy Bob's shift didn't start until nine and it was still ten minutes to. Duguid sat hunched over his desk, a slew of papers spread over every available surface except for that occupied by a laptop computer, at which he was furiously two-finger typing.

'Believe it or not, I've other cases to attend to, you know. And sorting out DI Carter's paperwork from my own before I can get started on it.' There was some truth in what he said, but McLean omitted the fact that he'd not yet begun the task. 'What's got you in so early, sir?'

Duguid looked up, his brow furrowed in a frown. Or maybe his eyesight was failing. 'Going through missing persons records from 'seventy-six. It's much easier now everything's been digitised. Be even easier if it had been indexed by someone with half a brain.' He went back to his laptop, hammered away at the keyboard again. McLean reckoned he'd have broken the thing by the end of the week.

'The Pentland Mummy?'

'The same. The old post-mortem report's got enough

detail about the man's physical features to at least start looking for him.'

'You've got the report there?' McLean strode over to the desk as Duguid grabbed a sheaf of papers and handed them to him. He scanned down the old typewritten pages, complete with black smears from the carbon paper. Noticed with a wry grin that his grandmother had carried out the examination. Had she come home at the end of that day, having cut open and examined this man's innermost secrets, then sat down beside his bed and read him a story before putting the lights out? Very possibly she had.

'What are you grinning at? Makes you look even more of an idiot than normal.'

McLean looked up from the report to see that Duguid had stopped abusing his keyboard.

'Just thinking about my gran.'

'Aye. She was a good pathologist. Took her time. Which gives me hope there might be some point in pursuing this.'

McLean put the report back down on Duguid's desk, then crossed the room to where a whiteboard was beginning to be covered in barely legible scribbles. 'Do we know what happened to the body?'

'Not yet. If we're lucky he was buried. Should be a record of where.'

'And if we're unlucky?'

'Cremated. Have to hope they've kept tissue samples for DNA. We find any possible candidates in the database then we can see about matching it to a relative. If the poor bugger's got any left alive, that is. 'Seventy-six was a long time ago.' Duguid shuffled some papers, went back to peering at the laptop screen. 'This chap looks like a possible, mind you. Daniel Calton.'

The name meant nothing, so McLean walked around the desk and peered at the mugshot on the screen. A dour-looking fellow scowled out at him in blurred black and white. To say he was nondescript would have been generous.

'Who is he?'

'Was, I'm guessing. He was about sixty when he went missing. No chance of him being still alive today.' Duguid clicked the trackpad and brought up another screen, as competent with the laptop as Detective Sergeant Mac-Bride. 'He was a merchant banker, apparently. It's a bit light on detail. Never showed up for work one morning; family say he left at six, same as every day. That was the last anyone saw of him.'

'So why didn't his name come up in the original investigation?'

'Apparently it did, but was discarded as improbable.' Duguid fished around on his desk until he found the paperwork he was looking for. 'Mostly because he went missing in nineteen seventy-two.'

''Seventy-two?'

'What? Is there an echo in here?' Duguid growled the familiar insult.

'Sorry. Force of habit.' McLean gestured at the papers strewn across the desk. 'That's good work.'

'You seem surprised. I wasn't always a pen-pusher, you know. Getting my head around a problem like this. It's very satisfying.'

'The joys of promotion. More time in meetings and less

out there solving crimes. Now maybe you understand why I've never really been all that keen on a DCI job.'

'Aye, and it's no' as if you need the money like some of us mortals.'

McLean let that one go. On balance he preferred the acerbic but productive Duguid to the shouty one. 'What's the plan then?'

'I'll have a chat with the mortuary about a DNA profile. Then when Grumpy Bob gets in we'll see if we can't track down some living relative of Mr Calton. Get a sample from them and do a cross-check. If all goes well we'll have ticked a box. On to the next one.'

'Did I hear my name being taken in vain?' Grumpy Bob came in through the open door, rolled up newspaper under one arm, cup of delicious-smelling coffee in his hand. The aroma reminded McLean of his meeting with Marchmont earlier, its unsatisfactory conclusion.

'I'll leave you two to track down Calton's family,' he said by way of an answer. 'I need to find DS MacBride.'

'He's up in the CID room, sir,' Grumpy Bob said. 'But you'd better hurry if you want to catch him before Carter does.'

'They've actually given Carter a case? That's brave. Anything interesting?'

Grumpy Bob raised his coffee in mock salute. 'I didn't ask. The less I'm involved the better.'

# 38

McLean found Detective Sergeant MacBride in the CID room, sitting at his desk in the far corner and staring at a large computer screen that partially hid him from the rest of the room. The lack of other detectives suggested either that DI Carter had already been in or word had got round that he had an active case to investigate.

'Morning, Stuart. I was hoping I might find you here.'

MacBride looked up with a start, clicking at the mouse to hide whatever was on the screen, even though from where he was standing McLean could only see the manufacturer's name emblazoned across the back.

'Ah. Morning, sir. I heard about the SCU. Thanks for the warning, by the way.'

'No reason you should have been dragged into it, but I reckoned Brooks wasn't going to let that stop him shouting at anyone who's ever spoken to me. Thought you'd be better somewhere else.'

'I was, actually. We found the missing teenager holed up at a mate's house in South Queensferry. How's the ghost squad coming along?'

It took McLean a moment to work out what MacBride was talking about. Then the name sank in. 'Ghost squad? Is that what they're calling us?' He was about to add what a rubbish name, then realised he actually quite liked it. 'That's not bad, really.'

'Can't be easy working with Dagwood, though.'

'We haven't come to blows yet. Early days, mind you.' McLean looked around the empty room. 'Quiet in here.'

'Aye. Carter's taken a load of DCs off to look into a break-in over in Grange. I managed to keep out of his way. Had to do this for DCI McIntyre anyway.' MacBride indicated the screen, which McLean still couldn't see.

'Any chance you could do me a favour while you're at it?'

MacBride didn't answer, which was the next best thing to saying yes.

'John Smith. The guy on the sex offenders' register. Can we access his tagging locator from here?'

MacBride reached for the mouse. 'Should be able to, sir. But I thought you weren't working the SCU any more.'

'It's . . .' McLean didn't quite know how to justify it. This was about as far from sanctioned use of police time and resources as he could get. Involving MacBride was a step closer to getting himself suspended or worse. 'I just wanted to see what he's been up to. Call it professional curiosity.'

The detective sergeant said nothing again. He didn't need to; his face was speaking volumes. All the same, he set about the task. McLean stepped around the desk so that he could see the screen and the various pages that came into view as MacBride brought up the relevant records.

'Here we go, sir. John Smith, Dockside Apartments. Tag appears to be active. He's at home.'

McLean looked at the data for a few moments before admitting to himself he had no idea what any of it meant.

'Is there a history of his movements over the past . . .' How long had it been since he and Ritchie had last seen Smith, when the tag was fitted? 'Week?'

'Let me see.' MacBride tapped away at the keyboard, swivelled the mouse around some more. The data on screen didn't seem to change appreciably. 'That's odd.'

'Odd? How so?'

'Well, the tag's active and doesn't appear to have been tampered with. Those things are sensitive. We'd know if he'd even tried to cut it off.'

'I'm sensing a "but" here, Stuart.'

'Well, he doesn't appear to have moved out of the flat for the past five days. Doesn't appear to have moved out of his bedroom.'

'Why are you even looking into Smith? He's strictly the SCU's business. Hardly an unsolved crime, either.'

McLean had called Ritchie as soon as MacBride had double-checked with the security firm that what he was seeing on the monitors for John Smith's tag was correct. Luckily for him, Jo Dexter was out of town, otherwise he was sure that the DCI would have been the next to know, and a lot less polite in her criticism. Instead, Ritchie had cadged a lift in a squad car from HQ over to the station to meet him. It was possible she had his best interests at heart and was trying to put him off doing something stupid, but he suspected she just wanted to get out for a bit.

'It's probably nothing, I was really only looking to find out where he was so I could have a quick chat with him about who invited him to the party.'

'Again with the question why, Tony? The case has been put to bed. Nothing's going to come of pestering Smith except maybe a formal complaint. You so keen to be busted down to sergeant when a DCI post is within reach?'

'I don't think it has been. Put to bed, that is. Oh, the DCC's got his report and the Fiscal's not going to pursue the matter any further, sure. But this isn't the sort of thing you can bury so easily. It's going to come back to bite us and I want to have all the facts to hand when it does.'

Ritchie rubbed at her eyes, pinching the bridge of her nose in a manner McLean had seen Jo Dexter do a hundred times or more. He knew he was pushing his luck, knew too that he could quite happily survive if he was sacked but others on the force didn't have the luxury of a wealthy inheritance.

'I'd go see him myself, not involve anyone else, but this data from his tag. It doesn't look right.'

'OK. We'll both go and pay him a visit. But it was my call all along and I only asked you to come with me because you were SIO when we arrested him.'

'Fine. Thanks.' McLean relaxed a little. This was how he'd intended justifying the visit anyway. Ritchie paused before answering, and for a moment he thought she was going to change her mind. Then she gave him a wicked smile.

'And we'll be taking your car, too.'

The residential blocks were part of the redevelopment of Leith Docks, tied into the government offices at Victoria Quay. Originally the trams had been intended to come all the way down here too, giving the civil servants easy access to the airport right on the other side of the city, but the financial mismanagement of the project meant that they stopped a good mile and a half short. The whole area was still under development, too, lending it a slightly seedy, unfinished air. One more victim of the financial crisis. It would be nice when it was finished, but McLean wondered whether it would have any soul. It was too far from the beating heart of the city, stuck out on the coast like a leper colony. Out of sight and out of mind.

And expensive. John Smith was obviously not short of a bob or two if he could afford to live in an apartment with a sea view. McLean couldn't remember what it was the man actually did for a living. It was probably somewhere in his file and he really should have checked. If Smith was a computer genius, then that might explain the failure of the tracking device.

'Still no answer from his mobile?' he asked as he pressed the buzzer for the main entry to the apartment block. Ritchie had been trying the number ever since they had left the station, her annoyance that McLean hadn't let her drive evident in the way she stabbed at the screen of her phone.

'Nothing. He's not answering the land line either.'

McLean studied the names on the buttons that operated the entry system. There was a camera too, so that whoever was inside could check before letting anyone in. Smith had still not answered, so he selected another flat at random, pressed that. A few seconds' delay and then an electronic click as the door unlocked. So much for security.

'I'm beginning to get a bad feeling about this,' Ritchie said as they climbed the stairs to the second floor. McLean cast his mind back to the last time they'd been here, when Smith's tag had been fitted, trying to see if anything had changed. There was an odd smell about the place, slightly sickly sweet as if someone had been spraying air freshener to cover something else.

'Want to call in some back-up?' he asked, but Ritchie gave no reply.

Four apartments opened on to the second-floor landing, two looking out across development land to the docks. No doubt soon another block of flats would sprout out of the ground, spoiling that vista, but the apartment Smith occupied had an uninterrupted sea view. Lovely at this time of year, perhaps less so in the depths of winter. McLean knocked on the door, the hollow sound echoing about the landing as he listened for noise of anything going on inside.

'Wasn't he due to report in this week anyway?'

'Not 'til tomorrow. I checked. Hearing's still a couple of months away, too.'

'So long? It's almost as if someone doesn't want this incident talked about at all.' McLean knocked again, then tried the door handle. It clicked open. Unlocked.

'Mr Smith?' He pushed the door wide, stepped into the hallway, wrinkled his nose at the stench. Something he'd smelled before, all too often. He remembered the layout of the apartment from his previous visit and pulled a pair of latex gloves out of his pocket as he stepped into the living room. The door was slightly ajar. Peering in, he saw a mess remarkably similar to how it had been before. The electronic control box for the tag sat on its table beside the phone, winking a gentle green light. There was no sign of Smith, though, and neither was he in the kitchen.

'Oh Christ. Over here, sir.' Ritchie stood across the hall by the door into the apartment's single bedroom.

'You don't have to call me sir, remember. We're the same rank.' McLean crossed to where she was standing, got a good look over her shoulder and wished he hadn't.

'Sorry. Force of habit.' Ritchie turned her back on the scene, pulling out her phone as she did so. 'You going to call it in or should I?'

'Probably best if you do.' McLean finished pulling his gloves on, took one step into the bedroom the better to see. Not that he particularly wanted to, and breathing wasn't easy either.

John Smith hung in the open doorway between the bedroom and its en-suite bathroom, held upright by what appeared to be a piece of lamp flex nailed to the door frame and tied around his neck. At first McLean thought he was wrapped in an old bin liner, but the more he looked the more he realised what he was seeing was actually some kind of latex body suit, rucked up over one leg to reveal the bulky electronic tag. Smith hadn't been a fat man, but the suit bulged alarmingly where his body had begun to swell with the trapped gases of decomposition. His head was uncovered, but he wore something that looked a bit like a dog's muzzle with a billiard ball in it, forcing his mouth open. Flecks of dried drool glittered on his chin and chest, dribbling down the smooth material to the party piece. Smith's flaccid member, protruding from a hole in the suit no doubt cut for that very reason, put McLean in mind of Eric Parker, and the idea that the two deaths could be somehow linked left a cold sensation in the pit of his stomach.

'Back-up's on its way. I think we'd better leave this to forensics, don't you?' Ritchie put a hand on his shoulder, though whether to stop him going further into the room or simply to ease the tension he couldn't tell. He turned his back on the sordid scene, nodded once, then followed her out of the apartment and on to the communal landing. Closing the door behind him, he took a deep breath of the fresher air.

'I told you this wasn't going to stay buried.'

'Auto-erotic asphyxiation. What a way to go, eh?'

McLean was back in Smith's bedroom, only this time he was dressed in the full Scene of Crime bunny suit and watching as Angus Cadwallader inspected the dead man.

'You reckon he did this to himself?'

'Well, there's nothing that immediately shouts to me that he had help. And the fact that he's dead suggests there wasn't anyone with him when it happened. I'd have thought your experience working with the Sexual Crimes Unit would have broadened your mind a bit, Tony. This is the preferred embarrassing death of rock stars, actors and politicians, you know.'

McLean knew his old friend was teasing him, but it didn't help much to be reminded of the SCU. It had taken the Scene of Crime team an hour to get there, Cadwallader a little longer, and McLean had spent the entire time trying to work out his justification for visiting Smith in the first place. It helped that Ritchie had come with him, but even so it wouldn't be long before someone asked him just what the hell he'd been doing there.

'So you reckon cause of death is strangulation, then?'

'Ah, you always ask. Next you'll be wanting to know when it happened. I can say probably, and at least four days. The rest will be revealed once we get him back to the examination theatre. Then this fellow will spill all his secrets. Provided we can get him down without him spilling them here.'

'You done examining him, then?'

'I think so, yes.' Cadwallader straightened up from where he had been inspecting the late John Smith's backside. 'I'll send some strong lads in to cut him down.'

McLean watched his old friend go, then looked around the bedroom, slowly taking everything in as the crime scene photographer's flashgun popped away. It was a good-size room for a change; most of these modern apartments had bedrooms barely big enough to stretch in. The bed itself was unmade, black silk sheets confirming most of what he already knew about the dead man. It stood against the wall at right angles to the bathroom door, the opposite wall taken up mostly by an enormous flat-panel television screen. As someone who rarely saw his bed for more than a couple of hours a night, McLean had never quite understood the appeal of having a television in the bedroom.

Behind the bed, two mirrored doors slid open to reveal a large walk-in wardrobe. Smith clearly hadn't been here long, as most of the drawers and hanging space were empty, just a bright yellow duffel bag on the floor. McLean crouched down, the gusset in the crotch of his bunny suit causing momentary anguish until he was able to adjust the waistband. The bag was unzipped, and opening it up revealed more latex gear, a couple of bottles of baby oil and a long black rod with wires coming out one end.

'Careful with that, sir. Wouldn't want to give yourself a shock.'

McLean turned and looked up into the face of the photographer. He recognised Amanda Parsons, the forensic scientist who more usually got all the shit jobs, or played around with cars. She smiled, pointed the camera at him and took a photograph. No doubt it would appear at Christmas in some humorous capacity or other. Detective Inspector McLean and his sex toys.

'You know what it is, Miss Parsons?'

'You don't? I thought you worked Vice.'

McLean decided it was best not to answer that.

'It's an E-stim. You plug it into that box there, adjust the intensity and then stick it where the sun doesn't shine. Very good for arthritis, I'm told. That and milking your prostate.'

'I'll take your word for it.' McLean stood back up again as a couple of white-suited officers came in, one carrying a rolled up body bag under his arm, the other with a small folded stepladder. It might have been a decent sized bedroom, but there were limits.

'I'll leave you lot to it then,' he said and beat a hasty retreat.

Outside in the hallway, Acting Detective Inspector Ritchie was busy telling everyone what to do. She saw him approaching and made a strange motion with her arm. Too late McLean realised That she was trying to warn him.

'What the fuck are you doing here, McLean?'

If it had been Spence, he could have just faced him down. Even Jo Dexter's wrath would have been short-lived before she found something useful for him to do. But finding Detective Superintendent Brooks standing in the open front door was not something McLean had prepared for mentally.

'Is there a problem with my being here, sir?' Go for the innocent approach, it might work.

'Too fucking right there is. This is an SCU matter and as

far as I recall you were removed from the SCU precisely because you couldn't keep your nose out of other officers' business.'

It had gone very quiet in John Smith's hallway, the collected police and forensics experts all staring at the two of them. There was no way McLean was going to get out of this without at least a severe reprimand, but he was damned if anyone else was going to take the rap.

'Were you aware that there was a dead man in the next room?' He swivelled slightly, pointing back in the direction of the bedroom.

Brooks looked at him, a puzzled expression on his fat face that made him look like the kid at school everyone bullies. 'What's that got to do with anything? Of course I was aware.'

'And were you aware that the circumstances of the man's death are suspicious?'

Brooks started to redden about the rolls of flesh that made up his neck, swelling from the tight confines of his collar. 'I'm here, aren't I? What the fuck do you think?'

'So perhaps you're aware that the dead man is also central to an investigation I was SIO on. An investigation I signed off just a few days ago because we thought it was closed and done with.'

'I don't know what the fuck you're trying to say, McLean. This is an SCU matter. You've no business—'

'I've every business, sir. This man was my responsibility and now he's dead. It would be remiss of me to not be involved. Don't you think?'

Brooks narrowed his eyes in suspicion, but McLean could see the doubt flickering across his face too. He looked around the hallway, noticing his audience for the first time.

'Haven't you lot got work to do?' he bellowed, scowling at them all until they scurried back to their tasks. At the same moment the two white-suited technicians came out of the bedroom, struggling under the weight of the body in its black body bag until they managed to drop it down on to a waiting gurney. Something made a wet popping noise and a stench rolled out across the room like a wave of garbage.

'Oh dear sweet hairy Jesus.' Brooks covered his mouth and nose with a pudgy hand, backed out of the door on to the landing beyond. McLean went to follow him, but the detective superintendent waved him back.

'No you don't, McLean. Your responsibility, right? Well, get on with it. And I expect a full report for me and the DCC on my desk by tomorrow morning.'

Brooks stalked off towards the stairs and McLean turned back to Ritchie, who was staring at him open-mouthed despite the foul smell.

'Well, I think that went better than expected.'

# 39

She's not nosey, not really. No one could accuse her of not respecting the privacy of her house guests. It's one of the cardinal rules of being a landlady; you don't go into their rooms when they're out, don't pry. Unless they're making too much noise, of course. Or coming and going at all hours when they know the front door's meant to be locked at eleven. She's heard them moving about the empty old house in the dead of night, doing things they shouldn't be doing. What if they're stealing the best china? Or the silver spoons? She's checked every morning, of course, but it's the time you don't check that they're gone. No, she has to have words. It doesn't matter about their references. They were told the rules when they came.

The stairs are longer and steeper than she remembers. Strange to think how long she's lived in this house and never felt that before. She has to pause on the second landing, at the bottom of the narrow stairs up to the attic rooms. To catch her breath, you understand. Not to listen for low voices muttering in conspiracy. Of course not.

They had seemed such a nice pair, too. Polite and well-spoken. She had a kind face and he was quiet but helpful. Brother and sister. Twins, if you could believe that. Down from the country on some business or other. And of course they had the right references. Perhaps she should have expected something, given who had sent them. What had sent them.

She pauses on the stairs, halfway up. From here she can see that the door to their room is ajar, noises of conversation filtering out. A few more steps up and her old ears tell her it's not conversation but a low moaning sound. A couple more steps and she can see through the open door.

It takes her a moment to work out what is going on. The woman is sitting on one of the twin beds, back to the door and naked as the day she was born. Her skin is very pale and covered in tiny, livid flecks of scars. Her brother stands beside her, leaning in close. He has a knife and is cutting her skin with the delicacy of a skilled carver, mopping up the blood with a white handkerchief as he goes. With each cut, she lets out a moan, her shoulders shuddering at the pain.

And then, with a slow inevitability, she looks around.

'Oh, hello there.' Her smile is all teeth, her eyes two black pits. 'Why don't you come and join us?'

# 40

It took the rest of the day for McLean to escape the apartment down on the waterfront. Further investigation of the rooms had turned up some more sex toys and a collection of pornography that made his eyes water, and that was just looking at the covers. Even after the body had been removed to the mortuary, the whole apartment had to be checked to make sure that Smith had been alone when he died. The call came in from Control mid-afternoon officially assigning him the case, not long after the letting agent had turned up. A smartly dressed young woman, she had been horrified to find her immaculate serviced apartments swarming with police and forensics experts, but had confirmed the other three apartments on that floor were currently empty. McLean had sent a couple of constables to do door to door around the rest of the building, but he didn't hold out much hope of finding anything untoward. Everything pointed to a pathetic end to a life that nobody would mourn passing. Only his gut told him there was more to the case than met the eye.

He had spent the rest of the day waiting for the instruction to wrap everything up neatly and close things down, but it never came. McLean knew it would, sooner or later, so stayed on site to supervise the forensic examination personally. It wasn't until the last white-suited technician had packed up and left that he locked the front door himself with the key they'd found in the pocket of Smith's discarded trousers and drove straight home.

Ritchie had gone hours earlier, insisting she needed a shower to take the stench away, and a stiff drink to blur the mental images that would linger far longer than they were welcome. McLean could hardly blame her; he felt the siren call of hot water and a whole bar of smelly soap too. And if he was lucky Phil wouldn't have found the hidden stocks of whisky.

Jenny's little black car was parked outside the front door when he arrived home. McLean wasn't quite sure how he felt about that. It had been a long and harrowing day and normally he would have dealt with it by staring at the wall while the house grew ever more silent around him, or possibly while whatever music he'd been listening to morphed into the hiss thunk hiss thunk of the needle circling the innermost groove. A psychiatrist would probably have told him he spent an unhealthy amount of time in his own company, and he had to admit they'd probably be right.

Entering by the back door, he was greeted by the smell of cooking. Something spicy and aromatic that was clearly the equal of anything the takeaway might have had to offer. He'd not really had any appetite for food, the smell of John Smith's rotting body still clinging to him like body odour to a teenage boy. Now his stomach gurgled in anticipation, reminding him that it had been neglected since breakfast and that had hardly been much.

'Oh, hi, Tony. Wasn't sure when you'd be in. I made a big pot of curry for Rae and Phil. Reckoned there'd be plenty to spare. Hope you don't mind.'

'If there's a cold beer to go with it, I could kiss you,' he said without thinking. Jenny's blush most likely mirrored his own. She turned swiftly back to the pot on the stove, stirring furiously. It didn't take a genius to see that he'd touched a nerve. 'I expect Phil's drunk it all anyway,' he added quickly.

'Actually, probably not.' Jenny stopped stirring, but still kept her eyes on the pot. 'Changing a nappy with a hang-over's something you only want to do once.'

'I'll take your word for it.' McLean dumped his case on a chair. 'It wasn't something I was planning on ever trying out.'

This time Jenny stopped stirring, turned to face him. 'Really? Never fancied having children?'

He paused before answering, unsure whether he was comfortable with the way the conversation had turned. 'There was a time, years ago. I think it's probably a bit late for me now. And the hours I work.'

'Ah well. You can always be Uncle Tony in your spare time. Now, let me get you that beer.' Jenny pushed herself away from the Aga, heading for the fridge. 'Supper's pretty much ready, so you've timed it just right.'

'Not quite.' McLean shrugged his shoulders, pulling at the lapels of his jacket. The stench still clung to the fabric, or at least he felt like it did. 'I've spent all day at a particu-larly unpleasant crime scene. I badly need a shower.'

Once he had washed, changed clothes and shoved all his dirty laundry into a plastic bag so that the smell was con-tained, McLean returned to the kitchen to find Phil and Rachel seated at the table, places laid out for all four of them. Jenny's culinary skills proved to be most acceptable, the curry far better than the cheap takeaways that had been his staple diet for so long. Eating in the kitchen reminded him of days long past when he and Phil had relied on his grandmother's hospitality to help eke out their student finances. Something about having more company than just Mrs McCutcheon's cat helped to ease the stresses of the day. There was good conversation, no mention of his police work, and for a moment he was able to completely forget about the bloated, rotting corpse of John Smith, Heather Marchmont's strange advances, Jo Dalgliesh lying in a hospital bed and all the other things that were making his life so complicated at the moment.

Supper over, they all moved through to the library, Phil cradling the same glass of beer he'd been sipping at all evening, still only half-empty. Out of habit, McLean went straight to the drinks cabinet artfully hidden in one of the bookcases, fetching out a bottle of whisky that appeared to be as full as it had been the last time he'd seen it.

'Think I'll give it a miss,' Phil said to the offer of a dram, earning himself a smile and a pat on the arm from his wife. He was still sleeping in one of the other spare rooms, but it seemed the relationship was coming back together.

'What about you, Jenny?' McLean held up the bottle by its neck, sloshing the amber liquid around inside it.

'I can't. My car.'

McLean was about to make a comment about it being her loss, but Phil interrupted.

'Go on, Jen. You can get a cab home. Rae'll bring the car over when she comes to visit with young Tony Junior tomorrow.'

Jenny seemed to take a little too long to decide. Had he been interrogating her, McLean might have thought she was putting on an act.

'Maybe just a small one,' she said finally. 'Plenty of water.'

He did the honours, settling into his favourite armchair as Jenny sat demurely in the other one. Rachel and Phil were already on the sofa and by the look of them both would be asleep before long.

'It's been a while since this house had anyone in it, aside from me and the cat.' McLean looked around, half expecting to see the beast lying by the empty fireplace. At this stage of the evening, had he been alone, she would have wandered in, maybe prowled around the room a bit before finally curling up and going to sleep just far enough away from him to be aloof. 'Actually, where is the cat?'

'Probably asleep in little Tony's room,' Jenny said. 'She seems to spend a lot of time shadowing the cot. Almost as if she's protecting him.'

McLean thought back to the last house guest he'd welcomed in. Madame Rose and her feline army hadn't stayed long, but it had been a memorable time. Before that there had been dozens of the animals prowling his gardens, warding off anything untoward that might come his way. And behind them all the elderly black rescue moggie keeping her eye on him. Keeping him from harm.

'Never really had you pegged as a cat person, though, Tony. I see you more as a terrier man.'

'As an owner, or just because I won't let something go once I've got it in my teeth?' He raised his glass in mock salute, took a small sip.

'A bit of both, I guess.'

'Gran always had one or two cats around, but when I lived in Newington I didn't think it would be fair. Top-floor flat – I could hardly let it out if I had one. The hallway smelled bad enough without having a litter tray in the bathroom as well. And besides, I'm hardly ever in anyway.'

'So why this one? Was she your gran's? I never quite caught her name, either.'

McLean couldn't help himself from grinning. 'Didn't know you hadn't heard the story. I don't think she's got a name. Just "Mrs McCutcheon's cat". That's all anyone ever calls her these days. I rescued her – no, that's not right. She belonged to the old lady who lived on the ground floor of the tenement block. Adopted me when it burned down. She and I were the only survivors, as far as I can tell. To be honest I didn't even know she was a she until Emma mentioned it. And then the vet confirmed it when I took her in for her first check-up.'

Phil let out a loud snore at that moment. So loud indeed that McLean thought he was pretending, but then he slumped deeper into the sofa, nestling up against an equally comatose Rachel.

'I should really go.' Jenny placed her barely touched glass of whisky down on the table, stood up. McLean copied her.

'You sure?' he asked. He couldn't help thinking it hadn't been Phil's snore that had spoiled the moment so much as the mention of Emma's name.

'Lots to do tomorrow. Chloe's gone back up to Aberdeen, so it's just me in the shop. I'll need to get everything sorted before Rae turns up too. She's chaos personified.'

Jenny edged towards the door as she spoke, perhaps trying not to wake the sleeping couple, perhaps just keen to get away.

'I had noticed.' McLean followed her out, flicked on the hall light as they both headed towards the front door. A small pile of letters awaited him on the wooden chest in the porch but he ignored them. They'd only be bills and offers of timeshare holidays after all.

'This evening. It's been fun.' Jenny opened the front door, letting cool night air spill into the hall.

'It has. Yes. I'd almost forgotten what that was.' McLean followed her out on to the driveway and over to the little black car. 'Thanks.'

'We should do it again sometime, maybe.'

'That would be nice. Perhaps when the young parents are a bit more sociable.'

'Or maybe when they've a place of their own?' Jenny leaned close, gave him a light kiss on the cheek. McLean felt a moment's panicked embarrassment, and then she was walking around the car, clicking the lock, clambering in. He stepped away as she backed and filled to turn around, and then with a nonchalant wave she was gone.

He stood for a while, feeling the breeze on his face, the lingering scent of her perfume, and then something twined about his legs, nearly sending him flying.

'Bloody cat. You'll be the death of me, you know.'

Mrs McCutcheon's cat looked up at him once, then sauntered back in through the open front door. McLean followed her, scooping up the pile of letters as he passed. Back in the library, Rachel and Phil were still fast asleep, so he quietly retrieved both whisky glasses, pouring Jenny's into his own before retreating to the warmth of the kitchen. Only once he'd settled down at the table did he take up the pile of letters, leafing through them with the familiar mixture of hope and a certainty that it would be dashed.

# 41

'Subject is male, Caucasian, five foot eleven and a half. Discovered hanging by a ligature made from electrical flex. Initial examination suggests death by asphyxiation. Most likely self-inflicted and accidental, but we'll have a closer look, won't we?'

Bright and early, McLean found himself in the familiar surroundings of the examination theatre in the city mortuary. John Smith's bloated, discoloured body was laid out on the stainless steel table in all its glory. Shorn of its protective black latex sheath, his mottled skin bulged in strange places. His hands, lying by his side, were bloated and dark His feet too, squeezed out of shape by the pressure of fluids and gases building up inside. Looking at him, it was hard to reconcile this with the arrogant man they had busted in the brothel raid. The man who had moaned about his electronic tag as if he felt his behaviour warranted no more than a slap on the wrist.

Cadwallader worked his methodical way around the body, dictating notes as he went. He spent a long time examining the marks around Smith's neck, longer still on his hands, no doubt looking for any signs of struggle or coercion. Finally he turned his attention to the flaccid penis, lifting it up with a probe and peering perhaps more closely than was polite.

'A swab please, Tracy.'

He waited until his assistant handed it over, taking his time to run it over the hairy flesh at the base of the dead man's stomach.

'People use the oddest things as lubricants,' he said by way of explanation as Doctor Sharp presented a sample jar for the swab to be dropped into. 'This looks like dried saliva to me. Quite possibly his, only I didn't see anything on either of his hands.' Cadwallader picked up first one, then the other, checking the palms again. McLean leaned forward, expecting to see hair growing out of them.

'No, nothing. So either he washed them, or, well . . . We'll see.'

The pathologist returned to his examination, oddly fascinated by Smith's genitals. Or so it seemed to McLean.

'Give me a hand, will you, Tracy. I think we need to turn him over.'

McLean took a couple of steps back as the pair of them rolled the body expertly on to his side. Given the swelling, he had a horrible feeling Mr Smith might burst at any moment and he really didn't want to have to get yet another suit cleaned.

'Just hold him there a minute.' Cadwallader fetched some evil-looking tongs as Tracy held the body, then he set about Smith's backside with enthusiasm, tugging and tweaking at something McLean thankfully couldn't see. And then with a horrible farting noise, accompanied by a smell with which even the industrial strength extraction system in the examination theatre would struggle, the pathologist took a heavy step back.

'Well, there's something you don't see every day. Even in my line of work. Can't see how I missed it back at the scene, although to be fair it was lodged impressively far up.'

McLean sidled around the examination table, keeping his distance and trying hard not to breathe.

'You can let him down now, Tracy,' Cadwallader said. 'Poor chap probably needs a rest.'

'What . . . ?' McLean began to ask, then saw what the pathologist was holding, gripped in his stainless steel tongs and smeared liberally with blood and shit.

'I believe the technical term is a butt plug? Metal, I think. It weighs a ton.' Cadwallader waved the offending article around a bit, then deposited it on a specimen tray. It clanked heavily as he released it. 'Don't think I've ever seen one so big before.'

McLean was still trying to get the image out of his head hours later, bombarding it with the dull monotony of processing paperwork. But every time he stopped for a moment or scribbled a question mark beside some particularly creative overtime claim, the noise played over in his head and that heavy, metal object reappeared from Smith's arse. Quite apart from the depravity, no, the madness – how had he got it up there? – it was deeply uncomfortable just to think about and he found himself squirming on his chair, clenching.

The shrill electronic warble of his phone was a welcome distraction. McLean scrambled to find it, buried under a pile of papers, briefly seeing a number on the screen that he didn't recognise. He thumbed the accept icon anyway, grateful for anything to take his mind off John Smith and his ignominious ending.

'McLean.'

'Inspector. Tony. Can I call you Tony?'

'I rather think you just did, Miss Marchmont.'

'Heather. Please. I wanted to apologise for yesterday morning. You didn't catch me at my best.'

McLean took the handset away from his ear a moment, looking at the number. It was a mobile, but not the one he had programmed into his phone's memory. Was she using someone else's phone? Or had she picked up a new one just to call him? What did they call it, a burner phone?

'I got the feeling you were warning me off, Miss – Heather. Much like everyone else. Perhaps I should take the hint.'

'From what I've heard, that's not your style.'

McLean leaned back in his chair, looked around the tiny office half expecting to see a surveillance camera hidden in one of the sagging ceiling tiles. Or maybe waiting for the DCC and his cronies to come bustling in and ask him what the fuck he thought he was doing. He remembered the feeling all too well from school; that indefinable sense that he was doing something wrong and was going to get into deep trouble, even though he had no idea what or why.

'Have you been asking about me behind my back?'

'I'm sorry. I needed to know. That you could be trusted. That you weren't like all the rest of them.'

Now he was sure he was being wound up. 'Miss Marchmont. Heather. I'm not sure who you think I am, or what you think I can do for you. But I'm starting to get a little tired of the half-truths, the suggestions. You keep leading me on and then running away. What is it you actually want?'

The line was silent for so long McLean thought she

310

might have hung up. Not that there was actually a line, or a means to hang up. He knew from years of interviewing suspects that sometimes people just needed the space and the silence, the time to build up their courage enough to speak. And she'd phoned him, so it wasn't even as if he was paying for the call. He began counting slowly in his head, reached twenty before she broke.

'I want you to help me escape. Like you did before.'

'Like I did . . . What are you talking about, Heather? When did I help you before?'

'I can't . . . I've said too much already. They'll know. Tony, you have to be careful. They'll try to turn you. Make you one of their own. I don't want that to happen. Not to you.'

'But you want my help. How am I supposed to help you if you won't speak to me? Won't tell me what this is all about?'

'I . . . Just need to find somewhere safe. Not the cafe, they know about that now. Not on the phone. They'll be monitoring that too. Perhaps you could come round to the house?'

McLean almost laughed, then remembered who he was talking to.

'That wouldn't exactly be appropriate. Not after what happened there. And besides, if they're watching the cafe, surely they'll be watching your house?'

'Perhaps I could come to yours then?'

'Again, hardly appropriate. And I have house guests at the moment.'

'Is there nowhere we can meet? Or are you just trying to avoid me?'

McLean stared at the wall opposite, unsure quite what to say. Unsure why he wasn't arresting Marchmont for wasting police time. Or possibly stalking.

'I'm not trying to avoid you, Heather. I'm trying to help. Just let me know what it is you want from me.'

There was no answer, again. And then he felt a change in the tone of the silence coming down the line, knew that Marchmont was gone. He looked at the screen, wondered whether he should call back. Perhaps they could find somewhere to meet, but then what? She would lead him on, then stop short of saying what he really needed to know. Where had they met before? What had he done for her? And how was it he couldn't remember?

Shaking his head, he slipped the phone into his jacket pocket, looked at the paperwork he'd been burying himself in. It wasn't anything like as interesting now; he needed something else to take his mind off John Smith's backside.

It wasn't really on his way home, even McLean had to admit. Perhaps if he'd still been stationed at HQ and working for the SCU it might have made sense, but driving right across town to the Western General through the late afternoon traffic was a stupid thing to do. Going there to visit a journalist who only a few years ago he would have happily seen rot in hell was a surprise even to him. It wasn't until he was parked and walking into the building that he realised he could just have easily called. What if she was still unconscious?

'Afternoon, Tony.' Jeannie Robertson greeted him at the ICU admin desk. It wasn't strictly visiting hours, but most of the nursing staff knew him well enough to let him get away with it.

'Good evening, Jeannie. Is she awake?' He cocked his head in the direction of the ward.

'Dalgliesh? Well, sort of.' The nurse struggled with a heavy brown folder that made the paperwork on McLean's desk look amateur by comparison. 'The swelling on her brain's down, and they've stopped the drug therapy so she's coming back out. It's early days, though. She's not exactly lucid.'

'Could I see her?' McLean asked, then heard what the nurse had told him. 'Wait. Swelling on her brain? I thought she was in anaphylactic shock.'

'Aye, that was the trigger. You'll need to talk to the surgeon about it, but there were complications. For a while we thought we might lose her.'

'I didn't realise it was that bad.' McLean rubbed at his face, trying to force this new information into his tired brain. 'Is she going to be OK? I mean, will she make a full recovery?'

'Your guess is as good as mine. You've talked to Doctor Wheeler enough. You know what it's like with brain injuries. She might be fine, might have suffered irreparable damage. We're leaning towards the former. MRI scans are good.'

'And they still reckon it was an allergic reaction to something she ate?' McLean looked back at the closed doors to the intensive care ward, wondering if he really wanted to go in there now.

'That's the best guess. She a friend of yours? Only no one else has been asking for her, let alone come to visit.'

McLean was surprised by the question. Not so much in

itself as that he really didn't know how to answer it. Had he changed so much? Had Dalgliesh?

'Let's just say our paths often cross.' He thought of the meeting in the cafe, the coffee and cake. 'And I feel a certain responsibility.'

Nurse Robertson ducked down behind the admin desk for a moment, then stood up again and handed something to McLean. 'In that case you can give her this. When she wakes up properly.'

He held the slim plastic tube up, the better to see the writing and simple pictograms printed around its circumference.

'You know how to use it?' the nurse asked.

'An EpiPen?' McLean remembered endless First Aid training sessions stretching back years. He was probably overdue a refresher. 'Yes, but it's been a while.'

'They're pretty idiot-proof, really.' Nurse Robertson smiled. 'Need to be, with people like your friend Dalgliesh there.'

# 42

'What on earth are you doing here, Tony?'

McLean was walking slowly back to the hospital entrance, Jeannie Robertson's strange present in his jacket pocket, when a familiar voice pulled him up short. Turning, he saw DCI McIntyre standing by a ward door she had clearly just closed behind her.

'Could say the same for you, ma'am.'

'Don't you "Ma'am" me. It was bad enough when you were a sergeant.' She smiled at him, but McLean could see worry lines on her face.

'Everything OK?'

'Not really. Just been visiting Lucy. Chemo's a bastard sometimes.'

'I'm sorry. I had no idea. Is this a recent thing?'

McIntyre started walking and McLean fell in beside her. He'd met the DCI's partner once, not long after the news had broken out in the station that she'd left her husband of fifteen years for a woman. Having met her husband a few times before, he couldn't help thinking McIntyre had made the right choice.

'Routine scan a couple months ago, came up with a lump in her right breast. They hope they've got it under control, but it's not easy.'

'I can imagine. I'm so sorry. Not sure what else I can say but best of luck.'

McIntyre stopped in her tracks. 'You won't breathe a word of this to anyone at the station, will you, Tony?'

'Of course not. I wouldn't dream of it.'

'No. No, you wouldn't, would you?' She started walking again, a little more swiftly this time. 'So what brings you to this sorry place? Chatting up one of the nurses?'

'Ha. No.' Unbidden, an image of Nurse Robertson flashed across his mind. 'No, I was checking up on Jo Dalgliesh.'

McIntyre stopped so suddenly this time that McLean was a couple of paces on before he realised.

'You what?'

'Dalgliesh. The journalist. She ate something that disagreed with her.' McLean filled McIntyre in on the details, seeing the weary smile fade to something like astonishment.

'Why on earth would you care? Surely you'd be making plans for the funeral after what she did to you. That book about Donald Anderson.'

'You'd think that, wouldn't you? But, I don't know. I guess I'm not as good at holding a grudge as I used to be. And she did save me from that nutter back in the spring.'

McIntyre cocked her head slightly to one side, like a dog watching its owner being stupid. 'There's more to it than that though, isn't there? I've known you long enough, Tony.'

'Well, I suppose I feel a certain degree of responsibility. She ate the cake that was meant for me, after all. Two slices of it.'

'So she has an allergy and she's an idiot. That doesn't make you responsible for her.'

'It's not that, Jayne. She wasn't carrying anything, and I

don't ever remember her even mentioning allergies. Something like that, as bad as that, it'd be the first thing you mentioned, surely. In a situation like that. And who with a nut allergy scoffs two large portions of walnut cake?'

McIntyre frowned. 'It does sound a bit odd. So what, you think it wasn't an allergic reaction? You think the cake was poisoned?' The look on her face suggested it was far-fetched, and McLean had to admit she had a point.

'It's probably not the cake at all. Nothing to do with me either. It just seems . . . odd.'

'And odd is your stock in trade. Well, I'd suggest you speak to her colleagues, maybe her GP. Find out if your new best friend is just very stupid before you leap to con-clusions.'

'Aye, you're right. I've let things get to me a bit recently. Not enough sleep and all that stuff.'

'Oh aye? That nurse of yours keeping you up?'

'Ah, you're worse than bloody Phil with the innuendoes. No, I've house guests and one of them just had a baby boy. His lungs are surprisingly well developed.'

'You have my sympathies then.' McIntyre patted him gently on the arm, then left him standing in the entrance hall. He watched her walk out into the falling night and wondered why he hadn't spoken to her about it all before.

Traffic was worse as McLean headed back across town the way he had come earlier, the evening rush hour spilling everyone out of their offices and into the long slog home. The little Alfa was a noisy cocoon, far less cosseting than the modern pool cars he occasionally managed to use. Even the more modern Alfa GT he had bought when it had been away for repairs had been more comfortable over the potholes and cobbles that made up the bulk of the city's streets, the Bentley that had been the catalyst for that purchase yet more comfortable still. Just a pity the GT had ended up under part of Rosskettle Psychiatric Hospital.

The offices of the *Edinburgh Tribune* had relocated from the modern, purpose-built block down near Holyrood and the parliament building, part of a cost-cutting exercise that seemed to be working its way through all of the media as the internet drove down the price people were prepared to pay for news. Now the few remaining journalists worked out of a couple of rooms in a refurbished old tenement, mostly populated by start-up technology firms and other suchlike hopefuls of the new age. In different circumstances, McLean could have relied on Dalgliesh being there, peering myopically at her computer screen as she tapped out some sensationalist version of an otherwise dull story for tomorrow's late edition. He just hoped that at least one of her colleagues was as diligent. If she had any colleagues left.

At least getting in wasn't difficult. The front door was unlocked, a reception desk in the narrow hallway unstaffed. McLean glanced at the list of companies on the noticeboard, hoping that it reflected their physical position within the building, then headed for the narrow stairs. He found the offices of the *Tribune* just off the first landing, compressed into a room not much bigger than his library. Most of the desks were empty, but a bleary-eyed man looked up at him, face washed pale by the reflected light of his computer screen.

'Here, you can't just . . . Oh. It's you.'

The man hurriedly stood, knocking a sheaf of papers to the floor as he sidled around the desk and came across the room, cursing lightly under his breath as he did so. McLean knew all too well how he felt.

'Not sure if we've met before. I'm Johnny Bairstow. I take it this is about Jo?'

McLean recognised the man's voice from his phone conversation, but the face didn't fit what he had been expecting. Bairstow was young, for one thing, not yet out of his twenties if McLean was any judge. A dark shadow of stubble fringed his chin and cheeks as if he'd shaved the day before and not been to bed since. The state of his clothing and general air of a man on the edge only reinforced the image.

'I just stopped by the hospital. Spoke to one of the nurses.'

'You did?' Bairstow's eyebrows shot up in surprise. 'How is she?'

'Still unconscious. They're bringing her out slowly, apparently. Something to do with swelling on the brain. Wouldn't have thought it possible, but there you go.'

'It's a bloody nightmare, you know? Hard enough running a paper on the budget they give us, but lose my senior reporter?' Bairstow leaned against the nearest desk like a man whose legs have given up the ghost. He was very thin, probably ran ultra marathons for fun or something equally ridiculous. Still, McLean felt sympathy for him. He knew all too well what it was like trying to work with no budget and an almost non-existent team.

'I'll not waste any of your time then. Just had a couple of questions really.'

'Oh aye? The police looking into her collapse? Something suspicious about it?'

McLean mentally kicked himself for forgetting that Bairstow was a journalist, even if he was in editorial. 'Not the police, no. Not unless she dies.'

'Christ, you don't think it'll come to that, do you?'

'Jo Dalgliesh? Killed by a slice of cake? No. She's far too stubborn.'

'Cake?'

'That's what I stopped by to ask you. Everyone seems to think she reacted badly to something she ate. The only thing I can think of is the walnut cake she had in the cafe where we met that morning. Did you know she was allergic to nuts?'

This time Bairstow's mouth opened and hung there for a while as his brain tried to think of something to say. 'Nuts? But that's not possible.'

'She hadn't told anyone? Seems a bit daft to me.'

'No. It's not that.' Bairstow pushed himself away from the desk, walked around it until he was on the business side, pulled open one of the drawers and dragged out a bag. 'This is where Jo works when she's in. Not allowed to smoke in here and she hates nicotine gum. So she chews on these instead. Always joking that it's healthy.'

McLean looked more closely at the bag, recognising the label of a nearby health food store.

One kilogram of mixed nuts.


It was still just about light when McLean finally made it home after what felt like an unreasonably long day. No sign of Jenny's little black car, and when he walked into the kitchen, Mrs McCutcheon's cat stared up at him from her customary spot in the middle of the wide wooden table. Something about the air of the place, and that simple act of defiance, left him certain that the house was otherwise unoccupied. He vaguely remembered some muttered conversation about Rachel and Phil going out for the evening, but even so he was surprised young Tony Junior hadn't forced them back home by now. Unless he was staying over at his aunt's, he supposed.

'Just you and me then,' he said to the cat. She ignored him as usual.

One bonus of having guests was that there tended to be more food in the house than normal. Phil had begun to learn the hard truths of fatherhood too, and wasn't hammering the beer supplies as heavily as he might have done in the past. All of which meant McLean managed to find himself some supper without having to resort to the stack of takeaway delivery leaflets pinned to the noticeboard by the phone. He leafed through the post as he ate, still vainly hoping for a postcard from Emma, then finally tidied away his plates and went through to the library with a mug of tea and the preliminary report notes for the Pentland Mummy case. Nothing like a little light reading before bed.

He had hardly started reading when Mrs McCutcheon's cat came in and began prowling around the room. He watched her for a while, realising that he'd missed her company. She was halfway across the rug when she stopped suddenly, arching her back and fluffing out her tail in a manner that might have been impressive were she not so threadbare. She stared at the door to the hall as if a ghost were there, and then a few seconds later the doorbell rang.

McLean shoved the report back in his briefcase, went to answer the door. He had heard no car, which meant whoever was outside had most likely walked and was probably a local. Maybe even Mary Currie, the minister. He'd not spoken to her in a while. A quick glance at his watch showed it was well past the hour his grandmother would have considered late for receiving visitors, but it was always possible Phil and Rachel had just lost their keys.

'Umm . . . Inspector . . . Tony. I'm sorry. I really shouldn't have. Didn't know where to turn.'

Not Phil and Rachel. Standing on the doorstep, clutching a small canvas bag, the small, waif-like figure of Heather Marchmont.

# 43

'I should probably ask how it is you know where I live, but I'm guessing that's not a difficult thing for someone like you to find out.'

McLean leaned against the Aga, Heather Marchmont sitting at the kitchen table. It had seemed the best place to bring her, even though a part of him just wanted to call a cab to take her back home.

'I'm sorry. I know I shouldn't have come. It's just, I didn't know where to turn any more.' She sat like an embarrassed teenager, upright and with her bag clutched in both hands, sitting on her lap. She hadn't taken her coat off, which he hoped meant she wasn't planning on staying long. There was something altogether too unsettling about the way she looked at him. A desperate hunger in her eyes, or was it just his imagination?

'If someone's threatening you, you really should report it to the police.' McLean turned his back on her as he heard the kettle come to the boil. He set about pouring water into mugs, looking for milk and biscuits.

'It's not that.' Marchmont paused a while as if trying to work out what to say next. 'I had a visit today, from an old . . . well, I wouldn't exactly say friend. More an acquaintance. Someone I was close to a long time ago but haven't seen in a while.'

'School friend?' McLean placed a mug of tea in front of

Marchmont. She looked at it, but didn't move her hands from her bag.

'You could call it that. School. I guess. I certainly learned a great deal there.'

'So what did this school friend of yours tell you that prompted you to come round here?' McLean pulled out the chair opposite Marchmont and sat down. No sooner had he done so than Mrs McCutcheon's cat leapt up on to the table. Marchmont flinched.

'Oh. You have a cat.'

'Not sure she would agree. She tolerates me.'

'How old is she? She looks old.'

'I've no idea. She belonged to an old lady who lived in my tenement block, down Newington way. It burned down a couple of years back. Me and Mrs McCutcheon's cat were the only survivors. That's probably why we stuck together.'

Marchmont slowly took one hand off her bag and held it out for the cat to sniff. The movement shifted the collar of her coat, revealing something black beneath. Whatever she was wearing, it was very smooth, and clung to her like a second skin. The cat stood, stretched, then cautiously sniffed the proffered hand, rubbed the side of her face against a finger.

'She likes you,' McLean said.

'I like cats. Alice never did, though, so we never had them.'

'Alice?'

'My friend. Well, acquaintance. The one I saw today. I thought I'd left that place behind, but you can never really do that, can you? Never really escape.'

McLean picked up his mug and took a sip of tea. There was something ever so slightly mesmeric about Marchmont's

324

voice. He'd not noticed before, but her scent was beginning to fill the room too, overcoming the more usual smells of cooked food, spilled milk gone sour and cat litter needing to be changed. Sooner or later she would get round to the point, but for now he was happy enough to let her take her time.

'She reminded me of who I am. What I'm supposed to be doing. What I owed them, and what I owe you.'

Marchmont stood up swiftly, Mrs McCutcheon's cat leaping away in surprise. She put her bag down on the table and shrugged off her coat. She wore a one-piece bodysuit made from the same shiny black material that he'd seen in Stacey Craig's wardrobe. It hugged so tight to her that it looked almost like it had been painted on to her bare skin, and it creaked and stretched as she walked purposefully around the table to where he sat. He had always imagined her thin, but the latex gave her unexpected curves, hugging her long legs, accentuating her hips and the slight swell of her belly as she straddled him. McLean found himself trapped, unable to push back his chair and stand up before she was upon him.

'Please, Heather. This isn't—'

'Shh.' She silenced him with a single finger to the lips, followed it up with a kiss that was almost violent. He struggled to extricate himself, but her hands were everywhere, the shiny black material slippery and difficult to grasp. That intoxicating scent made it hard to think straight as her long black hair swept over his face, smothering the last of his resistance. It had been a harrowing day, a long month, difficult years. There was nothing wrong in seeking solace like this, surely? No harm in a little fun.

And then a noise in the distance broke the spell. Marchmont stiffened, broke away, her eyes furious as she glared past McLean towards the back door. Half-crouched, she looked very much like a cat deciding whether to defend its kill or run.

'Ah. Well. This is awkward.'

McLean twisted round in his chair, unsure if he could, or should, get up right now. Phil stood frozen in the open doorway, holding the baby car seat with young Tony Junior fast asleep inside. Behind him, Rachel was pulling the back door closed, blissfully unaware of what was unfolding in the kitchen.

'It's not what you . . . Ah, hell. Who am I kidding? Phil, this is Heather Marchmont. Heather, Phil Jenkins.'

Marchmont moved with a fluid grace back around the table to where her coat lay draped over the back of her chair. She seemed very different to the shy, slightly clumsy young woman in the cafe as she slid it back on. By the time Rachel nudged her open-mouthed husband out of the way and stepped into the kitchen, she was once more sitting down, hands clasping her bag like a regular at Jenner's Tea Rooms. Prim and proper. The scent that had filled the kitchen had gone too, as if she had sucked it all back inside her.

'Out the way, Phil. You're blocking the doorway. Oh.' Rachel stopped mid-shove as she noticed Marchmont. 'Didn't realise you had company. Hello.'

It was, McLean had to admit, an awkward mug of tea. Marchmont changed in an instant from the uninhibited creature back to the demure, slightly shy and vulnerable person he had first met. It was hard to meet her eye, knowing what she wore under her coat. Phil, too, seemed to find it difficult to know what to say. Only Rachel, who had missed it all before, behaved as might be expected.

'I'm Rachel,' she said, holding out a hand to be shaken. 'Do you work with Tony?'

'I . . .' Marchmont froze for a moment. 'I'm Heather. And no. Not directly, anyway. I've been helping him with a case.'

'How exciting. He never tells us anything about what he's working on. Says it's either too grucsome or too boring.'

Marchmont's gaze flicked momentarily from Rachel to McLean and then back again. 'I'm sure there's a lot he just can't tell you at all. The law's like that sometimes.'

'Oh, you're a lawyer, are you?'

'Commercial law, yes. Company contracts and dull stuff like that. I know enough about the criminal side of things, though.'

'Is the kettle long boiled? I'd kill for a cuppa.' Rachel turned her attention back to McLean. Enough time had passed that he thought it would be safe to stand, so he set about the task, glad of something to do.

'I should probably be getting home,' Marchmont said, clutching her bag tightly to her as if it were filled with gold. Or maybe the source of that heady scent, overpowered now by the smell of newly filled nappy.

'Can I call a taxi for you?' McLean asked at the same time as Phil said, 'Oops, looks like Tony's dropped a fresh one.'

Marchmont frowned, looking from one man to the other. 'Tony?'

'Young Anthony Junior.' Phil bent down over the car

seat and lifted out his infant son. 'I do apologise, but he's not house trained yet. Probably best if I deal with this back in the laundry.' He hefted the baby on to his shoulder and headed out the door. McLean couldn't help noticing the look on Marchmont's face as they went. Part wonder, part terror.

'There you go, Rae.' He plopped a mug down on the table, turned to Marchmont. 'You want that taxi?'

'I . . . A baby . . .' She stood up so sharply her chair tipped over, clattering to the floor. She didn't seem to notice, her eyes fixed on the door where Phil had just left. 'You never said . . . I never knew . . .'

'Rae and Phil are just staying here 'til they get themselves sorted out. They've been out in the US.' McLean wasn't sure why he bothered to explain, Marchmont was clearly not listening to him. She backed away from the table, somehow managing to miss the tumbled chair despite never taking her eyes off the door on the other side of the room. McLean caught up with her at the entrance to the passageway that led to the front hall, took her gently by the arm. At his touch, she seemed to regain a little control of herself, shuddering slightly as she looked at him. 'You never said.'

'He's not my baby, Heather. Come on. I'll give you a lift home if we can't find a taxi for you.' He cursed himself for the offer even as it was coming out. Close up, he could smell that delicate, heady scent on her, clinging to her like the latex he knew she was wearing beneath her overcoat. Bad enough the two of them alone in the kitchen. In the cramped confines of his car there was no telling what might happen.

'No. It's fine.' Marchmont pulled herself away, the apparent shock at seeing a baby beginning to wear off. 'It's a warm night. I'll walk. Goodnight, Rachel. It was nice meeting you.'

'Oh. Do you live nearby?' Rachel half stood, then slumped back into her seat.

'Near enough. Say goodbye to Phil for me. And little ... Tony?' She turned and headed down the corridor at such speed that McLean had to half skip to catch up. He reached her at the same time as she reached the front door and pulled it open.

'I'm sorry. I shouldn't have come here,' she said before he could speak. 'What I did back there. It was wrong. I can see that now. You're not like the others. I thought you were, but you're not. Don't let them make you like they are. Like I am.'

'Heather, I don't know—' McLean started to speak, but she put her finger over his lips to silence him again.

'Let it go, Tony. I'll explain it to them. They'll have to understand. You won't see me again.'

And with that, she turned and was gone.

'You sly old dog, Tony. Thought you were still burning a torch for Emma.'

Rachel had finished her tea and taken the baby upstairs, declaring herself exhausted. McLean felt the same way, and confused as well. He knew better than to leave his old friend in the dark, or worse, telling just his half of the story to his wife, who would no doubt then tell it to Jenny, so instead he had suggested a nightcap. Phil had said nothing until they were both in the library, drams poured and the door firmly closed.

'It's really not like that, Phil.' McLean held up his hand to stop the inevitable objection. 'Yeah. I know what you saw. Trust me, I know what I felt too. But it wasn't my idea and I certainly didn't invite her.'

Phil gave him his best sceptical frown. 'So who is she, your latex-clad beauty? That was some kinky outfit, you know.'

'I told you. Her name's Heather and she's a corporate lawyer. At least, that's what she says she is. I'm beginning to have my doubts about that. We interviewed her a few weeks back. You know I can't tell you why, but we didn't press charges in the end. Thing is, she's been calling me up ever since, trying to tell me something. I thought that was what tonight was about, when she showed up out of the blue. Turns out she had something else on her mind. Unless that's what she's been trying to tell me all along.'

'Some people get all the luck.' Phil let out a little wistful sigh, then took a sip of his whisky.

'You interrupted us, remember?' McLean had a drink from his own glass. 'For which I will be forever in your debt, by the way. That's not the sort of complication I need right now.'

'Really? Looked like kind of a fun complication to me.'

'You're a married man now, Jenkins. With a young son to think of. Behave yourself.'

'I will if you will, Tony.'

'Seriously, though. There's something going on there and I just can't work out what it is.'

'You mean aside from putting on a latex catsuit and throwing herself at you to get your attention?'

'No, it's not that. And if I was being mean I might say

she's a bit young for me anyway. There's something else going on, though. I can't shake the feeling I know her from somewhere, and she's clearly got some issues she needs help with.'

'I'm guessing this is the stuff you know about here that you can't tell me.'

'Exactly so. More's the pity.'

'Well, if you ever need a wingman to come to your rescue.' Phil raised his glass in a mock toast. McLean followed suit. Not quite like old times, but then you never could go back. This was the closest he was going to get.

'Don't worry, Phil. I know who to call.'

# 44

Bleary-eyed and thick of head, McLean pushed his way through the back door into the station, far too early yet again. He'd hardly slept a wink, drifting in and out of strange nightmares of writhing bodies, choking black hair and a whiff of unidentifiable perfume that still lingered on the air after he finally gave up, got out of bed and stood for a long time in a cold shower. He'd have preferred it hot, but it was too early for the boiler to have kicked in, and someone appeared to have drawn a long bath late the night before. He couldn't have said with utmost certainty that it had been Rachel, but he'd known Phil more than half of his life and his old friend had never been the most conscientious when it came to washing.

'Morning, sir. Heard the news?' A far too cheerful Detective Sergeant MacBride accosted him in the corridor leading to his tiny office, tablet computer tucked under one arm.

'Which particular news would that be, Sergeant?' McLean didn't really feel up to much station gossip right now, and hoped using MacBride's rank rather than first name would broadcast his current state of mind.

'The Pentland Mummy. You know how we thought it might be a bloke called Daniel Calton?'

It was news to McLean that MacBride was on the cold case team, but he wasn't unhappy about it. 'Duguid said he was trying to find living relatives so we could check DNA.'

'Aye, that's right. And he did find one. A living relative, that is.'

'He did? Never said anything the last time I saw him. Who is this mysterious relative, then?'

MacBride consulted his tablet computer, even though McLean was sure he had no need. 'Miss Eileen Prendergast. She's Calton's niece.'

'I take it you've got an address for her?'

'Aye. She lives in Duddingston. Runs a B&B or guest house or something.'

McLean consulted his watch, even though he knew exactly what the time had been five minutes earlier when he'd parked his car. 'You busy this morning?'

'That depends on whether I can keep out of DI Carter's way.' MacBride didn't smile, and McLean could tell he wasn't joking.

'Is he that bad?'

'Worse. I can't see him lasting much longer. It's the mess he makes while he's in charge that the rest of us have to clean up.'

'Well, see if you can rustle us up a car. I need to get a coffee first, then we can go pay this Miss Prendergast a visit.'

He had no idea how MacBride had managed to secure it, but the car was perhaps the newest McLean had ever sat in. Judging by the seats and the smell, it had only just been delivered. It was a BMW, and he spent the first ten minutes of the journey looking around the interior, wondering if something similar would do him as a less fragile alternative to his Alfa Romeo.

'You know much about cars, Stuart?' McLean patted the

dashboard in front of him as MacBride carefully turned on to Peffermill Road. The detective sergeant didn't answer, just let out a long, slow breath as McLean realised he'd asked the same question many times before. 'Sorry, I know. I'm just going to have to grit my teeth and get on with it. Can't keep driving that old Alfa around forever. There just never seems to be a good time to go and look at anything.'

'A lot of the junior detectives would be very upset if you did, sir. They'd lose their favourite way of taking the piss.'

'They would?' McLean considered a moment. Of course they would, that was how a copper's mind worked. 'Ah well. If it stops them picking on someone else.'

They fell into silence as MacBride turned down towards Duddingston and their destination. No point asking him if he knew where he was going; the detective sergeant would have checked a map before leaving. There was one subject he'd been meaning to broach, though, and this was probably as good a time as any.

'You get any further digging up info on Heather Marchmont?' He thought he'd dropped it casually into the conversation, but he could tell just by the way the detective sergeant stiffened, twitching the steering wheel, that he'd hit a nerve. MacBride looked up at the tall buildings surrounding them before answering, as if he too believed their every move was being watched.

'I really should know better than to do stuff like that for you, sir. Could have got me sacked.'

'Really? How so?'

'Soon as I put her name in the PNC my phone was ringing. Only the bloody DCC asking me what my interest was.'

'Call-me-Stevie? What did you tell him?'

'What could I? Said you'd asked for some basic back-ground for your final report on the brothel case. He said that was all done now, so I didn't need to bother. Sorry if I dropped you in it, sir.'

'Christ, no. It's me who should be sorry, Stuart. If I'd known she was flagged I'd never have asked.'

'I did manage to find a few things out, though,' MacBride said after a while. 'Did some searching on other systems, away from prying eyes. On the surface she looks like a nor-mal person. School records, Glasgow University, a stint overseas in an American law firm. It's a good cover. I'm sure some of it's even true.'

'I'm sensing a but here.'

'For the age and where she grew up, there's only one birth record with that name. The real Heather Marchmont died aged six weeks in April 1984. Whoever your new friend is, she was given the identity of a dead child, and given it a long time ago. Possibly when she was a child herself.'

'Witness protection?'

'That's my working assumption, but as a child?'

'Born in 'eighty-four. So she'd be ten in 'ninety-four.' McLean stopped talking as the pieces started to fall into place in his mind, the familiar chill sensation in his gut. Could it really be that simple? That obvious? Christ, but he could be an idiot sometimes. Just thinking about it, about her the night before, made his ears burn.

''Ninety-four?' MacBride asked, at the same time indicating and slowing as they approached a narrow lane flanked by tall hedges. 'What's so special about 'ninety-four?'

McLean was about to reply, but his attention was

grabbed by the scene in the lane ahead of them. Two squad cars sat half on the road, half on the pavement beside a gateway that he just knew opened on to the house they had come to visit. A couple of uniform officers saw them, one approaching, the other mouthing something into his air-wave handset.

'Looks like someone got here before us,' MacBride said.

McLean didn't recognise the uniform constable, which meant he was probably from the local nick. He was half-way through his spiel, telling them this was a secured area and they couldn't come in, before MacBride managed to interrupt him with his warrant card.

'Sorry, sir. Didn't realise. The car . . .'

Well, it was shiny and new, so the mistake was under-standable. MacBride pulled in on to the kerb behind the nearest squad car and they both climbed out.

'We were looking for Eileen Prendergast,' McLean said. 'I've a nasty feeling we're not going to be able to talk to her, are we?'

'The old lady? Aye. She passed yesterday. Up on yon hill.' The constable pointed to Arthur's Seat as his col-league approached.

'Was it an accident?'

'Search me. They only found her this morning. There's a team up there looking at her. Me and Bob got sent down to secure the house. Hadn't been here five minutes before Detective Inspector Carter showed up.'

'Carter's in there?' McLean nodded towards the large house set back from the road and mostly obscured by the tall hedge that surrounded the property.

'Aye, sir, and DS Langley. They're talking to one of the lodgers. Dare say they'll not be long.'

'Thanks, Constable. Let Carter know I was here when he's done, will you? I'd like to have a chat with him about Miss Prendergast.' McLean looked away towards the slope of Arthur's Seat. Halfway up, past the trees and Queen's Drive, he could just about make out the white shape of a forensics van. There wasn't really any reason why he should go and stick his nose in, apart from up there was where DI Carter wasn't. That and his gut telling him he needed to know what had happened. 'Meantime DS MacBride and me are going to go for a little walk.'

'Dog walker found her first thing. Said her spaniel wouldn't come out of the bushes. Cut herself something rotten trying to get in there and fetch the damn thing out.'

The climb up from Duddingston had been harder than he expected, and McLean found himself thinking of Mac-Bride's words about spending too much time sitting at a desk. At least the action all seemed to be below the road, a steady stream of white-overalled forensic technicians wending their way down a path cut through the waist-high gorse. He'd waylaid one of the uniform constables who were wandering about aimlessly.

'Who's in charge then?'

'Car . . . Detective Inspector Carter's SIO, sir. Only he's gone off to look at the old girl's house.'

'Any other plain clothes here? Any sergeants?'

The constable looked a little lost. He was young, early twenties at most. Probably fresh out of training college. His face was enough of an answer.

'OK. You've set up a perimeter? Keeping the public away?'

'Aye, sir. Not many round here this time of day anyway.'

'Good, well just keep at it. DS MacBride here will sort out teams and assign duties. Meantime I'd better go and have a look at the body. Just as soon as I've found a set of overalls.'

The Scene of Crime team had cut a narrow path through the gorse, but it still tore at his paper overalls as McLean followed the twisting route from the road down to the tent. A couple of technicians were on their knees, inspecting the ground. One of them looked up as he approached, smiled. He recognised Amanda Parsons.

'Morning, sir. Lots of shit round here,' she said with a wide smile. 'Mostly fox, a bit of badger and some dog. Got to love an outdoor crime scene.'

'Well, I'm glad someone's happy. OK for me to go in?' He nodded at the tent.

'Sure. She's not going anywhere. Just don't touch anything that looks like a clue, eh?'

'I'll do my best.'

He pulled aside the flap and stepped inside. The white plastic sides and roof of the tent filtered a lot of the light from outside, casting a gloom over the scene. It covered a small natural gap in the gorse that blanketed most of this face of the hill, centred around a large rock with a round, flat top. And sitting on the rock as if she'd been out for a walk and had just rested a while to enjoy the view was an elderly lady.

McLean focused on her face first, searching the features to see if he recognised her. It was very unlikely, of course, but not unheard of. Difficult to tell with the way the crows had pecked at her eyes and other creatures had gnawed at her lips, her hands and feet. It was quite possible that she had simply sat down and died, but she hardly seemed dressed for a walk on the hill.

A noise behind him distracted McLean and he turned to see the tent flap push open. Angus Cadwallader stepped inside.

'Good Morning, Tony.' He looked from McLean to the dead body. 'Well, as good as it can be. What have we got here?'

'Looks like she strayed from the path. Sat down to catch her breath and just died. Could do with knowing how long she's been here.'

'All in good time, Tony. Let me have a look at her first.'

'Of course. I'll get out of your way.' He shuffled around the corpse, back towards the entrance to the SOC tent, looking down as he did so to avoid treading on something that would get him shouted at later on. And that was when he noticed the dead woman's feet.

'Christ on a stick, where's her shoes? She didn't walk up here barefoot, surely?'

Cadwallader bent forward, peering closer. 'Can't see anything, but there's been a lot of animal damage. More blood than I'd have expected too.' He reached for one of the dead woman's hands. They sat as if they had been folded neatly in her lap, but all that remained of them was a red meaty mess. It pulled away from her with a horrible tearing sound that made McLean glad he'd missed breakfast.

'No. I don't like the look of this at all.'

'What the fuck are you doing here, McLean?'

As greetings went, it lacked subtlety, but then Detective Inspector Carter had never been the sharpest pencil in the box. McLean had been expecting some kind of hostility from the man, and he wasn't disappointed.

'And a very good morning to you too.'

'Don't fuck me around, McLean. This is my crime scene. I'm SIO here.'

'If that's so, then why did you leave the scene without handing over responsibility to another officer? Who's Crime Scene Manager? Why is there no one more senior than a constable here? Why has no one been assigned duties? Did you think a crime scene just ran itself? Have you never heard of procedure?'

Carter blanched, but only for a short instant. 'Hah. The great Detective Inspector McLean quoting procedure at me. Why are you even here?'

McLean pinched the bridge of his nose like he'd seen Ritchie do when she was dealing with someone unreasonable, usually him. It didn't help much, but it stopped him from punching a colleague.

'Miss Prendergast.' He hooked a thumb over his shoulder in the direction of the forensics tent. 'Her name came up in a cold case. I was going to speak to her, found you were already here. Don't worry, I'm not trying to take your precious case from you. Just wanted to find out if there were suspicious circumstances. Anything that might tie in to what I'm investigating, really.'

Carter sniffed, his expression one of a man unconvinced. Either that or a man with gut-ache, it was hard to tell the difference sometimes. He said nothing for a while, the thoughts churning slowly across his face.

'So what do you reckon then? Suspicious, or just an old biddy gone senile?' From the way he said it, McLean could tell how Carter had already made up his mind.

'You've seen her, I take it?'

'Aye. Not the prettiest of sights straight after breakfast.'

'Then you'll know it's not straightforward. Could be a tragic accident; that'd be the easiest answer. I guess you'll have to see what the pathologist has to say, eh?'

As if on cue, a commotion at the tent turned into two forensic technicians with a stretcher, bringing the body out. Cadwallader followed behind them, more sombre than McLean was used to seeing him. The pathologist eyed Carter with ill-disguised contempt, then addressed McLean instead.

'There's something very odd about this, Tony.'

'Odd? How so?' Carter asked. Cadwallader gave a tiny flick of his head, like a teacher reluctantly acknowledging the presence of a tiresome pupil.

'Well, there's where we found her for one thing. Not an easy place to get to. She's been dead at least a couple of days, too, but I won't be able to give you a better indication until I've got her back to the mortuary. Then there's the lack of shoes. She really does seem to have walked here barefoot. Unless someone brought her, of course.'

'You reckon that's a possibility?' Carter's face had grown

very dark, his brow creased in a deep frown. This was clearly not going the way he had hoped.

'Probably not, given the way we found her. If someone had just dumped her in the bushes she'd be lying down. And there's abrasions to the front of her legs that suggest walking through these whins. I'll have a look at what's left of the soles of her feet when we do the post-mortem, but there's really not much. Anyway, that's not the main thing bothering me.'

'It isn't?'

'No. It's the animal damage. There's too much blood. The ground around her feet's covered in it, and her lap's been soaked too, though it's mostly dried out now. I'm going to hazard a guess right here and suggest she bled to death.'

'You mean . . . ?' This time it was McLean's turn to frown.

'Yes, Tony. She walked up here, sat down and didn't move a muscle as something ate her hands and feet.'

# 45

It took a long time to extricate themselves from the crime scene. DI Carter might have been even more useless than a chocolate teapot, but he was cunning where it came to passing the buck, or the workload. It hadn't taken him long at all to figure out that the reason McLean and Mac Bride were at the scene, the need to talk to Miss Prendergast about her missing uncle, was no longer relevant. In Carter's eyes, that meant MacBride was available to manage the scene for him. McLean almost told the detective sergeant to take on the job – at least that way it would be done properly – but he knew better than to drop MacBride in it like that. In the end he'd used the threat of Duguid's wrath to persuade Carter he needed to find someone else.

'Thanks for that, sir. I really didn't want to get stuck with the blame for everything that's going wrong up there.' MacBride drove perhaps a little more swiftly than was wise or legal away from Miss Prendergast's house after they had retrieved the car. McLean said nothing, keen as anyone to put as much distance as he could between himself and the impending disaster. Working at the SCU, he hadn't really noticed just how bad a mistake Carter's promotion had been; seeing it up close and personal had been something of a surprise.

'What's the sweepstake on how long he'll last?'

MacBride glanced sideways for an instant. 'I've a tenner on him being demoted by the end of the month. You want in?'

'I think that would be very unprofessional of me.' McLean checked his watch, then noticed the clock on the dashboard right in front of him. 'I would like you to drop me off at the mortuary, though. Think I might have a chat with Angus about Miss Prendergast and the Pentland Mummy.'

MacBride smiled. 'And you'd rather not be at the station when Brooks finds out where we were this morning?'

'Something like that. You might want to keep a low profile too. I'm sure Dagwood could find something for you to do down in the basement until your shift ends. Oh, and put me down for next Tuesday, if no one else has got it already. A tenner, is it?'

The air-conditioned chill of the mortuary was a welcome relief from the muggy heat of the city outside. Less welcome was the smell of death, only slightly masked by the chlorine stench of floor cleaner. It normally didn't bother McLean, he hardly noticed it any more, but today it clung to him like a latex bodysuit. A lingering scent that haunted him with its familiarity.

He half expected to find Cadwallader examining the dead Miss Eileen Prendergast, but the examination theatre was empty of cadavers for a change, the pathologist in his little office typing up notes.

'Tony, what brings you down to my lair? Not our poor old lady, I hope. I've not had a chance to get started on her yet.' Cadwallader greeted him with his customary wide smile. He was dressed in green scrubs, only slightly stained at the front from whichever poor dead soul had most recently revealed their innermost secrets to him.

'Given we only found her this morning, I'd be surprised if you had. And anyway, that's not my case, so the less I have to do with it the better.'

'Not your case? But I thought . . .' Cadwallader gave him a confused frown. 'The crime scene.'

'No doubt I'll be getting a bollocking from Brooks later on, but the investigation is Carter's to cock up. I was there because I wanted to talk to Miss Prendergast, only she upped and died before I could.'

'Oh yes?' Cadwallader raised a greying eyebrow. 'What did you want to talk to her about?'

'Her uncle, Daniel Calton. We think he might be the Pentland Mummy.'

Cadwallader frowned. 'The Pentland Mummy? Bloody hell, there's a case I've not thought about in a while.'

'Please tell me you've still got a tissue sample. Too much to think you'd have the body itself.'

'Should be on the system. You have a case number? Since we never put a name to the poor fellow?' The pathologist tapped at his keyboard, peering over the top of his half moon spectacles at the screen. McLean looked around the tiny room as he pulled out his notebook, noticing what was missing for the first time.

'Tracy not here?'

'Off on a training course. I am, of course, bereft.' Cadwallader made a sad face as McLean located the reference number and read it out.

'You could have just emailed this, or given us a call, you

know. Not that it isn't always a delight to receive living visitors.'

'I couldn't really face going back to the station. Not right now. It was easier when I was at HQ with the SCU team. Play one angry boss off against the other.'

'Ah yes. Ever the diplomat.' Cadwallader turned his attention back to the screen, pushing his spectacles up his nose the better to see. 'Here we are. Before even my time, this one. Oh yes. One of your grandmother's. Now there was a pathologist.' He tapped at the keyboard a bit more, clicked the mouse. 'Yes, I thought so. DNA profile's been done already, which should save us a bit of time. I'll get a sample of poor Miss Prendergast sent off for testing once we've done her PM, then we'll see where that leaves us. Don't suppose it'll shed much light on how he ended up the way he did, but at least we'll have a name, eh?'

'I think that's about as much as we can expect this far on. It still counts as a result.'

'Fingers crossed then.' Cadwallader pushed his chair away from his desk, stood up. 'Oh, there was something I was going to tell you. Not sure if Tracy emailed it before she went on her course. Your man Smith, with the interesting sexual appetites.'

'What about him?' McLean shivered at the image that formed in his mind: the dead man hanging from his flex, the sound of the plug being removed from his nether regions.

'The swabs we took from his ... member? Thought he'd been using his own saliva as lubricant? Turns out it wasn't his.'

'Wasn't his? Someone else was ... Someone else was with him when he died?'

'Looks very possible. And not just anyone. Initial tests suggest it was probably the same person who did for your friend the priapic salesman. Eric Parker.'

'Why can nothing ever be straightforward with you, McLean? You're a bloody menace, you know?'

It had taken the rest of the morning and most of the afternoon to get the Eric Parker case reopened and merged with the investigation into John Smith's demise. DS MacBride was working his usual magic setting up the major incident enquiry room, and sometime around lunch Detective Superintendent Brooks must have heard the bad news. Not bad enough to interrupt his eating, but plenty to put him in a foul mood.

'I'm sure we all wish things were simpler than they appear to be, sir. Not quite sure how it's my fault, though.'

'Oh man up, McLean. You're SIO, of course it's your bloody fault. Now what are you going to do about catching this mysterious woman who can kill a man just by sucking his dick?'

McLean bit back the retort he wanted to give, counted to a silent ten before answering. 'We're reviewing the Parker case, sir. Checking for anything we might have missed. Looking for any links between him and Smith. Not sure if it's going to help, mind you. There's nothing obvious between them.'

'Apart from the fact they both died with a hard-on?'

'We're looking at the sex worker angle, yes, sir.' McLean pinched the bridge of his nose. It didn't make the idiot go away, sadly.

'Is that it?'

347

Christ, it was like dealing with a bloody toddler. 'It's early days. Only got the message from forensics this morning connecting the two cases. DS Ritchie's on her way over to coordinate the SCU side of things. I've got a meeting with Clarice Saunders lined up for . . .' McLean checked his watch. 'About half an hour's time.'

'What the fuck are you talking to her for? Bloody busybody.'

'Believe it or not, she's our best contact for a lot of the sex workers in the city, sir. Most of them won't help us, but they'll talk to her. It's a long shot, I'll admit, but we need to see if there's anyone turned up recently. Maybe come down from Perth or Inverness.'

'How d'you figure that?'

'Parker was a salesman. His last stop was Perth. Chances are he gave this woman a lift and she paid him back with favours rather than cash. If she's turned up in Smith's flat helping him fulfil his odd fetishes, then she's started working in the city, and not exactly as a secretary.'

'So just how is she killing them, this femme fatale?'

McLean stared at the detective superintendent for a moment, looking for a sign on his pudgy face that he was taking the piss. There was nothing but a slight tomato stain to one side of his chin where the canteen lasagne had missed his mouth.

'I don't think she's killing them at all, sir. Why would you even think she was?'

'Well, why are you looking for her then?'

Really? 'Because she was with both men shortly before they died, sir. Possibly when they died. And then she fled the scene.' McLean tried to stop himself from sounding

348

like he was explaining something to a child. 'We still don't have direct evidence that either Parker or Smith died anything other than accidentally, but there is a link between them and it's this woman. We have to investigate that.'

Brooks scowled as the room bustled with busyness around him, IT technicians bringing in computers and uniform constables getting in the way while they waited to be told what to do. 'Just keep an eye on the budget, OK? We're not made of money, you know.'

# 46

If McLean had thought that time and familiarity might have softened Clarice Saunders' attitude towards the police, then meeting her again in interview room two certainly disabused him of the idea. She was prickly to the point of offensiveness, despite the presence of Acting Detective Inspector Ritchie.

'What makes you think I'd share information like that, even if I had it?' she answered in immediate response to his query about whether any new faces had come to her notice in the past few weeks. 'And don't tell me you're not interested in arresting them, just talking,' she added. 'If I had a pound for every time one of you lot has told me that, I wouldn't have to go begging to the council for funding.'

'I'm really only interested in arresting someone if they've broken the law, Miss Saunders. Not sure that's the case here.'

'Aye? Well what about Stacey Craig then? She didn't last long after you lot picked her up, did she?'

'Stacey Craig?' McLean took a while to understand the connection. 'You mean when she was picked up in Leith?'

'I mean the reason she was down in Leith in the first place. You lot running around shutting down all the safe places for people like her to work.'

'We have to obey the law. Even if sometimes it's not the best answer. And I do feel sorry for what happened to

Stacey. But that's not why we're here today. Two men have died and we've reason to believe a sex worker has fled the scene of both deaths. I'd very much like to talk to her about that.'

'Arrest her, you mean. Throw her in jail when it's the men you should be locking up.'

McLean took a deep breath, let it out slowly. 'I can hardly lock them up; they're both dead. And there's no suggestion of foul play here, just a common factor that needs to be investigated. She didn't kill these men. I'm fairly certain of that.'

'Only fairly certain?' Saunders made a face. 'I'm fairly certain I know what you'll do to this poor woman if you find her.'

'I get the feeling you're not going to help us find her, Miss Saunders,' Ritchie said.

'I will ask around. But if she's new on the scene, chances are she'll not be looking for the sort of services I provide. At least not yet.'

'Thank you. That's all we're asking right now.' McLean stood up as Saunders did the same, accepting that the meeting was over.

'Just be sure and arrest the men forcing her into this work. They're the ones you should be concentrating on. The pimps.'

'If we can prove someone's profiting from immoral earnings, trust me we'll prosecute. You know as well as I do how hard it is to do that, though.'

'Aye, like that brothel you raided? Nice cover-up some-one worked there.'

McLean almost missed what Saunders was talking about,

then remembered her previous visit, to the SCU the day after they'd raided Heather Marchmont's house. Remembered Marchmont's own words about the house and how long she had been living there.

'Cover-up? It was a private party in somebody's home. We cocked up. Bad intelligence.'

'Aye, right.' Saunders let out a very unladylike laugh. 'And you believe that? So why was Stacey working there?'

'Stacey wasn't working there. As far as I've managed to find out she wasn't working at all.'

'Then why did you lot arrest her down in Leith? Charge sheet says soliciting in a public place. You threw her in the cells.'

'Prior to that we'd had no interaction with her for several years. That's why we let her go with a caution.'

Saunders grinned at some joke only she had heard. 'You really don't have a clue, do you? Stacey never gave up the sex work, she just moved up-market. Safer that way, and she wasn't trying to compete with the Eastern European girls who get trafficked in under your noses.'

'So you're saying Stacey Craig worked at Heather Marchmont's house?' Ritchie asked. 'People paid to have sex with her there? Rich people with a thing for rubber and whips?'

'Not just her, by all accounts. She said there were at least a half-dozen girls there the last time she worked one of their parties.'

Hearing it from Marchmont had been one thing, but this was corroboration he couldn't ignore. McLean sat down again, took out his notebook. 'Don't suppose you've got any names?'

This time Saunders' laugh was more bitter. 'And have them end up like her? Even if I knew I'd no' put them in harm's way like that.' She nodded in Ritchie's direction. 'Sure I don't think either of you were in on it, but if you can't see a cover-up when it's so bloody obvious, you'd best look for another line of work.'

'You know what'll happen if you even suggest reopening the brothel raid case, sir.'

Ritchie stood beside him at the front entrance to the station as both of them watched Saunders climb into a taxi. They'd offered her a lift in a squad car, but she'd just laughed. For some reason she seemed to find the two of them very funny all of a sudden.

'I know. I wasn't even going to mention it. I've a horrible feeling it's going to rear its ugly head soon enough, though. And what she said just confirms a lot of things for me.'

'You really think the DCC's part of some group of . . . what? Sex addicts? S&M enthusiasts? Swingers?'

'God, no. I think it's something much deeper than that. I doubt Call-me-Stevie's ever been unfaithful to his wife, and I've met her. Not the kind to join any group activity unless singing hymns features high on the agenda.'

Ritchie scratched at the top of her head with a thoughtful finger. 'You say that, but you never know. All those people we busted in the raid seemed normal enough folk. Bankers, management consultants, lawyers. Who knows what people get up to in the privacy of their own homes? Or other people's, I suppose.'

'Fairly sure it won't be sex with the DCC. I just can't see him being caught up in anything so tawdry. But someone's got something on him, or can give him something if he cooperates. Or maybe he just thinks he's doing a friend a favour. That's how it works, carrot and stick. Christ, I never thought I'd admit it, but Dalgliesh might well have been on to something.'

'Dalgliesh? What's she got to do with all this? I heard she collapsed. They took her to hospital.'

'Aye, she did. Doctors thought she had an allergic reaction. Nuts in a piece of cake she nicked off me. Only I spoke to her boss and she's not allergic to anything, far as he knows. Certainly not nuts. I've been meaning to look into it, but . . .' McLean shrugged, not quite sure why he'd not looked into it, except that he'd been busy. And it was Dalgliesh.

'Why's she suddenly your new best friend?'

'Very funny. She came to me a while back. Working on a story. Well, maybe not a story so much as a mad theory. Not sure I really understood it if I'm being honest. She was looking for connections, some kind of secret society. The more she looked, the more she found. Only they didn't go very deep.'

'Not sure *I* quite understand, sir. Deep?'

It was McLean's turn to scratch, only his finger was less thoughtful, more confused. 'Perhaps deep's not the right word. It's like the whole six degrees thing. A friend of a friend of a friend and suddenly you're connected to everyone on the planet.'

'Well, that's hardly news.'

'No, but Dalgliesh reckoned she was on to something. Someone using these connections to manipulate people. Blackmail some, promise others favours, all to some unexplained end.'

'Umm . . . Isn't that just how, you know, life works?'

Put like that, McLean had to admit Ritchie had a point.

'Yes, but there was more to it than that. As if people were being deliberately manipulated to cover up things like the brothel, and worse.'

'But she couldn't find out who was doing the manipulation? Just some kind of shadowy force?' Ritchie waved her hands around, fingers splayed slightly, to illustrate how seriously she took the idea.

'It was more along the lines of something emerging from the complexity of the system. It's grown so far-reaching, and for so long, it's almost as if it's alive.'

'You any idea how nuts that sounds, sir?'

'I know.' McLean shook his head as much at his own stupidity as anything. 'And when did you start calling me "sir" again?'

'Habit, I guess.'

'Not trying to distance yourself from the station pariah, then. That's what I'm going to be soon.'

'Oh aye? Planning on doing something that'll piss off Brooks and the DCC?' Ritchie laughed, and McLean smiled at the joke. He knew well enough that anything he did would piss off Brooks, and Call-me-Stevie wasn't much better, for all his faux camaraderie. What Ritchie didn't know was exactly what he was intending doing, which could indeed easily land him in the shit again, most likely covering anyone close to him with it at the same time. He checked his watch, surprised at how late it was.

'Knocking-off time, I think. Must be way past your shift by now.'

'Detective inspectors don't work shifts, remember? Acting

detective inspectors even less so.' Ritchie's grin was welcome relief at the end of a busy day.

'Aye, well, it's still time to go home. I can screw up my career again in the morning.'

# 47

'Terrible shame. Terrible. She was a sweet old dear. Wouldn't hurt a fly.'

McLean hadn't needed to visit the doctor too often, but he was pleased to see the standard decoration of a GP's consultation room hadn't changed all that much since he was a boy with a skinned knee. The walls were lined with posters informing him of an alarming variety of diseases, the importance of good personal hygiene, and the perils of smoking. Over in one corner, an examination couch was draped with a white plastic sheet not unlike the ones he saw too regularly in the city mortuary. Beside it, a replica human skeleton hung from a frame by a hook drilled into its skull. At least, he assumed it was a replica. You never knew.

'Had you been her GP for long?'

Doctor Gillespie looked as if he might have been present at Miss Prendergast's birth. His skin was thin and blotched, eyes slightly sunken in a face that had once been strong but was now succumbing to the ravages of time. A great profusion of yellow-white hair sprouted from his head in seemingly random tufts, as if he had been an early experiment in hair-loss remedies. He had a ready smile, though, and the kind of bedside manner you wanted in a man with whom you might discuss prostate problems.

'Eileen? Gosh, there's a question. Probably going on forty years. Maybe more.'

'And did she have a history of mental illness? Was she . . . ?' McLean broke off, uncertain quite how to voice the question.

'Going senile?' Doctor Gillespie offered. 'It's possible, perhaps. But only very slightly. She'd had a couple of falls recently I put down to old age, but they could have been symptomatic of something else.'

'You wouldn't have expected her to go wandering off into Holyrood Park without her shoes on, then.'

Doctor Gillespie considered the question for a moment before answering. 'I've other patients I'd have expected to do so before Eileen. She was always very lucid. When I saw her, that is. She didn't visit me very often.'

'What about her family? She had a sister die recently, did she not?'

'Esme? Yes, that was what, a couple of years ago? They were twins, you know.' Doctor Gillespie pulled a pair of spectacles out of the breast pocket of his jacket, slipping them on as he leaned in to peer at the screen of the computer sitting on his desk. He tentatively poked at a few keys on the keyboard, moved the mouse, poked a few more keys, moved the mouse again. Clearly he wasn't confident of using both at the same time, but eventually he found what he was looking for.

'I tell a lie. It was three years last April. Where does the time go?' He nudged his spectacles down his nose and peered over the top of them. 'She went a bit strange at the end, Esme. And it happened quite quickly too. So I suppose there's that to consider. Still, she didn't wander off without her shoes on.'

'How did she die?'

'Esme? Oh, she contracted pneumonia. But she had to be put in a home before then. Kept saying that old house of theirs was full of ghosts. You've seen the place, I take it?'

McLean nodded. 'From the outside. Surprised it's not been turned into flats, to be honest.'

'Well, it probably will be now. Though quite who'll stand to inherit, I've no idea.'

'Did she not have any family then?'

'No, just her and Esme. Well, after her mother passed away, but that was a long time ago.'

'And her father?' McLean could see as soon as he asked the question that this was what Doctor Gillespie really wanted to talk about. He had come in ahead of morning surgery, but the clock was ticking away. How many patients were out there waiting to be seen?

'Well, there's a question, isn't there? Of course the birth certificates all say that Esme and Eileen's father was William Prendergast. But their mother, Amy. Now she was quite a character, let me tell you. Must have been a looker when she was young, too. There was some scandal, though. During the war, when he was away in the Navy, she used to hold parties in that big old house of theirs. And she was always very close to her twin brother. Very close. That was the really shocking part of it. If even half the rumours of what they used to get up to are true then ... Well ...' Doctor Gillespie ran out of steam.

'Her brother being Daniel Calton,' McLean said.

'Oh, you know about it all then?' Doctor Gillespie perked up, his enthusiasm for salacious gossip reinvigorating him.

'We know he went missing in 'seventy-two. Think we might know what happened to him, too. Or at least where he ended up.' McLean peered down at his notebook and the scribbles he'd made on the open page. 'If what you say about Miss Prendergast's mother is true, then that's interesting. Sadly I don't think germane to our investigations, though.'

'The children of incest are highly prone to degenerative disorders, Inspector. Double recessive genes and all that. If Daniel Calton was Esme and Eileen's father, as well as their uncle, then that might go some way towards explaining how they ended up the way they did, wouldn't you say?'

McLean stood for a moment outside the GP surgery, wondering what the hell he thought he was doing. Chasing down Miss Prendergast wasn't his job, wasn't even his case. They already had the DNA sample from her that might confirm the identity of the Pentland Mummy; that was as far as his involvement with her should have gone. And yet he couldn't leave it alone.

Doctor Gillespie's words hadn't helped to dampen his curiosity either. It was conceivable that Eileen Prendergast had simply and catastrophically lost her mind, wandered out of her house in bare feet, up Arthur's Seat without a care in the world. It was entirely possible she might have sat down on a rock and simply stopped functioning as a human being, her mind completely gone. Either way, it didn't really matter. None of this really mattered to the Pentland Mummy investigation, except that both cases were too weird to be so easily explained away. Too weird, and too connected.

But what had caused it? What had made her snap? Or had there just been a little clock ticking away deep inside? An alarm just waiting to go off?

He really needed to see inside Miss Prendergast's house. Get an idea of who the old woman had been. It would be easier than asking DI Carter anyway. He just needed a way of justifying it. Visiting the GP was one thing, searching the house would be impossible without treading on toes.

But then they knew Eileen Prendergast was Daniel Calton's niece. Or maybe even Daniel Calton's daughter by his own sister. And Daniel Calton might just possibly be the man found mummified on the back of Scald Law in the long, hot summer of 1976. A man who had remained unidentified for almost forty years. What he was doing could, just about, be justified in terms of that investigation. And the DCC had put him in charge of the Cold Case Unit, along with its budget.

McLean drummed his fingers on the roof of his Alfa, staring off into the distance as he tried to make his mind up. Eventually he realised that he was staring sightlessly at a public library just across the car park. It was a long shot, and there were far more important things he was supposed to be doing, but then they involved being back at the station in a room with Duguid, or in his tiny office faced with a mountain of paperwork, or justifying his every action to Detective Superintendent Brooks. No, there were far better ways to spend his time.

'This'll give you access to the internet. Although I have to warn you that some sites are blocked. You wouldn't believe what the local lads try to look up in here. And with the wee kiddies running around too.'

Like a lot of the local libraries, at least those that hadn't been closed down already, this one was partly a place where you could check out books, and partly an impromptu day care centre. The duty librarian was a cheerful, round-faced woman with smiling eyes, who had laughed at his request for a computer with internet access, but shown him to a line of elderly desktop machines anyway. The one he was using appeared to have something sticky smeared liberally over its keyboard, and its screen was missing some of the colours the manufacturer must have put in originally, but it connected him to a search engine and from there to the archives he was looking for.

Scrolling through page after page, he reached for his phone, intending to call DS MacBride for help. Then he remembered where he was and slipped it away again. Given what he was searching for, he'd have been better off calling Dalgliesh, asking her to trawl through the paper's archives. Except that then he would owe her a favour. And she was in hospital, possibly still unconscious.

'Brought you a cuppa. You looked like you needed it.'

McLean looked up to see the smiling librarian standing beside him, two mugs of tea in her hands. She put them both down beside the sticky keyboard, then pulled up a chair alongside him.

'Looking for anything in particular? Only I thought we had it bad with the budget cuts. Didn't realise the polis were having to share too.'

It was meant as a joke, and McLean smiled, thanking her as he took his mug of tea. But it was also too close to the truth to be really funny. The police might moan about cuts, but they had a certain security. How long could places like this be kept open? And when they closed, where would the local youth go? What would they get up to?

'I just wanted to try and track down someone who lived around here a while back. I've a sergeant who's brilliant at that sort of thing, but he's busy right now.'

'Oh, aye? Anyone famous?' The librarian peered at the computer screen, then seemed to remember herself. 'Och, it'll be police business. Sorry.'

'No, you're all right. I'm really not sure how to start. Just a name, an address, a vague idea it might be important.' McLean took a sip of tea. It was surprisingly good, although it would have been improved immeasurably by the addition of biscuits.

The librarian stood up as a couple of young boys walked up to the counter across the big open-plan room. 'You'd be best starting off with the National Archive website. Costs money, but if you've a name and a birth year you should be able to find them.'

McLean thanked her, both for the help and the tea, but she was already bustling over to help the two lads. He briefly checked his phone, surprised no one had called him back to the station yet, then turned his attention to the computer. He searched first for the name Amy Prendergast, then Amy Calton and then, in a flash of inspiration, Amy Prendergast-Calton. Eventually he found a collection of obscure obituaries, indexed by someone with clearly far too much time on their hands. There wasn't much information on Eileen Prendergast's mother other than that she had died in a psychiatric hospital in 1979, having been committed there seven years earlier. McLean made a few notes, before turning to another site, a few more details. He tried not to let Doctor Gillespie's gossip colour his thoughts as he read the few articles he could find, but by all accounts she seemed to have been something of a firebrand in her youth.

'Oh, you're looking for mad Amy. You should have said.'

McLean twisted round too quickly, sending a twinge of pain through his neck and shoulders. The librarian had managed somehow to stalk silently back across the room and was peering over his shoulder.'

'Mad Amy?'

'Oh, aye. Everyone knows about her. Well, everyone my age or older, I guess. She was a character, I can tell you.'

'You knew her?'

'Back in the late sixties, mebbe early seventies, aye. She lived in yon big old house with her brother. She was an old lady by then, of course. We used to go guiseing up there on All Hallows and she'd give us biscuits that were well past their sell-by date. Then her brother went missing, and she went a bit mad. They ended up taking her to Rosskettle, out by Loanhead, you know?'

McLean nodded. He knew Rosskettle psychiatric hospital all too well.

'Still, the stories they used to tell. The parties they got up to in that house back in the war, before then, even. There were orgies that went on for days. Stuff you wouldn't believe.'

McLean only half listened as the librarian relayed the gossip, embellished and exaggerated by decades of retelling. He had managed to find a record of Amy Calton's birth, in 1912. Her age wasn't all that surprising, nor the fact that her parents were clearly well-to-do Edinburgh socialites. What sent a chill to the pit of his stomach was the single line stating where she had been born. Not the big house just up the road from the library where he was sitting, but another sizeable mansion across town towards the Forth in Newhaven.

Headland House.

# 48

'Did you know this? Is that why we're looking into the Pentland Mummy case? Because you knew all along where it would lead us?'

McLean had driven back to the station with perhaps undue speed, barely thought twice about where he parked his car, and scattered constables left and right in his haste to get down to the gloomy room set up for the Cold Case Unit, all in the hope of finding Duguid still there. He needn't have rushed. The ex-detective superintendent was hunched over his desk, peering at a dusty handful of papers recently lifted from an even dustier archive storage box. He looked up at the question, his eyes taking a while to focus.

'You'll have to be a bit more specific, McLean. Did I know what?'

'Did you know that your man Daniel Calton had a sister who was born at Headland House? A sister who was involved in orgies and all sorts of similar stuff in the nineteen thirties and forties?'

Duguid narrowed his eyes, shaking his head almost imperceptibly before replying just a little too slowly to be believable. 'Don't know what you're talking about.'

'Amy Calton. Check her name on your computer if you want. I don't think you need to, though.'

Duguid leaned back in his seat, clasping his long-fingered

hands together like a man at prayer. Like McLean's old and much-hated prep-school headmaster, now he thought about it.

'What are you suggesting?'

'What am I suggesting?' McLean paused, looked around, noticing Grumpy Bob at his desk on the opposite side of the room from Duguid. Unlike his normal resting position, with feet up and face draped by a decorous newspaper, he was alert, and even awake, eyes flicking between the two of them. Face almost impossible to read.

'I'm suggesting that no one knew the Headland House case better than you. Even if most of the paperwork's been conveniently lost, it's all still up there in your head. The report said that the owners of the house couldn't be found, but I think that was just another part of the cover-up. They were well enough known, just protected. You knew the name Calton, probably tried to track down any living members of the family. What I can't work out is how you thought coming at the investigation by the back door would help. Or did you just want to see how far I got before they shut me down like they did you?'

Duguid had been looking at McLean while he spoke. Now he steepled his fingers under his chin, swivelled his head slowly in Grumpy Bob's direction. 'What do you reckon, Bob? Lost it completely?'

'Don't get me involved in all this, sir. I'm just killing time 'til my retirement.'

'Coward.' Duguid turned back to McLean. 'You know what your problem is? You see patterns everywhere. Connections between people that most would just consider coincidence. And when you get something in your head you just won't leave it alone. It's right fucking annoying sometimes.'

McLean slumped against the door frame, the adrenaline that had propelled him all the way from Eileen Prendergast's GP and the library computer leaching out of him like the warmth from a forgotten mug of tea.

'On the other hand, you've a gut instinct that's more reliable than most. Probably the only reason I've tolerated you all these years. That and the fact you found that wee girl when everyone else on the investigation had been either told not to bother with the attic or were distracted from looking up there.'

'So you did know?'

Duguid let out a low grunt of a laugh. 'Oh, give yourself a big pat on the back. Of course I fucking well knew. Danny Calton owned Headland House up until he went missing in the early seventies. After that it went to a trust fund set up for his nieces. His sister married Bill Prendergast before the war and they lived in that massive pile of a place in Duddingston. Judging by the way you came storming in here, I guess you know the rest. Twin daughters, Esme and Eileen, both bearing an uncanny resemblance to their Uncle Danny, if the old black-and-white photos I saw twenty years ago were anything to go by. Not much of old Bill in them, but then by all accounts old Bill didn't get much of himself in Amy. He was more interested in young midshipmen.'

'Midshipmen?'

'Ah, the famous McLean echo. Knew there was something else I'd missed. Do I need to spell it out? He was gay. Liked barely pubescent young men, by all accounts. Of

368

course a career naval officer between the wars would have been expected to have a wife and family, so someone found young Amy for him. She was already shagging half of Edinburgh high society, her own twin brother Danny included, so it wasn't as if anyone was going to mind old Bill not joining in. He died in the sixties, leaving everything to her. She went a bit mad when her brother disappeared, died a few years later. The two sisters lived in the old house, kept afloat by their trust fund money and taking in the occasional lodger. You can shut your mouth now.'

McLean did as he was told, opened it to ask a question, then shut it again. He walked across to his own desk and slumped down into the chair, aware that unlike Grumpy Bob and Duguid's desks, his was clear of files and paperwork, the computer switched off.

'So how did you expect this to play out, then? We ID the body as Danny Calton, start looking into his affairs around the time of his death and bam! Suddenly the files on Headland House reappear? The people who shut down that investigation relent and let us reopen it?'

'To be honest I never thought we'd get this far. It's not the first time I've tried. Usually they're quicker off the mark.' Duguid picked up his sheaf of dusty papers and went back to reading.

'They?' McLean swivelled his chair around until he was facing Grumpy Bob. 'You knew about this, Bob?'

The detective sergeant looked at his hands and muttered something under his breath that might have been 'Maybe, a bit.'

'Fine. Well. Where do you want to take it next? Assuming your hunch is right and the Pentland Mummy is indeed

Daniel Calton. I mean, even if we get a positive identification from the DNA, that's as far as we can take it, right? Everyone connected to the case is long dead.'

'But they'd know we knew.' Duguid's voice was low, like the rumble of distant thunder. 'They'd know we've not given up. Know they can't have everyone dancing to their tune.'

McLean looked across at the ex-detective superintendent. A man he'd despised most of his working life, but whom he had at least thought he knew well enough. And yet there was something about Duguid now that was unlike anything he'd ever seen before. Or maybe he had, way back when he'd first encountered him as a young detective sergeant gaining a reputation. It was clear that he had changed after Headland House, almost as if bowing to authority had broken him. Had he harboured a grudge all of those years, nursed his grievance, working away at it like a sore tooth until the pain was far worse than the initial injury? Was this the real reason for Duguid's animosity, because McLean refused to yield to the same kind of pressure?

'We can't beat them. You do realise that, sir? Not sure there's even a "them" to beat.'

Duguid leaned forward, his balding pate shining in the light from his computer screen, eyes shaded and dark.

'Oh I know that, McLean. But that's no reason why we shouldn't try.'

'Looks like there's nobody home, sir.'

McLean peered in through the front door of Miss Prendergast's house, looking for any sign of the lodger DI

Carter was supposed to have spoken to. He'd tried the door already, finding it locked. Multiple rings of the doorbell hadn't been answered either. Someone, somewhere had a key, but asking for it would have attracted the wrong kind of attention, which wasn't what he needed right now.

'Top marks for observation, Sergeant.' He dropped down the stone steps to where DS MacBride was standing, head tilted back as he stared at the sightless windows. 'Let's try round the back, shall we?'

The house would once have sat in expansive grounds, probably backing on to Arthur's Seat itself given the location. Over time it had been whittled away by housing developments but it boasted a sizeable front and back garden. The latter still had a coach house, set a bit back from the main house. Looking at the condition of it, McLean wouldn't have been surprised to find an actual coach parked inside. There wasn't enough grass to graze a team of horses, though.

'Locked, sir.' MacBride rattled the back door. A pair of French doors opening on to a patio at the side had been similarly reluctant to let them in, the drawing room beyond them empty of anything but ancient furniture.

'Must be a key somewhere.' McLean looked around the courtyard, trying to decide which unlikely hiding place the late Miss Prendergast might have used. There was nothing under the bins, neatly lined up along one stone wall, nothing hanging from the rusty hook screwed in under the eaves of the little porch overhanging the back door. Even the upturned flower pot next to the boot scraper concealed only a snail. He was about to give up, call in a locksmith, when MacBride gave a little triumphant shout. Looking round, McLean saw him emerging from the coach house, clutching a heavy iron key in one hand.

'There's a wee key cupboard in there. Everything's labelled up. This should let us in, unless it's all some elaborate hoax.'

It wasn't, and soon they were standing in the back hall of the old house, listening to its empty silence.

'Can you smell that?' McLean sniffed at the air, trying to place the scent. It was faint, almost impossible to make out over the dust and furniture polish, the stale air of a house where nothing moved around much.

'Smell what?' MacBride raised his head. 'Can't smell anything much.'

McLean tried to pin it down, but the more he sniffed, the less he could smell. It sparked a memory, though; fleeting and difficult to place. More a feeling of unease. He looked around the hall, seeing a door to the kitchen, another to a boot room and a third that most likely opened on to a downstairs toilet. It wasn't all that different in layout from his own house, across the other side of the city.

'This way, I think.'

A butler's pantry opened out on to a long corridor, leading to the front of the house and the main entrance hall. Not much light filtered in from the kitchen, but it was enough to make out a series of doors. The one nearest the pantry opened on to a flight of narrow stairs, uncarpeted and hidden in the thickness of the wall. They led up to a passageway at the back of the house that opened on to the main landing and a half-dozen sizeable bedrooms. All were empty, and looked like they'd not been slept in for a while. It wasn't until they went through to the back of the house, above the kitchen and where the children would originally have slept, that they found Miss Prendergast's room.

McLean moved carefully through the tiny space between the single bed and the ancient wooden wardrobe, across to the window. A lace curtain provided privacy from the neighbours peering in, although all the nearby houses were bungalows, looked down upon from this lofty position. The bed was made, an old woollen cardigan draped over the back of a simple wooden chair beside a small dressing table. A couple of hairbrushes, glass scent bottle, nothing unusual for a woman in her seventies to have in her bedroom. On the floor, tucked half under the bed, a pair of sensible flat shoes lay side by side. Were these the ones she had forgotten to put on?

'We looking for anything in particular, sir?' MacBride asked.

'Not really. I'd have liked to have talked to the lodgers if they were still here. Easier than getting their contact details from Carter. Otherwise this was just a chance to see how she lived, if there was anything that might have triggered . . . You know . . . It.'

'I can't see anything suspicious in here. Looks a lot like my gran's room. Smells a bit like it too.'

McLean sniffed, catching that scent he'd noticed as they walked into the kitchen. It was almost overpowered by lavender and mothballs, old person's smell, but it was there. He went back to the corridor, following his nose until it brought him to a second set of servants' stairs, leading up into the eaves and the attic rooms. They creaked under his tread as he climbed slowly upwards, the light from a dusty window illuminating a narrow landing at the top. With each step the scent became more powerful, like the musk of some wild animal. It came from a small bedroom, the door standing slightly ajar, and for the first time since they had entered the house, McLean heard noise. Stepping into the room made his eyes water, but it was the sight that made him wince.

Two narrow beds had been arranged side by side, with a small bedside table between them. At some point they may have had blankets on them, but now there were only sheets, ripped and torn and covered in splashes of red. Flecks of it speckled the walls where they sloped with the roof. A pile of blood-soaked towels had been thrown into a corner and now they shimmered and shifted with the movement of a thousand happy flies.

Behind him, McLean sensed DS MacBride about to step into the room. He dragged his gaze from the charnel scene, turned just in time to see the detective sergeant's eyes widen with surprise.

'Back up, Stuart.' He held up a hand even though MacBride was already retracing his steps. 'Get on to Control. We're going to need a forensic team in here. Fast.'

## 49

'It's human blood all right. Quite a lot of it. Not sure it's enough to have killed someone, mind.'

Late afternoon, possibly evening if you liked a drink after work, and McLean was standing in the courtyard around the back of Miss Prendergast's house. The Scene of Crime vans had managed to take up most of the available space; everyone else kept to the front. A team of white-suited technicians were working their way through the room. He and DS MacBride had searched the rest of the house whilst waiting for them to arrive, finding nothing particularly out of place. Of course, given the size of it, there might have been bodies hidden anywhere.

'It looked like an awful lot,' he said.

'Aye, but it's not all been shed at once. There's dried stuff going back at least a couple of weeks. Some more recent and the latest probably from yesterday or even this morning. We've done a simple analysis and so far it all seems to be from the same person.' Amanda Parsons looked like she was in her element, dressed in the full white paper overalls, overboots and hairnet. McLean might not have recognised her, had she not accosted him with a cheery grin and a clear plastic bag filled with bloodstained towels.

'Any idea what's gone on in there? If it's not a murder scene, that is.'

'Not really. Not yet anyway. Looks like someone just

liked cutting themselves. Or cutting other people maybe, but not fatally. It's fair creepy, in a big old house like this too.' She looked upwards towards the overhanging eaves, the lengthening shadows not helping to dispel the sense of unease.

'Well, keep on it. We really need to know what happened in there, and if it had anything to do with the dead woman we found out on the hill.'

'We'll get a blood match against the database as soon as we can. DNA'll take longer.' Parsons hefted her bag and a faint echo of the smell from upstairs floated on the air. 'Now if you'll excuse me, I'm going to see what other bodily fluids might be lurking at the scene.'

'Jesus, Tony. What were you even doing here? I thought the Prendergast death was Carter's case.'

'It is, but her name came up in one of the cold cases we're reviewing. Thought I'd get a little more background on her while we wait for the DNA results. I didn't expect to find . . . well.' McLean didn't bother finishing. McIntyre had seen the room with her own eyes. Now they were sitting in the fusty drawing room and waiting for the forensic team to finish upstairs.

'Brooks isn't going to be too happy, you know.' McIntyre looked quite comfortable in the high-backed leather armchair. McLean wasn't quite so relaxed, perching on the edge of his sofa like a young man on first meeting his girlfriend's parents.

'Is he ever happy about anything?'

'Fair point. But these lodgers. Did anyone talk to them?'

'Carter and DS Langley were interviewing them, least

that's what I was told when we first turned up. I didn't want to interrupt, so we went and had a look at the body instead. The old dear was only a few hundred yards away up the hill.' McLean jerked his head towards the conservatory window with its view out towards Arthur's Seat.

'I hope for his sake he got their name and address. You think they did for her?'

'Miss Prendergast?' McLean was surprised by the question. 'It's possible, I guess. But why? And how? She took herself off up the hill.'

'So why did you come here? Really? Skulking around in the dark with young MacBride, sticking your nose into someone else's case?'

'I don't really know. She's tied in to the cold case we're looking into, like I said. But there's more to it than that. You know her mother was born at Headland House?'

It was McIntyre's turn to look surprised. 'Now there's a place I've not thought about in a while. Let me guess, Dagwood's been bending your ear about how they closed him down on that one.'

'Oh, it's more than that. I was there when they raided it. I was the one who found the little girl.'

'I know, Tony. You were promoted to inspector under my watch, remember? I've read your file more than once.'

'Do you know what happened to her? The girl?'

'Social services took her. No one could find out who her parents were, where she was from. She went into the system and disappeared. I think that was kind of the point, really. Make it so the people who'd put her in that house couldn't find her again.'

'Well, I think I know who she is. I think she's back.

Living in the city. And I think she's connected to what's happened here.'

McIntyre said nothing for a moment, just stared out into the distance. Had he gone too far? Finally she shifted in her armchair, brought her focus on to him.

'When was the last time you got some proper kip, Tony?'

The question brought him up short. The DCI had a habit of that; asking something completely tangential to what they were meant to be talking about. She had a habit of seeing through to the heart of the problem too.

'Does it show?' McLean sunk back down on to the sofa. He'd been fighting off the weariness with nervous energy, but that never worked for long.

'You look like you've not slept in a month. It's a wonder you're standing at all, let alone making logical decisions.' McIntyre pointed at the ceiling this time. 'Forensics are going to seal this off and call it a day soon. Nothing will have changed by tomorrow. Go home and get some rest. Some real rest, not sitting in that draughty old library of yours listening to old records and drinking whisky until two in the morning. We'll sort this all out tomorrow when we've all got clearer heads.'

'And the lodgers?'

'Believe it or not, there's a night shift who can look into them. We'll get a description from Carter and Langley. Nothing else you can do, unless you want to drive the streets in that ridiculous sports car of yours hoping you see them coming out of a pub or something.'

'It's tempting,' McLean said.

'You do and I'll make sure Traffic pull you over. Driving tired's an offence now, you know.'

'OK. OK. I take the hint. I'll go home.' He got up again, swaying slightly as the blood rushed out of his head and the room darkened. Maybe McIntyre had a point. 'Tomorrow then.'

'Aye, Tony. Tomorrow. Now go. The poor old dear will still be dead when you come back.'

Jenny's car was parked outside the front door when McLean pulled up the drive an hour later. He was so fixated on it, and the implications that came with it, that he almost drove into the small van in front of it. Swerving at the last minute, he parked up by the back door, then walked around the outside of the house to see what was going on.

'Oh, hi, Tony. You're home early.' Rachel greeted him like an unfaithful wife, standing at the door with another man's child in her arms. Young Tony Junior looked up at him with round baby eyes and smiled in a way McLean hadn't seen since the last time he and Phil had got heroically drunk together.

'What's up? You nicking all the good furniture?'

'Ha! As if. No. We got the flat back early. Tenants found themselves somewhere else to go. Thought we'd get in there and leave you to some peace and quiet.'

McLean wasn't quite sure how he felt about that. On the one hand there was an enormous sense of relief that he could have his old life back. He could come and go as he pleased without censure, not worry about disturbing people in the wee small hours by playing music, or be woken by the distant, muted but still impossible to ignore wailing of a small bundle of joy. On the other hand he had grown used to having someone other than Mrs McCutcheon's cat to talk to. A two-sided conversation was always nice, and it was easier to justify a glass of wine of an evening if there was someone to share the bottle with.

'You heading out tonight? Seems a bit sudden.'

Rachel laughed. 'God, no. Unless you're that desperate to get shot of us. Phil's been moving our stuff out of storage. Not that there's much of it. Me and Jen were planning on giving the place a deep clean tomorrow. Be out of here by the weekend, if that's OK?'

McLean was about to say it was fine, but Jenny came out of the front door before he could speak.

'Tony. Didn't expect you home for ages yet.' She enveloped him in a hug that was at once awkwardly familiar and surprisingly pleasant. Certainly a lot easier than running the gauntlet of the kiss on the cheek and then the uncertainty as to whether the other one needed a peck too.

'A bit of a rough day, so my boss sent me home early.' It was the truth, but it raised a smile in Jenny and Rachel both. Tony Junior just gurgled.

'Well, supper's in the oven and I've made enough for everyone.' Jenny took him by the arm, guided him inside. Out of the corner of his eye, McLean saw the pile of post lying on the wooden chest in the porch. His instinct was to grab it, shuffle through the bills and junk in the hope of a postcard from Emma, but it wasn't possible to stop. And as he was almost frog-marched across the hall towards the corridor leading to the kitchen, he realised that the hope was no longer as poignant as it had been, the disappointment less deep. Nevertheless, he broke free of Jenny's hold before she could drag him through the door.

'Food sounds great, Jen. But I need to change.' He

looked down at his trousers, imagining bloodstains all over the turn-ups. And that lingering scent he couldn't quite place. That he could place, now he thought about it. He had smelled it here, in his own kitchen, when Heather Marchmont had opened up her long coat to reveal what little she was wearing underneath. The tips of his ears burned at the memory and he was certain his cheeks must have been as red as a skelped arse. Jenny didn't help things by pulling him close, giving him a good sniff and then pushing him away again.

'Good idea. You might want to have a shower too. I'll put the rice on to boil and pour you a beer.'

By the time he'd showered, changed and come back down to the kitchen the promised glass of beer was poured and waiting for him. Jenny stood at the Aga, stirring something that smelled suspiciously like chilli con carne, a pot bubbling away on the side that must have been rice. Four places had been laid at the table, bowls of grated cheese, tomato salsa and soured cream sitting in the spot in the middle from where Mrs McCutcheon's cat usually greeted him. The table top looked well scrubbed.

'Reckon I could get used to this,' McLean said after he'd taken a long draught and wiped the foam off his upper lip with the back of his hand.

'The beer, or having someone around to look after you?' Jenny turned to face him, a mischievous glint in her eyes. He was spared the embarrassment of answering by the noisy arrival of Phil, closely followed by Rachel.

'He's sleeping now. I swear that baby keeps the same mad hours as you do, Tony.'

'Well, you could have named him after someone else. Called him Phil Junior, maybe. Then you'd never get him out of bed.'

'I'll have you know I'm a hard-working professor of bioengineering sciences. And unlike some people round here I keep sensible working hours.'

'You got the job then?'

'Confirmed today. I start at the beginning of the month.'

'What about California? They happy about you not staying?'

'Anyone would think you were trying to get rid of me.' Phil smiled as he pulled out a chair for his wife, then sat down beside her. 'No. That was only ever going to be temporary. And the cutting-edge stuff's all being done over here now. I missed the drizzle too. And the food.'

'Well, don't get used to it.' Jenny heaved a large bowl of chilli on to a mat on the table, followed it up with enough rice to feed an army. 'Once you're back in your own place, you two can look after yourselves.'

She sat down next to McLean, passed out plates and they all started tucking in. He wasn't sure it was the best chilli he'd ever tasted, he preferred a little more spice, but it was freshly cooked and flavoursome. Better than the impossibly hot concoctions Phil had come up with back in their student days. Sitting around the table sharing a meal and good conversation, it felt like they might have been students again. Were it not for the fact that three of them were on the far side of forty now, just Rachel flying the flag for a younger generation.

'You reckon you'll be able to cope here all alone?' Jenny asked.

'I'll muddle along. It's not as if I'm home often anyway.'

'You should find yourself a hobby. Something other than work to do of an evening. That job of yours will chew you up and spit you out if you're not careful.'

McLean tried not to sigh. She was right, of course. Although perhaps with Phil back in town he'd have more of an excuse to get out once in a while. He was happy enough on his own, but he could see how unhealthy a lifestyle that was.

'A hobby, you say? Like stamp collecting, perhaps? Or maybe I should build a model railway in the attic.'

'Or you could do something with that old car of yours. It's far too nice to be using about town anyway.'

'So everyone keeps telling me. I just haven't had the time lately to find anything more suitable.'

The conversation turned to cars, then vintage clothing, running a small business, raising children and a hundred and one other topics. Not content with the chilli, Jenny had also made pudding, and evening wore on into night without McLean once thinking about his work. It wasn't until much later, when Rachel had gone to bed and Phil was fast asleep on the sofa in the library, that the reality of the next day began to settle on him.

'I think I'd better turn in. Got an early start tomorrow, as usual.' McLean put down his empty glass, the taste of the whisky still peppering the tip of his tongue. Put his hands either side of the chair and pushed himself up on to his feet.

'I should probably be going. Long day's stocktaking tomorrow.' Jenny stretched in her armchair like a cat, then peered at her watch. 'Gosh, is that the time?' She stood up quickly, swayed slightly. McLean put a hand out to steady her and she leaned a little too heavily into his touch.

'You OK?'

'Just a bit light-headed. I've probably been sitting still too long.'

'You can stay, if you want. If you don't fancy driving back this late.'

'Why, Inspector McLean. If I didn't know better . . .' Jenny's obvious tiredness was part-banished by her smile. McLean was about to protest that he had plenty of spare rooms, meant nothing by the suggestion, but at that precise moment he wasn't really sure.

'But no. Thank you, Tony. I've stuff I need to sort out for the morning. And I always sleep best in my own bed.' She patted him lightly on the arm, leaned in and kissed him lightly on the lips before breaking swiftly away. 'Thanks for a lovely evening. It's so nice here. Relaxed.'

She cast a swift glance at Phil's softly snoring figure on the sofa, raised an eyebrow, turned and left.

## 50

'OK, people. Let's get things started, shall we? Sooner we're done here, sooner we can get out there and fight crime.'

Early morning in the Major Incident Enquiry room. McLean had missed Jayne McIntyre's pep talks. He'd missed working with a team that was more than a dozen detectives strong, too. The SCU had always been spread thin, but here there were plenty of plain clothes and uniform to go around. It helped that they were involved in three active investigations, of course.

'First up. John Smith. Any progress on the CCTV footage from the apartment block?' McIntyre leaned back against the table at the end of the room by the whiteboards. McLean stood beside her, DS MacBride sitting close by. The collected CID and support teams ranged all the way back to the windows. Most of the station seemed to be there, apart from a few notable exceptions.

'We've got the hard drives. There's quite a lot of footage, though. The place has more cameras than a Japanese tourist. I've been working with forensics and the tagging company to try and narrow down what we have to look at. Otherwise it's a lot of man hours.' MacBride swiped the screen of his tablet computer as he spoke.

'Sensible. Any luck finding links between him and Parker?'

'Not yet. We ran Smith's name and photo past Parker's boss and all the people in his office. None of them had heard of the man. Not surprising, really. They moved in very different circles.'

'What about the people from the brothel raid? Do we know if any of them knew Parker?' McIntyre asked the question, but no one answered. Then McLean realised that all eyes were on him. Fair enough; the brothel raid had been his fuck-up.

'We've not had a chance to talk to them yet,' he said after a while. 'It's a bit delicate.'

'What about the woman in charge? What was her name ... Marchmont?' McIntyre asked.

'She wasn't...' For a moment McLean thought the DCI was making fun of him; pretty much every other senior officer had done, after all. Her face was all seriousness, though. He'd been meaning to call Marchmont anyway, find a way to confront her about the past she had conveniently forgotten to mention to him. 'We've got the transcripts of all the interviews we did with them beforehand. I'll go through them, work out who's worth talking to. We'll have to get Jo Dexter involved, though.'

McIntyre nodded her agreement. 'OK. So that's Smith and Parker. What's the score with the blood at Miss Prendergast's? Have we found the missing lodgers yet?'

Silence descended on the room again. Looking around, McLean could see DS Langley was among the missing, DI Carter as well. It didn't really surprise him.

'I'll take that as a no then.' McIntyre pushed herself away from the desk, walked to the whiteboard and wrote 'Blood' in big red letters on it. McLean half expected the ink to ooze out of the lines, run down the shiny white plastic surface and drip to the carpet tiles.

'The night shift did some preliminary work on the one that Carter managed to speak to, an Iain Angus. Nothing for him on the PNC. Least, not one who fits the description.' MacBride swiped at his screen again.

'Did we get an address for him?' McLean asked.

'I'm not sure. Haven't been able to get hold of Carter or Langley this morning. I think they're both over in Strathclyde on some training course.'

'Who the hell sanctioned that? Aren't they meant to be heading up a suspicious death enquiry?'

Nobody answered, but then McLean hadn't really expected them to. It was clear that Miss Prendergast's death had already been written off as tragic, bizarre, but accidental. No doubt the powers that be hoped this incident would just go away too.

'Get on it then, will you, Stuart? We really need to talk to him. Anyone else who's stayed at that guest house recently too.' McLean looked around the room again, the collected ranks of detectives and uniform officers. Were they really all assigned to these cases, or had they come here because working in McIntyre's team was better than being shouted at by Spence? What a happy ship Detective Superintendent Brooks was running. It almost made McLean wish Duguid was back in his old office on the top floor, not lurking down in the basement and making mischief.

McIntyre stepped back in front of the table, raised her voice to address the throng like a minister preaching to the faithful. 'Right then. Anyone who's meant to be here, see DS MacBride for your assignments. I get the feeling it's going to be a desk day, so don't get too excited.' She paused a moment as the collected officers shuffled from foot to foot. 'As for the rest of you? Nice try, but I'm sure there's other places you're meant to be.'

McLean watched as half the officers filed out of the room, the other half forming a disorderly queue in front of MacBride. He covered his mouth to stifle a yawn, the memory of Jenny's light kiss and swift departure popping into his head for no accountable reason.

'Something keeping you up at nights, Tony? Or should I say someone?' McIntyre nudged him in the ribs to let him know she was joking.

'Not helping, Jayne. I know you think it's funny, but half the station think I've been sleeping with Marchmont. It doesn't really help my credibility.'

'Aye, you're right. My bad.' McIntyre shook her head in apology. 'I did tell you not to sit up all night drinking whisky, though. You should be rested, not yawning your wee head off.'

'Still got my house guests with the newborn. They're moving out soon, but until they're gone I'm hearing distant wailing in the night.'

'That would do it, aye.' McIntyre smiled. 'So what's your plan of attack then?'

For a moment McLean thought she was talking about Tony Junior and his early morning singing, then he remembered they were discussing the ongoing investigations.

'Pretty much like we said in the briefing. Parker and Smith are just a desk exercise at the moment. Scan the CCTV, keep looking for any links between the two of them. I'm waiting on word back from Clarice Saunders and her organisation about anyone new in town, but that was always a long shot and chances are we won't get good intel from them anyway. Apart from that, we need to go back over Parker's itinerary, and it'll help if we can find out who invited Smith to the party. I'll get Sandy Gregg on to it. She's good at being diplomatic.'

'Sandy Gregg? Diplomatic? She never stops talking.'

'You'd be surprised. People seem to like her. Far rather her and Ritchie talk to these people than some uniform constable who doesn't really know what's going on.'

'OK. What about you? Heading off down to the basement to go digging around in the archives some more?'

'And spend all day with Dagwood? Not if I can help it. Thought I'd go see how the forensics lot are getting on at the house. It would help a lot if we knew whose blood it was in there.'

'Good point. Might be worth talking to your pal Cadwallader about the old wifey. See if it's not her blood anyway.'

For a moment McLean believed it might be that easy. 'Reclusive old lady with a family history of dementia, goes mad, cuts herself up a bit then heads out into the wilderness to die?' He shook his head. 'Brooks would be happy if that was all there was to it. Me, I've a horrible feeling it's just going to get even more complicated.'

'Shouldn't you be hiding down in the basement with your new best chum?'

McLean looked up from the report he'd been scanning as he headed down the corridor towards his office. Too late he realised that the best thing he could have done was to have ignored DCI Spence, pretended he'd not heard him and carried on walking past.

'Should I, Mike? Why's that?'

'Only place you're any worth. Sifting through dead cases no one cares about any more.'

'Never realised you had such high opinions of my abilities, Mike. But then if your idea of a good detective is Carter . . .' He left the sentence unfinished. 'Never could quite understand what you saw in him.'

Spence's normally sour face tightened into a scowl that could strip paint. 'Detective Inspector Carter is a valuable member of the team. You remember teamwork, don't you, McLean?'

'Indeed I do, Mike. I was just thinking about it at the morning briefing right now. The one you didn't bother to attend. Didn't see Carter there either, for that matter.'

'We're not involved in any of your cases, McLean. Why would we be there?'

'Not involved?' McLean shook his head, as much to remind himself that he really shouldn't poke this bear as in disbelief. 'So the blood we found all over one of the rooms at Miss Prendergast's house is of no interest to you? Only, last I heard you were in charge of the investigation into her death.'

Spence's scowl deepened, then disappeared altogether, something of a thin smile forcing its way on to his face as an idea wormed its way into his brain. 'Keep on pushing, McLean. I don't care. Don't think you'll be here much longer anyway. Not once everyone knows about your girlfriend and her swingers' club friends.'

'My girlfriend, Mike? You mean the one someone started a rumour about not long after the brothel raid went south? The brothel raid that should have been a secret only known to senior detectives in the SCU and a select few others who needed to be in the loop?'

'What are you—?' Spence started to speak, the scowl returning to his face wearing the guise of a worried frown. McLean stopped him with a gentle pat to the elbow.

'It's OK, Mike. We all make mistakes. Mine was thinking Brooks was the problem and you were just following his lead. I'll be more careful next time.' He turned away, headed down the corridor, suppressing the urge to turn and see if Spence was still standing there, mouth hanging slightly open as he tried to think of something to say.

The forensic team were packing up when McLean finally made it to Miss Prendergast's big old house in Duddingston. Most of the expensive kit was piled up in the small courtyard, waiting to be stacked into the battered old Transit van. A few of the technicians were still dressed in white overalls, but most had taken them off, so he figured it was safe to go inside without suiting up.

He found Amanda Parsons in the room up in the eaves, kneeling down by one of the beds. The mattress was gone, revealing an old metal and heavy-gauge wire frame that reminded McLean horribly of boarding school.

'Thought you were all finished in here.' He looked around the room, seeing the dark splashes on the wall, some smeared slightly where they had been dabbed for sampling. The place had been stripped almost bare; anything that might have blood soaked into it and that could be removed was gone. Only the dark wooden floorboards and the bed frames remained.

'Hi, Tony.' Parsons scuffled around on her knees, her wide smile turning to a scowl as she saw him. 'Stay there. Don't come in.'

He took a step back on to the landing, moving his hands away from the door frame he'd been about to lean on. 'Not finished then.'

'Thought we were, but I found some interesting stains under the rug.' Parsons pointed at the floor, but the wood was so old and dark McLean couldn't make anything out.

'More blood?'

'Reckon so. But it's old. I'd really love to dig up these floorboards, though. Something gave them a real soaking once.'

'Old? How old?'

Parsons made a glum face. 'Decades, probably. Big old house like this is full of secrets just waiting to be revealed.' She levered herself up off the floor with a dancer's lithe grace. Or the ease of someone who's still the right side of thirty.

'So probably not really relevant to our investigation then?'

'Probably not. Still interesting though.'

'Sadly our budget doesn't stretch to interesting.'

'Aye, I know.' Parsons smiled again, pulled off her latex gloves with a snap and shoved them into a pocket over her overalls as she pulled the hood back and let her hair free. A prickling of sweat beaded her forehead and she wiped it away with a sleeve. 'Still, got to make the most of it, right?'

'This place'll be sealed up for a while. You never know, you might have to come back.'

'I like an optimist.' Parsons smiled, exiting the room and pulling the door closed behind her. 'You here for any particular reason? Not that it's not nice to see a friendly face.'

'I was just checking up on progress. Hoping maybe for an update on the bloodstains.'

'Well, it's human for sure. And from what we can tell it's all from the same person. Freshest was still damp when we got here. Oldest was probably from two weeks back, maybe three. We've sent it off for DNA analysis, but that's only going to be any help if we've already got it on the database.'

McLean followed Parsons down the narrow stairs to the first-floor landing. 'You any idea how long it'll take to get the screening done?'

'A week. Maybe ten days. Depends on how busy the lab is. Why?'

McLean stood on the landing, looked around at the doors to the empty bedrooms, the narrow corridor leading to the back of the house where Miss Prendergast had slept her last night. He sniffed the air, catching the faintest hint of an aroma. Remembered the first time he'd come here and noticed it then. 'Call it a hunch. Is there any way we can get the process done quicker?'

Parsons glanced back up the stairs to the room they had just left. 'Technically we can do a profile on one sample in about eight hours. We've been trialling a new piece of kit that can do it even quicker. But it takes longer to run it through the database. And it means sweet-talking the lab boys too.'

'What if I was to give you a sample to compare it with?'

'That would shorten the database search, for sure. Still

doesn't help with the lab boys.' Parsons gave an exaggerated shudder. 'They have wandering hands.'

McLean dug into his pocket, pulled out his keyring with its enamelled Alfa Romeo badge, dangled it in front of Amanda Parsons' suddenly fixed gaze. 'What if I was to give you a lift back to the lab, maybe have a word with them about harassment in the workplace?'

The evening was becoming dark as McLean drove home, turned in through the open gates and up the driveway to park at the back door. A long afternoon of sifting through paperwork, waiting all the while for the call from the forensic lab that never came, had left his brain frazzled. He wasn't sure he could cope with another night being friendly, so the empty kitchen and note on the table came as something of a relief.

*Spending the night at home. Back tomorrow to clear out and clean up. J left food in the fridge. Phil.*

McLean flicked over the page, half expecting to see something else written on the underside, but there was nothing. The paper had been torn from a lined notebook, and the pen used was a leaky black biro similar to the one on the small table where the house phone lived. He put the note back down and shook his head to try and switch off the detective part of his brain. It was a note from Phil, nothing more. And the gist of it was he'd have a quiet night for a change.

Mrs McCutcheon's cat clattered in through the cat flap and stalked into the kitchen, bent tail raised high as she sniffed the air. No doubt knowing the noisy people had gone, she leapt up on to the table and sniffed the note, then presented her head for scratching.

'Just you and me now,' McLean said, earning himself the briefest of purrs before the cat jumped back down to the floor and stalked off into the house. 'Suit yourself.'

He opened the fridge, peering in at the mass of bottles, salad vegetables, neatly labelled pots of leftovers and jars of half-used condiments. It looked like a normal person's fridge, but he doubted it would last. Some of the previous night's chilli was in a bowl and he pulled it out, along with a beer. Opened one and popped the other in the microwave before heading out to the front door and the day's post.

A sizeable pile lay on the old wooden chest by the front door, and it was only then that he remembered he'd not bothered checking it the night before. He sifted through it slowly, unsure quite when it had become such a ritual. The usual round of credit card offers and catalogues for old ladies' clothes was supplemented by a couple of bills and something from his solicitors that would no doubt make his head hurt, or cost a lot of money, or both.

The microwave pinged as he wandered back into the kitchen. Mrs McCutcheon's cat was back on the table, sniffing at his open bottle of beer. She looked at him as if to suggest drinking on his own was a slow, sad way to go.

'Everyone's a critic.' He snatched the bottle away, poured the beer into a glass and set about serving up his meal. He should probably have cooked some rice, but the chilli on its own was plenty. Eating it straight out of the bowl meant less washing up, too. The cat retreated to the rug in front of the Aga and soon the quiet was underscored by the gentle wet noises of her washing herself. McLean ate in silence with his food and beer and solitude. Soon he would go through to the library, put some music on and savour a slow glass of whisky. He might even glance over the interview transcripts and other work he'd brought home with him.

Or he could call Jenny.

The thought came from nowhere. Except that he was sitting at the table where they had all shared a cheerful meal just twenty-four hours earlier. A meal she had cooked, the leftovers of which he was now eating. He looked over to the small table and the phone, the notebook and leaking black biro. Stupid, really. He didn't even have to get up. Just pull out his mobile and call.

And then what?

He stared at the blank screen, listened to the dull gurgle of the Aga and the schlep, schlep, schlep of Mrs McCutcheon's cat as she cleaned her backside with her tongue. Around him the house was a quiet cacophony of creaks and ticks, all familiar, all welcoming. It was his home, his refuge.

Gently, he placed the phone face down on the table beside his plate, picked up his fork and started eating again.

## 51

The station was quiet as McLean walked the corridors from the back entrance to his tiny office, early the next morning. For the first time in as long as he could remember, he felt refreshed, a spring in his step that even a note on his desk summoning him to a meeting with Detective Superintendent Brooks couldn't dampen.

'You wanted to see me, sir?' he asked ten minutes later, having been admitted to the office by a terse 'enter'.

Brooks stared up from his desk, shaved pate shiny in the weak morning sun that filtered through the window behind him. He narrowed his eyes suspiciously for a moment. Either that or he'd forgotten to put in his contact lenses that morning.

'Ah, yes. McLean.' Somehow Brooks managed to make the name sound like some kind of insult. McLean was experienced enough at dealing with his superiors to ignore it.

'This old woman up on Arthur's Seat. Mrs Prentice—'

'Prendergast, sir. Miss Eileen Prendergast.'

'Yes, yes. Whatever.' Brooks waved a pudgy hand in the air, swatting at his irritation like flies. 'I understand she ran a guest house. Had lodgers.'

'Apparently so.'

Brooks flushed red around his wobbling jowls, never a good sign. 'Apparently so? What do you mean, apparently so? You interviewed one of them, man.' A report lay open on his desk and he pulled it towards him, peering at the close type. 'A Mr Iain Angus.'

'Errm . . . No. I didn't.'

'Of course you did. It's written down here.' Brooks swept the page with a pudgy hand.

'I think I would remember something like that, sir.' McLean kept his tone level. It hadn't taken him any time at all to work out what was going on, but Brooks needed careful handling if he wasn't going to get violent.

'You're saying you didn't interview the lodger?'

'Correct. Sir.'

'So you didn't fail to get a home address or contact number from him.'

'Again correct, sir.'

'Well, what the fuck did you do then?'

'Do, sir? In what way?'

'What have you contributed to this investigation so far? How are you planning on taking it forward?'

McLean waited a few seconds before answering. True, he'd worked it out, but still he couldn't quite believe what was happening. 'I think there might have been a bit of a misunderstanding, sir. Eileen Prendergast's death isn't my case. I'm not involved in the investigation.'

Brooks' eyes almost disappeared into the folds of skin around his face, so deep was his frown. If it weren't for the layers of fat, McLean reckoned he might have heard the wheels turning slowly in his head, the cogs slipping and gears crunching.

'Not your case? Then what the fuck were you doing there yesterday? What were you and MacBride doing nosing about the scene in the first place, for that matter?'

Take a deep breath. Count to ten. So much for feeling refreshed and positive.

'Really? That's your biggest problem with all this?' McLean reached forward and snatched the report from the desk, flicked through it in search of his name, scanned the brief couple of paragraphs before throwing it back down. 'I've a mind to take this to Professional Standards.'

Brooks turned an even darker shade of red. 'What the fuck are you talking about?'

'I never spoke to anyone in Miss Prendergast's house. I had no reason to do so once I knew she was dead. And yet this report says I conducted an interview with a lodger. Rather than shouting at me, I think you should probably be questioning Detective Inspector Carter about his creative approach to evidence. And while you're at it, you might want to ask him why he forgot to get contact details from the witness he interviewed. If it helps at all, DS Langley was supposed to be with him at the time. I was a half-mile away doing my best to secure the potential crime scene he'd walked away from without handing over responsibility to anyone.'

Brooks leaned back in his chair, sweat pricking out all over his forehead in shiny spots. Either he was going to burst a blood vessel or there was going to be shouting.

'You have nothing to do with this at all?'

'Not nothing, sir, no. Miss Prendergast's name came up in a cold case we were reviewing. A possible relative of someone we were trying to identify. That's why me and MacBride went to see her. Everything else is Carter's responsibility.'

'Who the fuck assigned him the case?'

McLean suppressed the urge to say 'How the fuck should I know?' Trading insults with Brooks wasn't going to get the problem solved. 'I expect someone at Control in Bilston Glen, sir. Carter's not exactly working a lot of cases. They probably gave it to the DI with the least amount of work. Or maybe it was DCI Spence. He seems to like Carter for some unaccountable reason.'

'But he's written in the report that you visited the house and spoke to the lodger. Why would he do that if it wasn't true?'

'I really have no idea, sir. Perhaps you should ask him, rather than me.' McLean paused a moment before adding: 'Was that all? Only I've a busy day ahead.'

Brooks' frown became a scowl. 'Busy? You're running cold cases. How can you possibly be busy?'

'I seem to be running around cleaning up Carter's mess for one thing.' McLean knew it was a low taunt, but he couldn't help himself. He waited until Brooks was about to shout at him before adding: 'Also two deaths linked by a sample found at each scene, sir. Ring any bells?'

'Oh, right. Your prostitute angle.' Brooks deflated, shook his head slightly, jowls wobbling at the effort. Sweat sprayed off his forehead, falling to the carpet in little arcs. 'Getting anywhere with that?'

'Still waiting on the DNA profiles to be completed. It's ninety per cent certain we're dealing with the same person at both scenes. I'd rather be a hundred per cent before committing too much in the way of resources. Post-mortem doesn't suggest foul play, just an unhappy coincidence. But we've still got someone fleeing a scene twice. And Smith was meant to be under supervision.'

Brooks squinted again, his eyes disappearing into the folds of skin that made up his massive face. 'Aye. You're right there. Not sure anyone's mourning his loss, mind. Don't think they'll be so happy if we waste a lot of money chasing down shadows.'

'I understand, sir. Just want to make sure we've done our best.'

'Aye?' Brooks didn't try to hide his disbelief. 'Well, fuck off out of my office then.'

'With pleasure, sir.' McLean turned and headed for the door before the detective superintendent could shout at him any more. It didn't work. Brooks bellowed a parting shot.

'And if you see that useless streak of piss Carter, tell him I'm coming for his head.'

McLean found DS MacBride in the otherwise empty CID room, hunched over his desk and swiping away at his tablet computer. One of these days he'd ask the detective sergeant where he'd got the thing from. Uniform officers carried clunky PDAs on patrol, along with tiny little printers to issue fixed fines and other notices, but MacBride had managed to get in on some technology program that as far as McLean knew had long since been abandoned. And yet he still had the tablet, which seemed to give him access to every police network there was.

'See that sweepstake on Carter? Who's got today as the date he gets knocked back down to sergeant?'

MacBride looked momentarily puzzled, then tapped at his screen a couple of times. 'Sergeant Gatford, sir. And the kitty's standing at almost eight hundred quid.'

'Lucky old Don.' McLean told the detective sergeant about his meeting with Brooks. MacBride's eyes grew ever wider, like a child at Christmas.

'How on earth did he think he could get away with that?'

'Perhaps he figured we were there, and that was enough. Maybe he even thinks we actually did speak to this bloke after he'd gone. Knowing Carter he probably realised he'd forgotten to get contact details and thought he could just shift the problem on to someone else. Or he could just be pissed off we stopped his first major investigation from crashing down around his ears. I'm going to hazard a guess it'll be his last, though.'

'Why did they give it to him in the first place? Who gave it to him?'

'Funny you should ask that, Stuart. Brooks wanted to know the same thing. Control hand out the assignments, but they don't just stick their hand in a hat full of names. No, this has probably come from DCI Spence, and I don't think it's any coincidence he handed it to his favourite whipping boy.'

'But I thought Spence was doing everything he could to keep Carter out of trouble. Why hand him such a complicated case?'

'Put it this way. If you wanted something investigated without any risk of embarrassing evidence coming to light or awkward questions being asked, who would you put in charge? From CID in this station?'

'Oh. I see.' Dawning realisation spread across MacBride's face, followed up with another puzzled frown. 'But why?'

'That's what bothers me. I don't know. Seems to me someone's trying to make all this go away. Much like someone tried to make the brothel raid fiasco go away. Like they swept the original Headland House investigation under the carpet.'

'You think they're all connected?' MacBride didn't even try to hide the scepticism in his voice.

'I know, Stuart. Said out loud it sounds mad. Worst paranoid conspiracy theory going. Still, I can't quite shake the feeling there's something to it. The coincidences start to stack up rather too conveniently.'

'But something like that? I mean, it's too big, surely. Something that well organised, over so many years. Someone would have said something. There'd be journalists all over it.'

Oh to be young and naive. 'That's the thing, Stuart. If you look at this as an organisation, then you're right. Someone would have spilled the beans, or uncovered a secret. The bigger something gets the more difficult it is to hide. But if you think of it more as an organism, something that's emerged out of its own complexity . . . Well, maybe Dalgliesh was on to something after all.'

'Dalgliesh? What's she got to do with all this?'

McLean pulled out his phone, thumbed at the screen in search of a number. 'I'm not sure. But if you're talking conspiracy theories, she's the expert.'

The phone rang far longer than he was expecting it to. McLean had visions of an office in chaos, short-staffed as it was and now down their star reporter. Of course it might have been that his name had come up on the caller ID screen and they were deciding whether or not they wanted to talk to him. Finally the dial tone clicked away. He was expecting a voicemail message, but a familiar voice answered instead.

'*Edinburgh Tribune.* Senior editor's desk.'

'Mr Bairstow? Johnny? Hi. It's Tony McLean here. Wondered if you'd any news about Jo Dalgliesh.'

'Detective Inspector? This is a surprise. Oddly enough I've just been on the phone to the hospital and they're optimistic she'll make a good recovery. Probably be a while before she's back at work, but I don't suppose you lot will mind that too much, eh?' Bairstow laughed, but even over a mobile phone connection McLean could hear the desperation in his voice.

'I'm sure I don't know what you mean, Mr Bairstow. I'm really pleased to hear she's going to be OK.' McLean was surprised to find that he meant it too.

'Is that all you were calling for? Only I'm a bit busy right now.'

'Sorry. No. Should have got to the point. The story Jo was working on, that she came to see me about. Had she spoken to anyone else about it? Told you?'

'Only the basics. You know what she's like. Plays everything close to her chest. I knew it was about corruption and influence. Think she was trying to draw a link between several high-profile cases. She muttered something about Beggar's Benison and secret societies too, but then she always had a bee in her bonnet about those sort of things.'

'Did she say anything about some cold cases? Seventies, eighties, maybe some early nineties?'

'I'm not really sure ...' Bairstow left the sentence unfinished, as if there were very many things of which he was unsure.

'I'll not mess you about, Mr Bairstow. We need the press as much as we hate them. There's two cases I'm thinking of in particular. Was Jo interested in the Pentland Mummy, back in 'seventy-six? Headland House in 'ninety-four?'

The silence on the line was answer enough for McLean, but he let it draw out for a count of ten anyway.

'Thank you,' he said. 'Next time you see Jo, give her my best. I'll try to drop round and see her soon.'

He ended the call. For a while he just stared into the middle distance, the implications of the conversation bouncing around in his head. Not least of which was that he'd just wished Jo Dalgliesh well.

McLean was almost at his office when his phone rang. He'd been meaning to call Marchmont, confront her about her past and the way it seemed to be coming back to haunt both of them. The number was a mobile, near enough hers that in his haste he was sure.

'Heather. I rather think you owe me an explanation.'

'Heather? Who's Heather? Have you been keeping secrets from me, Tony?'

Not Marchmont. McLean felt the tips of his ears burn as he ducked into his office and out of sight. There hadn't been anyone in the corridor to see his embarrassment, but that didn't make it any less bad.

'Miss Parsons. Amanda. Sorry. I thought you were someone else.'

'Clearly. I'm all ears as to this explanation you're owed. Sounds fascinating.'

'You've a better chance of getting your hands on the keys to my Alfa than my telling you that. I take it this isn't just a social call?' McLean shuffled round his desk and dropped into the chair, noticing the ever-growing piles of paperwork camped around the surface. Hadn't he cleared all this lot yesterday?

'Here's me trying to be friendly. Don't know why I bother really.'

'Sorry. Just had a difficult conversation with my boss. Shouldn't be taking it out on you.'

'Aye, well. You'll maybe want to sit down before I tell you what I've got.'

'Sitting already.' McLean picked up the nearest folder, peered at the letters typed across the top of it, then dropped it back on to the stack when he realised they meant nothing to him.

'I did like you asked. Ran the freshest of the blood samples through the new machine I was telling you about. It's still undergoing evaluation, so I was able to slip yours in without anyone noticing. Wouldn't be admissible in court, but it's a good profile.'

'And did it match?'

'It's not an exact science, you know. There's always a degree of uncertainty.'

'How much uncertainty are we talking about here?'

'Twenty per cent? Maybe a little less. There's some strange patterns in the profile I can't make sense of. We'll run things through the old-fashioned system to be sure, but that'll take a few days.'

McLean leaned back and stared at the ceiling, his brain not really able to process what he'd suspected all along. 'You're telling me there's an eighty per cent chance the blood came from the same person as the sample?'

'Thereabouts, aye. Unless they had a twin, of course.'

'A twin? Is that likely?'

'What? I don't know. I was just joking. I mean it's possible, but I didn't really mean it. The sample profile's from the guy in the car park, right? And it's the same as the sample from the bloke in the gimp suit. Chances are whoever did for them was staying in that attic room for the last few weeks.'

McLean did a quick count in his head. How long since they'd found Eric Parker? The timeline fitted, it was just any explanation that eluded him. At least any rational explanation.

'That's good work, Amanda. Thank you. I'd really appreciate it if you could get the blood samples profiled the normal way now. Soon as possible.'

'Already done it. Should have the official results by the end of the week. So, about those keys?'

# 52

Descending into the depths of the building was like fast-forwarding the seasons. The temperature dropped and light faded to a winter twilight as he approached the Cold Case Unit's offices. McLean was still reeling from the news about the blood sample, even if a part of him had known. The scent lingering in the house, easily overlooked unless you'd encountered it before. And he had. When Heather Marchmont had tried to seduce him it had been almost overpowering, but he'd noticed it even before then. She carried it around with her all the time, only fainter, more subtle. He'd smelled it in the cafe, and when they'd first met in her house during the raid. But it wasn't Marchmont's blood in Miss Prendergast's attic bedroom, and it wasn't her saliva on Eric Parker or John Smith.

Unless she had a twin.

Parsons had meant it as a joke, but now McLean wasn't so sure. The coincidences were stacking up, and he didn't believe in coincidences. He couldn't take them to McIntyre, though. Not yet. Not until the results had been verified, linking all three cases together and into something a lot more sinister than they realised. Duguid was another matter, though. He was deep into this, knew far more than he was letting on. McLean hated to admit it, but the ex-detective superintendent was exactly the sounding board he needed.

It wasn't until he was almost at the door that he heard the voices inside and stopped. Two voices, and one of them wasn't Grumpy Bob. Something about their tone suggested interrupting wouldn't go well for him.

'You've got to let it go, Charles. Stop digging over old ground. Nothing good will come of it, you know that as well as I do.'

'Thought better of you, Brooks.' Duguid's low growl of a voice suggested he wasn't in the best of moods. 'Robinson been spanking your arse again, has he?'

'This isn't your station any more, you know? You're only back here as long as you're useful. Keep stirring this up and that won't be for long.'

'They've really got to you, haven't they, John? What was it, carrot or stick? Carrot, I'm guessing. Nice Chief Super post, maybe DCC in a couple of years when Call me Stevie's retired? Well, it's not as if you couldn't do with going on a diet.'

'You think this is a joke? You think this isn't going to blow up in all of our faces? Fuck's sake, Charles. You let it go once. Why can't you let it go again?'

'You need to ask that then you're not the detective I thought you were. Sure, I can live with the disappointment.'

McLean had the sense to back up the corridor a few paces so that it looked like he had just arrived as Detective Superintendent Brooks came barrelling out of the room, face a dangerously dark shade of red. His jowls wobbled as he strode, head down, only noticing McLean at the last possible moment.

'What the fuck are you doing here, McLean?'

'My job?' McLean saw the look on Brooks' face, took a

step back. Perhaps not the right time to break the news about the DNA test to him. 'Sir.'

'And does your job involve skulking around in dark corridors, eh? Does it involve sticking your nose into other detectives' cases, eh?' With each 'eh' Brooks jabbed McLean in the chest with a finger. Not hard enough to hurt, but enough to make him step back until he was pressed against the wall.

'Walking down a corridor towards my office is hardly "skulking", sir. And as I explained to you this morning, the only reason I was at his crime scene was because Miss Prendergast's name came up in one of our cold case enquiries.'

Brooks stopped poking him, his scowl deepening. He clearly wasn't a man used to being questioned by his juniors.

'Have you spoken to Carter yet, sir?' McLean knew he was pushing his luck, couldn't find it in him to care any more. 'Only I'm not the first person to find fault in his performance. He wasn't much use as a detective sergeant and I really don't think he's cut out for the responsibilities of being a DI. I'm sure someone thought it was a good idea to promote him, maybe even had a word with you about that. I think we can all see it's not worked out, though?'

For a moment he thought the detective superintendent was going to hit him and he tensed, ready for the blow. Brooks shook like a man barely in control of his rage, stared at him with his narrow, black eyes set deep in his pudgy face.

'Get out of my way.' He barged past, knocking McLean's

shoulder like a primary school bully, then stalked off up the corridor muttering under his breath.

'Someone's not a happy bunny.' McLean rubbed at his arm as he stepped into the room. Duguid looked up from his paper-strewn desk. Over in the far corner, Grumpy Bob had the air of a man trying very hard to pretend he wasn't there.

'Never much fun being shown up by your junior officers,' Duguid said. 'Especially after having your ear chewed off by the DCC. Probably the only perk of seniority's being able to take that out on the lower ranks. No fun if they bite back.' If he saw the irony in his words, he didn't show it.

'So, you've been pushing forward with Headland House then. Judging by that.' McLean cocked his head in the direction of the departing detective superintendent.

'You've got a problem with that?' Duguid leaned forward in his seat, long fingers steepled under his chin.

'Nope. You know I've never been good with being told what to do. This shit's all been buried deep, but that just means it takes a bit longer to resurface and it causes more damage on the way up. Gets very complicated too.'

'You always were trouble, McLean. Pain in the arse from the first moment I met you.'

McLean opened his mouth, was about to complain, but then he saw the glint in Duguid's eye, the faintest twitch of a smile. Hard to tell when the ex-detective superintendent was paying you a compliment.

'Did you have any idea what a can of worms you were

opening with all this, though?' McLean waved his hand in the general direction of Duguid's desk as he walked across the room to his own. The ex-detective superintendent leaned back in his seat, sliding into the shadows like a cheap magician.

'You've found something.' It wasn't a question.

'Eileen Prendergast had a couple of lodgers at the time she died. They've both done a runner, but one of them left a lot of blood behind. DNA profile suggests she's the same person who links Eric Parker and John Smith. Our missing sex worker. Least that's what we thought she was. Now I'm not so sure.'

'Parker. Smith.' Duguid muttered the words as if trying to dredge them out of his memory.

'The priapic salesman and the auto-erotic rapist.' Grumpy Bob seemed happy to join the conversation now that Brooks had gone.

'Oh. Right. You're working on them being linked, then?'

McLean wasn't sure whether Duguid was just acting dumb or really didn't know. In the past he'd been on top of pretty much everything that was going on in the station, but that was when he'd been in charge. Down here in the basement with his dusty archive boxes it was just possible he'd not been keeping up.

'Both had traces of saliva on them from the same woman. She sat in the passenger seat of Parker's car, so we assumed she got a lift from him. Now her DNA turns up in blood at Miss Prendergast's place. You know how I feel about coincidences.'

Duguid frowned. 'You taken this to Brooks or McIntyre?'

McLean shook his head. 'The test's not conclusive. Still waiting for it to be double-checked. It's enough for me, though. I really don't like how everything's coming together here. And another thing—'

He was cut short by the electronic trilling of his phone. A glance at the screen showed the name he had been about to bring up.

'I have to take this.' He thumbed accept as he slumped into his chair. 'McLean.'

'Tony? Is that you?'

A shiver shook through him that was only partly to do with the chill of the basement room. He said nothing, thinking only of a figure-hugging black latex catsuit, a musk so powerful it could render a man senseless. A scent shared with the woman they were trying to find. How to ask the questions he wanted to ask? Where to even begin?

'I wanted to apologise for the other night. It was wrong. I shouldn't have.' Marchmont's voice was that of a little girl lost. Nothing of the sultry seductress about it.

'I know who you are, Heather. Who you really are.' McLean looked up to see Duguid peering through the glare from his desk light, brow furrowed as he tried to work out who was on the phone.

'I should have told you. Right at the start. When we first met.'

'And what about the other night? Were you going to tell me then?' McLean put his hand in his jacket pocket to stop himself from fidgeting. This wasn't an easy conversation to have. He felt something, a slim tube, pulled it out to look at it.

'Please. I understand you're angry. What I did. It was wrong. That's not you. I should know that, of all people.' Marchmont sounded agitated, more so than usual.

'I don't know what you hoped to gain. Blackmail? Cheap thrills?' McLean held up the tube to the light, the EpiPen Jeannie Robertson had given him. How long had it been in there? He'd chucked yesterday's suit in the pile for the dry cleaners, grabbed this one from the hanging cupboard without realising he'd worn it recently.

'It's not like that, Tony.'

Marchmont's silence was wretched, the unheard sobbing as loud as any wail.

'Look, Heather. I know you're mixed up in something that's difficult to extract yourself from, but you've come this far, from a much worse place. You can change, and don't let anyone tell you otherwise.'

'If only it were so simple. Perhaps, a few months ago, it would have been. If you'd raided . . . If we'd . . .' Marchmont's voice faded to nothing, then she added: 'Can you come round? Please? I'm at home. I need to tell you what's going on and I can't do that on the phone. It's important you know, that you understand. I couldn't live with you thinking what you must about me.'

'After what happened the other night, I'm not sure that would be wise.' McLean rolled the EpiPen around in his free hand as he spoke.

'Bring someone with you. Your colleague, Ritchie. She's not part of this, but I know she understands.' Marchmont fell silent for once more and McLean found he was doing the same. Only this time it wasn't an interviewing trick to get her to speak; he really didn't know what to say.

'Please, Tony. It has to be now. They're coming for me. They know.'

'Who are they? What do they know? Has this got anything to do with Eileen Prendergast? Her two lodgers?'

'Not over the phone. They're listening. Always listening.' Marchmont's voice was almost a whisper now. McLean pictured her curled into a foetal ball in a darkened corner of the dungeon basement, the paranoia eating away at her. She needed help, that much was abundantly clear. But she hadn't asked who Eileen Prendergast was, which suggested it was a name she had at least heard before. She knew, and the only way he was going to get the answers was to play along with whatever game she was playing.

'I'll see what I can do, Heather. No promises, though.'

He waited for a response, but there was only the beep beep beep as the call ended.

'Who the hell was that?'

McLean looked up from the blank screen of his phone to see Duguid leaning over his desk. He'd been so absorbed in the call he'd not noticed the ex-detective superintendent stand up and walk across the room. A quick glance sideways showed Grumpy Bob sitting far more upright than McLean had ever seen the old detective sergeant, his ears fair quivering as he strained to hear what was going on.

'I think you know damned well who that was. You're the one with all the facts about Headland House, after all.'

'Headland . . . ?' Duguid paused a moment, then pointed at the phone still in McLean's hand. 'Heather? Heather Marchmont?'

415

McLean leaned back in his seat, enjoying the look of confusion and alarm on Duguid's face. 'So you did know what her name was after all. Thought you were lying to me about that.'

'But how? Why's she calling you?'

'When was the last time you spoke to her?' McLean asked.

'Spoke?' Duguid looked surprised at the question. 'Not since 'ninety-four. When we handed her over to social services. I wanted to interview her that night, but they wouldn't let me. Wouldn't let anyone talk to her. They made her disappear. My chief super told me it was for her safety. Didn't believe him, but there wasn't much I could do about it.'

'You found out where she was, though. Kept an eye on her.'

'For a while, yes. But she dropped off the radar a few years back. I figured she'd made it past twenty, so she was probably going to be all right. How the fuck do you know her?'

McLean dropped his phone on to the desk, noticing as he did that the screen showed the number alongside the name associated with it. Edinburgh local code, Stockbridge, not her mobile. So she'd been telling the truth when she'd said she was home.

'She lives in Stockbridge. It was her house we raided thinking it was a brothel. She was there, but not participating.'

'Not participating?' Duguid asked, then his brain caught up. 'Oh.'

'I recognised her. First time I saw her I was sure I knew

416

her from somewhere. Of course the last time I saw her before that she was only ten, so I couldn't put a name to her face. It took MacBride and his magic computer to fit all the pieces together. They gave her a dead child's identity. That's the sort of thing Witness Protection do.'

'But why's she calling you?' Duguid paced around the room, ending up at his own desk. He leaned against it, faced McLean with an accusing stare. Then something else slid across his face, something like horror. 'Christ, is that what Spence meant about your new girlfriend? You've not been fucking her, have you?'

'What? No. Give me some credit, won't you?'

'So what does she want? Why call you now?'

McLean picked up the phone, rolled it around in his hands. 'She wants me to go round to her place. Says she's something important to tell me. Only the last half-dozen times she's tried, she's bottled it at the last minute. I've no idea whether this time will be the same.'

'But you're going to go and see her, right? Even though that's probably the stupidest thing you've done in a long career of idiot moves.'

'I wasn't planning on going alone. Ritchie is—'

'An acting detective inspector with good promotion prospects despite all you've done to ruin her career progress. You'd do well to leave her out of this.'

'I wish I could, but Marchmont trusts her. And this all started off with the SCU raid. I need to let her know I'm going at the very least.'

Duguid let out a weary sigh, but McLean could see it for the act it was. True, the ex-detective superintendent had never much liked him, but this was a chance to get to the heart of a mystery that he'd been chasing for over two decades. No way he was going to sit on the sidelines and watch.

'Bob. You go over to HQ and talk to Ritchie. Let's keep this out of official channels for now. We'll meet you over at this house in Stockbridge. All of us'll go and visit wee Heather Marchmont together.'

## 53

They parked in the same spot across the road from the front door that McLean and Jo Dexter had taken the night of the raid. Only that time it had been an SCU pool car, not McLean's tiny red Alfa Romeo. It had been strange driving across town with Duguid in the passenger seat. He would far rather it had been DS Ritchie or even Grumpy Bob. Duguid had spent most of the mercifully short journey muttering under his breath about the 'ridiculous car', but he had never once tried to persuade McLean not to come. Not until now.

'You know doing this will get you fired, right? Probably be the end of my retirement plan, too.'

'You didn't have to come, sir. I'm not so stupid I'd go in there alone.'

'Aye, but Grumpy Bob and Ritchie're no' here yet, are they? How long are you going to wait for them? Knowing Marchmont's in there? Knowing who she is and what she can tell you?'

McLean had to admit that Duguid had a point. Despite what he'd said, he would almost certainly have gone in already had the ex-detective superintendent not been with him. Waiting had never been his strongest point.

'I've already retired. Don't mind if they fire me.' Duguid unclipped his seatbelt and clambered out of the car with surprising agility given both his age and its ride height.

McLean scrabbled to follow, then remembered the Alfa didn't have modern facilities like central locking. By the time he'd sorted everything out, Duguid was already across the road and approaching the stone steps that led up to the front door, still showing signs in the chipped black paint of where it had been battered open.

It was a big house. McLean remembered it from the raid, but that had been at night and with scores of policemen milling around. Standing in the quiet, empty street he could take in the sheer size of the front windows and the high ceilinged rooms behind them, count the storeys climbing up to the grey autumn sky. He remembered the basement, too, with its faux torture dungeon complete with hanging cage. This was far too big for a large family, let alone a single woman to live in. And yet it was becoming increasingly popular with the city's wealthier inhabitants to return these massive New Town houses to their original specification from the apartments or office blocks they'd been converted to.

'How the other half live, eh?' Duguid hopped up the steps and rang the doorbell. There was a moment's silence, as if the city held its breath, and then the door opened a crack. A single eye peered suspiciously through the gap.

'Miss Marchmont? Heather? I'm Detective Superintendent Charles Duguid. I believe you've been in communication with my colleague, Detective Inspector McLean?'

Marchmont shifted slightly as she moved her gaze from Duguid to the street beyond, finally noticing McLean at the bottom of the steps. She opened the door slightly, still not exactly welcoming.

'I was expecting—'

'Acting DI Ritchie is on her way.' Duguid took a step back. 'Miss Marchmont. Do you remember me?'

She looked him up and down, eyes widening. 'You'd better come in.'

The kitchen was pretty much as McLean remembered it; something that could have come straight out of any designer homes magazine or broadsheet weekend supplement. Their feet had echoed across the cold, empty hall, breath almost misting in the frigid air, but here there was at least the semblance of warmth, of somewhere people actually lived. Marchmont poured coffee from a glass jug, fetched milk from a fridge big enough to hide several dead bodies inside. She said nothing all the while, waiting until they had all perched on uncomfortable stools at the breakfast bar before finally speaking.

'For a long time I hated you, you know?' She looked from McLean to Duguid and then back again. 'Both of you.'

'Why's that, Miss Marchmont?' Duguid asked.

'Heather, please. At least I think Heather. It's the name they gave me when I was old enough, and it's all I really know. Before that I was just "girl" if I was anything at all.' Marchmont took a long, slow sip of her coffee. 'I hated you because you abandoned me. You saved me and then you abandoned me to them.'

'Once you were given over to social services it was out of our hands. I was lead investigator and I wasn't even allowed to know your name.'

'But you found out anyway, didn't you?' Marchmont looked straight at Duguid and for the first time McLean saw something like life in her features, a defiance worn

421

down by years of abuse. A lifetime.

'I did. McLean knew nothing. He was too young, too junior to be involved. And besides, he'd been sent up to Aberdeenshire on six months' training. They made it look like a good career move, but the truth is they just wanted him out of the way.'

'I know that. Now. Back then it was different. I was only a girl, and all I'd ever known was abuse. My earliest memories are of . . .' Marchmont paused, her eyes going out of focus for a moment. Then she shuddered. 'I don't want to think about it, but you can't begin to imagine. And then you came along, rescued me like a knight in shining armour. Or at least a black police uniform. It was good, for a while. The family they fostered me to, they were nice, to start with. But you can't run from the people who put me in that cage. You can't escape from them. They found me, claimed me as theirs. They didn't abuse me any more. No doubt they had other toys to play with, and I was probably getting too old for them by then. But they owned me. They helped me through college, got me my job, but they owned me. Never let me forget that, and what I owed them.'

The silence that settled over the kitchen was a blanket of misery. Looking at her now, McLean could see clearly the little girl he had found in the cage in the attic of Headland House, all those years ago. He really should have tried harder to keep an eye on her, find out where she was and check from time to time that she was OK. But that was something the Tony McLean of today would think to do. Back then he'd been a different person.

'I—' He started to apologise, knowing that it would

sound insincere, but the doorbell's ring interrupted him. Marchmont tensed, her hands tightening around her coffee mug so that the liquid inside slopped over the edge.

'That'll be Ritchie.' Duguid slid off his stool with a groan of relief. 'I'll go let her in, shall I?' He didn't wait for an answer, just headed for the door. McLean waited until he was gone before speaking.

'I'm really sorry for what happened. If I'd known . . .'

Marchmont reached out her coffee-dampened hand and placed it over his. 'It was never your fault, Tony. I'm not sure it's really anyone's fault. It's just the way the world works.'

'You can't believe that, surely? It was men who put you in that cage in the attic. Well-connected men who were going to do unspeakable things to you.'

'Men?' Marchmont cocked her head to one side as if it was the first time she had considered the subject. 'I suppose. In a way. Men, women. They came and they went.' She let her head droop a moment, as if trying to suppress some particularly unpleasant memory. 'You'll probably find it hard to believe, but I was one of the lucky ones. I had a twin brother, once. Long ago. He died.'

Something about the way she said it suggested to McLean that it hadn't been an accidental death.

'They killed him?'

'You keep saying "They" as if you want to label them, identify them. Track them down and punish them. But it's not like that, Tony. This isn't some secret society of perverts doing unspeakable things. It's bigger than that, not so much organised as organic.'

McLean couldn't help but hear the echoes of Jo

Dalgliesh's words, her mad theories. 'But there are connections, links between people. And someone has to own places like this house, Headland House.'

'Oh, there are organisations, yes. There are little groups and less formal networks everywhere. It's the nature of the beast.' Marchmont looked him straight in the eye as she said the last word. 'You went to boarding school, right? You'll know the things the boys get up to. The initiations, the stupid little ceremonies. You had to do them, or nobody would talk to you. Right?'

It was a long time ago. He'd been painfully young, not really over losing his parents when his grandmother had packed him off to his father's old prep school. A draughty old country mansion in rural Hertfordshire, surrounded by too much emptiness to ever think of running away, no matter how miserable he had felt there. The regime was brutal, bewildering, the teachers one minute sympathetic the next unaccountable rage. He remembered the little traditions, though, the things that formed a bond between you and your fellow pupils. The shared depravities endured because the alternative, to refuse, was both unthinkable and to court humiliation. They'd seemed innocuous at six, but later, at the big school? Not something he was all that proud of. And by the time he reached university he'd developed the outsider's mentality, no longer wanted to be part of that club. Many others had, though.

'That's how it starts.' Marchmont seemed able to read his thoughts. 'It's part privilege, part a coping strategy. Those bonds you form in childhood mark you. If you're lucky or brave or strong, you can say no. But deep down everyone wants to be part of the team. Everyone wants to be loved. And once you've joined in it can be very hard to stop. Some people don't even want to.'

'I'm not sure how this links into what's happening here,' McLean said, although deep down he was pretty sure he understood.

'You're not part of this, Tony. You never were, I can see that now. But so many successful men and women are. Their success is bred from a mixture of hard work and opportunity, greased by the oil of those connections made in childhood, at school and university, and all held together by the mutual fear of what they have all done together, of it ever coming to light. You look for secret societies running things, pulling strings, letting people commit terrible atrocities, but the truth of it is it's much more passive than that. It's a framework within which atrocity can breed as easily as charity. Self-perpetuating and with highly evolved strategies for defending itself when threatened.'

McLean leaned back on his stool, not quite sure how to take in what Marchmont was saying. 'So how do you fit into this, then?'

'She's one of those highly evolved strategies. At least she was, for a while.'

He turned too swiftly, knocking over his stool and almost falling to the floor as he tried to see who had spoken. She stood in the doorway, dressed in an outfit that could have come from the wardrobe in Stacey Craig's master bedroom. At first he didn't recognise her, the shiny black material all too distracting as it revealed everything that it hid. Then she stepped forward into the room and he remembered the surly waitress who had served him coffee and cake in the cafe around the corner. Cake that

Jo Dalgliesh had eaten rather than him. Behind her, ex-Detective Superintendent Duguid stumbled into the room, pushed forward by a man who could only be the woman's twin.

'Alice.' Marchmont spat the word out like an angry cat. 'You said you were done here. You were leaving.'

'What can I say, Heather? I lied.' The woman nodded once, then turned her gaze on McLean. 'And this must be the fabled Tony McLean. If it isn't the very man I've been looking for.'

# 54

McLean stood motionless, unsure whether he couldn't move or had just forgotten how. He hadn't noticed the scent before, but now it grew stronger, filling the room with that heady musk. It coated the back of his throat, squeezed his lungs until breathing was almost impossible. The kitchen, the table, Heather Marchmont, all faded from his vision until all he could see was the woman with the dirty-blonde hair.

'Help me.' Duguid struggled past her, tried to get to McLean but stumbled sideways into the table, knocking more chairs over in the process. His voice was slurred like a man who's had a couple of whiskies too many. Or a man in the throes of a seizure. The movement and sound broke partially through his stupor, and McLean was able to take a step back, shaking his head to rid himself of the fog.

'What have you done to him?' His voice was distant, like somebody else talking. The woman – Alice, wasn't that what Marchmont had called her? – stepped lightly across the room, her hips swaying in a parody of provocation. She crossed over to where Duguid was thrashing around on the floor, and McLean could only watch as she knelt down, took hold of the ex-detective superintendent's chin and pulled him around to face her.

'Poor little old man. Looks like something he ate didn't agree with him.' She pouted as she slipped one finger into her mouth, pulling it out glistening with saliva, then ran it over Duguid's lips as if she were a weary mother silencing an unruly child. He struggled for a moment longer, then went limp. When she stood up, releasing her hold of him, he slumped motionless to the floor.

'I like an older man, but just for starters.' She stalked towards McLean with that slow, exaggerated, predatory walk. He took a step back and found himself pressed up against something. His eyes darted to the door where the man had been standing. Somehow he'd managed to cross the kitchen without McLean noticing, and now stood directly behind him. Strong hands grabbed his arms, pinned them behind his back. He struggled then, couldn't quite understand why he hadn't before. His thoughts were slow, as if they waded through deep water, his hearing muffled.

'Don't fight. It only makes things worse.' Whether it was Alice who spoke, her brother or Heather, McLean couldn't have said. The effect was the reverse of its intention, though, and he fought all the harder. Dropping his chin to his chest, he hurled his head backwards as hard as he could. The crunch of breaking nose was satisfyingly meaty, but the lock on his arms held strong. If anything the man gripped him tighter, letting out the slightest of grunts as if pain meant nothing to him.

'Tony, Tony, Tony. Calm yourself.' The young woman stood directly in front of him now, reaching for his face with a well-manicured hand. He flinched at her touch, but it was soft, caressing his cheek like a mother with a new-born child. The smell of her was overpowering; a mixture of flowers and wine and darker, earthy tones that seemed to bypass his nose and connect directly with his hindbrain.

'Who . . . ?'

'Shhh.' The woman pressed an unlicked finger to his lips and the taste of her made it almost impossible to breathe.

'You know who I am,' she said. 'You of all people. I am Aphrodite, Goddess of Love. I am the spirit of the forest in spring. I am the sap that rises in the trees, the birds that sing in the air. I am life itself.'

Her scent was everywhere, filling his lungs, overwhelming his senses. It was crushed grass, flowers freshly picked on a summer morning, loam disturbed by sporulating fungi. It was the stench of decay, of dead things rotting in the dark.

'What . . . What have you done to Duguid?' McLean struggled against the iron grip holding him fast, tried to drag his eyes away from the young woman's face to the prone form behind her.

'What do you care about him? He hates you, doesn't he?' She pinched his cheeks together, forcing his gaze back to her. 'You hate him.'

'Not . . . Hate . . .' McLean forced out the words with the last of his strength. He could hardly breathe for the stench filling the room, drowning him in a miasma of filth. How could this have happened so quickly? How could they have overpowered him and Duguid both?

'No?' Alice raised a disbelieving eyebrow. 'It's no matter. I'm going to enjoy this. You should too. Everyone should die happy.'

She pulled him forward towards her, leaning in with a slow inevitability. McLean was powerless to resist as those shiny red lips parted to reveal perfect white teeth, a darting, flicking tongue.

'You can't have him. He's mine!'

The words cut through his stupor like a bucket of ice-cold water to the face. Still slow, he couldn't work out where the knife handle had come from that jutted out of the young woman's chest. A dark red stain oozed out and she let go of his face, looking down as if she too couldn't quite understand what was happening. And then McLean felt the grip on his arms release, so suddenly he lurched on unsteady legs.

'Alice! No!'

The young man caught his sister as she started to fall forwards, and only then did McLean notice Heather Marchmont standing just to his side. There was a look on her face of utter horror, and she held her right hand up by her head, fist clenched where she had gripped the knife. The knife she had stabbed into the young woman's heart.

It took long moments for McLean to recover his sense of balance, longer still to realise that the cloying scent had faded almost entirely. The young man had lowered his sister gently to the floor and was fussing about her head and neck. She was so pale as to be almost white, face, neck and hands stark against the black rubber of her skin-tight outfit. Blood slicked around the wound, the tip of the knife protruding from her shoulder blade like an ugly wart.

'No, no, no, no, no.' His voice was quiet, desperate, echoed by the sobs escaping from Marchmont as she too sunk to her knees. McLean staggered back, bumping into the stool he had been sitting on just moments earlier. It felt like a lifetime had passed since they had been talking, since Duguid had gone to answer the door expecting Ritchie and Grumpy Bob. Where the hell were they?

Duguid.

As he remembered the ex-detective superintendent, McLean looked across the kitchen to the dining table, saw him sprawled on the floor, chairs toppled all around him. He staggered over, knelt down beside the prone figure. Duguid's face was dark red and swollen, his lips slightly parted as if he was trying to breathe but couldn't. His eyes were open, and he stared up at McLean with a look of terror, tried to say something but failed.

McLean fumbled at Duguid's neck, loosening his tie and undoing the top two buttons of his shirt with one hand while he scrabbled at his jacket pocket with the other. His brain was still not working properly, but he could remember just an hour or so earlier. He'd taken it out while he was talking to Marchmont, but for the life of him he couldn't remember if he'd put it back again, or left it on his desk. His hand closed around the slim plastic tube and he let out a short laugh of relief. Pulled out the EpiPen and whipped off the lid. A swift jab to Duguid's leg, hold for a count of ten like they'd shown him in the training session. He chucked the used syringe away, rubbed at the spot where he'd just injected, hoped to hell that his hunch was right.

'Oh my dear, sweet Heather. You really shouldn't have done that.'

The words sent a chill through McLean as cold as the person who spoke them. He looked up to see the impossible. Alice stood slowly, helped to her feet by her brother. Blood smeared the front of her bodysuit, slicked the floor where she had lain. There was no way she could stand, no way she could still be alive. Unless she hadn't truly been alive to start with. The room began to fill with her scent

431

again, the odour of decay, the unemptied bins, the dead badger rotting at the verge. Death in all its many forms.

Marchmont backed away, but the stool McLean had knocked over stopped her and she was pinned against the counter. Alice reached up to the handle in her chest, gripped it firmly and pulled out the knife with a horrible sucking sound. It should have been excruciating, but she just smiled as it slid out, a drop of deepest red blood hanging from the tip. McLean knew he needed to move, but his legs were tree trunks, rooted to the floor.

'Here, cousin. Let me give you this back.' Slowly, oh so slowly, she twisted the knife around in her hand. Then, swifter than any snake, she jabbed it forward, hitting the exact same spot on Marchmont's chest as it had pierced her own. It sunk in up to the hilt, driven with such force that Marchmont fell to her knees, letting out a dreadful shriek of pain that quickly turned to a bubbly cough. She looked down at the knife, up at the young woman, then across the room to where McLean still crouched. And then the light seemed to fade from her eyes as she toppled forward to the floor.

Where the rage came from, he couldn't say. One moment he was crouching beside Duguid, head still thick with the fug that filled the room like a haar on the Forth. The next, he was on his feet, one of the dining chairs in his hand, launching himself across the room with a scream that echoed throughout the house. He brought the chair crashing down on the young man's back and shoulder, catching his head as he turned to defend himself. It shattered into a dozen pieces, jarred McLean's arms right up to his shoulders, but the young man merely shrugged it off as if he'd been hit with a feather pillow. He pivoted on one foot, reached up and grabbed the chair leg that was all that was left in McLean's hand. McLean twisted around, holding on with all his strength, stuck a foot out and used his opponent's momentum to bring him crashing down. He fell awkwardly, grabbing at the nearest stool, clipped his forehead on the breakfast bar. The noise of him hitting the floor was out of all proportion to his size and bulk, but then so was his strength. McLean stood over him, waiting for him to push himself back up. Too late he remembered the woman.

'You really shouldn't try to hurt my brother. It only makes him angry.'

He turned on the spot, foot slipping in something that might well have been blood. She was so close it was no stretch at all for her to reach out, grab his lapels and steady him. He put his hands out to fend her off, felt the front of her outfit wet and warm. She shuddered at his touch, closing her eyes for a moment and breathing in deeply. McLean could smell the aroma oozing off her in waves, mixed with an earthy, copper tang and something darker, more menacing. He tried to step backwards, get away, but the wall was immediately behind him. And then the wall grabbed his arms, twisted them around and up behind his back until he couldn't move at all. He risked a sideways glance and saw the young man's face, impassive, close. A gash across his forehead leaked red into his eyes, down his nose. A drop pooled on the tip and then fell, splashing on the dark tweed of McLean's jacket.

'I think he likes you, though.' Alice reached up with a hand smeared red. Whose blood it was, her own or

Heather's, McLean couldn't say. He tried to shy away from it, but it felt like he was being held in place by a mountain. Her touch was soft, slippery as she gently stroked his cheek, gazed into his eyes with a half-smile on her face as if plunging a dagger into Marchmont's breast were some kind of joke.

'You won't get away,' McLean said, even though he knew it was a lie. 'Back-up's on its way.'

The woman frowned. 'Shame. I would have liked to have spent some more time with you. Got to know you better. There's so much about you that is fascinating.' She leaned towards him, the musk rising as she came closer, crushing her body against his. Her breath was like cut grass heaped into a pile and slowly decaying on a summer's day, her lips cool as they brushed his.

The kiss was long and intimate. McLean tried to struggle, but he was overpowered by her scent, by the warmth of her body, and by the strong arms pinning him tight. Her tongue pushed past his lips, exploring his mouth in tiny, hesitant jabs. The taste of her was at once intoxicating and abhorrent, the pressure building in his head as he fought to get away, fought to have ever more. He knew then what had put Stacey Craig in a coma. Knew how Eric Parker had died, John Smith too. Even Eileen Prendergast, old and on the verge of senility. They had all succumbed to this heady pleasure. Now he would die too. It would all be for nothing. It would all be over.

And then she was gone, pulling away from him, releasing her hold on his face. Everything felt distant, muffled. Behind him, the young man released his hold and McLean slumped to the floor, his legs unable to take his weight. He struggled to lift his head, saw Heather Marchmont lying on her back, the knife sticking out of her chest, blood seeping into the light oak polished floorboards. Her eyes stared sightlessly at the ceiling and she wasn't breathing.

'We're done here. Come, Iain. It's time to go home.'

McLean forced himself up on to his knees. The room swayed about him as he reached out, tried to stop the twins from leaving. The young woman, Alice, stopped at the kitchen door, turned back to him and winked. 'It was fun. We should do it again some time.'

And then she was gone.

Duguid's groan woke him from his stupor. McLean shook his head, trying to get rid of the scent clinging to him like cheap aftershave, spat out the taste in his mouth. Looking over, he saw the ex-detective superintendent lying on his back, taking deep breaths as if he'd just finished a marathon. At least he was alive.

Alive.

He crawled on all fours over to where Heather Marchmont lay. The pool of blood on the floor beside her was darkest red. He felt its warmth as it soaked into the knees of his trousers, far too much of it to be healthy. The knife was buried deep, no way he was even going to try getting it out. But the hilt quivered rhythmically, a slow, shallow breath.

'We need an ambulance. Quick.' McLean croaked out the words, not really expecting them to be answered, but then he heard the tones of a mobile phone being dialled, Duguid's wheezing one-sided conversation as he put a call in to Control. McLean eased Marchmont over on to her side, raised her up towards him as gently as he could and tried to check for a pulse. She stirred at the movement, eyes flickering open. As she saw him, the faintest of smiles ghosted across her face and she reached up a bloodstained hand to his cheek.

'You came back for me.' It wasn't the voice of the woman he had met just a few weeks earlier, but the frightened little girl in a cage in a dusty attic twenty years before. With the words came blood, bubbling out through her lips in bright, vivid contrast. Her last coughed 'Thank you' was little more than a whisper as the light faded from her eyes and she fell limp in his arms.

Behind him, McLean heard a commotion at the kitchen door, the familiar voice of Acting Detective Inspector Ritchie exclaiming 'Oh fuck!' But all he could see was Heather Marchmont's black, dead eyes staring back at him.

## 55

'Have you any idea how bad this looks? What it means for the force? For Police Scotland?'

McLean hadn't often sat on the wrong side of the table in an interview room. Once or twice during training, of course. And there'd been that time when he'd been hauled in front of Professional Standards accused of taking bribes and having a bad drug habit. But never in front of the deputy chief constable. Never straight from a crime scene. Never with the smell of blood still in his nose, the stain of it still on his fingers and in his clothes. Never with the image of the light fading from someone's eyes still fresh in his memory.

He didn't think he would ever be able to forget that.

'Nothing like as bad as it is for Heather Marchmont.'

Her dying eyes haunted him. That final, whispered 'Thank you'.

'Of course, if you'd left well alone when you were told to, then chances are she'd still be alive.'

McLean clenched his fists under the table, aware that leaping to his feet and attacking the deputy chief constable would probably not do his career prospects much good. If he had a career at all. It hadn't escaped his notice that this interview was taking place without any witness to the proceedings, though. No one from Professional Standards was anywhere to be seen, and as far as he knew the cameras were disconnected, the voice recorder switched off. So perhaps there was hope.

'If you hadn't shut down the brothel raid investigation she'd probably still be alive too. What are you doing about catching the woman who attacked her?'

The deputy chief constable stopped mid-stride, turned to face McLean. 'What woman would that be? This mysterious woman who somehow managed to overpower Charles Duguid and you? Who managed not only to survive being stabbed in the chest herself, but also to then extract the knife used on her and turn it on her alleged attacker? Have you any idea how far-fetched that sounds?'

'Duguid was there. He saw it all.' McLean knew this was a lie, but he was clutching at straws. This wasn't how things were supposed to have panned out. There should have been a city-wide search for Alice and her brother Iain, but every time he had tried to mention them people had looked at him in that horrible, sympathetic way. That same look he remembered all too well from when he had found his fiancée's dead body. It wasn't accusatory, at least not fully. More pitying, and perhaps a little fearful. He was tainted with death and no one wanted to be associated with that.

'As I understand it, Charles had a bad allergic reaction, probably something he ate while you and this Marchmont woman were chatting to each other. Lucky you had an EpiPen on you, really. Not quite sure exactly why you were carrying one, though.'

'A friend of mine almost died from anaphylactic shock recently. The nurse in the ICU ward gave it to me to pass on when she's recovered.' McLean wasn't sure why he was justifying his actions, except that reason seemed to have been locked out of this room along with any witnesses to the proceedings.

'The point is, Tony, Charles was unconscious or as good as. Just you and Miss Marchmont and a knife. That's what it looks like to anyone coming in from the outside.'

McLean froze. The implications were horribly clear. 'You can't honestly believe I ?'

'Murdered her?' Call-me-Stevie smiled like a cartoon shark. 'No. You're not a murderer. To be honest, I don't think you'd even kill in self-defence. But let's face it, the woman was obsessed with you. I know her boss. She's been shunning her work, digging up every last piece of information she can find about you these past couple of months, constantly calling you, arranging meetings and then running out on you when you turn up. She's a classic stalker, and she couldn't cope when you didn't react the way she wanted you to. I'm willing to bet the coffee she served you and Charles was drugged; that's what knocked you both for six. She probably tried to seduce you, then got violent when you rejected her. Drugged, you can hardly be blamed if the knife she attacked you with ended up in her chest. I've seen it all too often. It's why we try to stop people carrying knives in the first place. Nine times out of ten it's the one carrying the damn thing gets hurt.'

McLean looked down at his lap, his hands balled into fists. Smears of dried blood still caked his skin in places. His fingers shook as he tried to relax the tension and spread them wide. He was dimly aware that the DCC had stopped speaking.

'I never touched the knife, so it won't have my finger-prints on it. There will be prints, though. Marchmont's and those of a second person.' McLean looked slowly up into the bland face of his boss as he spoke. 'A simple forensic analysis of the blood found at the scene will confirm there was at least one other person present, sir. A more detailed DNA analysis of that blood will confirm it to be the same as was found in the attic bedroom of Eileen Prendergast's house in Duddingston. It will also match saliva found on the bodies of Eric Parker and John Smith. I believe DNA profiling can also confirm the gender of the person in question, but I'll save them the time. It was a woman. She was there, and if you try to pin the blame for Marchmont's death on me, I'll make damned sure everything comes out in court.'

Call-me-Stevie flinched slightly. 'Court? You misunder-stand me, Tony. This isn't a matter for court. Nobody really thinks you had anything to do with Marchmont's death. I'm just pointing out how it looks to those of us who weren't there.'

'So what are you doing to catch the person who did it, then?'

The DCC acted as if he hadn't even heard the question. 'There'll have to be an enquiry, of course. A woman's died in violent circumstances and that will need thorough inves-tigation. Think I'll put DCI McIntyre on the case, she needs something to take her mind off her situation at home. You'll have to be suspended while we clear things up, I'm afraid. Shouldn't be more than a couple of weeks. Month tops. And it'll be paid. Not that it matters to you, eh? Can't really spare you for longer than that, though, if I'm being

440

honest. Far too few good detectives these days. Too many DI Carters. Well, PC Carter, perhaps I should say. No idea how he managed to persuade the promotions board he was capable. Mike Spence speaks very highly of him, of course.'

McLean slumped back in his seat as the DCC wittered on, clearly rehearsing a story for the inevitable press conference. Another couple of run-throughs and Call me Stevie would have it down pat, maybe even actually start to believe it. So that was how it worked, when all was said and done. Not some sinister shadowy organisation manipulating people with blackmail and promises; more everyone acting in their own self-interest, protecting what was theirs at the expense of what was right.

He knew what had happened, and Duguid knew some of it too, but it was their word against the deputy chief constable's. And their word had the whiff of something inexplicable about it. He could try to call them out, shout to the world how Heather Marchmont had really died, but he knew it would be pointless. Nothing could ever be proved. If he so much as mentioned Dalglicsh's theories they would call him mad, pension him off, sideline him.

He was damned if he did and damned if he didn't.

Dimly aware that the DCC was still talking, McLean pushed back his chair, scraping the legs noisily on the concrete floor as he stood up.

'What do you think you're doing?' Call-me-Stevie asked, interrupted mid-flow.

McLean straightened his jacket, spots of red blood darkening the material. He'd not seen himself in a mirror, but if there was that much on his cuffs, his face was probably covered in it too. Why had nobody taken his clothes from him for analysis? So much for procedure; the investigation was dead before it had even started. 'You're not going to arrest me, sir. You said as much already. Sounds like you don't want to fire me either. So I'm going to go home and have a shower to clean off all this blood and the stench of corruption. Then I'm going to find a bottle of good whisky and see if that helps to wash away the bitter taste in my mouth.'

He'd meant to go home. Walked out of the interview room hardly hearing the deputy chief constable's protestations, through a station full of staring faces, accusing faces, worried faces. Out into the car park where his little red Alfa Romeo had been carefully parked in a reserved space. Someone else must have brought it back from Marchmont's house, probably Ritchie. He vaguely recalled giving her the keys, her handing them back to him later. He'd been in no fit state to drive then, still wasn't, if he was being honest with himself. And for all he'd told Robinson he wanted to go home and wash away the day's horror with whisky, the idea of being alone with a bottle grew less appealing with each footstep.

So he walked. He'd always enjoyed walking; the rhythm of his feet on the pavement helped him think, helped him puzzle out exactly what was going on. What had happened.

He had spent a long time in Marchmont's house, sitting quietly in the corner of the kitchen while Ritchie and Grumpy Bob had secured and processed the crime scene. Duguid had left in an ambulance, shaky from whatever drug Alice had used on him. Alice and Iain. The twins. He had no idea who they were, where they had come from or where they had gone. Thinking too hard about them, about what they represented, just made his head hurt.

So he walked. Walking helped clear his mind, movement the antidote to the toxins fizzing in his bloodstream. The memories started sorting themselves into proper order, even if nothing really made any sense. He had stared at Heather Marchmont's dead body, lying in a drying pool of her blood, until a paramedic had covered her over with a sheet. He had wanted to uncover her face then. To see her just one last time. To tell her he was sorry.

Which was probably why his feet had brought him here.

'Tony. Good God, man, you look like you've gone ten rounds with Cassius Clay.' Angus Cadwallader was dressed in a fresh pair of green scrubs, ready to perform yet another post-mortem. Too early for it to be Heather, of course; she'd only just have arrived at the city mortuary. McLean looked over to the wall of cold-store cabinets, wondering which one she was lying behind.

'Sorry, Angus. I shouldn't be bothering you while you're at work. It's been a bit of a shitty day.'

Cadwallader pulled out a chair from a nearby desk. 'Sit down, man. You look ready to drop.'

McLean sunk into the chair gratefully, watched as his old friend skirted around the desk and opened a drawer, came out with a bottle and two fine crystal tumblers.

'Haven't you got work to do?' he asked.

'It can wait. Not as if my customers are going to complain.' Cadwallader poured two stiff measures, handed one

443

over. McLean sniffed the powerful, peaty aroma of Islay malt.

'I probably shouldn't. Going to have to drive home soon.' He tipped the glass back and took a long sip, letting the unwatered spirit burn away some of the bad taste in his mouth.

'I heard what happened,' Cadwallader said after a while. McLean noticed he'd not drunk from his own glass, just held it in one hand.

'You'll not have had a look at her yet, though.'

'Actually, we've had the X-rays through already. She's scheduled for tomorrow morning, but I can bring that forward if you want. Not sure you should be here when I do it, though. Not given the circumstances.'

McLean shook his head, feeling the whisky already. The bottle had no label on it, he noticed. Something from Cadwallader's private supply. 'I don't want to, Angus. I know what killed her. Who killed her. I saw it happen. I was there.'

'And did you know she was pregnant?'

The question hit him like a punch in the gut. McLean put his empty glass down slowly on the desktop, his mind suddenly very clear as the final piece of the puzzle slotted into place.

'Pregnant?' he asked. 'Are you sure? How long? Would she have known?'

'Obstetrics isn't really my area of expertise, Tony. I tend towards the other end of medicine.' Cadwallader smiled at his joke, but it was as thin and weary as McLean felt. 'That said, I'd imagine she knew. She'd be about four months in. Just starting to show.'

'Four months,' McLean echoed, his mind racing through the calendar. Long before they even knew about the brothel. Round about the time Stacey Craig was picked up in Leith and let off with a caution.

'A double tragedy, really.' Cadwallader finally raised his own glass, knocked back the whisky in one. 'She was carrying twins.'

## 56

He still had her blood on his hands. It was underneath his fingernails, caked around the cuffs of his shirt, soaked into the front of his jacket. Christ, it was probably all over the steering wheel of the car, maybe the seats too. So much blood. So much wasted life.

McLean wasn't entirely sure how he'd made it home. He knew he shouldn't have done, not after drinking Cadwallader's whisky, but he'd walked back to the station and then driven. He wasn't drunk, just shell-shocked. He had a vague memory of changing gears, turning corners, indicating. How he'd managed not to crash he had no idea. Maybe someone up there was watching him, making sure he came to no harm. Just everyone around him. Everyone who ever got close.

He was sitting at his kitchen table, the scrubbed wooden surface almost completely bare. He didn't remember opening the back door, walking through here, pulling out the chair and sinking slowly into it. He didn't remember sinking his head into his hands and sobbing uncontrollably. Or maybe he did. Maybe that was all part of the dream.

Something nudged at his hand, distracting him. He looked up to see Mrs McCutcheon's cat standing in the middle of the table, head bowed and bobbing slightly as it – she – tried to get his attention. Instinctively he reached out, scratched her behind the ears. His reward was a deep rumbling purr that for once was not judgemental in any way.

But he still had Heather's blood on his hands.

'I did my best, you know?'

The cat said nothing, just turned her arse towards him, arched her back. He stroked her a couple of times, and then she stalked off across the table, jumped lithely to the floor before setting about her food bowl with determined enthusiasm. It occurred to McLean that her newfound affection had nothing to do with his current state of mind and everything to do with the fact that all the noisy house guests had gone.

'Fine. Be like that then.'

His legs and arms ached as he left the kitchen and uncaring cat behind, slowly climbed the stairs. He stripped off bloodstained jacket, trousers and shirt, dumping them in the bin rather than the laundry basket. Even if they could be cleaned he never wanted to wear them again. The shower was hot, the first swirls of water red with Heather Marchmont's blood, spiralling down the drain like so much wasted life. Soap and shampoo washed him clean, but he stood under the water until it started to go cold, his fingers and toes wrinkled like flabby white prunes. The drumming sound on his head helped to blot out the memories, but it couldn't last. Those dying eyes still haunted him, that whispered almost silent 'Thank you'.

Dressed, McLean went back down to the kitchen, looked into the fridge out of reflex even though he wasn't really hungry. The evening had barely begun, a time when he would more normally be looking forward to a couple of hours' peace and quiet at work. Now he was at a loose end.

Nothing to distract him when he sorely needed distraction. He went to put the kettle on and saw that his hand was shaking. Christ, but he didn't need to be alone right now.

It took a while to find the number, buried in the arcane filing system of his phone's address book. He hesitated before hitting dial, partly out of uncertainty, partly because the shakes made it hard to tap the right patch on the screen. The phone rang four agonising times before it was answered, and a part of him prayed it would go to voice-mail.

'Hello?'

'Hi, Jenny. It's Tony here. Tony McLean.'

'Hey, Tony. How's things? I've just literally walked in from helping Rae and Phil get themselves organised. I swear I don't know who's the biggest kid of the two of them. Pity their poor child.'

'Sounds like Phil. Some hope that fatherhood would have made him start behaving like an adult.' McLean tried a laugh but it sounded hollow even to him.

'You OK, Tony? You sound kind of down.'

'Sorry. I really shouldn't be bothering you. Just came home to an empty house, and it's not been the best of days.'

'Hey, what are friends for if not to call when you need cheering up?'

'Aye, well, I don't like to impose.'

Jenny laughed, her voice a welcome ray of light in the darkness. 'My sister's been imposing on you for the last two months, Tony. I think you're due a little payback.'

'Thanks. I guess I'm just not good at asking for any-thing. Too used to looking after myself.'

'Badly. I've seen the state of your fridge.' Jenny laughed again. 'Here, have you eaten yet? There's a new place on Clerk Street just opened up. Really good Thai food. I think you'd like it.'

'I . . . Yes. Maybe. That would be nice.' McLean wasn't sure what he felt, wasn't sure why he had called Jenny except that he'd not been able to think of anyone else. Or was he kidding himself, just the same way the deputy chief constable seemed to make a lie the truth just by repetition?

'Sounds like you really shouldn't be left on your own. Tell you what. If you're not keen on Thai then I'll come over. You can order something from one of your favourite takeaways. Fair?'

He looked up from the phone, seeing the empty kitchen table, Mrs McCutcheon's cat sitting beside her food bowl and cleaning one foot with her tongue, the corkboard by the house phone with the menus pinned to it.

'Sure. Why not?'

He spent twenty minutes after hanging up wandering from kitchen to library to drawing room to hallway, half-heartedly tidying a house that hadn't really been untidy to start with. It was true that Phil and Rae weren't the most house-proud of parents, and McLean knew too that children were little vortices of chaos that no amount of self-discipline could tame, but someone with a bit more world experience had made sure the madness didn't spread too far.

It didn't take a genius to guess who.

He kept his phone with him as he paced the house, expecting it to ring at any time, for Jenny to have found some excuse not to come and share his misery. He could hardly blame her if she did. Every so often the image of Heather Marchmont's dying eyes stopped him in his tracks. He could have sworn he could hear her voice in the empty silence of the big old house.

And then a more concrete sound broke the stillness, the unmistakable crunch of car tyres on gravel. He was back in the kitchen now, and saw the spray of headlights across the blackened glass of the window. Somehow night had fallen while he wasn't looking. Somehow winter had arrived.

He flicked on lights as he set across the hall, only then noticing the pile of mail lying on the doormat unchecked. He scooped it up, thoughts of postcards long forgotten, and dumped it all on the wooden chest. The car was pulling away as he unlocked the front door, reached for the switch that would flood light over the porch, threw open the door to welcome Jenny in. It was only as he was doing so that he realised Jenny would most likely have come to the back door, would not have needed to be let in to a house she'd visited many times before in the past few weeks. Jenny would have driven over in her own car, too. It would be parked here in front of the door.

And then he saw that it wasn't Jenny at all.

'Hey, Tony. Did you get my postcard?'

She had changed in two years. Was it really two years already? Her hair had once been short, spiky and black as the night. She'd let it grow long before she left, but now it was short again, and shot with grey. Travel had hardened her features, but not cruelly. Rather they gave her a distinguished look, someone with a story to tell. She wore clothes that were practical, a long leather coat covering jeans, walking boots, baggy jumper that had seen better days. A large canvas bag was slung over one shoulder, and behind her McLean could see the taxi driver had left one even larger still. All of these details he only registered on some subconscious level, his attention fixed entirely on her face.

'Em?' He took a step forward, the light from the hallway spilling out from behind him, adding to the illumination. 'You came back.'

# 57

A light dusting of snow carpets the hallway, blown in through the broken windows either side of the door. She doesn't notice it, nor the cold seeping in through her boots, the chill wind whistling around her legs. The dull ache where the knife wound puckers her skin is the only thing she feels. That and the sadness.

'It's good to be home.'

Her brother says nothing. He has said nothing since they left the city, his mood surly. Almost as if the blow to his head has turned him back into the little boy she knew so many years before. He moves past her, heavy feet leaving dark imprints in the white. She follows him to the bottom of the staircase then stops, watches him climb slowly up the wooden spiral and disappear into the darkness above. His footsteps echo on the floorboards, fading away to nothing, leaving only the sighing of the wind in the trees that surround the house.

She lets him go, then sets off through the house. She's not ready to sleep yet, still buzzing from the city, the life that surges through its streets.

Her footsteps take her through rooms long abandoned, but she doesn't see the decay, the plaster fallen from the ceilings, the curtains furry with mildew, the fireplaces filled with twigs left by birds long dead. This has always been home, she was born here. It can never change.

Beyond the tumbled-in patio doors, the snow has begun to settle on the lawn. Thick flakes float down in the near-darkness, settling on her head, her shoulders. She ignores them as she walks to the edge of the trees, follows the short path to the clearing she has visited so many times before. The gravestones poke from the ground like rotten teeth, small and simple as the bodies whose last resting place they mark.

Kneeling before one, she presses a finger against the scar on her chest. Softly at first, but then harder, parting the flesh where it has begun to heal. The pain surges through her whole body, making her shudder, and a low moan escapes from between her lips as the blood begins to ooze sluggishly from the cut. She draws a name on the headstone in childish letters, scarlet and sticky. Adds some dates.

Heather
1984–2015
'Girl'

The job done, she stands, barely able to see the words in the failing light. Behind her the house is dark, silent, brooding. The trees that surround it seem to close in tight, a protective wall from the world outside. She turns away from the graves, walks back through the snow to the open door. Up the stairs to the room she has always shared with her brother. He lies in the one bed, eyes closed, still as a corpse. The bag sits on a table at the end, open, and she feels inside it until she finds the dress. The fabric is strange beneath her fingers, soft and dangerous. Swiftly she undresses, then pulls it on, smoothing the rubber over her scarred skin. Her fingers follow the curves, delighting in the sensation for long moments. Then she gently pulls back the covers, climbs in beside her brother. She will sleep now. They will both sleep now.

Until they are needed again.

# Acknowledgements

For all that it's my name on the cover, producing a book is a team effort. I may spend months alone in a dark room with my thoughts and a typewriter, but others then take my fevered imaginations and soothe them into something you can actually read. A huge thank you to Alex, Tim, Viola and all the team at Michael Joseph for all their hard work they have put in over the years. The success of these books has been in no small part down to your efforts.

I am forever indebted to my agent, the indomitable Juliet Mushens, and her ultra-efficient sidekick Sarah Manning. Without them Tony McLean would probably still be a beat constable.

Thank you to Barbara, who keeps me sane and has put up with me for far longer than I deserve, and thanks too to Stuart MacBride, whose advice all those years ago to give up writing dragon fantasy and to have a go at crime fiction has turned out to be very wise indeed. Even if I only half followed it.

# The *Sunday Times* bestselling

*'His writing is in a class above
most in this genre'*

**DAILY EXPRESS**

# nspector **McLean** series

*'Oswald is among the leaders in the new batch of excellent Scottish crime writers'*

**DAILY MAIL**

# He just wanted a decent book to read ...

Not too much to ask, is it? It was in 1935 when Allen Lane, Managing Director of Bodley Head Publishers, stood on a platform at Exeter railway station looking for something good to read on his journey back to London. His choice was limited to popular magazines and poor-quality paperbacks – the same choice faced every day by the vast majority of readers, few of whom could afford hardbacks. Lane's disappointment and subsequent anger at the range of books generally available led him to found a company – and change the world.

*'We believed in the existence in this country of a vast reading public for intelligent books at a low price, and staked everything on it'*
**Sir Allen Lane, 1902–1970, founder of Penguin Books**

The quality paperback had arrived – and not just in bookshops. Lane was adamant that his Penguins should appear in chain stores and tobacconists, and should cost no more than a packet of cigarettes.

Reading habits (and cigarette prices) have changed since 1935, but Penguin still believes in publishing the best books for everybody to enjoy. We still believe that good design costs no more than bad design, and we still believe that quality books published passionately and responsibly make the world a better place.

So wherever you see the little bird – whether it's on a piece of prize-winning literary fiction or a celebrity autobiography, political tour de force or historical masterpiece, a serial-killer thriller, reference book, world classic or a piece of pure escapism – you can bet that it represents the very best that the genre has to offer.

## Whatever you like to read – trust Penguin.